I0612590

Dark Ones Take It

A Stormclouds/Harbingers fantasy novel

Being the origin story of Caedon and Maeldoi

Jane Wiseman

Shrike Publications

Albuquerque and Minneapolis

Copyright © 2020 by Jane M. Wiseman

All rights reserved. No part of this publication may be reproduced, distributed or transmitted in any form or by any means, without prior written permission.

Shrike Publications
Albuquerque, New Mexico
Minneapolis, Minnesota
www.janemwiseman.com

Publisher's Note: This is a work of fiction. Names, characters, places, and incidents are a product of the author's imagination. Locales and public names are sometimes used for atmospheric purposes. Any resemblance to actual people, living or dead, or to businesses, companies, events, institutions, or locales is completely coincidental.

Book Layout © 2017 BookDesignTemplates.com

Dark Ones Take It/ Jane M. Wiseman . -- 1st ed.
ISBN 978-1-7355068-1-4

For Will and Wallace

He himself ran in terror. Reaching the silent fields, he howled aloud, frustrated of speech, foaming at the mouth, and greedy as ever for killing, still delighting in blood. His clothes became bristling hair, his arms became legs. He was a wolf, but kept some vestige of his former shape, the same violent face, the same glittering eyes, the same savage image. . . .

–OVID, METAMORPHOSIS I (modified from the Kline translation)

Trigger warning: *This book is a work of fiction and fantasy, but it includes some graphic violence and reflects some harsh realities about sexual abuse. Please take care of yourself if such references cause you distress.*

Contents

The World as Caedon and Maeldoi Know It

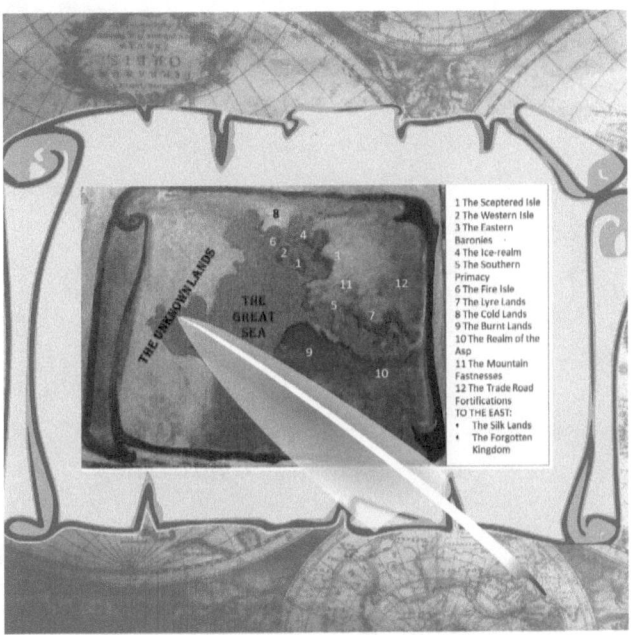

1 The Sceptered Isle
2 The Western Isle
3 The Eastern Baronies
4 The Ice-realm
5 The Southern Primacy
6 The Fire Isle
7 The Lyre Lands
8 The Cold Lands
9 The Burnt Lands
10 The Realm of the Asp
11 The Mountain Fastnesses
12 The Trade Road Fortifications
TO THE EAST:
• The Silk Lands
• The Forgotten Kingdom

THE UNKNOWN LANDS

THE GREAT SEA

Part I: CAEDON

CHAPTER ONE

Strangers

Where do they live, the Dark Ones, and who are they?

Many a villager asked such questions, in those parts, as they huddled around the turf fires. Especially they asked each other in winter while the prowling wind outside nuzzled at the oiled fish bladders covering the windows with their cloudy translucence.

The village tale-tellers and muckspouts scared the little children with tales of the Wild Hunt, and the Dark Rider who went out before it on a stallion black as night, galloping over a nightmare land. "The Dark Rider," they whispered. "One of the gwrgi."

Cae and his brother Maeldoi and his mother didn't ask questions like these. They too were huddled around a turf fire, chafing their hands, crowding together to keep from freezing in their tiny thatched, turf-walled hut on the unprotected wind-buffeted edge of the moor.

They didn't ask the villagers' frightening questions about the Dark Ones because they already knew the answers.

Sometimes their father came to visit them. To visit their mother really, not the boys. As he pushed aside the hide covering the door to the hut, and came in, and spotted the boys, his too-red lips would draw back from his too-pointed teeth in a grimace, the way you'd grimace at vermin scuttling to the safety of the cornerboard. He'd put his hand on their mother and force her up the ladder to the loft.

When he'd had his fill of her, and when she had fed him what meager food they kept, he'd disappear back into the night, and they wouldn't see him again for many seasons. Sometimes for nigh on a year. Now not at all.

He always came at night.

He was a hard man, his features carved into his face and set there, as if he were made of stone. His lank dark hair was pulled back from his pale face and tied with a leather thong.

Their mother feared nothing and no one, only their father.

Sometimes he hit her. If the boys got in his way, he hit them, too.

Their mother hit them.

Maeldoi beat Cae routinely, because he was the elder and the bigger and stronger. Because he could.

But their father was the worst.

This last time, he stayed the whole night. Cae clapped his hands over his ears. He lay trembling in the corner of the hut where the boys rolled themselves in blankets to sleep during their father's visits. Otherwise, they slept in the loft huddled up to their mother. But this night, the sounds of combat from the loft were too disturbing even for Cae. He wondered if one of his parents might kill the other. He wondered which would emerge the victor.

In the early light of dawn, their father came down the ladder from the loft. He strode to the boys and shook Maeldoi awake, hauling him up by an arm. He dragged Maeldoi stumbling after him behind the hut.

Cae woke in confusion, and then he stole out too. He knew his mother wasn't dead. He could hear her scolding and cursing from the loft. Even when he stepped outside the hut, he could hear her. He crept to one of the barrels they used to catch rainwater, and hid behind it to watch.

He watched while their father beat Maeldoi bloody and did the gods knew what else to him. "I'll have satisfaction out of this night, some kind of satisfaction, that I will!" their father kept shouting.

Cae, hiding behind a barrel, wasn't sure what he was watching, just that it was terrible and dangerous and vile.

Then something strange happened that he didn't know how to describe. He watched while Maeldoi clawed whimpering away from their father. Watched his father feel for a fallen branch on the ground. Lift it high. Bring it down.

Watched Maeldoi crouch low to the ground, then seem almost to swell in size. Watched him spring snarling for their father's throat, and fasten on. His father was roaring and beating Maeldoi away from him, trying to pry Maeldoi's jaws off him. He batted Maeldoi to the ground and rushed at him, to stomp on him. Maeldoi was screaming in a vibrating high-pitched crescendo. The sound hardly seemed natural.

Their mother dashed out of the house then, interposing herself between father and son. Maeldoi was on the ground, cursing and spitting. Their father was prowling around looking for a way to get at him.

Their mother had a stout crock in one hand and a stick in the other. She laid about her with a fury. Maeldoi sprawled in the dirt. Their father went flailing back and fell and hit his head, maybe on a stone. So it seemed to Cae while he watched, out of breath behind the barrel.

And so at the end, both of the combatants lay still.

Their mother stood over the two of them, breathing hard and muttering to herself.

Cae didn't dare come out. He crouched behind the barrel. He found he had pissed himself.

After a long moment of staring from father to son, son to father, his mother went back into the house.

A bit later, his father sat up, shaking his head in a baffled way. He brought himself into a crouch, then pulled himself unsteadily to his feet, putting his hand to his throat. It came away bloody. He looked down at Maeldoi. Then he went into the house.

Still Cae couldn't move.

After what seemed like a long time, his father came out again, a bandage wrapped about his head, his neck bandaged. He moved to Maeldoi again and stood over him, fingering the knife at his belt. Their mother pushed aside the hide at the doorway and screamed something and ran at him again with the crock. So then he backed off. He went off down the road, weaving a bit, and soon he was lost to Cae's sight.

Cae's gaze strayed to his brother, who had not risen. Maybe he was dead.

Eventually their mother went to his brother and helped him sit up.

So not dead, thought Cae. He wasn't sure whether he was glad or sorry.

Their mother led Maeldoi like a little child back into the house.

She came out again, looking around. When she spotted Cae behind the barrel, she tried coaxing him out, but he just flattened himself further behind the barrel against the hut's turf wall. Finally she produced a piece of bread from her apron and held it out to him. When he lunged out to grab it, she grabbed him instead, by the ear, and hauled him inside. Later she beat him, for his cowardice. He cursed himself for an addlepate. By now, he knew to be wary of any coaxing of hers.

Eventually, Maeldoi came around, although he sat by the fire for a day or two, his eyes blank as stones.

Their mother felt him all over, especially his skull. Maeldoi sat listlessly and let her. That's how Cae knew he was not himself. Maybe not even in there, Cae thought.

"No head wound," his mother remarked matter-of-factly. "So it's the other thing."

What other thing? Cae wondered.

"Nigh a man," said his mother. "Makes sense."

Nothing makes sense, Cae thought.

That was only the worst of their tussles, and the last. Even without their father home, the three of them had had their noisy brawls.

They stayed away from the neighboring villagers, and the villagers stayed away from them.

The villagers knew. They could hear the commotion on the edge of the village, although they never came around to investigate.

The neighbors could see. The eyes. *Gwrgi*, they whispered to each other. *Not our look-out. Leave them to themselves.*

Cae wasn't sure what that meant.

"We are gwrgi," Maeldoi told him at last. "And they are afraid of us. They see we are different."

"Different?"

"Look at my eyes, you ninnyhammer."

Cae looked into his brother's face. He hesitated. He was still puzzled.

"Do you see anyone else with eyes like these? We have them. You do. Mother does. None of the neighbors do. Only us."

Cae thought about it. He had made a friend, once, not very long ago.

Another boy, from the edge of the village, who had ventured beyond the village blackthorn hedge one day. He had come to the stream behind Cae's mother's hut, and was splashing around in it. Cae saw him from the back window in the hut and came out to stand by the stream.

The two boys had stared at each other a long time.

Cae started splashing in the stream. After a while, they were splashing together. Then Cae told the boy to be quiet, and then he taught him how to tickle a trout. The boy's name, he told Cae, was Duiset.

But later, Duiset's mother had caught them together. The two of them had begun examining each other's bodies, and touching each other. They were doing this behind the blackthorn hedge, and she caught them at it. She had cursed at Cae, and brandished a stick at him, and run him off.

He didn't see Duiset again, except at a distance.

Duiset's eyes had been blue.

But ours, Cae remembered whispering to himself when Maeldoi pointed out this difference. *Our eyes are amber.* Duiset's eyes were like the sky. *Our eyes*, he told himself, *are like the barley in the field.*

"Our eyes are like barley? Are you daft? Who'd think such a thing. Our eyes are like the wolf's," said Maeldoi, when Cae told him his thoughts. "Or like a dog's. And that's why they fear us."

Then he had punched Cae, and had chased him away from the nicest spot under the tree behind the hut, and had taken it for himself.

After that, Cae sought out still pools and looked at himself in them. His reflected face wavered back at him. He wasn't sure what he was seeing.

It's not just about our eyes, Cae told himself, of the villagers' abhorrence. *We're not from these parts. Strangers. It's about that, too.* He didn't know how he knew it. He just did.

Life got better for Cae when he and Maeldoi were finally separated, but it didn't happen the way he thought it might, and life didn't get better all at once.

"You're nigh manhood, son," their mother said to Maeldoi one day. It was shortly after the fight between Maeldoi and his father. Cae had heard those words out of her lips before, as Maeldoi sat senseless at the fire.

"Nigh a man," she continued, "and now I've sent word. I can't deal with you. I shouldn't be expected to. Maybe someone can."

It was about that time of year when the sun, having swung down into the dark places of the Spheres, was poised to climb out and up again.

"In two days or thereabouts, some men of our people are coming to have a look at you," their mother told Maeldoi.

The next day, she skinned the dirty clothes from both boys, brushed their matted hair, and made them wash. Not in the stream. In water she had heated over the fire.

A good thing, too, Cae thought. *If she'd made us wash in the stream at this time of year, we'd have froze our plumstones off.*

She made them splash the hot water liberally on themselves, and then she rubbed them raw with a rag.

Maeldoi protested and struggled to get away from her, but she had him by the ear, and then by the cullions. That settled him down. His mouth worked, and tears streamed down his cheeks.

Cae stared at his brother with interest, wondering if he'd transform himself into that bestial thing again, but he didn't.

When his mother came after Cae with the rag, he stood still and let her wash him. Far the wiser course, he thought.

She threw their ragged clothes in the fire. The clothes reeked as they burned.

Then the boys had to sit around naked while she rooted around in a chest and a bag of hers to find other clothes. Clothes neither of them remembered ever seeing before.

She held these clothes up, clucking her tongue. Sniffed them. Washed them in the bathwater and draped them over the blackthorn to dry.

"I'm cold," Maeldoi whimpered, leaning protectively over his privates. She ignored that.

Cae decided he wouldn't say a thing, although he was shivering.

Finally, she'd had enough of Maeldoi's whining and handed them the woven blankets of the sleeping loft to drape over themselves.

"You'll begin to stink again, and just when I've gotten you clean," she muttered, more to herself than to them, but still she handed them over.

A whole day later, the wet clothes had dried, at least enough to put on. Their mother dried them a bit more, by the fire, which thawed them out. They'd frozen stiff, spread over the blackthorns.

The boys stepped into the unfamiliar, scratchy trousers and pulled the unfamiliar tunics over their heads. Cae's hung on him, but Maeldoi's were too tight in the shoulder and too short in the leg.

She looked at them both and sighed.

Cae saw then that she, too, was wearing her best kirtle, not the stained and patched one she usually wore. He'd never seen the clothes he was wearing now, but he had seen his mother in her best kirtle. Sometimes she had to go to the market town, and when she did, she put this kirtle on, and a headcloth to cover her hair.

Now she took the headcloth from the chest and smoothed it out. She wound it around her head, binding up her hair.

Cae sniffed. She smelled good. Like sweet herbs. He realized she too must have washed. It unnerved him, though. She didn't smell like his mother.

She stalked around the two of them, looking them up and down. "It will have to do," she said.

Then she made them take the clothes off. "You'll not get them dirty again, after all the trouble I went to."

The brothers spent the rest of the day huddled in the blankets.

The next morning, they all put on these best clothes of theirs again.

Soon after they had broken their fast, a noise of feet crunching down the icy path to their cottage warned them someone was coming.

"More than one," said Maeldoi. He reached for the stout stick they kept over the door. The one his mother had used on him and their father during their fight.

"No," said his mother. "These are the men I told you about. They are guests."

Guests, thought Cae in confusion.

Three men shouldered into the tiny single room of the cottage. Each of the men had the amber eyes that Cae and Maeldoi and their mother did. *Gwrgi. These men are gwrgi like us*, thought Cae.

Maeldoi had gone into a crouch with the stick.

Their mother gave Maeldoi a look, so then he reluctantly put the stick back up on its pegs.

She hastily thrust the porridge bowls onto the one shelf and turned to make an awkward curtsey to these strangers. "Bow," she hissed at Cae and Maeldoi.

The two boys eyed the men, who were all three wrapped in warm cloaks.

Cae stared at these cloaks. He wanted one of them. He'd be warm then.

Maeldoi made the men a stiff little bow from the waist, and Cae watched him and copied what he did.

Their mother showed the visitors to places around the turf fire of their hearth. Cae and Maeldoi hung back in the corner, licking the porridge off their fingers.

Their mother stood before the men, twisting her hands in her apron.

"Sit, daughter," said the oldest of the men.

Cae thought his mother was probably not this man's actual daughter. Although he had no idea whose daughter she was. He'd never thought of his mother as a daughter with a mother of her own.

Their mother seated herself hesitantly on the stones beside the men.

"A headcloth," said the leader of the three men, the visitor who looked to be the oldest, and in charge. "That's not our way. Remove it."

The boys' mother snatched the headcloth off and then her long stringy hair fell free down her back and about her shoulders. She folded the headcloth in her lap and fingered it nervously.

"Your elder son is of age. You were right to get us word. We'll need to examine both boys," said the leader.

"Maeldoi," said their mother sharply, ignoring Cae. "Come here to us."

Maeldoi straightened from where he was slouching against the hut's lintel and came to the fire and stood there.

Cae saw that for all his bravado, his brother was afraid.

"Your man did wrong, bringing you here," said the oldest visitor to their mother. "You're too far from us. When we leave on the morrow, we're bringing you back with us. All three of you."

Cae felt his eyes growing round. He peered over at his mother. She sat impassive.

The man now turned to Maeldoi. "What is your name, boy?" he asked.

"Maeldoi," said Cae's brother.

"'Maeldoi, sir,'" corrected the man.

Their mother gave Maeldoi a fierce look, so then Maeldoi said, in a reluctant voice, "Maeldoi, sir."

The man grunted. "And how old are you?"

"I don't know," said Maeldoi.

"He's of age," said their mother. "Or near to." To Maeldoi, she hissed, "'I don't know, sir.'"

Maeldoi ignored this.

The man scrutinized Maeldoi. Maeldoi was beginning to show a shadow of beard on his pale cheeks, and a little on his upper lip. "Yes," he said. "I see you're right. And after what you told us—."

In a moment, he turned his eyes on Cae. Cae shrank back. "And the little one?"

"Ten summers, maybe?" she ventured.

The leader of the men stared at Cae for a long time.

Cae began to fidget.

His mother rapped him smartly on the knuckles. She stood him before the men.

The leader took Cae's chin in his hand and stared into his eyes. Cae stared back. What the man saw—Cae wasn't sure what it was. He wanted to know. When he had stared at himself in the pools, he had wanted to know.

The man stepped back and looked to the boys' mother. "We'll only take one."

"Take the elder," she said.

The man nodded and glanced at Maeldoi again. "With this one, it seems we're just in time."

He turned to the other two men and said something to them in a low voice, something Cae didn't quite catch. He looked back to their mother. "But all three of you will travel with us. Even the little one should not grow up here, among these barbarous people." The man began speaking nonsense now.

Cae felt his eyes growing bigger and bigger.

He was even more startled when his mother began speaking nonsense too. A kind of babbling that was like speech but wasn't, quite.

"I'm glad to see you have not forgotten, daughter," said the man, "but you were remiss in not teaching our tongue to your sons."

"Life has been hard," she murmured.

The three visitors stood, and so did their mother.

"Make yourself ready," said the oldest man. "Pack what you need, but don't pack much. We leave before daybreak."

"There's little enough here," she said, sticking out a defiant lower lip. "I'll take none of it."

Then, struck with a thought, she asked, "And my man?"

"Gone," said the oldest visitor, giving her a shrewd look.

"That's done, then," she said.

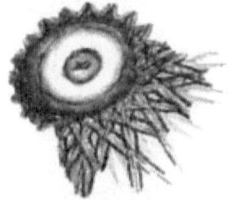

CHAPTER TWO

Just in Time

T he next day passed for Cae as if it were a dream. He did things he didn't believe it possible to do. They all did.

Just as the leader of the three strange men had said they would, the men showed up before sunrise the next morning. They were there to lead Cae and his family away from their cottage. Forever, Cae realized.

The night before, Maeldoi had plied their mother with questions. Cae remained silent, but he listened.

"You'll know soon enough." That was their mother's answer to most of Maeldoi's questions.

"Who are these men, and why are they going to make us leave?" Maeldoi insisted.

"These are our people," said their mother, worn down at last. "We belong with them, not here where your father brought us. So now they'll take us back."

"What will Father have to say about that?" said Maeldoi.

"He's gone," said their mother.

"Gone where?" said Maeldoi.

She wouldn't answer.

"Why did they say they'd take me and not Cae? Looks like all of us are going," said Maeldoi.

"They're taking all of us back to our homeland, but once we get there, they'll take you to a special place for boys they need for special tasks."

"What tasks?"

She was silent.

Cae was glad only Maeldoi would have to go off with the men to do these tasks. He was glad he didn't have to, although he wished the leader of the men had spoken about what he'd seen inside Cae.

He'd looked inside Cae, and he had seen something.

Cae didn't dwell on that. He imagined the new hut they'd have in the new place where they were going, a better hut, maybe. He imagined life would go on pretty much as before. Except without Maeldoi. A good thing. Maeldoi wouldn't be able to beat him then or take the best piece of meat out of the pot for himself, on those days when they had meat.

The three of them spent a restless night of it. Cae felt he'd hardly gotten to sleep when his mother was shaking his shoulder and making him rise in the dark. They all put on their strange new clothes in the dark. They wrapped their feet in rags, because the frozen soil would numb their feet as they walked the lanes.

The men who'd come for them were already waiting outside as Cae and his mother and brother finished putting a few of their belongings into a sack. Their mother had decided to take a few things after all. She shouldered the sack, and then Maeldoi followed her out into the dim mists and stinging cold of predawn.

The only possession Cae wanted to bring was a carved little bird. The boy Duiset had given it to him. No one knew he had it. He had kept it in a hollowed-out place behind the shelf with the porridge bowls.

He wanted no one to see it. It was private. It was only his. No one must touch it. No one must even know of it.

He hung back as Maeldoi and his mother crept from the hut, and he scrabbled behind the shelf to find it. He secreted it in his palm, and then he eased it into the top of his trousers, where the twine tied about his waist made a kind of pouch.

"Get out here, Caedon," his mother called from the other side of the hide at the door, her voice sharp with annoyance. "Or we'll leave you behind."

Cae burst through the doorway. A wall of cold air hit him, and he felt his teeth begin to chatter in his skull. He wished they had brought the blankets, to wrap around themselves, but their mother had made them leave the blankets behind.

"Quickly, now," said the leader of the three men. "Before your neighbors see."

He hustled the three of them ahead of him, and the other two men came after. Cae saw how these others kept a watch for anyone coming up behind them.

The stones of the path bit through Cae's rags and hurt his feet. But he daren't lag behind. One of the men came just on his heels with a stout stick and a stern look about him.

The little group of them swerved away from the village into the rough ground out on the moor, where the wind blew straight through their clothing.

Once more Cae wished he had one of the men's cloaks for himself. He was thinking of sidling up to Maeldoi and suggesting they snatch the men's cloaks from their shoulders and take off through the pastureland toward the nearest tor. Mikkle Tor, it was called. The highest one around. They would outrun the men, and then they'd have the cloaks.

Before he could maneuver to Maeldoi's side, they reached their destination.

"Quickly, no lagging." The leader was standing at the head of a small gully, and he was using his walking stick to point Cae's mother, and then Maeldoi, down into it and out of the wind.

"Quickly," the man said again. "The sun is nigh to rise."

Cae, too, stumbled down the gully in the dimness. To his astonishment, he found himself headed into a narrow rock-lined passageway. How was it he'd never known this place? He thought he had explored all the land around the hut and the village.

He crowded in beside Maeldoi and looked over at his brother.

"Aye," said Maeldoi. "The fougou."

Cae didn't know what that meant. He saw his mother and brother knew about the place, though, and that reassured him a little.

Now the three men were there in the passageway too.

"Stand before us, daughter. And you boys, stand by your mother. Look to the opening of the passage. The sun will rise, and you will see his beams," whispered the leader.

He grasped Cae by the shoulders and pushed Cae to stand beside his mother and brother.

Just as the man said, the entrance to the passageway—the fougou, Maeldoi had called it—began to lighten. Then the first beams of the sun caught them all full in the face.

And then.

Later Cae couldn't explain to himself what happened to him, then. It was as if he, and the world around him, began to attenuate. It was as if he could see into the earth around them, all its striations and strata of rock. It was as if he had dissolved into these rocky layers and had melted through them.

In less than an eye's blink, he found himself on a hillside, with the sound of the sea beating in the distance. He felt his mouth dropping open.

"Here we are," said the leader of the men. "Follow me."

The air was much warmer, in this place they'd somehow come to.

Cae realized later it was because the passageway led into a vast cave. But the cave was. . . where?

Cae couldn't think how to put what he was feeling and seeing.

The cave was somewhere else. Not on the moor. Not near the village. Some completely different place.

As he later learned, the air and the earth outside the cave were as cold, at least, as at home. Outside, as at home, it was the deep midwinter.

But inside the cave where they now found themselves, the air was only cool. Great fires burned from one end of the cave to the other, the smoke of them rising to the cave's ceiling—so then Cae knew there must be smoke-holes or crevices for the smoke to escape to the outside—and near those fires, the air was very warm.

He and his mother and brother stepped to one of these fires, invited by the men. After they had warmed themselves with many others standing there, almost all of them women and children, the leader pulled them aside.

"My companions and I are going now," he said to the boys' mother. "We're taking Maeldoi with us. This is your choice?" He looked to her.

She nodded.

"Make your farewells to your mother and brother, Maeldoi." He gave the boys' mother another hard look. "From this moment, speak only in our tongue, daughter. Otherwise the young one will never learn, and when he is turned out, he will not be able to make his way."

Their mother nodded again. Cae saw she had made up her mind about a hard thing.

Maeldoi turned from the men and looked at Cae and their mother. Cae thought he looked surprised. "Farewell," he said.

They took him by the arms and walked him away.

Cae didn't see him again until many years afterward, and their mother never saw him again, ever.

They didn't know that then.

Cae thought Maeldoi would be back with them after a while, at least to visit.

Later, he wondered what their mother would have said in that moment, if she'd known her son was being taken from her forever. Cae wondered if she would have protested. She never grieved for Maeldoi, in any way that he could see.

Maybe, thought Cae. Maybe she knew. Maybe she had known from the moment the men arrived in their hut on the moors.

That hut was many leagues away from where they now found themselves—hundreds of leagues, and across a sea. So many leagues that Cae didn't know how to think of it.

Whatever Cae's mother knew or didn't know, she let some of the women around the fire lead her by the arm into the warren of tunnels branching off from the cave.

Cae, terrified he'd be left behind in the maze of tunnels, hurried after them, although no one looked to make sure he was following.

One of the women gestured to a bed-shelf in a niche in the rock and gabbled nonsense.

Cae's mother replied in the same sort of gabbling noises.

They all turned to Cae now, as if they'd forgotten his existence and now they remembered.

The woman who had spoken put out her hand to Cae's cheek and ran the back of her hand down it.

Later, Cae's mother told him what she said.

"This one will come of age pretty soon. It won't be that long, I'm thinking," she had told Cae's mother. "As for your older boy. Looks like they took him just in time. If the council had waited, he would have been too old. And then I don't know what would have become of the three of you. Certainly I don't know what would have become of him, your older one. You and your family are lucky, mistress. The older one could have been turned out, friendless and alone."

"Maeldoi," whispered Cae's mother.

Cae understood that word, at least, when she whispered it.

He realized that if he listened carefully, he could understand quite a bit of what the woman said, and the others. But they talked so rapidly that it seemed a babble to him.

"They'd have turned your Maeldoi out," said the woman. Cae's mother told him this later. "And all of you living so far away and so isolated from us, he wouldn't have known how to keep himself, mistress. You must thank The Three that the council got to him in time, and saw in him what they saw."

Cae's mother nodded mutely.

"This one," said the woman, turning back to Cae and staring at him. Listening hard, Cae understood she meant him. "He'll have a few years to learn. Maybe he'll be fine, when the time comes. Maybe one of the bands will accept him."

Cae's mother murmured this rapidly to him as the other one spoke.

One of the bands, he thought in confusion. He didn't know what the woman meant.

"Maybe not," muttered one of the other women. "A strange child like that, with no decent language, no understanding."

His mother didn't translate that, but Cae could tell from the woman's expression and tone of voice that something like this must be what she was saying.

The first one rounded on her. "Then he'll just have to figure out how to keep himself, won't he?"

Cae's mother rapidly translated this.

The woman turned back to Cae. "Learn, boy. You'd better." Cae knew exactly what she meant. She said it slowly, with menace in her voice. He understood.

"Caedon," said his mother, speaking to the women at last. "His name is Caedon." And that was clear to him, too, what his mother was saying.

All of the women, three or four of them, looked hard at Cae, their eyes narrowed.

"What kind of name is that," said the second woman, the one who'd expressed her doubts about Cae. Cae understood these words, too.

"His father named him that," said Cae's mother. "It's from his people." She said it again to Cae in their language back where they'd come from.

But Cae was beginning to hear now. The two languages were much alike.

"Ah," said the first woman. "I see it. Your man is from out there, one of the bands of the Fastnesses." She gestured.

Cae got the gist of it. Not about the bands in the Fastnesses, though. He only learned that part much later. Where his father came from.

"Yes," said Cae's mother.

"A good thing they took your other boy. He has a proper name. He'll learn. He'll make you proud, mistress."

The women walked away. A few looked back over their shoulders at Cae and his mother.

His mother straightened his tunic so it didn't droop so. "That woman said, good thing they took Maeldoi and not you. Maeldoi has a proper name. Maeldoi will make me proud."

And I won't, thought Cae, seeing it all. *These women think I'll end up some outcast.* "I understood what they said," he told his mother.

But for the first time, he wondered about a difference between Maeldoi and himself. *Maeldoi has a proper name and I do not. What does that mean?* he wondered. *My name is from our father's people. Maeldoi's is not.*

Cae's mother sat down on the bed shelf and didn't speak or move or explain any further.

After a while, Cae threaded his way back through the tunnels to the fire. Someone thrust a bowl of hot stew into his hands, and he ate it.

That part of his new life was very good. His belly was usually full.

In the day, he huddled around the fire. At night, he found his way back to the bed shelf and slept there rolled up in a cloak beside his mother, at least at first.

Clothing was not a problem in the cave. At one end, large chests were lined up. Cae discovered you could go to these chests, rummage around in them, and find yourself clothing, even a cloak. Even boots. If they fit, you could take them and wear them.

He was never sure what his mother did all day. He never saw her. Did she stay sitting on the bed shelf all day long? He knew she must come out to eat. Beyond that, he didn't know what she did.

But as for himself, he found the company of other children. For the first time in his life he had—well, not friends. Companions, maybe. These half-grown children all kept together, three or four groups of them.

Cae attached himself to one of these groups. He wasn't even sure how. Maybe this was the only group that would let him near.

In very short order, he could understand what they were saying. His old language fell away from him like the rotten scraps of clothing his mother had scraped off his dirty body, back when the men came to get them. And the new language, so similar, draped itself about him like the better clothing his mother had taken from her chest back in their old hut. Ill-fitting at first, but very soon, just right.

The groups of children fought each other. Within the group, the oldest preyed on the littlest. Cae recognized that.

But if another group menaced one of theirs, even the smallest of them, they went to war to protect their own. Sticks, stones, fists. If their wars got too noisy and bloody, the older people of the cave chased them outside.

When the weather got better and warmer, the children were always outside, and only came in for meals and sleep.

Inside the cave, the very little children kept close to their mothers and slept on the bed shelf with them. The older children were more likely to take their cloaks down some disused corridor and bed down together there, curled up like pups. Dogs, maybe. Or wolves.

Pretty soon, Cae was there curled up with them.

The women ran the cave, organizing the cooking and cleaning and discipline.

There were no men except old men, and a few men who were too impaired to do anything but sit by the fire. A man who had lost a leg and could only get around by leaning on a stick. A man not right in the head. A blind man.

But perhaps once every turning of the moon, some of the hale men of the cave returned, bows slung over their shoulders, knives at their belts. They found and claimed their wives, and took them off alone down various corridors, before disappearing again for another moon or season or so.

Fairly often, then, a baby would be born in the cave, and the women organized the birthings. If the baby and mother were fine, the mother would be exempt from all but the lightest work for a few years until the babe was weaned. If the baby died, one of the attending women would take the small corpse away and no one ever saw it again.

If the mother died, in childbirth or for any other reason—a fall from the sea cliffs, maybe, or a fever, or an evil swelling in this or that part of the body—the whole community would process outside to a place above the sea—for this land lay on a rocky coast—and burn the body.

One older woman led the cave. As the body burned, this leader would say prayers to the goddess known as The Three. Cae didn't know who this goddess was. Just that The Three was Their name.

Sometimes an older child would die. That corpse would simply disappear the way dead babies did, and no one would say prayers over it or burn it. If its mother grieved much, too visibly, too noisily, the other women would turn on her and beat her.

Cae realized later that his mother must have been assigned tasks in the cave and must have performed them. Otherwise, she would have been cast out, and Cae with her. He didn't know what these tasks were. Cooking. Gathering firewood. Washing and mending clothes. Things like that, probably. Some of the women went outside the cave to gather herbs and roots.

But most of their food came from the returning men, who always brought meat from their kills and dropped it at the fire for the women to butcher and clean and cook before the men hauled their wives off down one of the tunnels.

Sometimes no man came to the cave for a long time—in winter, especially—and those were lean times for all the inhabitants.

Cae was not one of the smaller children, but he was the newest, and he was strange to the rest of them, and not very robust.

The leader of his group of children was a large strapping girl. Early on, some of the other children caught Cae and grabbed him and hauled him before her. Her name was Rimoete.

"You must serve us," she told him. "Or you're out. You can't even speak right. You're here on sufferance."

One of the big boys stepped to Cae then and hit him in the face as the others held him. "Understand?"

"Yes." Cae gasped this, spitting out blood and a piece of tooth.

Then the big boys took him off with them into a remote corridor and took turns pleasuring themselves with him. They threatened him and told him never to look them in the eye.

Cae was too ashamed to look anyone in the eye, after that. He lurked at the fringes of the group, cowed, and whenever one of the older boys felt like it, he'd summon Cae to him and abuse Cae's body for his own pleasure.

For a while there, Cae actually missed Maeldoi. He knew Maeldoi would have protected him against bigger boys like these. Not against himself. But he would have, against outsiders.

Cae remembered a time when some village boys back in their old land had chased him, and then Maeldoi had risen up from the brush with his baleful eye and his fists like rock, and they had run pell-mell away.

But Cae had no protector now.

In time, though, as he became more accepted, and as he grew older and felt the changes in his body, he took turns with the others in abusing the little boys.

None of the big boys abused the girls, though.

"First, because Rimoete would kill me," one of them explained to Cae, warning Cae never to try it. "And second, because the girls become women, and then the men take them for themselves, and if they find we have had to do with them, the men will kill us. And they won't care which of us they kill. They'll go after any they can get their hands on, whether he's the fucker or not."

Cae nodded to show he understood.

He never spoke much. At first it was because, as they said, he couldn't speak properly. Later it was a habit. Besides, to speak was to give up power to the other.

Every now and then, one of the children in his group, one of the older ones, always a boy, would disappear. For a while, Cae couldn't figure out where such a child had gone to. And he was afraid to ask.

Gradually he realized where. As a boy came of age, the women of the cave drove him out.

Cae heard a commotion one day and hid behind some rocks to watch.

In shock, he saw a member of his own group being chased by a number of the cave's women. They had stout sticks, and they beat him and drove him off, screaming at him.

The lad stumbled away down the rocky path by the shore, his face bloody, looking behind him in terror. When the women were certain they had run him off, they turned and went back into the cave.

Cae waited a while to see if the boy would come back. He wasn't a friend. None of them were. But he was a member of Cae's group, and Cae and the rest of them helped any of their own who were hurt.

Even though Cae waited a long time, the boy didn't come back, and Cae didn't go after him, to find him and help him. Cae waited until after dark, and then he slowly made his way back to the cave. The next day, the boy was not there. No one spoke of him. No one seemed surprised that he was gone.

"Where do they go?" he whispered to his mother the next night. He never questioned her. Hardly spoke to her at all. But he felt he had to know, and she was the only one safe to ask.

"They are driven off, when they come of age."

"What happens to them then?"

"They find a band of men to join. If the men will have them, they are safe. If the men will not, then—" she paused. "Then I don't know what becomes of them."

"Will that happen to me?"

His mother was silent for a long time in the dark. "Yes," she finally whispered back.

"And Maeldoi? Is that what happened to him, because he was of age?"

"No. They took Maeldoi with them, those three men who came to our village. Took him off to train."

"But why?"

"They saw something in him. They'll take one of a woman's sons to train. Not every woman's. And then, if they do, only one. He was the one they chose."

Not me, thought Cae. Then he thought, *But Mother was the one who did the choosing.*

What happened to the girls was no big mystery. In the early spring, the women got together and tallied up which of the girls had begun her courses since the last spring.

At a certain time in early spring, men began gathering. Some of them men of the cave, but many were strangers. It was a festive time, meat enough for all. The spits turned the haunches all day long. The men sang into the night and passed around a potent drink called chouchenn. There were games of strength and chance. Some of the men fought each other.

When the moon grew to full, the elder woman of the cave waited for exactly the right night decreed by the goddess as the night of Choosing.

"The elder had better hurry herself up about it," the women muttered to each other. "These men are getting so full of their own juices that they are going to start fighting each other to the death, not just in play."

"And you know what happens then," one of them said with a dark look at the others.

Cae, overhearing, shivered. He remembered what happened, when Maeldoi fought their father.

At last the cave's elder pronounced The Three satisfied.

The men had barely been able to contain themselves, waiting for this moment. Now they nudged each other and laughed out loud, throwing back their heads. Their teeth flashed white. They set aside all their petty hostilities and belligerent challengings and tauntings of one another, all their posturings, as if they hadn't meant any of it.

At the old woman's signal, everyone went outside the cave into the mild springtide air. The men built a big bonfire, and they danced, their oiled bodies gleaming in the firelight, while the women watched with shining eyes.

Then, one by one, the girls who had reached womanhood were brought to the fire, and the men bid for them. When a man won one of these girls, he led her off to cheers and bawdy remarks into the recesses of the cave, where the man made her a woman indeed—his woman. Most men only had one or two women. It was too expensive to have more than that.

The bride price went to the leader of the cave, and she used it to buy necessary things for the community, things that couldn't be gathered or hunted. Iron pots, for example. Things like that, to be found out in the wider world.

Most of the younger men didn't have brides of their own. It took a long time for them to scrape together enough gold to bid on one. They had to make do with furtive gropings and couplings with village women, any who would have them. They didn't dare touch any women of their own kind.

After that night of feasting and bidding on and bedding brides, the stranger men left again for their bands, taking their new wives with them. And the life of the cave went on.

The neighboring bands held their own Choosings. Throughout the springtide, the men of the cave came stumbling home drunk in twos and threes, bringing brides from the neighbor bands.

A few of their own men attended their own Choosing to bid on one of their own new brides. Not many. "I might bid by mischance on my own daughter," Cae heard one of the men say with a laugh.

It was said that one man, the richest of all of them, all the gwrgi, went from Choosing to Choosing, accumulating brides. No man of their band. Maybe it was just a story.

Cae's mother had had to come out to the bonfire for the Choosing. Everyone did. Cae came to her after the bidding was over, the brides carried off, the fire burning low. "Is that how it was? How our father got you for a bride, and you to make me and Maeldoi?" Cae asked her.

"Not exactly. Not the same," said his mother. "Your father didn't come from one of our bands. He came from—" She waved her arm vaguely eastward. "They have different ways, there."

"Is that why he took us to the place where we lived before, by the moors?"

"That—" she faltered. "That was different. His band had run him off. He took us there to live."

"Is he dead now?"

Cae's mother looked him in the eye. "Yes," she said. "His band found him and killed him. He thought he'd gotten far enough away that they'd never find him. But they did."

"Did that make you sad?"

"No," said his mother. "It made me glad."

"Did you even want us?" Cae burst out. "Me and Maeldoi?"

She stood and smoothed down her kirtle. She turned to walk back to the cave. She looked back over her shoulder. "Not you," she said, and then she would never talk about it again. She never had said much at even the best of times. Now she said hardly anything at all. It was as if she had only so many words inside her, and now she had used them all up.

As Cae traveled closer and closer to his manhood, he wondered how it would be, with him. The girls he knew would all go to a Choosing, sooner or later. The boys, run off by the women, would find bands of men to join. The boys in his group knew some of the men in the other bands. Had known them from early childhood. But he knew none of them.

What will happen to me? he wondered. *How will I live?* As for women. He realized he wanted none of them.

"Ah, ya addled lad, that will change," one of the other boys told him with a grin.

Cae didn't think it would.

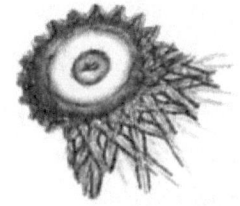

CHAPTER THREE

Tribute

In time, Cae no longer found his new life strange. It was just life. It was as if he had always led such a life. The years rolled by, and he didn't bother to count them, and he didn't know how many. More than two. Three? Maybe.

He was never a leader in his group of children, but he was respected. The younger children gave way to him. The older children knew not to mess with him. Children in other groups knew not to mess with him, and if they did, he didn't even need backup from children of his own group. He wasn't large, he wasn't especially strong, but he fought his own battles.

He had almost forgotten the way of his childhood speech, not so very different from the speech of his band. But as always, he was mostly silent.

Later, thinking about it, he knew he should have been prepared for the change that was about to overtake him. Since he lived in a kind of eternal present, he wasn't.

He wasn't often with his mother any longer. Sometimes at meals, though, he brought his bowl over to sit beside her and eat.

During one of these times, a few of the older women of the cave saw them and moved to them.

Cae clambered to his feet. All the children knew to show respect to such women, or they'd be beaten.

He made his bow. When he straightened, he nearly jumped back from them. One of them was running a hand down his cheek.

Cae felt an involuntary shiver. Someone had touched him like this, once. He barely remembered when. One of the women, when they'd first come to the cave.

The woman who had stroked his cheek looked past him, down at his mother. "Nigh time, for this one," she said. She and the others didn't smile. They walked on.

Cae sat down again to finish his stew. He caught his mother's eye on him.

He put up a hand to feel his own cheek, which had begun to roughen up. His skin was no longer the smooth skin of a child. "They mean I'm near manhood," he said to his mother.

"Yes."

"Then they'll run me off."

"Yes."

"I don't know where I'll go," he said to her. She didn't answer, and he didn't expect her to.

He took his bowl to one of the washing tubs and gave it to the woman there. Then he went to the mouth of the cave and stared out.

When? he wondered. *How much time do I have?*

From watching, he knew these events usually happened around the full of the moon. Not always. Recently, the women had run off one of the boys he'd known since his first arrival at the cave, and he watched how they did it.

Maybe they'll wait a bit, before they do it to me, he thought. So maybe he had near a moon's turning to think what he would do. Maybe.

Now he felt panic as he realized how little he knew of the other bands. He did know one was fairly close to theirs. A band whose members lived in a forest, not a cave. That was a strange thought to him.

Some of the children in his group knew some of the stranger men who came for the Choosing each spring. He had seen them scurry up to men from other bands, and speak to them as if they knew them, and run little errands for them.

He wondered how they knew to do such a thing. He realized they were making connections with other bands. But it was harvest-tide now, at least out in the world where there were harvests, and he knew he wouldn't last til another Choosing to study how it was done.

He did remember, at the last Choosing, how one of his group had nudged him, pointing out one of the strangers, a young man in a green jerkin, his weapons oiled and keen. "See that one? He was in our group. When I was but little, I remember him. One of the older boys. He has risen fast in his new band, so they say."

But Cae had no such memories and connections to draw on.

He figured he wouldn't be helpless, out there beyond the safety of the cave. All of the cave's children knew how to fight. All of them knew how to hunt. They weren't the hunters the men were, but they could trap a rabbit for the pot, or bring down small game. He didn't think he'd starve.

The cave's midden was the children's armory. When the men of the cave came back for their visits to their wives, they tossed aside broken weapons and worn-out leather armor. Then, between bouts with their wives, they crafted new ones. Not swords or knives. If they had those, they had gotten them out in the world, where there were smiths and bloomeries.

But bows. Many of the men were skilled bowyers and fletchers.

Bows wore out. The men tossed them in the midden.

Then the children fought over them, and the lucky winner of a fight like this would have a valuable prize. Cae himself had won one of these broken bows. He had carefully repaired it. With some of the other lucky boys who had gotten bows from the midden for themselves, they set up butts for practice.

Cae knew he had become a fair archer. More than fair. He had laid in shoulder muscle. He had learned how to fletch, finding the right sticks for arrows, bone for arrowheads or even ones chipped from stones, feathers to affix to the arrows. And he knew his hands to be clever. He could trade his arrows with some of the less-clever boys for other things he wanted. A sling. A snare.

His best prize was a knife. Its edge was blunted and notched. He spent many candle-measures sharpening it on the cave's head cook's whetstone. With cast-off, worn-out leather from the midden, readily available, without even a fight for it, he had made himself a leather cuirass and a leather sheath for his knife and a leather quiver for his arrows. From the chests at the front of the cave, he had found himself leather boots that actually fit him. Maybe not for long.

Don't think about that, thought Cae. *Think about now. Think about soon.*

The moon had gone to dark. Had shone a crescent. Now it began to wax.

Not long now, thought Cae. The unknown expanse of time after that was frightening to him. But he knew that at the very least, he could feed himself. Maybe he could show off his skills to this neighboring band, the one that lived in the forest, and they'd take him.

It was a haunted forest. Cae had heard all the stories. In ages past, malign spirits had imprisoned Merlin the great mage there, barking him up in an oak tree. Cae didn't want to go in there, underneath the great trees. *But I'll have to*, he told himself.

He asked his mother about the forest, and the great mage. She didn't know much about it.

"Myrddin?" she said.

"It's Merlin, I think."

"He goes by many names," she told him.

Privately, Cae wondered whether the mage really existed. He might be just a story.

He was beginning to feel genuinely afraid, even though he knew he was maybe more prepared than most to be cast out utterly on his own.

One night, he stepped to the cave's entrance to look up to the sky. He did this every night, calculating with a cold trickle of sweat how much time he might have left to him. The moon was rounding up into a fat oval. Nearly to full.

One of the older women was strolling past. "That's right, boy," he heard her say under her breath. "Not long now."

Her words caused a fury to rise in him. Before he could caution himself, he had whirled on her with a snarl, and had raised a fist to her.

She stood arms akimbo, not taking a backward step. "This is why we need to cast the likes of you away from us. This," she hissed. "Unruly young men. We need you gone from us. Unrestrained. Unlawful."

A passing older boy from one of the other children's groups saw a fine chance to get in some blows at Cae. He rushed up and jabbed Cae in the ribs.

The woman shrieked curses at them as the two boys circled each other. Cae retreated a little, enticing the other boy to think he could get under Cae's guard. When he tried it, Cae landed a flurry of blows on him so fast and so hard that the fellow bellowed and tried to get away.

But something rose in Cae. Some red fury. He'd never felt it before. He felt himself snarling like a beast. Crouching. Preparing to spring for the other boy's throat.

What he would have done then, he did not know.

Before he could act, a throng of women came rushing past the two of them. "To the fires!" one of them called out to the fighting boys and the woman standing there cursing them.

"It's the baron," one of these women exclaimed. She picked up a stave and started beating Cae and his opponent with it. The first woman stepped in and separated the boys. "Stop this wrangling," she said. "We can't have this now. It's the baron. You cross him, you're dead, the both of you."

The other lad scuttled away, looking back fearfully over his shoulder at Cae.

Cae stood, breathing hard, and the strange feeling inside him began to subside.

The woman was staring at him, even though almost all the others were congregating around the fires.

"The baron," he said to her. "Who is that?"

She didn't answer him, just continued to stare. Finally she spoke. "I see it. You're almost past the safe point. You nearly went past it, just now. We'll need you gone. Maybe tonight. Not tonight," she said, as if talking to herself. "The baron is here. Tomorrow, or maybe the day after. I'll let the others know." And she walked away.

Cae saw that all of the cave's inhabitants had gathered by the fires. He was the only outlier. He shook his head, hard, trying to clear it.

The cave's elder was standing at the central fire, her arms raised.

Cae inched over to one of the outermost of the fires and stood at the edge of the crowd of others to listen. When they noticed him there, several of the women moved away from him.

While everyone is occupied, maybe I should get myself away this very night. Before they can chase me, Cae thought. He'd heard of a few of the older boys who'd done the same.

Across the fires, he spotted his mother and felt—he wasn't sure what. Some wistful thought half-formed itself inside him, to go to her and tell her farewell. He brushed the thought away.

Most of the boys he knew seemed to understand a day would come, and they'd be driven out. Some prepared for it. Others clung to the illusion that they themselves would somehow prove an exception. That they'd be allowed to stay. He saw how such boys might have a closeness with their mothers, or they might have two, or three, or even more sisters and brothers at the cave. A few seemed to be close with some of the cave's men. Maybe they knew they were these men's sons. Such boys had good reason to want to stay, maybe even a hope they'd be allowed to. A hope that their fathers might love them enough to want them there.

Not Cae. He had no father. His mother didn't want him and never had. His brother was far away. Somewhere. Maybe. And now, the strange thing that had happened during his fight with the other boy had done for him.

Even if they didn't drive him from the cave—this, Cae suddenly realized, the moment that, later on, he saw was the moment he moved out of boyhood and took a first step into manhood—he needed to be gone from it.

These thoughts rolled one after another through his mind so fast, he barely had time to recognize them.

Because something was happening at the fire.

A wavery, smoky figure was beginning to solidify beside the elder of the cave. Or maybe it was just a trick of fire-bedazzled eyes. It seemed the figure wasn't standing there, and then it seemed he was.

The elder's voice rang out, quieting the rising murmurs around the fires. "Our baron has come to us. Hail, Most High," she said. She turned to him with a cloak and wrapped him in it. This man who had appeared so suddenly.

Many of the cave dwellers repeated her words. "Hail, Most High."

Cae craned his neck to see better. He stepped closer to the central fire.

"Women with unweaned infants, come forward," the elder commanded.

A number of the women, their babes in slings around their necks, sidled closer to the elder and this strange new figure. *The baron*, the leader had named him. He stood holding the cloak around himself, as if he might be naked underneath.

"As you may recall," said the elder, and her voice penetrated throughout the cave. "This is the year our band has the privilege of giving tribute to the baron. Because of our kind, he has made us special dispensation, and for that we are always grateful."

She paused.

Murmurs rose from those in the cave, hesitant and faint. Mostly women. The children all stood gaping.

"All of us thank you, Most High."

The man beside her, who had said nothing yet, spoke then. "Mistresses of the gwrgi, I thank you for your gracious welcome." The man's voice was smooth and rich. He spoke with a lilting kind of accent.

Our tongue is not his, thought Cae. *He's not one of us.* Peering at the man in the firelight, Cae could see his eyes were dark. *Not like ours.*

"Good mistresses, you know that of all kinds of tribute, I prize a child of six years the most."

Murmurs rose around Cae.

"This is the best age for a child to enter my service," the man went on. "Especially a boy. Yet if that cannot be, I prize an infant. Infants can serve me in their own way. I prize girl infants most."

"Here are infants, Most High," said the elder. "Choose which you will." She motioned.

The mothers with infants in arms lined up and filed silently past the strange man. Even standing a little way off, Cae could see that some of the women brushed away tears.

The man put his hand on each infant. Smiled at each mother. "I know this is hard for you mothers of the chosen. If you will, you may come along with your child, to my service. A use will be found for your milk."

When he said this, Cae felt a shiver crawl up his spine. What could the man's meaning be? Wouldn't the baby need the milk?

This man, this baron, pointed out five or six of the seventeen infants brought before him. The mothers put them into his hands, and he examined each, casting aside their swaddling, prodding at them, holding them up at arms' length. Bringing them close to smell them. Ignoring their howls of outrage and fear.

"These three," he said at last. "And the mothers?"

Two of the women stepped back quickly, leaving their infants with the elder and an assistant she had summoned to help her hold the babes. But one mother stood with her babe before the baron.

"Brave one," said the baron admiringly. "We will use your capabilities well, and you will find yourself well-rewarded," he said to her. Then, looking out into the crowds, he said to the assemblage, "In the morning, I'll leave with my entourage. You other two mothers, please stay with your infants to suckle them before my departure."

Cae could see how reluctant these two mothers were to stay back with the elder, the assistant, the baron, the mother who had volunteered herself. And the three chosen infants, all girl-children. The two mothers who had given up their children looked terrified.

The baron murmured something low and reassuring to them, but still Cae could see how frightened they were.

Now the baron motioned. The elder, the assistant, the mothers with their babes, all made off toward one of the cave's corridors, leaving the baron standing by the central fire.

And all the other cave-dwellers began edging away from him, as if, should they turn their backs on him, something bad might befall them.

Cae looked startled over his shoulder at the jingle of harness. Just outside the cave's entrance, he could make out a troop of mounted men. He was sure they hadn't been there not so long ago, when he stood looking out at the moon. How had they come there so suddenly?

When he turned back to the fire, Cae saw with shock that only he, a few others already making away, and the baron himself were left by the fire. Cae saw he had unconsciously moved closer to the central fire, with his burning need to see and understand.

From the fire, the baron spoke to him. "You, boy. I see you have more courage than the others. Come closer and let me look at you."

Cae shoved down a jolt of panic. He looked around quickly to see if the baron could mean someone else.

"You. I mean you," said the baron, crooking a finger.

Cae couldn't say how it happened, but his feet took him closer to the baron. Very close. Too close.

The baron eyed him. His eyes widened. "Oh, my," he said softly.

Cae couldn't have spoken if someone had taken a poker from the fire to him.

"You have a brother, boy," said the baron.

Cae nodded, his mouth gone dry.

"A brother named Maeldoi."

Cae nodded again.

The baron's eyes roved up and down Cae's body. "What a pity you're not younger. But still—"

The silence stretched between them.

"I believe your people must be on the point of casting you out. Isn't that so?"

For the third time, Cae nodded.

"They'll have to do it fast. You're right on the point of changing." He stared into Cae's eyes. "It won't do for me to just, you know, take you. Of course I could." The baron seemed to be talking to himself now. "What I could do with you," he mused. "But The Three will be most displeased." He seemed to decide something. "Boy. When the time comes—maybe tomorrow, maybe not, but very soon—and they chase you from this place, wait at the foot of the sea cliffs. Wait there. Do you understand me? I'll send someone for you. Then you'll belong to me. If you come to me of your own free will, The Three can hardly object. Can they?" He looked intently into Cae's eyes. "Speak."

"No," Cae heard himself croaking out. "They can't object, if I come to you because I make up my mind to do it." Even after all this time, he had no firm idea who these Three might be. He'd heard the name, heard the cave's elder invoke Them. Some sort of goddess.

"Will you give yourself into my keeping?" said the baron. "A gift freely given?"

"Yes," Cae said.

So then, only a day later, Cae belonged to the baron.

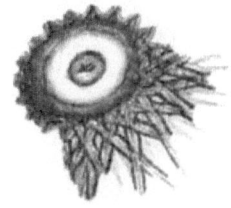

CHAPTER FOUR

All the More

At first, Cae wasn't sure what the baron wanted him for. The Baron Gilles de Rais, the most powerful lord in the Eastern Baronies. He didn't know what that was, the Eastern Baronies, not then, although he realized in a vague way that it must be the name of a realm (as it turned out, the realm where he'd been living, all along—just in a remote part of it). But he was about to learn.

At first, all he could do when he woke up each morning in his soft bed at Gilles's huge stone pile of a dwelling was laugh. His life had changed, once, from misery to a slightly better misery. But now his life had changed again.

When he found out about the tales the ordinary folk told each other around the hearthstones—because until now, he had never heard any—he realized his life had changed the way the pig boy wakes up to find a kind magician has turned him into a prince.

Each morning, he went to a room where servants bathed him and rubbed him with fragrant oils and dressed him in rich clothing. He went to board in the great hall of the baron and dined on the finest cuts of meat, the most delectable dishes of fruit and savories and sweets.

He was completely idle. He wandered in beautiful gardens and stared up in wonder at the tall towers of the baron's dwelling. His castle. That's what the servants called it.

Le château. Cae made the words with his lips.

For a few turnings of the moon, he didn't even see the baron except at a distance, hurrying through the corridors of the castle. For an entire turning of the moon, not at all.

"He's traveling," said one of the servants, when Cae questioned him.

Cae began to worry that he was going soft. *When this man tires of keeping me, I'll still have to make my way in the world, and maybe by then I won't know how*, he worried.

He began teaching himself things. He taught himself to negotiate the many interlocking courtyards of the castle's grounds. He came upon one courtyard that was barred to him by a gate. Beyond it, he could hear voices. Children.

He remembered then the strange way the baron had appeared at the central fire of his band's cave. How he had chosen unweaned babies to take away with him. Where had he put them? Maybe here.

What did he want with them? That was a puzzle.

"Is this where his lordship keeps the children that mothers give up to him?" he asked the guard at the gate, forming the words carefully. These people at the castle spoke a different language from his, and by now he had picked up a little of it. It wasn't the tongue of the cave, nor the similar tongue of the land where he'd lived before the cave. Some other very different tongue.

"Yes, young master, this is where," said the guard.

"But the babies," said Cae. "What do they eat?"

The guard stared at him. "There are no babies."

"But he took babies," Cae insisted. "He took them from the mothers."

The guard gave him a sidelong look. He shrugged. "That's nothing to do with me," he said at last. He turned to Cae. "Some of the mothers, they come along. Did you know that?"

"Yes," said Cae.

The guard said something rapid about the milk they had and giving out of milk and what they did then, but he spoke too fast and Cae couldn't really follow anything he said.

"Like cows!" the guard said, chuckling.

Cae backed away from the man. He didn't understand. He didn't want to.

"He pays me well," the guard shouted after Cae. "Don't think I'm not grateful."

Cae didn't reply. He turned his back and started walking away.

"Puts food on the table," the guard shouted after him. "Don't go telling anyone I'm not grateful."

Suddenly the guard was right there beside him, grabbing at Cae. Shaking him. The man's eyes were panicked. "Don't go telling anyone I'm not."

"I won't," said Cae, shocked.

The man's hands dropped from Cae and he stepped back. With a look half-ashamed, half-defiant, he leaned down to pick up his pike, which had fallen to the grass, and he went back to his post.

Cae made his way back to his own room and sat at the hearth there, shivering. What he had seen was frightening to him. The guard's panic, his shame.

For the first time since he had come to the baron, Cae thought about that last night in the cave. The baron summoning him. The baron extracting a promise from him. Then the baron suddenly not there, only a wisp of smoke.

How he had cried out in fear and wonder.

How he had turned to find his mother standing close beside him. "Should I go with him?" he asked her, feeling something inside him twist and sicken.

"It's the only way," she said. "You won't be in any danger. Only the little ones are in danger." She had given him a long look. Picked up his hand and pressed a leathern bag into it. "There, that's the only thing I have from my family, before your father took me. It should have been your brother's. . ." She trailed off. "It's yours now, Caedon." She had made her way back to the corridor where she slept and disappeared down it. That was the last Cae had ever seen of her.

Now, in his room at the baron's castle, remembering, he stood and went to a chest where he kept his things. He felt around the bottom, underneath his clothing, and pulled out the leathern bag. He sat back down at the hearth and tipped the contents out into his hand. Four small glittering objects. One six-sided, a little amber cube. One glowing red, spiky and four-sided. One many-sided, the blue of the sky. The last one nearly round, with a sort of pebbled texture. Depending on how he held this one up to the light, it wavered sometimes bluish, sometimes greenish. Away from the light, it was a flat gray. He wondered what the little objects were made of. He wondered about his mother's family, and his mother, and why his father had taken her, and how.

After a while, he dropped the little objects one by one into their pouch and hid it away again underneath his clothes in the chest. He was glad he had the glittering objects, and not Maeldoi.

Shortly after that, the Baron Gilles de Rais came back from his travels. Soon, he summoned Cae.

Cae stood before him in a large hall of stone with high, echoing ceilings. By now, he had been all over the castle. Not in this particular room, though. He looked around, taking it all in.

The baron sat at his ease in an elaborately carved chair raised on a dais. Against one arm of this chair leaned a young boy of around six or seven years.

Cae wasn't sure what to do. He remembered the men who had come to his mother's hut so long ago. "Bow," she had told him. He remembered watching his brother, and copying him. Cae bent his body at the waist. Then he straightened up.

"My boy!" said the baron to Cae. "How sorry I have been that duties elsewhere have prevented me summoning you before now. You have much to learn. Courtly manners," he said, smiling. "But we'll deal with those later." He reached out a hand to caress the boy standing at his elbow.

Cae couldn't think what to say to this, so he stayed silent.

"I'm glad to see you've been learning on your own, though. I thought you might. You have an eager mind, Caedon. These past turnings of the moon must have tried your patience, but you have learned quite a bit of my language. This pleases me."

Cae could tell the baron had slowed his speech so that Cae could follow along.

Now the baron turned to the young boy. "Raoul, welcome your new brother. Caedon."

The boy looked into Cae's face and smiled. "Welcome, Caedon. Brother."

His eyes were wide and gray. He was beautiful. Cae felt filled with a strange emotion. Part joy. Part jealousy. In some dim hidden part of himself, he remembered Duiset.

He knew the only brother he had was Maeldoi, so this boy, this Raoul, wasn't his birth-brother. He realized he and this young boy, this Raoul, would become brothers in the baron's eyes. That's what the baron's words meant.

If this were one of the little ones of the cave, I'd chase him down and master him, and he'd know me for the stronger, Cae thought savagely.

Raoul's eyes widened and he took a small backward step.

"You mustn't be frightened, Raoul," said the baron to him, taking the boy's face in his hands and turning his gaze to the baron's. "Caedon is one of the gwrgi. Look at his yellow eyes. But don't be frightened because a creature is a different creature from yourself."

Raoul dropped his eyes from the baron's. He hazarded a glance at Cae, then dropped his eyes again.

What do I see there? thought Cae. He remembered the fear and hatred of many in his boyhood village. But he remembered Duiset, too, and how Duiset had no hatred toward him. Duiset had been drawn to him, and he to Duiset.

Cae had a moment of panic. Where was Duiset's little carved bird? He realized he didn't know. He realized he had lost it.

What do I see? thought Cae again, scrutinizing Raoul. Perhaps this boy wouldn't like it, being told to become a brother to Cae. But Cae didn't see hatred in Raoul's eyes. A little fear, perhaps? Not jealousy.

"Run along, now, Raoul," said the baron to the boy, giving him a gentle push with his fingertips. "Run back to the courtyard and play with your fellows."

"Yes, my lord," piped the boy, and gave the baron a graceful little bow.

I must learn to bow like that, thought Cae.

"A kiss first, though," said the baron.

The boy came to the baron's arms, and the baron kissed him.

Cae looked hastily away. It was a kiss like one he'd seen a man give his bride on Choosing night.

"That's my lovely boy," said the baron softly, and released Raoul, and then Raoul ran from the room and, as he went through the doorway, Cae saw him give a little skip.

The baron sighed. His eyes roved back to Cae. "I love that boy," he told Cae. He leaned toward Cae and his voice dropped into a menacing snarl. "And you are not to touch him."

Cae stood taken aback.

"I'll send other boys to you." The baron waved a negligent hand. He had transformed in an instant back to completely gracious and benign. "They don't stay around long, most of them. Some of them are delectable, though, in their moment, before I require their services. Or girls. I could send you girls." He gave Cae a long, considering look. "But I think not."

"And now I'll begin your education," said the baron after an uncomfortable silence. "You must learn to control the thing inside you. I watched, you know. How you went after that other boy, in the cave, when he goaded you. I'm sure you've learned how to defend yourself. But that was a new emotion, was it not? What you experienced that night?"

Cae looked at him, uncomprehending. *Emotion*, he said to himself, letting his tongue roll around the word. It was unfamiliar to him.

The baron began again. "Was there ever a time," he said, "when your brother Maeldoi transformed before your very eyes from ordinary, with an ordinary rage, to something with the rage of a beast?"

Cae thought to that time he had witnessed, the fight between Maeldoi and his father. That fight, he realized, was what had impelled his mother to summon the men of the cave to take them.

"Yes," he said.

"I thought so. I know so, in fact, because I see what is within you, Caedon. Never think to withhold any thought from me. But what I see here is your understanding. You may not be able to name what you saw, but you saw it, and you understood it was out of the ordinary."

"Yes," said Cae.

"Good," said the baron. "That rage you saw. That is the way of the gwrgi, the male of your kind. You need to learn to control it, as your brother is learning to control the rage inside him."

"That's what his training is for?"

"Indeed."

"But they wouldn't give me that training."

"It's arduous, Caedon. They can't offer it to everyone. The rest of you must simply make do, when your rage overtakes you. And then hope that kindly others will see you past the insensible time that follows. Your kind is very vulnerable, at that moment. Enemies among you wait their chance to catch you at such a moment and end you. It's easy for them to do, then. Or for any other enemies of yours, even wild beasts. Even if they don't understand why you just sit there waiting for them to destroy you. It's a curse, you see. A double-edged sword. Unnatural strength and ferocity gains you an advantage against an enemy. Then the abject weakness that follows might deliver you helpless into some other enemy's hands."

Cae remembered how blank Maeldoi's eyes had been after his fight with their father. If only he had realized, Cae thought. Maeldoi, the stronger. No, in that moment, Cae had been the stronger, and he could have—.

"Ah," said the baron. "So much anger. I can use that, Caedon. I can turn that to my service."

"I am entirely at your lordship's service," said Cae. He had heard one of the servants say this to a visiting noble. It seemed like a good thing to say, so he said it now to the baron.

The baron laughed aloud, delighted.

"We will do well together, boy," he said.

After a moment, he continued. "So. An education. All of it will help you control what's inside you. I myself will teach you letters. You are quick. You'll pick them up fast." He summoned Cae to him and reached out to Cae, caressing his cheek.

Cae shivered, remembering what he had seen between the baron and Raoul.

"Oh, yes," whispered the baron. "That I'll teach you too." His hand lingered on Cae. "You know how to wield a bow, I see, and a knife. But I'm going to set you to a fencing master, Caedon." He smiled at Cae, and his lips parted to reveal his teeth, a bit more pointed than the ordinary. "Look at you. Hard, lithe, quick. You're perfect."

"I don't have a lot of strength," said Cae, trying not to think of those teeth and the feelings they roused in him. Thinking instead of a few of the burliest boys in the cave, and how they would have been able to beat him into submission if he hadn't been fast enough to elude them.

"That won't matter. Not a whit. Well, you do need strength for swordplay. Of course you do. But you have enough for that. I doubt the mace or the club would be your weapon of choice." The baron laughed. "The bow. A fine weapon for the yeomanry. But I have nobler things in mind for you. As for the knife. There are quite graceful, quite deadly methods of fighting with short sword and dagger. I'll find an arms master to teach it all to you. Not just fencing for display. That too. But arms training to refine you from rage-filled boy to honed weapon."

Now the baron began tallying items off on his fingers. "Letters. Arms training. Courtly manners. Horsemanship. Falconry. Music." He stopped. "Hmm. Music. I'll find a tutor to teach you the harp of your native country. After a while, you'll have to put it aside. As you and I come closer to one another—" Here Cae nearly quailed back, because the naked hunger he saw in the baron's face was too baffling and too frightening— "sadly, music becomes a casualty. There's always a price to pay, boy. Never forget that. A small price, in the scheme of things. For now, though, the fingerings of a harp will help refine your dexterity. Do you have any questions of me?"

Cae mutely shook his head.

"Fine, then. We'll begin with letters tomorrow. Attend me in the library. You know your way there? Good. Right after you break your fast." The baron rose from his chair and stepped from the dais.

As he moved past Cae with a hiss of his silken robes, he stopped and put a hand on Cae's arm. He scrutinized Cae.

"How strange that your people should pass you up in favor of Maeldoi. Wonder why. Maybe they didn't see how they would channel your rage. Too strong for them. But with Maeldoi, they did. That could be it. Or maybe, when they found the three of you, it was simply that Maeldoi was ready for their training and you would have required waiting. Yes," said the baron. "That must be it. Considering the urgency of their need." The baron shrugged and smiled at Cae.

Cae stirred uneasily. He knew the real reason. It was because his mother chose Maeldoi, not him.

"Their reason doesn't matter." The baron was still staring at Cae, his gaze roving up and down over Cae's body. "We have a saying in the place where I come from. 'Your loss is my gain.' There's another very like it. You'd usually say this when someone else has rejected a fine piece of meat at a wonderful meal. 'All the more for the rest of us,' you might say with a smile. But when I say it, boy." The baron looked deep within Cae's eyes. "I mean by it, 'All the more for me.'"

His tongue, pointed and red, protruded a bit from under his upper lip, and flicked back. He took his hand off Cae, and Cae nearly fell to the stones of the floor.

He left the chamber—Cae was not quite sure how—and Cae stood trembling there until one of the servants led him back to his own rooms.

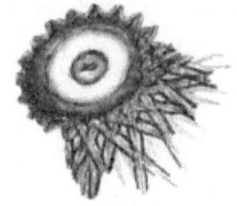

CHAPTER FIVE

An Education

In the castle's library the next morning, Cae began his lessons with the baron.

Cae had looked into this room, the library, in his explorations of the castle. It was a mysterious room lined with shelves, and on these shelves were ranged odd-looking objects. They looked like narrow stacked leather boxes.

There were tables, too, with large unrolled sheets of animal hide, perhaps. But these sheets were too thin to be animal hide, surely. And they were covered with strange marks.

Sorcery. Cae had shivered, laying eyes on those marks of power.

Now, as he came into the room to start his lessons, Cae stepped over to one of these tables to stare down at the unrolled substances. He put out a hesitant finger to touch one. Not cloth. Too stiff to be cloth. Too thin and fine to be hide.

"You were right the first time, Caedon," said a voice just behind him. "They are animal hides. Or were."

Cae startled and whirled around. "My lord," he said and made his stiff little bow.

"Never react fearfully to my presence, Caedon," said the baron. "As far as you know, I'm ever near you. As far as you know, I'm ever in your head, overhearing your thoughts. I may not always be there. My attention may be elsewhere. But I always could be."

The baron regarded him keenly. "Does this frighten you?"

Cae thought to himself, *I must be honest. It won't matter if I lie. He sees my thoughts.*

"Yes, my lord," he whispered.

"Good lad. You understand how it is. And so you see that you need never fear, as long as you are honest."

"Suppose my thoughts displease you, lord?" Cae got out.

"Then you may be sure I will punish you," said the baron. "And so you'll learn always to strive to please me."

"Suppose I fall short."

"Well, then, I'll see that, won't I?" The baron gave him a kindly pat on the shoulder. "That you've tried. Now look—these really are animal hides," he said, pointing down at the table. "But they are scraped very fine. We call this substance by a particular name, parchment, or sometimes, depending on the type of hide, vellum."

"What are they for?" asked Cae.

"You must always address me as lord."

"What are they for, lord?"

"Here, I'll show you something a bit easier to understand, before I answer that," said the baron.

He took Cae by the shoulders and steered him toward another of the tables. When Cae stirred nervously under his touch, he laughed, a low grating sound.

So then Cae knew it was true, that the baron always saw what he was thinking, and he felt himself break out into a sweat.

"Oh, lad," said the baron, his voice tinged with amusement. "It won't do to have you always fearing me this way. Put your mind at rest. This very night, after the evening meal, I'll show you what I mean, by my touch. Then you'll no longer fear it. You'll know what to expect. Partly, anyway. But here. Look here."

Cae looked at where the baron was pointing.

One of the rolled out animal hides had something marked on it that Cae did understand. The mysterious marks, to be sure, as he'd seen before.

But also a picture.

Cae put out a finger and touched it. It was a drawing of a small flower, and all of its parts. Floret. Stem. Roots. And the mysterious marks.

"This scroll is an herbal," said the baron. "It explains the medicinal and also the magical properties of certain plants. It shows the parts of the plant—" The baron reached around Cae and tapped his own finger on the drawing. "—and it explains them in words." He pointed out the mysterious marks.

"Words. I don't understand," said Cae.

The baron was very close. Cae could smell him. He smelled . . . odd, Cae thought. Then he tried frantically to close that thought down.

Beside him, the baron smiled. "Words. Thoughts. Words are thoughts you have—" The baron tapped his fingers on Cae's skull as Cae carefully kept himself from cringing away. "—and these thoughts come out here." The baron moved his finger to Cae's lips.

He pressed his finger softly against Cae's lips, and a strange tingling moved through Cae.

"And then I hear these words of yours." The baron continued to explain past Cae's disquiet. He moved his finger to his own ear. "I hear them, and understand them, inside me." He tapped his own skull.

Cae nodded. *Yes*, he thought. *That's what happens.* Then he thought again of how the baron could read the thoughts in his mind.

Usually.

"Very good," said the baron, smiling again. "You understand. Be at ease, Cae. You please me. So very much. Now suppose, Cae. Just suppose the person who wants to know your thoughts isn't there to hear you speak them. Unless he's me, of course."

Cae nodded along, seeing what the baron was getting at.

"How would you let such a person understand your thinking? Unless he's me," the baron added.

"I wouldn't be able to," said Cae.

"Not if he were a beast. Or a gwrgi."

Cae felt a dull flush seep up his neck and into his face.

"The usual gwrgi," the baron amended, patting him comfortingly. "or the usual peasant, for that matter. The usual noble trained for war. But a scholar? Or a mage like myself? There's a way to make yourself known to such a one."

A prickle of understanding made Cae stand up straighter and lean forward over the scroll. His excitement edged out his anger. "With these marks!"

"Exactly. The marks act much like the picture of the plant. But they are able to do more than a picture can." The baron stopped, considering. "No. That's not it. Let's just say the marks are able to tell you things in a different way than the way of a picture. I will teach you how to use these marks. We will look at the marks on these animal hides—the parchment scrolls here on the table. And also—" Here the baron stepped to one of the shelves and took down one of the oblong leather objects. "—in these." He flipped open leather covers to reveal, not the box Cae expected to see, but many leaves of the parchment substance, made together into a kind of block. Each of the leaves was covered with the marks. "Can you imagine it, Caedon? Conversations with thousands upon thousands of people, most of whom you'll almost certainly never meet, and they are all bound between these leather covers for you to discover."

Cae felt a bit dizzy. "Magic," he breathed.

"Of a sort," the baron agreed. "Sit here beside me, and we will begin."

By the time of the evening meal, Cae's head was swimming with the glory of it all. Only a few turnings of the moon earlier, the baron had taken him from one sphere of existence and had set him into another, the luxurious surroundings of the castle. But these surroundings were just a gateway.

A gateway into a strange and mysterious and marvelous realm, and the baron had just handed Cae the key.

At the evening meal, the baron had Cae sit close by him. Not many others were at board that night, just a few noble guests. The baron conversed with them about matters of state.

Under the table, though, his hand rested on Cae's thigh, and from time to time he stroked Cae's thigh reassuringly. Cae did not feel reassured. He felt some different emotion.

After the meal was over and the servants moved in to remove the boards from their trestles, the baron took Cae by the hand.

"And now I will show you what I meant when I told you today that you should not fear my touch. Come with me, my boy."

He guided Cae down a corridor that, Cae knew, led to his private quarters. The servants had pointed the way out to him once.

"Here," said the baron, pushing open a large carved door. He ushered Cae into a room blazing with beeswax candles on prickets, and a warm fire crackling in a huge hearth built into one wall of the room and faced with large stones.

On a bench by the fire sat the boy Raoul.

He jumped up as the baron and Cae came in.

"I'm here, my lord," he said, making his graceful little leg to the baron.

"Raoul, I won't need you tonight," said the baron.

"Yes, my lord. And tomorrow?"

"I'm not sure when I'll need you next, Raoul. You may go off to your own rooms," said the baron.

"Thank you, my lord!" said Raoul.

Cae was amazed to see the surge of joy and relief that burst over the boy's features. He practically ran from the room.

The baron chuckled. "See how he runs before I can change my mind." He turned to Cae. "Raoul is—" he paused delicately. "—shall we say, a bit reluctant to serve me in certain ways. But all the more savor in it when he is made to do so."

Cae felt himself begin to tremble.

"Now, Caedon," murmured the baron. "No need for fear. All you need to do, boy, is please me."

And then he had overmastered Cae, and Cae found he couldn't do anything to stop him. The puny anger he was able to summon to his aid was snuffed out the way one might snuff out a candle, and Cae had to stand apart from himself and watch it happen.

Afterward, the baron led him to the fire and sat him on the bench. He brought out a fur robe and tucked it tenderly around Cae, and stroked the hair back from Cae's face, and bound his hair with an embroidered band, and kissed him.

It was like the times in the cave when the older boys had cornered him and forced him, thought Cae. Then again, it was nothing like that.

"There now," the baron soothed. "There now. How greatly you have pleased me, Caedon. And later on, you may in your turn take anyone here at the castle for your pleasure. Anyone at all. I'll let it be known. They won't resist you. But Raoul. Not Raoul. Do you understand?"

Cae nodded that he did, but he hardly knew what he was agreeing to. He could hardly think at all.

As day followed day, Cae continued with his lessons in the library. Just as the baron had promised, lessons in fencing, in courtliness, in many other arts, the art of music, the art of dressing well—all were added to Cae's education.

As night followed night, the baron's other kind of education proceeded as well.

By the end of a moon' s turning, Cae knew he had years of study ahead of him in all the arts he learned by day. The thought of all those years did not daunt him.

They thrilled him to think of.

By night, though, he thought he had learned all he needed to learn, and was proficient.

How wrong that turned out to be.

What he was learning at night was merely a preliminary.

One evening, just after the meal, when only a few guests were present, the baron arranged for Cae to show off his apprentice skills with the harp.

Cae and his music master had practiced a short and simple but pleasing piece until Cae felt he could play and sing before a few people without disgracing the baron.

The servants cleared away the board, and Cae took his place on a seat by the hearth of the great hall. The guests gathered around, the baron called for silence, Cae drew a deep breath to steady himself.

He took up his harp and struck a note.

He played and sang.

It was a song about flowers and May, fitting because the winter winds were howling about the castle, and everyone was longing for spring.

Come, my dear love, walk through the woods of May.
My dear love, walk with me.
Listen, the sweet birds with their voices sweet
Calling from tree to tree.
Nightingale the beautiful, that ceasest never.
Take away all grief, for Time, we know. . .
Time, thou fleetest ever.

Then a refrain with just the harp. Short and sweet.

Cae's fingers dropped from the strings, and he was heartened when everyone around him smiled and applauded.

"Wonderful, my boy. Truly wonderful!" the baron exclaimed.

He introduced Cae to all of the guests as his adopted son. Cae noticed the guests exchanging knowing glances, at this.

Soon after, the guests left, and the baron led Cae off, as was his custom, to his private quarters.

Cae prepared to take his clothes off.

"I'm very gratified by you, my boy, the progress you've made in all your studies. No, leave your trousers on," said the baron. "You have worked hard with the music master to improve your skill with the harp, and it shows. You have a very captivating voice, has he told you that?"

Cae felt himself glowing with pleasure.

"Ha, ha, no need for false modesty, my boy."

"I don't know how I sound, lord. I can't hear myself."

The baron turned serious then and led Cae to the bench by the fire. "I'll tell you a thing, Caedon. I can't hear you either. Oh, I can hear that you and your instrument are making noise. That's all I can hear. I know you sounded well tonight, though, because I could see it in the others' eyes, when you sang. And the music master has told me the same. He thinks you are one of his more promising students. He thinks, should you wish it, that you could become an accomplished musician."

"I didn't know that, my lord."

"You won't, though," the baron went on. "Become an accomplished musician," he continued at the question in Cae's eyes. "Do you know why you won't?"

"Because I don't have the talent for it, in spite of what the music master thinks?"

"That's not why. It's the same reason why I can't hear you, lad. Once you begin serving me in the way I expect you to, you'll have to give up your music. Those of us possessed of certain powers must give up certain things. Music is the first to go. Almost always, it's the first. I tell you this so you won't be disappointed, later. Of course, if you choose not to serve me, you might still practice that art."

"But I will always serve you, lord," said Cae.

"Good answer, Caedon," said the baron, "and when I look within you, I see you mean it sincerely. Because if you were dissembling about that, I'd see it, you know."

Cae nodded. "I do mean it," he said.

"In spite of having to give up music?"

Cae nodded again.

"What about giving up many other things?"

"What things, lord?"

"Ah, I see you're not as certain now," said the baron, and his eyes had a disturbing glint in them.

"I am completely at your disposal, lord," said Cae. His lips felt numb.

"Giving up your choice in love? Will you give that? I don't mean possessing whomever you wish. You may have that, that's nothing. Less than nothing. But love?"

"Yes, it's yours, lord," said Cae.

"I hear duty there, Caedon, not conviction."

"Do I have a choice?" said Cae.

"You have a choice. Only a gift freely given can please me."

"You said that once before, lord." Cae remembered.

"That's right, I did. The day I took you away from the gwrgi, who were about to abandon you. You might have thought, then, what do I have to lose? I'll give myself to this noble lord." Gilles regarded him narrowly.

"You see into my heart, lord," said Cae, with a sinking feeling. No use in lying or prettying up the truth. "But truly, I hardly know what love is."

The baron nodded thoughtfully. "You're right, you don't. You hardly do know it. But one time, it touched you. Do you remember when?"

"Duiset," said Cae dully. He didn't know that was what he was about to say, but as soon as he had said it, he knew it to be true.

The baron gave him an approving smile and took his hand. "You are honest with me, Caedon. I value that. Yes. The young boy you knew, so long ago. No love from mother and father and brother. Love from that boy."

"Yes," said Cae, feeling downhearted.

"Here," said the baron and held out a small object to Cae.

Cae could not stop himself exclaiming. Duiset's little carved bird, the one he was sure he had lost.

"Keep it always, Caedon, as a token of love, not just from that boy, but from me." Then the baron said softly, "I see you value this little object more than any rich jewel I might have given you."

The tears poured from Cae's eyes, and the baron pulled him over and stroked him and let him cry.

"I'm sorry," said Cae, after a moment. "I just—"

"No need for apologies, my dearest lad. However, as I mentioned, there's a price to pay, and you must pay it."

"Give up my music."

"Give up your music only because you are about to give me what I need. And after that, music will be abhorrent to you. As it is to me."

"I don't understand, lord."

"You will fear music, after this. I don't fear it, but that's because I have strong wards that I place between me and it, so I can listen with every pretense of enjoyment but feel nothing."

"After what, lord?"

"This," said the baron, and he drew Cae toward him again, and then, through Cae's ear, he insinuated a chill penetrating presence of himself that bored rapidly to Cae's brain and spread throughout all the branching structures of Cae's body.

As the baron withdrew from Cae, he withdrew a thin essence of Cae himself.

It resembled a long fleshy thread.

Cae's body shuddered as the baron withdrew this thread from him. His entire body shuddered after it, at its withdrawal.

The baron held him while he vomited.

"No fear, lad. No fear. Not so bad, this time. I'll let you get used to it gradually. But know this. I enjoyed the taste of you very much, as I fed. Very much indeed, as much as I thought I might. You are my best beloved, Caedon. I look forward to feeding from you again."

Part II: MAELDOI

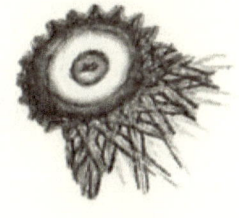

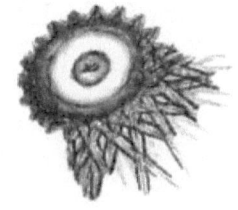

CHAPTER SIX

An Education

A fter their small family's journey from their home on the moors in a distant land, to the mouth of the cave where they had all somehow appeared, Maeldoi stood on the threshold of a new life. The three strange gwrgi, their three visitors, led Maeldoi away from his mother and brother. Just outside, four horses were tethered.

"Can you ride, boy?" said the leader of the three to Maeldoi.

Maeldoi stared at him in consternation.

"No, I suppose you can't," the leader said with a sigh.

The others muttered in gibberish.

Maeldoi couldn't understand what the others were saying. At least the leader spoke in his own language. At least Maeldoi could understand one of these strange gwrgi.

"We'll have to teach him everything, rector." That's what one of the other gwrgi was saying to the leader in an undertone. "Is it—is this—"

"Worth it? Worth the effort? We're told it is. So we must try with the lad," the leader said in their own language. Not Maeldoi's.

From listening carefully, Maeldoi began to realize that *rector* must be the leader's name. Or maybe his title. That was just about the only thing he understood, in the midst of all their gabbling speech. He could sort of make it out, but they spoke too fast. Just the same, he understood they were talking about him in tones of dismay and dismissal.

"You know," the rector was saying to the other two after a moment of silence, "Once we deliver the lad to the rectory, it will be up to him. He won't be your responsibility any longer. He'll still be mine, I suppose. I'll step away from him and watch. He'll be given his chance. If he does not measure up—" Here the leader, the rector, turned his eyes on Maeldoi. "—well, that's his lookout, not yours. Not mine either."

The other two nodded.

They're saying something about me. And it's not good, thought Maeldoi. *Something about not measuring up.*

One of the gwrgi, the one who had talked so earnestly to the rector, approached Maeldoi, while the other two got on two of the mounts.

"Here, boy." He led Maeldoi around to the left-hand side of the horse. Maeldoi understood that much. "I'll make my hands into a sort of step, see. Come over here to the near side of the horse. Put your foot in the step, and I'll hoist you into the saddle. After that, just hold on." He must have seen Maeldoi hadn't understood much of it, so he demonstrated in gestures.

Maeldoi had looked up at the horse and had taken a little lurch backward. Then he saw the glint in the man's eye. *He expects me to fail. He expects me to be afraid*, thought Maeldoi.

Maeldoi approached man and horse nervously.

"No, the left foot," said the man, and Maeldoi saw with anger that he was suppressing his exasperation. *I must not get angry*, he told himself. *This man thinks I'm stupid, but it's just that I don't know his speech.* He realized the man wanted his other foot, so he put his left foot into the step the man's locked hands made for him, and he grasped desperately at the mane of the animal as the man boosted him into the saddle atop the beast's back.

As the horse sidestepped skittishly, Maeldoi grabbed at the reins. He'd seen the others with their hands on these long leather thongs.

"Easy, boy," said the gwrgi who had helped him mount. Maeldoi didn't know whether the man was addressing these words to him or the horse. Maybe both.

Once the horse had quieted, the man moved to Maeldoi and guided his foot into the stirrup on the near side of the horse. Maeldoi got the idea and stuck his own right foot into the stirrup on the off side.

"There. You're set," said the man, giving Maeldoi a sour smile. "Don't fall off."

Maeldoi understood right away what the man had told him. He gripped the padded wooden saddle between his knees with the strength of panic, collected the reins in his left fist, and held on to the high pommel for dear life with his right hand. He managed to achieve some kind of precarious balance.

The man handed up a stout cloak to Maeldoi, and he pried his hands loose long enough to wrap it around himself. It helped against the bite of the wind. Then back to his panicked clutching of saddle and reins.

"We'll take it slowly," said the rector in Maeldoi's own language, and headed off down the path that led away from the sea cliffs and the cave. "Nice and easy. No fear, boy."

The other two rolled their eyes. Maeldoi saw.

By the time they reached their destination that early evening, Maeldoi was sore, exhausted, and terrified. But he had done it, and he was alive.

One of the men helped him down into an inn yard.

"I suppose we can count this as your first lesson, lad," said the rector.

"Doesn't talk much, does he?" said one of the others.

Maeldoi didn't catch what the other man was saying, speaking in that strange liquid-syllabled language of theirs. But he caught the man's tone, and his fists clenched at his sides.

"Maeldoi," said the rector.

Maeldoi turned his eyes on the rector.

"Don't look in that sullen way at me."

Maeldoi tried to rearrange his face and realized, from the reaction of the other man, that he must not be doing a good job of it.

"Listen, lad. This is the last time anyone will speak to you in that barbarous language of yours from across the sea. I know your language, and the cave's language, too, from an unfortunate episode in my past, and that's why they sent me to you and your family, the gods help me. That's why we get the honor of your keep here at the northern rectory and not the one to the south. But almost none of the rest of us know your language. These two men were born here on the peninsula. That's how they know the cave's language, and it's very much like your own. That's why they came, too. But none of us will be by you after today. I might come by the rectory from time to time. Not often. You are going to have to learn to speak properly, and learn fast. I mean by that the language of the ordinary people in the inland baronies, where I'm taking you. And that language, boy, is very unlike your own. Tell me that you understand."

"I understand," said Maeldoi, even though there were things he didn't understand in what the man was telling him.

" 'I understand, sir,' " the man corrected.

Maeldoi made himself say it.

"Good," said the man. "Follow these others. They'll take you to a place where you can eat something, and relieve yourself—" Here he stopped, for Maeldoi had turned aside to unlace his britches. "Stop."

Maeldoi looked up startled from his pissing.

"You must not do that here. Do it in private."

Maeldoi gave him an incredulous look.

One of the others made some remark, and the other started laughing.

Maeldoi turned to them with his fists ready.

"Maeldoi. Stop. Stop or I'll have you whipped and locked up."

Maeldoi lowered his hands.

"You have much to learn, Maeldoi. What we were saying back there, the others and I. We were saying we doubt you'll be able to learn fast enough. We were saying we think you'll fail. And will you?"

Maeldoi stared at him hard in the light of the inn yard's torches. "I won't fail." He hardly knew what he was promising, though. What task was he being set to? He had no idea. But he did know one thing. This man and these sneering others would not win. He'd win.

"Good. You have a lot of work to do, then," said the rector. "You must study what others expect of you. You must understand that you'll have to undo the habits of your entire life. And if you get angry about it, especially if you offer violence to any, you can expect harsh punishment. If your faults continue, and your superiors judge them irredeemable, you will be cast out. Or worse. Are we clear?"

"Yes," said Maeldoi. "Sir," he added. Then, "May I ask a question?"

"One," said the rector.

"Why am I here with you and not with my mother and brother? Sir."

"We have chosen you for training, Maeldoi. You will likely never see your family again. If you fail, you will be cast out. You will probably die. If you succeed. Well, then."

The rector turned away, handed the reins of his horse to a waiting groom, and stalked away.

By gestures, the others made him understand where to sit inside the inn.

Maeldoi accepted a bowl of stew. He accepted bread and ale. He gobbled the food down, holding the bowl to his lips and shoveling the food in with his hands. He bolted the ale, aware that the others were regarding him with disdain. *But I don't care*, he told himself.

That rector told you that you have to care, he said to himself after a moment. So then he watched how the others ate, and tried to copy how they did it, even though it made no sense to him, eating in such a prissy way as that. Even though, when he tried using the implement he later knew as a spoon, he got more stew on him than in him. He cast it away with a muttered curse.

After they had eaten, the man who had helped him mount his horse took him by the elbow and led him to a room with a bed. He, the other two gwrgi, and two of the ordinary folk there at the inn settled down together for the night. The two strangers looked with alarm over at Maeldoi and his companions, and moved as far away from them as the bed allowed. Maeldoi paid them no mind. He slept like someone gone to his grave.

In the morning, one of his companions—keepers, really—cuffed him to make him hurry to break his fast. Maeldoi schooled himself to take it, and to do the man's bidding.

Then back on the horse. They were riding far inland, and soon they were making their way up into some mountainous terrain.

"There," said one of Maeldoi's two keepers. The man pointed.

Nestled into a valley, the stubby red stone tower of a building rose through the trees.

Not much longer afterward, they were dismounting in the courtyard of a stone building with several towers and a long stone gallery pierced with arched windows, giving views into an enclosed garden at the center of the structure.

The men motioned to Maeldoi to follow them. They led him into a doorway under the nearest and highest tower, into a stone hall. Maeldoi had never been inside such a large closed-in space. Groups of men and boys stood about. All of them gwrgi.

One of these other men moved to them. Maeldoi's companions, or keepers, or whatever they were shoved Maeldoi in the man's direction, spoke to him rapidly in a very different tongue, and went back outside.

Maeldoi turned his head to look after them. He never saw them again. The rector, not for a long time afterward.

"You. Boy. Maeldoi."

At the sound of his name, Maeldoi swiveled to the new man standing before him.

"Kneel," said the man, and shoved Maeldoi down with a hand on his shoulder.

Maeldoi struggled for a moment, then realized and knelt.

The man directed a long string of incomprehensible language at him—truly incomprehensible this time, not the halfway intelligible language of the rector and his keepers on the road—and then hauled him back to his feet. He motioned to Maeldoi, led him outside to a kitchen shed, and soon Maeldoi found himself occupied in scouring a row of pots almost as big as he was.

The task took him all day. He thought of trying to get away through the big gates, but instead he bent to the task and kept at it until his hands were raw.

At the end of this work he'd been assigned, some other man spoke some command to him and pointed. A line of boys—boys just on the point of becoming young men—were lining up outside the kitchen. Maeldoi understood he was meant to join them. He made his way to the end of the line. When he arrived at the front of it, he was handed a battered tin pan with some stew in it, a piece of bread, and a cup of ale.

The usual fare.

The line wended out into the garden at the center of the buildings. All the boys sat on benches with their stew. Their spoons. Their cups of ale.

Maeldoi set his spoon down on the bench, lifted the tin to his mouth, and slurped the stew down.

He noticed some of the other lads looking sidelong at him. "What?" he said to them. They weren't men placed over him. He didn't care what they thought. Dimly he thought of the inn and the way those keepers of his had eaten, and how he had copied them. But these were just stupid boys. Why should he conform his actions to theirs? He made a rude gesture at one of them.

Almost immediately, he and the other lad were rolling about on the stones of the courtyard, gouging and biting and getting in a fist whenever they saw an opening.

Until they were pulled apart by two of the men set over them.

Maeldoi stood under the hand of one of these men, heaving up deep breaths, staring down the other boy with satisfaction. He wondered if he looked as battered as his opponent. Blood dripped from some cut into his eye, and he wiped it away.

The men questioned both lads sharply. The other one answered, elaborating with gestures and outraged exclamations. The men sent him away.

Then they turned on Maeldoi and directed their stream of language at him.

Maeldoi stood looking stonily at the stony pavement.

One of the men shouted something in his face. The other hustled him away to a little dark room, shoved him inside, and barred the door.

Maeldoi tried it. It didn't open. It was shut fast. So he sat down on his haunches against the wall to wait.

No one came.

He pissed in a corner. He slept in the little room, huddling into himself for warmth.

A long time later, some different men opened the door, and morning light streamed in. Then he knew he had spent all night in the windowless room.

These men stared down at him.

"Get up," said one.

Maeldoi didn't understand the words, but he understood what the man wanted just the same. Supporting himself against the wall, he got to his feet. He felt his whole cramped body begin to loosen and unfold.

"Come," said the man who had spoken.

Maeldoi stored that word up. He saw what it meant. If someone said it to him again, he knew he'd recognize it. He shambled out of the room, and the men laid hands on him and walked him down a long corridor and into the courtyard of the afternoon before.

Rows of boys—others like him, he supposed, brought here to learn how to perform some mysterious task—stood silently. He recognized one or two from the evening's meal. And there, his face bandaged, was the boy he had fought. He directed a sneer at this boy, who looked away.

At the head of the rows of boys stood a man in a long robe, a man with an air of authority. Beside him, a man with a leather whip.

In one way, all of those in the courtyard were like him. *We are all gwrgi*, thought Maeldoi, looking around him. *We all have the eyes.*

In another way, there was a big difference. Two kinds of people stood in the courtyard. All the others, filling the courtyard. And then the one who was different. Maeldoi.

Those accompanying him took Maeldoi to the end of the courtyard where stood the two men who seemed to be in charge, and stepped away from him, leaving him there.

The man in the long robe made some pronouncement to the assembled boys. Maeldoi examined this man's robe with interest. It was not fur. It was cloth, but cloth with a soft nap, almost fur-like. He wanted to touch it, to find out what substance it might be made of.

But the man was saying something to Maeldoi. Maeldoi looked up. The man's eyes were severe.

"Maeldoi," he said.

"Sir," Maeldoi replied. He had learned this.

The man gabbled at him. Maeldoi didn't know exactly what he was saying, but he knew approximately. The stern man was gesturing at the man with the whip.

They're going to beat me, Maeldoi thought. *Nothing my father hasn't done many times over*, he thought.

The man with the whip stepped to Maeldoi and grabbed him by an arm. He cast Maeldoi down before a bench. He leaned over and with a leather thong, he tied Maeldoi's wrists to this bench. Then he grabbed Maeldoi's tunic at the nape of the neck and ripped it apart. The cloth tore under the man's hands. The cloth of the tunic his mother had made him wear, too tight about the shoulders. It tore easily. Maeldoi figured the cloth of it was not of the best quality, and who knows how long it had lain in that chest of his mother's? It was probably rotten already. Now it fell away from him in shreds as the man's whip came down about his shoulders and back.

For a while, Maeldoi successfully kept from crying out or making any sort of resistance. But then he passed some point where all he could see was a red haze before his eyes, and he felt himself fighting and struggling and kicking out with his legs, which weren't bound. Then nothing beyond some wailing and roaring and agonized moaning coming to him from a long way off.

He spent he wasn't sure how many days afterward in the small windowless room.

When he finally knew himself again, his back was throbbing and he was horribly thirsty. He hoped they'd left him a pail of water. He remembered it from before.

As he crawled to the corner where he remembered it standing earlier, he was aware someone else was in the room with him.

"You've come back to us, Maeldoi," said a voice out of the dark.

Maeldoi heard his name. Beyond that, he understood nothing else.

"Can you stand?"

A hand yanked him to his feet.

Maeldoi stumbled and nearly fell.

"Easy," said the voice.

Maeldoi understood that. One of the men who had taken him from the cave had used that word to Maeldoi's horse. Maeldoi stored the word up. Now he knew two or three of their words. *Come. Sir. Easy.* And of course he knew his own name.

The door to the room creaked open and through the crack of light that streamed in, Maeldoi, slitting his eyes against the unaccustomed brightness and the pain that throbbed throughout his body, saw a man, a fairly young man, lounging against the lintel. This was the man in the room with him, the man who had just pushed the door open.

"I'm your tutor, Maeldoi. Your last-chance tutor. The rector and his assistant figure you're not going to learn. Never going to adjust. You have these natural abilities, and they want that. But maybe they're locked too tightly inside you, Maeldoi. So the good men of the rectory are debating. Turn you out? Or maybe just put you down. Like a mad dog, Maeldoi. But then they say, Aleron, you take him on. See what you can do with him."

None of this beyond his own name penetrated to Maeldoi. The man's voice was strangely soothing, though. Maeldoi felt his agitation lessen.

The man leaned toward Maeldoi. He patted his own chest. "Aleron," he said. His face was long and lean, his yellow eyes glinting with amusement.

"Aleron," Maeldoi repeated. He understood. It was the man's name.

"You won't have training with the others. Just with me. Then, when I say you're ready—if I say you're ready—you'll join the others. But Maeldoi, if I may speak freely, I don't like your chances. You're little more than a beast." The man laughed and poked Maeldoi in the chest as he said it. He emphasized the word. "A beast of the caves. Even if you progress, you'll never catch up with these others. But maybe if you work hard, you'll make a minor place for yourself, enough for a bed out of the rain, hey? The rectory always needs kitchen servants and stable boys. Always a need for someone to muck out the jakes, hey?"

What's he telling me? Maeldoi thought. He saw that same expression the others had worn on their sneering faces. Skeptical. Half-appalled, half-amused. *He's telling me how I will fail. He's telling me I'm no good. In fact,* Maeldoi realized, *he's telling me I'm an animal.*

"I'm not—" Maeldoi began. He thought about the journey, how the horses had shied at the scent of some beast, how the minders had scouted around and had repeated this word back and forth, *beast.* Here was the same word, and the man standing before him with a sneer on his face was directing it at him. In a burst of understanding, Maeldoi realized what it meant. *Beast.*

Maeldoi pointed to himself. "Maeldoi," he said. Then, carefully, picking out a few words he had figured out, and adding this new one. "Not a beast."

The eyebrows of this Aleron arched in surprise.

"No beast," Maeldoi repeated firmly.

"Let's get you cleaned up, then, like a person, not some stinking animal. Let's get you something to eat, then," murmured Aleron, guiding Maeldoi out of the little room.

As they moved together down the corridor, the boys they passed swerved out of their path. The boys looked over their shoulders at Maeldoi with round yellow eyes and gaping mouths.

"You're the talk of the rectory, Maeldoi. Here. Before we go further—" Aleron moved him down a side corridor to a little smelly shed. "This is the jakes. Here is where you—" Aleron demonstrated. "Nowhere else. Do you understand?" When Maeldoi looked back at him, puzzled, he pointed to the jakes, said the word again, *jakes*, and mimed again what was to be done there.

Then he pointed outside the jakes, acted out a little scene. Squatting to shit, slapping his own face, standing up, rushing to the jakes—and so on.

By then, Maeldoi felt a grin stealing across his face. "Jakes," he repeated. "Shit here." He realized he had learned another word, too. *Shit.*

"Piss here too," said Aleron, mimicking.

"Shit and piss," said Maeldoi. "Here." He pointed.

"Excellent," said Aleron. "Lesson One accomplished."

No, thought Maeldoi later, when he had the language to mull it over. That other man had told him. Lesson one, get on a horse. This was lesson two. But now he nodded at Aleron, not really understanding, but understanding enough.

"Nine Spheres," Aleron was saying to himself. "How did this lad come here at all? How in the name of The Three will he make his way?"

Maeldoi's ears pricked. The Three. That god. He'd heard that god's name. This man, he thought, was calling on his gods for strength. That's how terrible he thought Maeldoi was. He thought of the word the man in the robe had hurled at him many times, as he was about to be beaten. *Bad.*

Maeldoi stopped and thumped his chest again. "Not bad," he declared of himself.

Aleron regarded him for a moment. "We'll start there, then," he muttered.

After that, Maeldoi found himself in the bathing shed. He remembered the bath his mother had forced on him. He made himself endure this one, as the bathing servant washed him and exclaimed in disgust. He made himself not struggle. The water felt unexpectedly good against his skin, even though it stung all the places that had been whipped raw or beaten with fists or bitten.

Next, Aleron took him into the kitchen to be fed. Outside in the courtyard, he glimpsed the other lads breaking their fast. He started toward them.

"No," said Aleron, shaking his head firmly. He led Maeldoi to a small bench at the back of the kitchen next to the big hearth. They ate there.

Between the bath water and the hearth and the hot food in his belly, Maeldoi felt himself begin to thaw.

He was only in ragged and blood-stained trousers. He knew his tunic must have been in tatters by the time that man with the whip had finished with him. The shreds of it must have been dumped in the midden.

After they ate, he followed Aleron to a storeroom with a chest. Aleron rummaged around. "Try these." He thrust a new pair of trousers, a new tunic, a cloak at Maeldoi. Maeldoi stepped out of the old trousers and kicked them away. His skinny wiry body pimpling in the chill, he drew on the new trousers and pulled the new tunic over his head. It fit him. He furled the cloak around himself and leaned his face into a comforting fold of it. If he had still been a little boy, he knew he would have cried. But he made his face into a stone.

"Before we can learn, we must be fed and warm," said Aleron softly.

They ended in a room with a small woman puttering over a shelf with various herbs and potions ranged along it. She looked up as they stood in her doorway.

"Maeldoi," said Aleron.

Maeldoi turned his eyes on his tutor.

"Pull up your tunic so the healer can see your back." Aleron demonstrated.

Maeldoi turned around and eased up his tunic.

He heard the woman behind her, clucking with her tongue. Then cool fingers spreading cool salve along the welts and hurts.

"Get him shaved and bring him back to me, Master Aleron, and I'll go to work on his face," she told his tutor.

"Probably not til tomorrow," said Aleron. "One step at a time, with this one. I might have to get help to hold him still, if the bathing man is to shave him."

"Crop his hair while you're at it. No place for vermin to hide." The healer regarded Maeldoi with her head cocked. "He looks like a beast of the caves," she said.

Maeldoi put his hand on his chest. "Maeldoi," he told her. "No beast."

And so Maeldoi's education began.

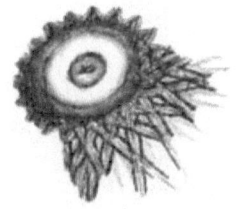

CHAPTER SEVEN

A Step At a Time

In very short order, Maeldoi knew enough of the strange new language that he could converse with Aleron.

At first, all they talked about was fighting. Along with the basic things, like what a jakes was for and how he needed to bathe every day—"Every single day," Aleron insisted, hauling him off to the bathing shed—and how to use a spoon, they talked about combat. Incessantly about combat.

At first Maeldoi was skeptical. At their first sparring session, their hands wrapped in leather strips, dressed in light trousers that came only to the knee, their hair tied back with thongs, he sized Aleron up and thought, *I can take this fellow.*

Aleron was older by five years. He weighed more than Maeldoi and was taller. But his torso wasn't a mass of scar tissue, as Maeldoi's was.

He hasn't fought the way I have, Maeldoi thought. *I'll bet I'm faster,* he thought.

Maeldoi was right about the first, wrong about the second.

Aleron did not fight the way Maeldoi did. He fought smarter, and in a completely different style. And he was fast. So fast. Sometimes Maeldoi could swear he hadn't even seen Aleron's fist coming before it laid him out in the dirt.

After the first, second, maybe third humiliating defeat, Maeldoi steeled himself to ask it.

"Aleron, master," he said.

"Yes, Maeldoi?"

"Will you teach me this, what you do?"

"I thought you'd never ask, Maeldoi," said Aleron with a grin. "You are so stubborn I think your head must be made of wood."

Maeldoi felt himself flushing.

Aleron stood quietly and watched him.

Maeldoi wanted to rush at Aleron and pummel him for those words. Then he thought, *No. He's waiting for me to do exactly that, and then he will strike me down again.* "Yes," Maeldoi made himself say. "But I am ready to learn."

"Now," said Aleron. "Now we progress. Only now can we do it."

Maeldoi nodded. "Yes," he said.

"You have the will, the strength, the quickness. Everything, Maeldoi. It's born in you. You only lack tactics and strategy. I'll teach you what I know. Then you'll be the one defeating me."

Maeldoi had been staring at his feet, ashamed. Now he raised his eyes to Aleron's. He saw respect there. He smiled at Aleron, and Aleron smiled back.

"That stubbornness of yours, Maeldoi," said Aleron. "It's your enemy now. But I will show you how to make it your friend." Aleron held out his hand.

Maeldoi gripped it with his own. He had seen others make this gesture, with their hands. He had never done it himself. Now he saw what it was. A promise. A vow. A bond.

After that, Maeldoi's combat training progressed in a long smooth upward curve. Maeldoi used to wake each day to misery, so much a part of him that he'd never recognized it for what it was. Now he woke each day to a fierce kind of joy.

To this point, all of the combat training was hand-to-hand.

One day Maeldoi finished eating with the others—for now he was judged civilized enough to do that—and made his way out to the little area behind the rectory where Aleron taught him. Normally this practice would take place early in the morning, before they went in to break their fast. But today Aleron told Maeldoi to meet him at the practice area after the midday meal.

Shortly after noontide, Maeldoi found Aleron under a tree at the edge of this area. He looked at Aleron, his brow quirked up. "I'm here, Master," he said only.

"Here's something new, Maeldoi." Aleron nudged a long, cloth-wrapped package with his toe. Maeldoi had come to the rectory in mid-winter. Now the year had moved into late springtide. They sat together comfortably basking in the mild spring-tide sun.

"Maeldoi, by now, you can defeat me seven out of every ten passes. I'm sure you will surpass me entirely as you progress further," Aleron began.

"Yes," said Maeldoi.

Aleron laughed. "And your manners have improved, despite some rough edges still."

Maeldoi waited, to see where this conversation of theirs would lead.

"It's time for a new phase of your training." Aleron leaned forward to unwrap the package. A sword of glittering metal. A long knife. A club. A bow. "Weapons training. Look at these weapons. Get a feel for them in your hands. Tomorrow we'll begin to practice with them."

Maeldoi reached for the sword and felt the heft of it. He put it carefully down. "Master Aleron?"

"Yes, Maeldoi?"

"What would you be doing, if you weren't training me. Would you be training the others?" Maeldoi had watched the other boys as they lined up each day for their own training with the rectory's arms master and his assistant. The men worked them hard, then released them for the rest of the day to eat and play.

Once Maeldoi had gone with some of them toward the nearby village of ordinary people. The other students didn't all hate him or fear him now. Some of them had made overtures of friendship, although Maeldoi was cautious around them. This day, he followed a group of them as they made their way to a little woods.

"Now watch," said one of the boys to the others. Maeldoi edged in to watch, too. The boy raised his hand for silence. After a long wait, he hissed, "Here she comes."

A young peasant woman, a yoke on her shoulders from which hung two pails, one on either side, came walking down the lane in the woods that led to the nearby village of ordinary folks.

"She can't get away from us very easily," whispered the lad who had taken them there. "She's burdened by her pails and that yoke. See anyone about?"

"No," whispered another of the lads. "I've been looking. She's alone."

With a yelling, the whole pack of them had leaped from the underbrush and had taken her down, one of them smothering her cries with his hand. They all quickly took their turn with her.

But Maeldoi had hung back in the woods, still watching.

When they released her, stunned and sobbing, they had all rushed back past the place where Maeldoi stood. He had turned and had run to the rectory with them. The rest sat about the rectory's well, laughing and boasting.

One of them had turned to Maeldoi. "You don't like women?"

"I do like women," said Maeldoi.

"He likes boys," joked one of the others.

"I don't like boys," said Maeldoi, reddening.

The others had looked at each other. They probably remembered what had happened, when one of them had goaded him.

"You didn't take a turn. Scared?" said one of the bolder ones.

"I didn't feel like it," said Maeldoi, and made himself walk away before he could strike that lad.

The scene played itself out before Maeldoi's inner eye, and he felt himself cringing. He couldn't have said why.

But Aleron was speaking past this memory unscrolling itself in his head. Aleron was answering the question he had asked. "No, I wouldn't be training the other lads," Aleron said.

"So tell me," said Maeldoi, wrenching himself from the troubling memory with an effort. "Why are you training me? We've never talked about it."

"When the rector and his assistants went to your home across the Narrows," said Aleron, "they were there to examine you. Your mother had sent word that you were becoming a man. They needed to see for themselves."

"I don't see them doing that with anyone else."

"No," said Aleron, hesitating. "You did know your father, true?"

"Yes," said Maeldoi.

"Tell me about him."

"He was a terrible man. He beat us. Me and my little brother. He beat my mother. He—" Maledoi shied away from another memory even more painful. What his father had done to him, that last time.

"Did you know much about him?"

"No. Just that he came to us a few times a year, and that we dreaded to see him, when he came. I think my mother hated him."

"He was from the Fastnesses. He is dead now," said Aleron, watching him.

"Good," said Maeldoi. He felt something rising up inside him. "Because if he were alive, I'd find him and kill him myself." He didn't know those words would come bursting out of him. They did.

"The enforcers of the Fastnesses hunted him down and did the job for you," said Aleron, his tone dry. "He had done a very wrong thing. Your mother was not his to take, and he took her. Maeldoi—" He looked at Maeldoi carefully. "You may not be that man's son. You may be the son of the man he killed, when he took your mother. It's impossible to say."

"I'd like to think it is true," said Maeldoi, low.

"It would make sense," said Aleron. "You have the name of one of the cave bands. Your brother has a name from the Fastnesses. From that man's people. The man you've believed to be your father."

"So his people killed him for his crime, and then your rector came to take us all to the cave band."

"Yes," said Aleron. "But then they saw something in you. In your brother as well, but they could only take one of you to train."

"Why me? Why not Cae? My brother," he added.

Aleron shrugged. "He was too young, maybe. They wouldn't have been able to start his training right away, but they could start it, with you. And then—then maybe you don't have that man's blood. Maybe you have the blood of our own bands in you."

"My mother chose," said Maeldoi suddenly, remembering. "She said, Take the elder. So the rector took me and not Cae." He thought briefly of his brother, with pity, but then the thought flitted away. He never thought of Cae. Almost never. "So all of us at the rectory are here to be trained. Trained for what?"

"You probably don't know much about the life of the men in the cave and forest bands. They hunt. They provide for the band.

They take wives from the neighboring bands. But we gwrgi are more than animals living in caves and forests. We are prized throughout the realms for our abilities. Monarchs vie with each other for our services. Some don't want to have anything to do with us, especially those realms to the west and north. They're afraid of us because we are not their kind. But many of the barons, many of the monarchs of the Fastnesses, the Lyre Lands, the Burnt Lands want our cohorts to do their fighting, or fight alongside them in their battles. And there are special tasks we do, that only we can do. None better."

"So do you fight with these cohorts?"

"Yes, I am captain under one of the cohorts' generals."

"Yet you've been taken away from your cohort and set to train me. Doesn't that anger you?"

"I won't deny it, Maeldoi. It did at first. Then I saw that the rector was right to try, with you. Even if it didn't work. Even if you were too far gone into a life of savagery, it was worth it to try."

"A savage," said Maeldoi. Now he was able to smile at it. "You thought I was a kind of animal, when you first saw me."

"I did. But I soon saw I was wrong. Almost immediately. Do you remember?"

Maeldoi turned inquiring eyes on Aleron.

"You pointed to yourself and said—"

Maeldoi smiled. "Not an animal. I remember." He hesitated. He turned to Aleron. "And so. You are training me, and we are progressing. What will come of it? For me. For them." He spread his arms out, taking in the entire rectory.

"You'll go through several years of training here. Preliminary training. Then the rector will come back to examine you again. If you pass his examination, he'll send you to more advanced training. If you show you can fulfill the strict demands of this training, you'll become one of the professed. Then the council of the gwrgi at our capital will place you where you can do the most good."

"Several years."

"With the other lads, it's usually three, and that's just for the preliminaries. I told myself, with this one it will be five, six— maybe he'll never learn, and then what?"

"And then what?" Maeldoi repeated softly. "Turn me out? I hear of these things from the other lads. This one will say, 'If I don't do well here, they may turn me out.' That one will say it. They look afraid, when they say it."

"Maybe we would turn you out, yes. But if we did, you'd have all of these skills, dangerous skills with no refinement, unlike the others, who know what is expected of them, so—"

"So kill me."

Aleron looked down at his hands. "But it hasn't come to that, and it won't. You are going so fast, Maeldoi. You're drinking it in, all this training. You've started far behind. The other lads have been at it, their preliminary training, since early childhood. But you're catching up faster than I've seen anyone do it. I'm glad I've been assigned the task to train you. In spite of these bruises you keep giving me." Aleron grinned at him. "And maybe when the time comes, you'll fight by my side. There are other tasks you might be set to do. Fighting in a cohort is only one of them."

"When training here is over, what comes next?"

"Well," said Aleron. "Some of these lads won't make it to a co-hort of fighters, much less any of the special tasks. Such lads might be put to work at one of the rectories. Stableboys. Kitchen boys. Things like that. The ones who pass their examination will enter one of the cohorts. But some—"

"The special tasks you mentioned."

"Yes, but let's not think of those. Let's not get ahead of our-selves. Let's just get you started on these weapons. What do you think?" Aleron nudged the cloth on which the weapons were ranged.

Maeldoi leaned forward to look at them. He put the special tasks out of his mind. He put *afterward* out of his mind. He looked at the weapons, examined them carefully. Finally he picked up the knife, wicked and curved. "I like this," he murmured.

Aleron regarded him narrowly. "You'll learn them all, Maeldoi, and later on, spear and pike. But this knife. Yes, I think it's you, Maeldoi. I think this is going to be your weapon. Let's see, shall we? Starting tomorrow, we'll take the next step."

"Tomorrow," said Maeldoi. He felt a rising excitement.

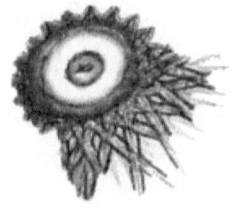

CHAPTER EIGHT

What It Takes

Aleron was going away. The very thought filled Maeldoi with desolation.

He'd never had a friend. Now he had one. He'd never had a teacher. Aleron was the teacher he had needed, the best teacher.

But Aleron's time as his teacher was ending.

"You've surpassed me, Maeldoi," said Aleron with a rueful look. "There's not much more I can teach you about fighting and weaponry, and the things you need next aren't things I'll be very good at teaching you."

Maeldoi thought about all the skills he had learned.

Hand-to-hand combat. Combat with the sword, the bow, the club, the axe, the knife. Especially the knife.

And last, horsemanship. That had taken the entire year past. Horsemanship, and the use of the spear from horseback. At first Maeldoi was sure he'd never catch up to the others in the skill of the horse. The others had all been riding since childhood. After a fortnight of training, though, he surprised himself. He caught up, and fast. From that time on, he yearned always to be on horseback.

He heard what some of the others said, behind his back. "He's a beast himself. Of course another beast would submit to him."

When Maeldoi told Aleron this, Aleron only laughed. "Let them talk. They're half-right, you know." At Maeldoi's expression, Aleron put his hand on Maeldoi's shoulder and turned him to look him in the eye. "Maeldoi. You have a kinship with the horse. The horse is an honorable creature. These others may have had it bred out of them, or maybe they're just not as talented. You are. This is an important connection you're making, you and your brother the horse. Use it."

When the time drew near for Aleron to leave the rectory, Maeldoi found himself growing melancholy. "You'll be glad to get back to your cohort," said Maeldoi.

"Will I? I'm not so sure," said Aleron. "I've been away three years. Another man has taken my place as captain. I'll have to fight hard to regain what has surely slipped away from me by now."

"Will you not think of me with resentment, then?"

"Never, Maeldoi. I count you as a friend. The rector saw something in you, and he was right. I count it an honor he called on me. For if he hadn't—"

"He thought of just getting rid of me," said Maeldoi.

"He did. Then he thought you were worth a try. And you were. And he was right. But now you have more to learn. I'm not sure how you'll do with these other matters you'll need to learn. The other lads have studied them from boyhood."

"Letters," said Maeldoi.

"For most of them, just a smattering is enough. Most of them need at most a turning of the moon or so to refresh the basics they learned as children. But you are starting from the beginning." Aleron regarded him seriously. "That's been the way all along, though. You start from behind, and soon you've mastered everything we've asked you to do. Fighting comes naturally to you, though. This, not so much, maybe."

"You yourself, you're lettered?"

"Yes, my father thought it important, so he made sure I was sent to a rectory known for its learning. This one is not. Later on, I came to this rectory for some special training one of the arms masters could give me."

Maeldoi felt a wash of relief. "I'll have to learn some of it, letters. But in this rectory, not very much."

On the other side of the mountain, he knew, there was an annex of their rectory that housed children. Gwrgi whose children were chosen sent them at a young age, six or seven, to be taught and nurtured carefully there. Then the most promising were brought here to the main rectory. The others were sent back to their families.

Not only had Maeldoi been brought to the rectory late, as he began to change, in adolescence, but he had been brought from one of the savage cave and forest bands. That in itself was unusual.

Although, in truth, he hadn't even spent a day among the people of the bands. He hadn't even had that much.

Cae will grow up in the bands, he thought. *At least he'll have something to build on, when he reaches manhood. But I came from nothing.* He thought of his brother and realized something that surprised him, although it shouldn't have. *By now, Cae has reached manhood,* he told himself, marveling.

"Maeldoi, listen to me." Aleron broke into his thoughts.

Maeldoi turned his attention to Aleron. He knew to pay attention, when Aleron took this serious tone.

"You may not like it or think it very important to learn your letters, but you'll need that skill if you're to do the most important tasks. I think you should strive for one of them."

"I want to join a cohort, like you, and rise through its ranks, and become a leader, like you."

"But I—" Aleron hesitated. "I aspired for more. It wasn't to be. I'd like you to go further than I have. You have it in you."

"What are these tasks? You hint at them, but you never tell me what they are."

"We gwrgi. The Three treasure us. They protect us. They tell us that we have a unique place underneath the Spheres. Ordinary people are dedicated to one of the four great star-Children,

Earth, Water, Fire, Sky. Each is necessary for balance, and balance is what holds up the Spheres."

Maeldoi gave a quick glance to the sky, to the sun blazing high above them. The sun hung by its golden chain from one of the nine Spheres. And the moon. And the stars. He knew that much. He wasn't sure what these celestial orbs had to do with his own life. They were just there. "But the tasks?" he insisted.

"You have to understand balance to understand the tasks. If not for that tension of the elements the star-Children control, the thing we name balance, then the Spheres would collapse, and everything in them and under them would be flattened and destroyed. The Three are bigger than any of the Children. They Themselves are balance, Maeldoi. Serenity and strife, together creating harmony."

"Three," said Maeldoi. He ticked them off on his fingers. "Serenity. Strife. Harmony."

"No, not like that. They are inseparable. No one part of the Three is serenity. No one part strife. And harmony builds from both."

"I don't understand."

Aleron sighed. "I'm no priest. Neither do I. Just know that in the eyes of The Three, we gwrgi are closer to the matter of the Spheres than regular people. We seem like animals to these ordinary folk, but that's because we are part of the natural world, as they are not. In their separation, they look down on us and fear us. The Three sees how valuable we are, and They treasure us." Aleron examined his hands as if he were examining the stuff he was made of. "And we are not the only beings. There are a number of kinds. The ordinary folk. The gwrgi. And there are the eala. There are the mages. The witches. Each type of being has its role to play in the balance of the Spheres."

"I know of ordinary folk. And I know of us, the gwrgi. I've never heard of these others. Well," said Maeldoi, thinking. "I've heard tales of the others, but they seem like children's stories told around the fire."

"We gwrgi seem like stories to them." Aleron laughed.

"Frightening stories," said Maeldoi, remembering his boyhood and the suspicious villagers nearby.

"Yes. So. We gwrgi have our tasks. The most talented among us take on the most important tasks. The same with the other beings. Most ordinary folk—I'm sure you've seen it—live in villages and guide plows and take goods to the market and haul on the oars and the ropes of sails that send ships over the sea. But the most talented of them are set to rule realms, or serve the Children as priestesses and farwyds, or captain the ships."

Aleron looked thoughtful. "At least, that's the way it's supposed to work. Ordinary folk have strayed from the ideal. Those who rule them often aren't the most talented. Just the ones who have managed to grab the most power. But The Three have kept tight control over the gwrgi. Only those chosen by Them perform our own most important tasks."

"Your task is important."

"Yes, to fight. But there we have maybe strayed a bit from the ideal. We hire ourselves out to the rulers of the ordinary folks' realms. There are other tasks, more important, more controlled. To serve as priests. That's one of the most important. To serve as go-betweens and councilors. To become rectors and train the young. I had hoped to become one of these go-betweens, ambassadors of a sort to other beings. But instead I—" Aleron stopped and smiled to himself.

"What?"

"I fell in love. To be a go-between is to be solitary the whole of one's life. Instead, I linked my life to another's."

Maeldoi blinked. He thought of his father and mother, linked in a terrible way to each other, damaging each other, producing offspring they hated.

As if he could read Maeldoi's thoughts, Aleron put out his hand and laid it on Maeldoi's arm. "That was your father's great crime. He performed this act, which is supposed to be an act of love, on a person unwilling, your mother. One of the three most heinous crimes we recognize. The Three Unpardonable Crimes. He was punished for it. Not before he damaged your mother, your brother, you. He deserved his punishment."

Maeldoi, remembering how his fellows had run down and imposed themselves violently upon the village girl, felt a surge of some terrible emotion.

He didn't know what it was, couldn't name it.

But it was bad.

"Maybe I'm like him," he got out.

"Maeldoi, I know what some of the other lads do. They think they won't be found out, but they will. Then they will be punished. Foolish lads. They don't realize what they are risking. Not just because what they do is evil. That too. But because it gives all gwrgi a bad name, and The Three deplore that. You, though. I don't believe you do these things."

"No, but—"

Aleron waited.

"But once, I watched. And did nothing to stop the ones who did do the bad thing."

"And afterward?"

"Terrible dreams."

"Did you ever go with them again, on their sneaking travels to the villages?"

"Never."

"You learned."

Maeldoi nodded miserably. "And you? You don't behave dishonorably to women. You love a woman."

Aleron laughed. "Why do you think the one I love is a woman?"

"Oh," said Maeldoi.

"I miss him very much. Every day."

"Soon you'll be with him again."

"Yes!" said Aleron, and his face lit up as if there were some lamp inside him and someone had turned up the flame. "Haldemarus. That's his name."

When he said the name, it was as if his voice caressed the person who carried it.

Maeldoi felt confusion. He felt jealousy.

"But you're my friend!" he burst out.

"Of course I'm your friend!" said Aleron. "There are different friendships. Different loves. I'm thinking, Maeldoi, that if you felt the kind of love I feel for Halde, you'd feel it for a woman. Am I right?"

Maeldoi felt himself blush. "Yes, but I'm not around any women, so I—"

Aleron laughed.

He nudged Maeldoi. "Maybe sometime you'll find a real woman and not that fantasy woman you carry around in your head. Much more gratifying, I promise you. Not speaking from experience, of course. But I'm not blind. I see others in the cohort who love women just as intensely as I love Halde."

He turned to Maeldoi, regarding him intently. "Love, Maeldoi! As your teacher, I'm demanding you learn it! If you connect your life with a woman, though, completely connect your life with another's, that's different. You'll take yourself out of contention for some of the most important tasks. So think about that."

"Do you regret connecting your life with Halde?"

"Never," said Aleron, low. "No matter what the cost. Never."

"What a hardship for you, taking me on," said Maeldoi, feeling gloomy.

"No, because I have made a friend. Friendship, too, is precious, Maeldoi. Besides, I'm able to get away from time to time." A secret smile played about his lips. "But anyway, Maeldoi. Learn your letters, even if you find the task unpleasant. To be a go-between, you need to be lettered."

"You think I have it in me, to be one of those?"

"I know so," said Aleron. "I've talked to the rector about it. He thinks so too. Who better suited for that life than you? Already you've managed to stride two different worlds. The rector and I both see you have what it takes."

CHAPTER NINE

A Test

Life at the rectory without Aleron was much harder, Maeldoi thought. For maybe the thousandth time he thought it. He missed his teacher fiercely. His friend. He felt pangs of jealousy over Halde, Aleron's lover. Halde was with Aleron. He, Maeldoi, was not. He didn't want to be the lover of any man; he was not made that way. But he'd never had a friend, and now that friend was gone.

The feelings of the others at the rectory towards him, teachers and pupils both, ranged from fear and scorn to indifference. None of them could deny his skills in combat, though.

Letters, on the other hand. Letters came hard to him. At first he didn't see the reason to learn them. By now, he knew the language of these parts and could communicate fully. What need to write the words down, as well?

His teacher called him stubborn and wooden-headed. Maeldoi thought, *If he dares, he will call me little more than a beast of the caves. But he does not dare.*

After that first day at the rectory, when he had attacked the other boy, the others at the rectory had treated him gingerly. *They thought I'd be sent away,* thought Maeldoi. *Done away with, even. But before that happens, I might seize their throats in my jaws and drain their blood, so they are afraid. Yet here I still am. Not sent away. Not done away with.*

Thanks to Aleron, he realized.

The boy he'd attacked had been demoted to the kitchen, although not through anything having to do with Maeldoi, thank The Three. The lad gave him black looks even now, so that Maeldoi always wondered, when one of the kitchen help handed him his bowl of stew, whether that boy he'd fought had maybe spat into it.

In spite of that early incident of violence, Maeldoi was still allowed to be with the boys receiving training. Aleron had reported to the rector, and the rector had allowed Maeldoi to continue.

Maeldoi could barely remember the rector, how he had taken Maeldoi away from his family and the familiar landscape of the moors far across the Narrow Sea. Brought him here. Maeldoi hadn't seen the rector since that day he'd ridden away. But Aleron kept telling him. *The rector sees something important in you, Maeldoi.*

This new teacher saw only that Maeldoi was a burden and a dullard.

Maeldoi was sitting in the sun of the rectory's courtyard, his slate and chalk in his hand, attempting to write out the morning's lesson. All the while, he was yearning to be on the forested hillsides, hunting. Or on the practice field, sparring with the others.

He wrote his name on the slate. *Maeldoi.*

He looked to the book beside him on the bench. *I must copy out these lines*, he told himself, and set himself to it. His letters straggled across the slate. He wiped them out and began again.

Gossuin, his book. Maeldoi copied the words down. *A picture of the world*, he wrote.

He put aside the slate and chalk and squinted at the little book in his hand. Here were the elements of the Children, just as Aleron had described them to him.

Earth, water, fire, the air of the sky. A small diagram stood beside each description of an element. Beside *earth*, a small cube. Beside *water*, a pebbled round shape. Looking closer, Maeldoi saw the little spherical shape had so many facets, it just appeared pebbled. Beside *fire*, a spiky three-pronged shape. Beside *the air of the sky*, a many-sided shape.

The world is a ball, he read. He looked around himself in confusion. The world did not look like a ball to him. He wrote it down on his slate just the same.

When the eala appear before you, they are shining bright. You cannot gaze at them. You would fall down dazzled if you did, Maeldoi read.

The eala. Aleron had spoken of them. One of the many kinds of beings in the world.

His teacher walked past.

"Master," Maeldoi called out to him. "I do not understand this book."

The teacher looked over at him and sighed. "Keep trying, Maeldoi," he said, and walked on.

Letters. They were necessary if he wanted one of the higher tasks Aleron was always urging him to consider.

I suppose maybe I'll just join a cohort, like Aleron, if I pass my examination, thought Maeldoi. *Why would I want to do one of these other tasks, and forever have to squint my eyes at these tiny marks on these little pages?*

He knew he'd much rather fight. Then again, he trusted Aleron and Aleron's judgment.

The examination was coming up fast, and Maeldoi still found himself having to puzzle out every word in the books given to him to read.

Suppose he failed. Would his combat skills alone allow him to pass?

"Oh, don't worry," said one of the other pupils about to take his examination also, one more friendly to Maeldoi than most of the others. "I only know my letters from the things we were given as boys to read. The cat sits on the mat. The quick brown fox jumps over the lazy dog. Things of that sort."

That fox would have to be quick, thought Maeldoi. Even the laziest dog would jump up and snap—

That's the problem, he thought. *None of this makes any sense. Why are we reading these things? Why do we have to?*

Just the idea, that the words in his head and his mouth could be put into these marks in a book, was absurd.

He thought about what the other pupil had told him. *Maybe the other boy would pass his examination with the cat sits on the mat and the quick brown fox,* he thought, looking over at the lad bent over his own slate in the sun. *They all think you'll pass. It will seem right to them that you pass.*

But I. Maeldoi gripped his chalk tighter, so hard it snapped in two. He leaned over to find the pieces. The scholar-teacher would be angry. As he almost always was, when he stared at Maeldoi's work on the slate.

In spite of the uselessness of letters for fighting, Maeldoi wondered if his failure there would make a convenient excuse for his superiors to claim he had failed his trials and must not move forward. He knew he'd be held to a higher standard, unless somehow the rector came back to vouch for him, or even Aleron.

But Aleron was off fighting a war. He had written to tell Maeldoi this. As for the rector, from the day the rector brought him here, he'd never seen the man again. No one would be here to speak for him. No one here cared. He'd be stuck in some menial position, maybe.

"Nah," said the other pupil. "You'll be sent to the wars. Everyone sees how good you are with fists, with the club and sword and knife."

Then Maeldoi could relax his vigilance a little. Still, he worried.

But now he put his book carefully down on the bench and felt within his belt pouch. He pulled out a much-folded piece of parchment. *Here's a reason to know my letters,* he told himself, smoothing the parchment out and reading it again. The letter from Aleron. *Here's a use for that skill.*

"My dearest brother," Aleron wrote. Maeldoi made the words silently with his lips. "How I miss you," Aleron's marks on the parchment told him. "Take your studies seriously so you can join us soon in these wars. I will speak to my general on your behalf and take you into my own cohort as soon as you pass your examination. But Maeldoi, remember the higher matters we discussed."

Reading, re-reading this letter, then reading it again heartened Maeldoi. Aleron believed in him, and each mark on the piece of parchment was a physical sign that he did. As Maeldoi cast his eye on each mark, he felt the force of it inscribing itself deep inside him, as if Aleron were there beside him, pressing with his finger on Maeldoi's self with each stroke.

But the assistant rector, the man who led the school, looked on Maeldoi with a severe and disapproving eye whenever it chanced to light on him. Then he'd look away with an expression of distaste.

No matter how good I am at combat, this man thinks I don't belong here. He thinks the efforts to teach me are a waste of his valuable time. He thinks I belong in a cave with the savages. He has thought so since the day he had me beaten, thought Maeldoi, and sank again into a melancholy.

His scholar-teacher thought so, too. "Here, Maeldoi," he said with a sigh. "Take this book back to the library tower. You've done as much with it as you're capable." He handed the book about the world being a ball to Maeldoi. Maeldoi turned with it to the tower where all the rectory books were housed, and trudged up the steps spiraling around the inside of it.

At the top he paused. He'd never been up here. Big windows let in light and air. Sitting so that the light of one of the windows fell across her book was a tall, narrow woman. Reading.

"Mistress, here's a book I'm supposed to bring to you," said Maeldoi, remembering at the last moment to make his bow. He had seen the woman before. She tended the books.

She looked up slowly. With her finger, she marked the page she was reading. "Bring it here, child," she said.

Maeldoi came to her with the book.

She took it from him and turned it over in her hands. "Gossuin on the properties of the lands underneath the Spheres," she said. "Did you read this book?"

"I tried."

"And what did you find out?"

"The world is a ball, mistress."

"Did you find the book interesting?"

"No, mistress?"

"Why not?"

"I don't know my letters well, and the book was hard for me to make out, and my scholar-teacher said it's because I am a wooden-head and a dullard, and I come from savages, and I am no good, mistress."

"My, my," said the woman. "Did you believe what he said?"

"No, mistress. Well, some of it. I suppose. Maybe most of it."

"Tch. Look over there on my table. See that book, the one with the red cover? Bring that to me," she said.

Maeldoi did.

"Now sit here beside me. My eyes are no longer the best. You are to read to me. Start with page one."

Maeldoi opened his mouth to argue. He was expected down below, in the courtyard. He had other things he should be doing. But then he shrugged and sat down beside her instead. He struggled to read the first page aloud to her.

"Now we will talk about what you just read. What did it say, Maeldoi? That's your name, is it not?"

"Yes, mistress. This book says that I am about to read a song of mighty deeds. By a great warrior. His name is. . ." Maeldoi struggled.

After a moment, the woman put her finger under the word and helped him make the sounds.

"Guillaume," he said finally.

"Excellent," she said.

"And then it talks about his nephew Vi—something."

"Good enough. His nephew. And what do they do?"

"They fight, mistress. They fight against a fell enemy."

"Very good. Read me another page."

Maeldoi did. And another. And another. He read five pages, and they talked about the doings in each.

"Now then," she said. "I want you to sit quietly. Can you do that? Good, many boys can't. Sit quietly and read those pages again, inside your head."

Maeldoi did. His lips moved silently over the words.

"Excellent. I am going to ask you a favor, Maeldoi. My eyes are so bad these days. I am going to request of the assistant rector that you be assigned to assist me one candle-measure out of the day, when the light is good. You will come up to my tower and read to me. Are you willing?"

"Yes, mistress." Maeldoi surprised himself. He was willing.

After a few days, he realized another surprising thing. He was having an easier time with the scholar-teacher's demands. And if he didn't understand something the scholar-teacher was making him read, some dull thing, he could take it up the stairs of the tower and the tall, narrow woman would help him with the places that were difficult. Sometimes the dull thing turned out to be interesting after all. But mostly he didn't want to, he wanted to puzzle out the scholar-teacher's readings on his own, because the mighty deeds of Guillaume and his nephew Vivien were getting to the good part, where a giant shows up to help them fight the foe, and that's what he wanted to read, not the schoolbooks, when he went up the tower stairs for his candle-measure of reading with Mistress Pereta.

"A giant," he said to her. "Another being underneath the Spheres. Ordinary folk, we gwrgi, the eala, the mages. And see here, the giants." He showed her the place in the book.

"The giants, yes. But the giants are in the past. They no longer walk the lands," said Mistress Pereta.

"This is an old book, then, mistress."

"No, but it's an old tale."

One day only a moon's turning from the examination, the porter of the rectory called Maeldoi to him. "Here's a parcel for you, Maeldoi."

Maeldoi took it and hurried to his tiny room with it, wondering what it could be.

He sat down on his bed shelf, undid the twine of the parcel, and unfolded the waxed cloth. A book fell into his lap. He stared at it, stupefied.

A piece of parchment fluttered from the book, and Maeldoi bent to retrieve it. He held it up to the light filtering in from the single window. A message from Aleron!

Maeldoi spoke the words of the message silently to himself. "My dear brother. Here's a book you may like."

Maeldoi opened the book and glanced at the woodcut on the frontispiece. He looked harder. He began to wonder, and then he began to smile, and then he began to read. The next day, he brought it to Mistress Pereta, and they read more of it together.

The day of the examination was one of those clear chill days with a high blue sky. Not too hot, not too cold. No rain. Perfect for demonstrating the skills of combat.

Maeldoi marched with six of the others to the practice field, to demonstrate his mastery of those skills. First, hand-to-hand combat. Then combat with a weapon of one's choosing, and of course Maeldoi chose the knife. Then horsemanship, and the use of the spear from horseback. Finally, hunting.

At the end of the session, he could see in the eyes of the examiners, even the assistant rector's, that his mastery was without question. Without question, he was the best of the six. He was pre-eminent in hand-to-hand combat and in the use of the knife. He was an excellent hunter. His horsemanship was beyond good. It was inspired.

He thought wryly of the first time he had mounted a horse, and how terrified he had been. These others had been in the saddle since childhood. Then the strange feeling of kinship that he had discovered. And now he and his horse were one.

"Next, the examination of your letters," said the assistant rector, leading the lads to be examined back inside the rectory. Maeldoi's ebullient mood dampened into a dull despair.

The six to be examined headed for the courtyard and sat on stools at the front.

Just there I was beaten before the entire rectory, thought Maeldoi, glancing at the bench beside them. Being beaten there again might be easier than what he was about to do with book and chalk and slate. Less humiliating, even. If given a choice—examination in letters or a beating—Maeldoi was sure he would choose the beating.

The other pupils filed into the courtyard and stood in their rows. The assistant rector and the scholar-teacher of letters stood before them. They handed each of the six to be tested a slate, a chalk, and a parchment.

"Copy what you see on the parchment onto your slates, and wait for me to examine them," directed the teacher.

Maeldoi balanced his slate on his knee and took up his chalk. He stared at the parchment and then tried to copy it as neatly as he could. He began to sweat. Glancing sidelong at the boy next to him, he saw that his own letters looked ugly and ill-made in comparison.

He concentrated on the parchment. Something about the gods and the elements and the little shapes known as the solids. He remembered seeing the diagrams of them in that book about the world being a ball. Cube, tetrahedron, icosahedron, octahedron. And one more, the mysterious dodecahedron. Laboriously, he wrote down what he saw.

When the teacher called time, he hadn't finished, so the final words on his slate were a hurried scrawl.

The teacher went from pupil to pupil. Maeldoi was fourth.

"Very good," the teacher said, nodding to the first pupil. He nodded to the second pupil. Pursed his lips at the third but finally nodded. He came to Maeldoi and held out his hand for Maeldoi's slate.

Maeldoi handed it over.

The man stared at it in silence, his eyebrows raised. The assistant rector stepped over to look. They gave each other a glance, and the teacher rolled his eyes. The teacher handed the slate back to Maeldoi and moved to the next pupil.

Maeldoi knew he was flushing red. He felt a kind of roaring in his ears. He knew he must tamp it down. *Here's the confirmation they needed*, Maeldoi thought, staring down at his slate. *Good in a fight, but too stupid to be of much use.* That's what they were thinking, he told himself. Maybe he'd be allowed to go as a foot soldier. Maybe they'd make him a porter. That would be a waste of his combat skills, though, so maybe—

But the assistant rector's voice brought him back into the moment. "And now," said the assistant rector, "we will examine your reading skills."

They started with the first pupil, handing him a book and asking him about it, then bidding him read from it.

Maeldoi tried to listen, but there was a buzzing in his ears, and his heart began beating fast. He thought of his own halting attempts, and how they'd scorn him when it came his turn.

Too soon, the two of them, assistant rector and scholar-teacher, came to stand before Maeldoi skulking like some criminal on his stool

"Here is a book, Maeldoi," said the teacher, handing him one. "Open it, please, and describe what you see."

Maeldoi took the book, fumbling it, nearly dropping it. "Sorry," he muttered.

The teacher gave him an exasperated look.

With clumsy fingers, Maeldoi opened it to the beginning.

Then a feeling amazing to him began to unfold inside him.

He felt his mouth beginning to twitch into a smile, and he worked hard to suppress it.

"What do you see there?" prompted the teacher.

"A picture."

"Explain to me what you think the picture shows."

Maeldoi held it up. "It's a picture of a creature. A man in armor, but he has the head of a wolf or a dog."

"What does that say to you, Maeldoi?"

"I believe this is a book showing what ordinary folk think when they look at us, the gwrgi. We don't really have dogs' heads, but that's what they think, when they think of us. And see? This dog-headed gwrgi wields a sharp sword. They think we are dangerous, too."

"Very good, Maeldoi," said the teacher, surprise in his voice. Then his eyes narrowed. "Open to the first page and read what it says there, if you please."

Maeldoi heard it in his voice. *Now you will fail, boy.*

Maeldoi opened his mouth, and the words of the book came rolling smoothing out of it. "Now when Man-Dog Rough-Gray marched out to fight the king—"

He read on, until he felt the hand of the assistant rector on his shoulder. "We've heard enough, Maeldoi. That will be all."

The two men went on to the next pupil, leaving Maeldoi stunned on his stool

The book. It was the book Aleron had sent him. The book he had read avidly, one of the first books he'd ever read so. A book about the gwrgi and their terrible deeds. Their terrible, magnificent deeds. As dear to him as the book about Guillaume and his nephew and his giant.

The examination was over, but the six being examined had to sit quietly on their stools while the assistant rector and the scholar-teacher conferred.

The eyes of the entire rectory were on the six of them. Maeldoi tried to make his face a blank. Even with this performance of his at the end, he had no confidence the examination would end well for him.

Their quiet conference ended, the assistant rector and the scholar-teacher now stepped into a little curtained alcove at the very head of the courtyard.

It contained, Maeldoi knew, chairs and a table and writing implements. If an important visitor needed to consult privately with the assistant rector, this is where he'd be brought. Maeldoi and the other pupils had peeked inside it when they were younger, sure it held many secrets. But it did not. Just a bare table and chairs, a quill, an ink-stone, a few sheets of blank parchment. One of the pupils had been whipped for making an obscene drawing on one of the blank sheets of parchment. *That was a long time ago*, thought Maeldoi. *Three years and more.*

Two men stepped into the alcove. Three stepped out. The third was the rector himself.

Maeldoi gaped over his shoulder at the man. He remembered those keen eyes. That mouth, which had curled so scornfully.

The assistant rector gestured to the rector, who now moved past him to face the assembled pupils, his back to the six on the stools, waiting to hear their fates.

He was dressed sumptuously in velvet. Maeldoi remembered how he had stared at the assistant rector's velvet robe, when he'd first been brought to the rectory, and how he didn't know what it was, and how he wanted to touch it to see if it were some kind of fur.

A gold chain of office hung about the rector's neck.

"Students of the Northern Rectory," said the rector to them all. "This is a day for celebration. Six pupils have taken their examination, and now the six of them are about to go out into the world to serve our people." One by one, he began naming the pupils on the stools, and as each one was named, the assistant rector brought the young man to stand before the rector.

The named person knelt before the rector, and then the rector said where the young man would go. Where his life would now lead him. Then he would rise, bow again, and be taken off to gather his belongings from his room and wait at the big doors of the rectory for directions where he must travel.

The first of them, to a cohort in the Lyre Lands. The second, to a similar cohort in the Burnt Lands. The third, a porter in the halls of this very rectory. He wouldn't have to travel, just move from one room to a different, lesser one in a different, lesser part of the red stone buildings.

Maeldoi braced himself. It was his turn next. The rector had said six would go out. That must mean he had passed. He felt a rising tide of joy inside him. It still didn't mean he'd be given anything important or even interesting to do, though.

Then Maeldoi frowned in confusion. Maybe he had misunderstood. Mis-heard, somehow.

The rector passed from the third to the fifth. Passed over him sitting on the fourth stool to the next lad, the fifth. The fifth would go to a company of archers. The sixth, the friendly lad, to teach the little boys of the annex on the other side of the mountain. *The cat sat on the mat*, thought Maeldoi. *The quick brown fox jumps over the lazy dog.* That's all the lad really knew of letters, and that's all he'd be required to teach the children there. But maybe such a life would content him. And he was kind. The children would like him.

By now, only Maeldoi remained on his stool. *Will they drive me off?* he wondered. *Is this how it happens, when they do?*

"Maeldoi." The rector named him.

He got up from his stool, came before the rector, bowed, knelt.

"Maeldoi, what a long way you have come. What a journey," said the rector.

Maeldoi hazarded a look upward. The rector was smiling.

"You have done well, my lad. Stand and face these others."

Maeldoi stood, and the rector took him by the shoulders and turned him to face the assembled pupils.

"This, your fellow pupil Maeldoi, has made me proud today. He has far outshown any of the rest of you in combat skills, and I suppose you already know that. He has learned his letters. Not perfectly. That will be remedied. But he is ready for a higher training. For some of the most important tasks we're called to perform. Congratulate your fellow-pupil."

The others in the courtyard all stamped their feet obediently in approval, although some of them did not look happy about it. The assistant rector and scholar-teacher did not look happy.

"Go to your room, Maeldoi, and collect your things. You and I will ride out as soon as the kitchen has packed some provisions for our journey."

Maeldoi bowed again and went off in a daze to collect his things. Especially his little book. *Should I hide it*, he wondered. He'd never hidden that he was reading it, but then again, it was likely no one had bothered to see what it was he was reading. *I was given this book*, he realized, *so I would be ready. So there would be no question I'd pass my examination. Is that wrong?* he wondered.

He hastened to the big doors of the rectory with his few belongings in a small sack—change of clothes, the letters from Aleron, the book, not much else. He left his slate and chalk behind, glad to see the last of them.

The doors stood open. The rector was already mounted.

Maeldoi knew he must risk the man's impatience. He bolted up the steps of Mistress Pereta's tower, taking them two at a time.

"Mistress Pereta—"

"I heard, Maeldoi. I knew you could do it! Come to me for a blessing, then hurry. You don't want to keep the rector waiting."

He rushed to her and knelt.

She put a cool hand on his forehead. "May The Three keep you in Their care, Maeldoi. May They exalt into the highest Spheres all those who see your true worth. May They strike down into a dung-heap any who would try to make you think you are a wooden-head and a dullard, or come from savages."

"A dung-heap?" said Maeldoi, dumbfounded.

"A really nasty one, stinking and vile," she said, nodding. "And now go on, boy. Think of me sometime."

"I will always think of you, mistress," said Maeldoi. He turned and rushed down the stairs of her tower, getting himself in hand. It would be shameful to shed a tear. Wouldn't it?

He burst out into the courtyard. The rector gestured to the horse Maeldoi was to ride. But Maeldoi's steps faltered.

He stepped to the rector's stirrup and stood, head down. "Lord rector. Sir."

"Speak, Maeldoi."

"I believe you knew. That I had read the book they gave me, at the examination. That it was familiar to me."

"Yes. Indeed. I made sure to tell the assistant rector to examine you with it, and I made sure to have Aleron send it to you well beforehand."

"So, really, I didn't succeed at this examination through my own merits."

Part of Maeldoi was telling him, *just shut up and take your good fortune.* Another part of him was saying, *no. I want this on my own merits, or not at all.*

"Maeldoi. I know what I saw in you, and then Aleron told me how you had triumphed over every obstacle. Mistress Pereta has told me the same. I came here to see for myself, from time to time."

"I didn't know that, lord."

"I made sure you didn't."

"But letters, lord. They are hard for me still."

"I know that. Aleron told me they would be. I thought, give him every chance to show what he can do. And you did. You could have tossed the book aside, when Aleron sent it to you. Your skills could have been so poor that even with the best will, you might not have been able to read it. We needed to know that you could. We needed to know how hard you would try. You tried on your own, and you tried with Mistress Pereta. So now we do know that."

Maeldoi thought of the book about Man-Dog Rough-Gray, and how that book showed him the important things that letters could bring to him, when most other books had failed to do so. The book about Guillaume, his nephew, his giant had showed him. He had thought, *what good is this skill? Just some useless game.*

Aleron's book had taught him otherwise. Mistress Pereta had taught him otherwise. Guillaume had taught him.

But still.

"The others didn't get that chance," he said.

"They didn't need such a chance. The examination was just a ceremony, for them, to confirm what we already knew about them. No matter how they performed, they would have ended up in the places we put them."

"I, too."

"No, there you are wrong. It may seem to you that we rigged your examination for the result we wanted. Not so. Some think of an examination as a way we teachers torture our pupils one last time. One last petty display of power over them. Some think of an examination as a rote parroting back—you know of parrots, Maeldoi? No?—but a repetition, as exactly as possible, of the things we teachers have said to them, a kind of memory test. That can be useful for certain skills. Some think of an examination differently. I do. In certain cases, an examination is one more chance to learn. I wanted to see what you'd do, when someone gave you a chance to transcend your limitations. The test told me that. Get on your horse, Maeldoi."

Maeldoi slung himself easily up onto the back of his horse, feeling the bunched muscles, the power of the animal beneath him, almost a part of him. Recently he'd learned how to guide his horse using only his knees and a light rein, just a braided rope, no saddle, no stirrups. He wished he were riding this horse that way, he wished always to ride that way, but he knew that in the long journey to come, he'd be glad of the saddle and stirrups, and the horse would be glad, too.

He turned his horse's head to follow the rector toward the place that would become for him a new life. He settled himself and his horse to the rhythm of the road, and his dark hair, bound off his pale, intent face with a thong, streamed behind him in the wind.

At the joy of a difficult enterprise new-begun, the amber of his eyes gleamed.

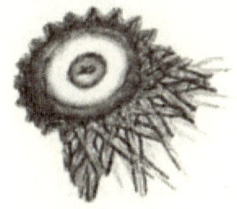

CHAPTER TEN

Mastery

Maeldoi sucked in his breath and tried to keep every muscle as still as possible. He tried to hold his pose beyond what his body was telling him. His body was telling him no. His will was speaking to his body, telling it yes.

Life at the physical training quadrangle was hard. These tasks, to instill discipline, were hard.

He had thought, with the end of his time at the rectory, that his training had ended, too. But for him and the other chosen lads, it had just begun.

The worst of it was not being allowed to see Aleron. The lads in the quadrangle were allowed a bed-shelf, a piss pot, and a bucket of water. They were not allowed to speak, not to each other, not to anyone, unless one of their instructors specifically ordered them to. They were not allowed visitors. Once a sen'night they were allowed a bath, and they were taken from their tiny rooms one by one on bath day, the only day they did not engage in their arduous exercises. A minder shaved their cheeks smooth. They weren't allowed to touch the blade. The minder made sure their hair was cropped close to the head. The mark of a trainee, Maeldoi realized after a while.

How is this different from a prison? Maeldoi wondered. By comparison, his room at the rectory had been luxurious. But the door of his room at the quadrangle was not locked. He supposed he could have walked free away from there, and he wondered how many did, when the rigors of training finally broke them.

He hadn't been given any reasons for the conditions he faced at the quadrangle. He had been told only one thing, by the Training Chief who had welcomed him there when the rector handed him over. "Obey, Maeldoi. That is your only task. If you succeed in obedience, perhaps you will be allowed to take the next step."

When? Maeldoi thought desperately. There were no candles to measure time, and no way to tell much about the passage of the seasons. After a while, he began scratching a small mark on the wall of his room for every bath day. Every sen'night. Then he had a rough idea how long he'd been there.

A long time.

Every day, the trainees were brought into a central courtyard under a high ceiling. Was it springtide outside? Harvest-tide?

Winter? Summer? No way to know, except by hints. One of the guards, or minders, or whatever they were, exuding a frosty air as if he'd just been outside in the cold. A messenger rushing past the lads, brushing grass from his cloak.

The Training Chief's admonition was the last anyone talked to him, except the instructor demonstrating the poses they were to assume in the courtyard of the quadrangle, and mostly the instructor did this silently, through gesture and example.

In the quadrangle, the lads were set to endless exercises. Difficult poses for their bodies to assume, held endlessly. When the body failed, through weakness, inattention, or hunger, the lad lay where he had fallen til the end of the exercise.

For session after session, candle-measure after candle-measure, Maeldoi had lain against the cold stones. Each morning, when he assumed the required position, he strove to hold it longer. He strove not to fall.

Each day, after the session ended, he lined up with the others to receive a piece of bread to take back with him to his room. At least the breakfast was hearty. Meat, cheese, some sort of gruel with field greens mixed into it.

Once, an amazing piece of fruit. Maeldoi didn't know what to make of it. He didn't know what it was called. It was round, with a dimpled skin. It glowed like a little sun, only duskier. Orange, he thought the color might be called. He watched one of the others peel the skin of it off, so then he copied the gesture. The juices of it were sweet. He could feel his whole mouth blooming as he bit into it. The flesh of it was in sections. He licked the juice from his fingers. He wanted to keep the skin of it, so he could put it to his nose always and inhale its odor, but the minders went through and took the skins away with the porridge bowls.

As the seasons wore on, as they surely did outside in the world, Maeldoi began to notice the quadrangle thinning out.

It's some sort of endurance test, he realized. He wondered what it took to be removed from the group in the quadrangle. Too many falls? Too soon into the session? Someone complaining? He'd never heard anyone do that.

Maybe the disappeared ones were not the failures. Maybe they were lads who had succeeded, and were being allowed to move back into the world.

But somehow, he thought the removed lads were the failures or the ones who had given up.

Every morning, after breaking his fast silently with the others, relieving himself, and coming to the quadrangle, he strove to last a little bit longer. And a little bit longer.

Why? he asked himself, collapsed onto the stones. *Why keep trying?*

They want me to fail, he realized. *I will not do what they want.*

Every time he fell, he wondered if he'd be hauled off, kicked out of the physical training. *Why don't I want them to do that?* he asked himself. *Why am I terrified, each time I fall, that they will?* He had no answer.

One morning, his terror magnified a thousand-fold. He could hear the minders going from room to room, bringing food to the lads to break their fast in the quadrangle so they'd be ready to face its usual torments. But no one came for him.

He was left sitting on his bed shelf for the better part of the day.

When he heard footsteps echoing down the corridor of his dormitory, he knew fresh terror. Were they coming for him, to throw him out? Did he want them to, or did he hope they passed him by?

When they stopped outside his door, he had his answer.

The minder crooked a finger at him from the door.

Maeldoi rose from the shelf and followed him dumbly out.

The minder led him down the winding corridors that rimmed the outside of the quadrangle

The minder handed him off to another man, who took him outside. The air was mild. Maeldoi took a deep breath of it. It was so delicious to breathe outside air that he nearly wept. He followed this man through the streets of the city to a portico where a man waited at a small table, with parchment before him and a quill in his hand.

"Bow," whispered the man who had brought him.

Maeldoi did.

"Maeldoi, is it?" said this man, looking down at his parchment and back at Maeldoi.

Maeldoi straightened and nodded. He wasn't sure he was allowed to speak.

"You have a visitor."

Someone stepped through a door and approached them.

"Aleron!" Maeldoi shouted and launched himself into the arms of his friend.

"Breach of discipline," said the man at the desk, but when Maeldoi whipped his head around in fear, he saw the man was smiling.

"Maeldoi, you have passed this test," Aleron told him, beaming. "They're allowing me to tell you."

Maeldoi sagged against Aleron in relief.

"May I take him outside and feed him, sir?" said Aleron to the man at the desk. "He looks like he's about to collapse from hunger."

"Oh, this one," said the man. "He never collapses. Well, he does, they all do. But not if he can help it. He summons the very gods to keep himself upright."

"I knew it," said Aleron, his eyes shining.

"Take him, Aleron. Then, after he's eaten, bring him back to me," said the man.

Aleron took Maeldoi by the hand and led him out of the portico under the sun to a sunny garden with tables and people, people buzzing with talk.

Maeldoi hung back. It was too much. Too bright. Too many voices.

"Oh, my friend. My dear friend. I see what you need," said Aleron, motioning to someone at a table. He led Maeldoi down a shady walkway into a small secluded arbor. He pushed Maeldoi gently to sit on a bench. The person at the table had followed them there.

"I'll bring the food here, shall I?" said this other person, a young man as tall and dark as polished wood.

"Thanks, Halde," said Aleron.

Maeldoi looked after the young man's retreating figure. *So that's Halde,* he thought, and couldn't suppress a pang of jealousy.

Aleron saw it and laughed. "Now, Maeldoi, you must not worry. Halde will be your good friend," he said.

Maeldoi felt an unwilling smile creeping across his lips. He wanted to say something, but somehow, he didn't know how. Finally he croaked it out. "I'm not sure I know how to talk any longer. Not much talking, in there."

Before he could say more, Halde had returned and was pressing a miraculous object into Maeldoi's hand.

"The orange fruit!" Maeldoi exclaimed. "We had these, once. They are—"

"Delicious, no?" said Halde with the flash of a grin.

Maeldoi glanced up at Halde cautiously as he peeled the fruit with shaking fingers. He felt an emotion he didn't know how to name. He'd never felt such an emotion before. He dropped his eyes, fastening them on the orange.

"My shy friend," said Aleron with amusement, nodding at Maeldoi and taking Halde's hand to press it. "Be gentle with him, Halde. He's like a new-hatched chick."

After a while, Maeldoi found he could relax a bit around the two of them. He ate well. He drank ale. They moved into the sunshine, and Maeldoi found himself basking on his bench like a cat.

"The two of you are so big and stalwart," he said to them, admiring them. They both glowed with health and vigor. They were dressed in leather cuirasses. They were soldiers, professed soldiers, their hair long, drawn away from their faces with embroidered bands.

He looked down at himself and saw how pale he was. How scrawny.

"Oh, Maeldoi," said Aleron, reaching over and feeling his upper arm between practiced thumb and forefinger. "You're all muscle, you know that? Honed down completely to muscle. Feel that, Halde."

It was strange, feeling the hands of these men on his body. Maeldoi had a dim recollection of other hands on his body, how he fought and snarled and spit. If he had learned anything during his time in that training quadrangle, he supposed, he'd learned how to be still.

"Will they let me join your cohort now, Aleron?" Maeldoi heard himself blurt out.

But before he'd even finished speaking, he saw with dismay how Aleron was shaking his head no.

"I'd like nothing better than to fight beside you, brother," said Aleron. "But they—" he inclined his head to indicate the tall buildings of the city government that surrounded them on all sides. "—they have other ideas. You remember? We talked of this."

"Special tasks," said Maeldoi.

"Yes, and now you've passed the first hurdle. You've shown how disciplined you can be within your body. For, Maeldoi, if there's one thing we gwrgi lack as creatures, it's discipline. Control of that thing inside us all."

"Beasts of the caves," Maeldoi whispered.

"Control of the cave beast," said Halde with a laugh, the amber of his eyes sparkling. "I like that idea."

"Suppose I say I don't want these special tasks," said Maeldoi. "As you did."

He watched as Aleron put out a hand and laid it on Halde's knee. Watched how Halde's face closed.

"As I did." Aleron nodded. "And I don't regret it. Not for a moment. Not for an instant of my life." Aleron was saying these words to Maeldoi, but Maeldoi saw they were really meant for Halde. After a moment, he said, "Yes, Maeldoi. Even now, you can reject these tasks. After all you've been through."

"Will I be punished, if I do?"

"No. They see how valuable you are. If they'd had any doubts before, they have none now."

"They'd let me join your cohort."

"Yes. I believe they would." Aleron looked down at his hands for a long time. He raised his eyes to Maeldoi's. "But if you choose instead to do one of these tasks, you will serve our kind in ways no one else can. I'm not sure what they'll ask you to do. Only that it will be hard, as hard as the experience you've just come through. So no one will ask you to choose such a life lightly. No one will force you to it. In this next phase of your training, you'll be given every opportunity to reflect on your choice."

"Is that when you decided against it and instead took a role in the cohort?"

"A lesser role. Yes, this is the time I decided it. A lesser role as the world counts these things. Not as I do." Once again, his hand moved to Halde.

"You decided it during this period of your training, the one I'm about to begin?"

"Yes."

"That means you passed your physical training. You knew that quadrangle as well as I do."

"Oh, yes," said Aleron with a grim smile.

"Did that figure into your decision, then? What you endured?"

"No. It was all this big fellow here," said Aleron, and he grinned at Halde. "I met him during this new phase, the training of the mind."

"And you, Halde, sir—"

"Please," interrupted Halde. "Just Halde. I hope we will become fast friends, brother."

Maeldoi felt something ease inside him. "You, Halde—were you undergoing the same training?"

"Me? Not me," Halde scoffed. "Poring over some book. Standing still like a tree or a water bird or a dog all day long til I fainted dead away. Are you crazy, man? Who'd want that?"

"Don't listen to him, Maeldoi," said Aleron. "He was so good at his letters that they decided he should become a priest. So bright they knew he'd be a scholar."

"I didn't want that life, either. They kept urging me and urging me. One day, as I walked down that street there—" Halde pointed. "I saw what I wanted most in life. Then I knew. And I never looked back." Halde and Aleron shared a smile so secret it made Maeldoi shiver, looking in at it from the outside.

He'd never felt about another person that way, and he figured he never would.

"Well, brother," said Aleron at last to Maeldoi. "I promised that man back there I'd get you to him before the sun went down. Let's go." He and Halde walked Maeldoi back through the city streets to the little portico and the man behind the desk.

Maeldoi turned to them. "Will I see you again soon?"

"Of course. As often as you like," said Aleron. "This phase won't be anything like the last, I promise you. This phase, they actually tell you what they're doing to you, and why." He grinned at Maeldoi.

Then the two of them embraced him and left him with the man at the desk.

"Maeldoi," said the man.

"Sir," said Maeldoi, and bowed.

"You have achieved physical mastery. Now it's time for a different type of mastery, even more important." The man stood, came around his desk, and tapped Maeldoi on the forehead. "Mastery in here," he said. "Follow me."

So Maeldoi did, to a comfortable, sunny room that would be his for the next several years, and to a discipline harder to come by, in its way, than the discipline of the quadrangle.

Part III: TWO PATHS

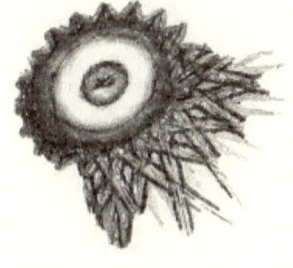

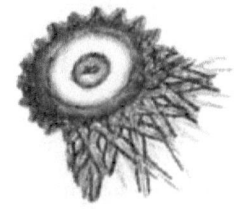

CHAPTER ELEVEN

An Encounter

Maeldoi stared across the narrow defile to the other man. A crevasse separated them. Physically, the gap was not much, although wide enough to prevent the man from stepping over, or even leaping over, to Maeldoi's side of it. They were close enough to speak across, though.

In another way, the crevasse might as well have been as wide as an ocean. Maeldoi saw it right away, the gulf stretching between them. But he wasn't sure what, exactly, he was seeing. His mind was mazed with trance, his sense of what was real and what was dream blurred.

A young man, a bit younger than himself. Another of the gwrgi. They stood close enough to see the yellow of each other's eyes. There the similarities stopped.

A lean and muscular young man, not lean in the way that Maeldoi was lean. Lean in the way that young rich men are lean, given vigorous exercise, the most nourishing food, the best clothing.

Maeldoi was lean in the way that starving men are lean. He wasn't starving, not technically. He was fasting. He wondered, briefly, if the other might have stepped out of some vision. During his vigil, he'd had visions. Many. Whenever they came, he blessed them and shouted out greeting.

This man looked too solid to be a vision. Maeldoi thought he was not. And the feelings the man aroused in him were disturbing. Disturbing not in the way of stirring up hopes and challenges. Disturbing in the way the sight of the man stirred up some deep rottenness.

The man across the crevasse was smooth-shaven, the planes of his face handsome and proud. Maeldoi knew what he himself must look like. He'd seen himself in a pool of the spring where he went to draw water. His hair and beard long and matted. Dressed more or less in rags. At least he had a cloak to keep off the weather and wrap himself in for sleep. Even that was getting thin and worn.

"Maeldoi," the other man called across.

Maeldoi stared at this intruder, a long, measured stare.

Out of the deep, disturbing thoughts, a recognition emerged. "Cae."

"Come to my side of the crevasse and talk with me. Can we not sit down to talk?" The voice held a wheedling tone. Maeldoi wondered how long the man—his brother—had been shouting across the expanse. Maeldoi thought maybe he'd just now begun to realize that words were proceeding out of Cae's mouth, and that he was hearing them. "I can come around. Go down the valley, make my way back up to your side."

"No," said Maeldoi. A fear smote him.

"But why?"

Looking across to his brother waiting for a reply, Maeldoi found he was making one, at the same time something inside him was reacting in horror. *Stop!* this something was saying. But Maeldoi found himself speaking. "I'm not supposed to be talking to you at all, not even this way. It's my vigil." With a jolt, Maeldoi realized what he had just done, speaking, replying. Hastily, he turned his back, his thoughts in a whirl. He'd have to report this to Master Bertran, his shamanic guide, when the good old man arrived next. Maeldoi knew with a chill he'd have to take his punishment, even if the breach of his vigil's commandments wasn't really his fault. *Not my fault!* he kept insisting to something inside himself, and that something kept replying, *Your fault.*

"Maeldoi! I'm your brother! Your own brother, and you won't talk to me?"

"Go away, Cae," Maeldoi shouted back over his shoulder, just as he realized he'd do better to stay silent.

He got himself well out of the choppy hillside of crevasses and tangled vegetation, up into the hills above his camp. He squatted there, watching. With an effort, he made himself a blank inside, but underneath the blankness, he felt a rising panic. He had betrayed his vigil.

The teachings described a temptation like this one, and he had just fallen for it. Part of Maeldoi still felt he was experiencing some sort of vision.

The rustling of foliage below him insisted that Cae was no vision.

It didn't take his brother a candle-measure to skirt around the crevasse and back up to Maeldoi's side of it. From his height on the mountainside, hidden, Maeldoi watched Cae stand irresolute, looking around him. Then go on a sweep of the territory uphill, until he stood at Maeldoi's camp.

Maeldoi watched while Cae, just below his hiding place, poked around Maeldoi's meager belongings—the cape that served as a blanket, the cooking pot, the small fire tended in a circle of stones.

"I know you are near, brother," he heard Cae say, in almost a conversational tone. "Brother, you must come down here and speak to me. I come on an important errand."

Maeldoi squatted motionless. He knew how to do it. He'd make no noise. Cae would never spot him here, would never hear the least sound out of him.

Why are you here? Maeldoi beamed the thought at his brother. *Why are you not back at the caves where you belong? How have you come by this clothing, the sword at your belt?*

He wanted to know. But curiosity would be his undoing, if he gave it mastery over him. Even this thinking and wondering was a betrayal of his vigil. He'd have to take the consequences for that, too, when the shaman came.

He tried to focus his thoughts elsewhere. He stilled his breathing. In the quiet of the early harvest-tide landscape, even his breathing might be heard by someone listening hard. Maeldoi knew how to keep that from happening. He fixed his eyes on the clouds forming and re-forming in the mountain up-drafts.

But Cae's voice would keep intruding, breaking into his peace.

"Look at me, brother. I've been taken in by the baron. Baron Gilles de Rais. I'm treated as his adopted son. I have everything. But you—look at this trash." Cae stomped around the campsite. "How by the gods, whoever they are, did you come to this? You were supposed to be the lucky one. I was supposed to be the despised son, the misfit, tossed away into some cave with the savages."

In spite of himself, Maeldoi lowered his gaze from the treeline to the camp, where Cae was kicking at his cooking pot.

If he breaks it—

Well, then, Maeldoi told himself. *If he breaks it, I'll have to do without.*

"The baron has sent me to find you." Cae raised his voice. A group of small birds at the edge of the forested ridge flapped up, startled, into the sky. "Come back with me, Maeldoi. The baron wants you. Wants to help you, as he has helped me. We are brothers, you and I. We led a hard life, in childhood. It doesn't have to be like that. The baron has sent me here to fetch you to him."

Maeldoi resolutely swatted away from him the memories that now came crowding in. The low hut. How he had dominated his small brother and gotten a mean sort of enjoyment out of it. Their mother, her misery. The terrible visits of their father, especially the last. The way that last confrontation, and what his father had done to him, had evoked the building, bestial thing inside him, the thing his training was designed to master.

Then the day the rector and his men had come.

And he had walked away from his mother and brother. He had rarely thought of either of them again.

Cae's presence threatened that training. This new phase of it, training the mind, not just the body.

Maeldoi turned his gaze inward, stopped his outward hearing. He assumed a more efficacious pose, Hillside of the Mountain, and held it. It was dusk before he came out of it.

Looked down to the camp.

Cae was gone.

Now he spent a candle-measure or more on the exercises to bring himself out of his inward state.

By the time he'd finished them—and no good rushing them, he'd just pay in body and mind if he did—it was too late to find something to eat. He'd sleep hungry this night.

Hungrier.

At least Cae hadn't stamped out his fire or broken his pot.

Maeldoi gritted his teeth. There Cae was, back inside his head again. Maeldoi banished him from it. He knew it might take as much as a turning of the moon to regain his equilibrium, and before that happened, the shaman would pay him one of his regular visits and examine him.

Maeldoi dreaded it. But welcomed it, too. The shaman's punishments would help him banish Cae's taint from him for good and all. The shaman's generosity of spirit would help him regain his sense of himself. Master Bertran knew him through and through. Valued him. Helped him. He thought about the time he had spent at the rectory. He thought of Mistress Pereta. She had believed in him when others did not. And so did Master Bertran. And Aleron. So did Aleron. Maeldoi felt himself honored and valued. So many helpers. He praised The Three.

In the meantime, waiting for the arrival of his shaman and the penance he would prescribe, an experience both unhappy and healing, Maeldoi took himself through the penitential exercises the shaman had taught him so far. He ate even less than before. He deprived himself of his few pleasures. Bathing in the stream. It was beginning to get too cold for that, anyway.

He shivered, anticipating melting the snow and using it for hasty washing before the fire.

I need to build myself a winter shelter, he thought vaguely.

Then brought himself resolutely back to the penitential practices that would cleanse him of his brother.

When the shaman arrived a fortnight or so later, Maeldoi was so deep into his trance that he didn't notice. Carefully the man brought Maeldoi back to his ordinary self.

"Master Bertran," said Maeldoi, kneeling to his guide, the man who had taught him so much.

"Rise, Maeldoi. Here. Eat this. You've just about starved yourself to death. Good thing I've come along when I have."

Given the permission, Maeldoi wolfed down the bread, downed the ale in a single draught.

"Easy, Maeldoi. You'll make yourself sick. Come to the fire, trainee. Ah," said the shaman, dismay in his voice. "And you've let the fire go out. It's not winter yet, but this is dangerous. You have my permission to speak."

"A bigger danger has assailed me, master."

"And?"

"Someone visited me. I spoke to him."

"Tell me who this someone was, to make you break your training." The shaman's voice had gone cold.

"My brother."

"Your brother came here? And he did not realize what he was doing, coming here?"

"No. I don't know how he found me. I haven't seen him since we were boys, when the rector took me away and I left my mother and brother behind."

The shaman knew his history. "Have you had any contact with your brother, over the years?"

"None, master."

"Why, then? Why do you think?" he prompted, when Maeldoi didn't answer.

"I can't think why. We were not close, as children. I was not a good brother to him. In his place, I'd be relieved never to have to see me again. Yet he found out where I am. Somehow he did. And he came. And I was startled, and spoke."

"What did you say?"

"I told him to leave."

"Anything else?"

"No, just that." Maeldoi thought about it. "I spoke his name. I asked why he had come, told him I was breaking my vigil, talking to him. That's when I told him to go away. He kept talking to me, explaining about his new life and how it could be mine. So then I hid from him. I got myself away and waited all day in my pose, until he did leave."

"Which pose?"

Maeldoi described it.

"Very good," said the shaman. "Exactly the right thing to do. I'm thinking your punishment won't be severe. I see it now. I see you have already begun the penitential exercises, even to the danger of your well-being."

"Yes," whispered Maeldoi, miserable.

"Better that, than endanger your training."

Maeldoi nodded.

"I see this visit of mine is greatly needed. No mere form."

"Yes," said Maeldoi.

"Tell me what your brother said to you, Maeldoi. What is the name of this brother?"

"Cae," said Maeldoi. Then, thinking about it, "Caedon," he amended. "That's his name."

"Go on."

"He told me that the Baron Gilles de Rais had adopted him as a son. He told me the baron sent him out to find me, that the baron wants me as well."

Maeldoi, who had dropped his eyes, looked up startled at the shaman's hiss of indrawn breath.

"Did he offer you any inducements to go away with him?" the shaman said at last.

"He told me he lived well. That I could live that well, too. I could see that he did live well. Well-dressed, like a noble, with a sword of fine steel at his belt."

"How did that make you feel, Maeldoi?"

"Frightened. I blocked the words from my mind."

"Frightened that you'd be tempted to go with him?"

"No, master. Never. Frightened that he had made me speak. Frightened that I had broken my training."

The shaman stepped to Maeldoi and took him by both shoulders. Looked deep within his eyes. "I see you are speaking the truth, Maeldoi. The Three be praised. This is a minor setback only. You will be fine."

He dropped his hands from Maeldoi, and Maeldoi felt himself trembling.

"You know, Maeldoi—your third training year in my care is nearly over. It's nearly time for you to return to the city."

"But this. This will delay things. Change things," Maeldoi whispered. "When I was so close."

"Maybe a delay," said the shaman. "Not very long, Maeldoi. I have every confidence in you. If anything, this incident has proven to me how much you can withstand. How deep an attack. Do you know this baron? The Baron Gilles de Rais?"

"I have heard of him, master. The most powerful of all the realm's overlords."

"Nothing beyond that?"

"No, master."

"I'm of two minds here. You know nothing of the baron, nothing important. Let's keep it that way. That's my first thought. But if the baron really has sent this other one, this brother, to find and take you, then you are in danger. So I think I must go with my second thought. Explain to you about Gilles de Rais." As he'd been talking, the shaman had swiftly re-lit Maeldoi's fire and was fanning the embers into a blaze. "Sit here by the fire with me. Here," he said. "I brought you a new blanket. The old one is practically rags." He held it out to Maeldoi.

Maeldoi took it and wrapped it around himself and sat by the fire. Until that moment, he hadn't realized how deeply he was chilled.

After several moments of silence, the shaman spoke. "Gilles de Rais is, as you say, the most powerful overlord of the Eastern Baronies. But he is more. Much more. He is a mage. In fact, one of the most powerful underneath the Spheres, and above them, too."

"Why would he want me, master? Why has he adopted my brother?"

"The mages are powerful. Three of them the most powerful. Merlin stands at the head of them, at least for now, as long as he can keep control. His right-hand man, John Dee, not quite as powerful. And the other most powerful is Gilles de Rais. Let me describe their roles to you, Maeldoi, so you will understand."

Maeldoi nodded, listening.

"Merlin is the faithful servant of The Three, dedicated to preserving and fostering Their harmony," the shaman said, watching Maeldoi carefully. "Dee supports him completely. Gilles is nearly as powerful as Merlin. In a head-to-head contest, who knows which would win? Gilles subtly opposes and undermines The Three, carefully staying—I'm using their own phrase, although I must say I don't understand it—'under the radar.'

That is, he stays just so far over the line into compliance with Their wishes that They don't come after him and destroy him. But Dee, while not as powerful as either, is Merlin's ally. Together, he and Merlin are able to overmatch Gilles."

"I see," said Maeldoi, although, actually, he really didn't. The words, the very ideas, were alien to him.

"This is hard for you, I know," said the shaman, smiling. Underneath his smile, Maeldoi saw how disturbed he was. "You're to learn all of this very soon. I'm telling you some of it now."

"Why I need my letters," said Maeldoi glumly.

"Why you do," the shaman affirmed. "And when you return, you'll need to spend some turnings of the moon, maybe even a season or so, brushing up on them."

Maeldoi nodded his obedience. Thinking of holding a slate and chalk again made his hands itch. He flexed his hands and stared down at them. Easier to do that than to look into the shaman's eyes.

"Look at me, Maeldoi."

Reluctantly, he did.

"Maeldoi, this mage Gilles takes men—often he takes children—and he uses them as conduits for his magicks. He must be using your brother. He feeds on their force, their juices, and brings them into himself. From what you've told me, it's clear to me he intends to do that to you, if he can."

Maeldoi felt a shiver creep up his spine. He didn't know what the shaman meant, *feeds on their juices*, but he knew how it made him feel. Frightened to his core. "I wouldn't go with Cae. I didn't. I wouldn't, ever, even if I just thought I'd be going to an easeful life."

"Don't let your brother near you. I fear he is lost to you." Master Bertran peered into Maeldoi's eyes. "Ah," he said. "I see something in you I've never adequately been able to explain to myself. I see it now. I see the guilt over him that you bear with you. It lies deep inside you. You've never confronted it, and in an ordinary world, you would, because it eats into you like a canker. But now, lay that aside. Your brother has become too dangerous to you. Weighing the alleviation of your guilt against this danger, you must choose your own survival."

Maeldoi tried to look inside himself. Guilt over Cae. It rang true, and he felt a deep remorse.

"I'm not sure what Gilles can do to reach through others to touch the one he wants. It's beyond my knowing," said the shaman. "But I know he does it. I'll send you to someone at the House of Penitence, when we get back there. Someone who can give you full instruction, one of the priests trained in penance. I suppose you'll need to put yourself in the hands of the Penance Board. Your penitential exercises are good—the right thing for you to do. But after this." Master Bertran shook his head. "I'm thinking you'll need to do more, after this. You'll need exercises beyond my powers of instruction, if you're to stay safe from the threat of Gilles de Rais."

The shaman stood then and began pacing around the little camp. He stopped. "In fact, Maeldoi. Pack up your things. I'm taking you back with me."

"So I have failed. This—thing—my brother was hoping to inflict on me has caused me to betray my training." Maeldoi tried and failed to keep the bitterness from his voice.

In childhood, he had dominated Cae. Now, it seemed, his brother had overmastered him. Maybe it was justice that he did. Maeldoi's mind flicked back to some of the things he'd done to Cae, a helpless small boy. And now this baron, this mage, had taken possession of his brother. Maybe Maeldoi's mistreatment had opened up some fatal vulnerability in his brother that the mage could then exploit. A wave of guilt as bitter as nausea overwhelmed Maeldoi.

"No, my lad," said the shaman. There was genuine affection in his voice. "By no means have you failed. I'd say this incident means you have passed your training, if in an unorthodox manner, and I believe they'll see it my way, at the House of Penitence."

"They'll decree punishment. I deserve it."

"I see your thinking better than you do yourself, Maeldoi. You're not saying this because you spoke aloud and broke your vigil. Those deep things are rising in you, to accuse you. You must not dwell on your faults, Maeldoi, without expert help. The Penance Board will help you atone for them in the proper way. One thing is certain. You must not be left out here at your camp to do penance. You'd be defenseless if your brother or—The Three forfend—Gilles himself were to come on you out here as you went into your trance. It's luck I got to you in time."

Maeldoi stumbled after the shaman down the mountain. He wasn't sure he'd be able to mount a horse, weakened as he was. But he did it.

As the ramparts of the city began looming over them, as they rode in through the big gates, only then did Maeldoi feel himself in some measure safe. In some measure, at peace.

His shaman had guided him through the last few years, and Maeldoi trusted him completely.

He was right to trust that Master Bertran loved him and wished the best for him.

But both of them were wrong to trust in the guidance of the Penance Board. The Board did not wish the best for Maeldoi, and neither Maeldoi nor Master Bertran could know that.

Both of them were soon to learn that painful lesson, Maeldoi in the harshest way possible, or close to.

CHAPTER TWELVE

Discipline

Newly come out of the penitential cells, Maeldoi didn't know how to think about himself now that he was back in the world.

Almost an entire year gone by since the misfortune of his encounter with his brother. Maeldoi blinked in the unaccustomed sunlight. His wounds itched and some of them still burned, but worse than that was the feeling that violent hands waited to snatch him back inside.

As a penitent, he'd entered the cells as dirty as he was when he'd come off his vigil, his hair and beard as long and matted and rank.

He'd expected to walk back out some days later, cleansed in body and spirit, ready to resume his training. His shaman guide, Master Bertran, had believed the same.

That's not what happened. His hair was shorn. But he stayed as dirty as when he went in, and only got filthier.

Maeldoi disappeared into the cells as completely as if he'd never existed.

Now, many seasons later, he was out. He'd been bathed. He was clean. His hair was clean, and he had been cleared to resume his training. Although his hair was shorn prison-short, he didn't think it differed much from the style appropriate to a trainee, so he didn't think others could take one look at him and realize where he had been. As long as he kept his tunic on, and the sleeves well pulled down over his damaged hands, he didn't think anyone would notice. Not at first glance.

Yet he imagined that every person he passed on the street was cringing away from him, sensing his guilt.

His first thought had been to find Master Bertran and get guidance on how to think of what he'd been through. He desperately needed it. But one of the conditions of his release was to have no contact at all with Master Bertran.

If he violated those conditions, he'd find himself back in the cells. He might endanger his spiritual guide as well. A man who only wanted Maeldoi's welfare and had acted in good faith. Maeldoi was sure of it.

Suppose Master Bertran thought Maeldoi had somehow betrayed him. Surely Maeldoi had endangered the good old man. From some words spoken by the men of the Penance Board, he thought Master Bertran, too, had been punished. Maybe not too severely, not as severely as Maeldoi, surely not, but still, the very idea of it catapulted Maeldoi into an agony. He had to keep the thought far away from him.

At least he'd been released from the forbidding walls of the House of Penitance to a pleasant room in the capital. It was a bare little room, but its cleanliness and the light and air coming in through its only window were a balm to him. Inside, he still might feel himself imprisoned. At least now he was free in body to come and go. He remembered how it felt to exchange his ordeals in the physical training court for a less rigorous existence. What he was feeling now was something like those remembered days. By now they seemed very long ago.

But unlike that heady burst of freedom, and the first pleasant and easy days of his mental training, he couldn't settle to enjoy this new freedom. If that's what it was. He rattled restlessly around the room, and then he took to walking the peaceful streets and courtyards of the gwrgi city, situated high on a mountain, shielded from ordinary folk by thick walls and steep, near-inaccessible roads.

It was the capital. It kept gwrgi safe from their prying, superstitious neighbors.

When they'd come off the mountain of his vigil together, his shaman master had blessed him and handed him off to the penitential priests for their chastisement, never thinking they'd remand Maeldoi to anything but the Lesser Penances. Rigorous, of course, but necessary if he were to understand what had just happened to him during his encounter with Cae. A necessary healing.

Instead, the Penance Board had taken him immediately into the Penitential Order. The most severe of all sentences the clerical court meted out, short of execution. And there was nothing Maeldoi or Master Bertran could do about it.

The penance priests had probed into Maeldoi and had seen what Master Bertran had seen. But they'd put a very different construction on it.

Unlike his gentle master, they decided Maeldoi needed atonement not just for the few words he had spoken to his brother Caedon, but for Caedon himself.

"If not for your mistreatment, Caedon might not have fallen prey to the baron," one of the priests explained to him. "And there are other things we don't like. They lead us to bring a third charge against you. You need to atone for all three, but the third most of all."

"If he even can," one of them muttered under his breath.

The three members of the Penance Board presented a severe united front as Maeldoi stood before them, trying to understand what they were telling him. This third charge. Aiding Insurrection. What did it mean, how could they think such a thing of him? Maeldoi tried to keep his mind even and under control. It would do no good to rail at the injustice he saw they were determined to do him. In fact, it would make things worse if he presented anything other than a face of silent obedience to them. An obedient stance. A posture of utmost contrition, even if he didn't know for what.

"Your spiritual guide, Master Bertran, was very wrong to suggest to you that you'd receive a light punishment," the Penance Board members told Maeldoi. "Master Bertran will need to reflect on that. It was not his place to make such a judgment. It's ours. Aiding Insurrection. A most heavy charge."

Maeldoi remembered his down-heartedness when he heard those words. He'd be punished, not under the relatively mild rubric of the Lesser Penances, but under the authority of the Penitential Order itself. Meanwhile, his own offense had put Master Bertran in danger. He'd come to respect and love the old man.

But his own punishments. When he heard the Penance Board pronounce the charges, a cold hand touched him.

The punishments of the Penitential Order took a while. They were profound, as he knew they would be. He could never have imagined how painful. Now that he was out of their hands, he tried not to think about what they'd done to him. He was luckier than some. Some went into those cells and never came out.

Maeldoi was out, and he was grateful, but he had no master.

He was adrift, and deeply bruised by what he had undergone. He wondered how much damage he had sustained. The shock of it was just beginning to wear off. There might be unhealed lacerations he'd bear for the rest of his life. Inner lacerations. The outward scars were nothing to those.

Aleron and Halde were off at war. He'd hoped he'd see them, but they were far away, fighting in the army of the Great City of the Lyre Lands. Seeing them would have been some consolation. Aleron might have been able to help him understand what had happened to him, and why, and he had not been forbidden to see his friend. Not expressly. But Aleron was not there.

During the year Maeldoi was sitting his vigil, letters from Aleron had come for him, and the shaman had carefully kept them. Maeldoi was allowed to hear nothing from the world while he was in that last phase of severe mental discipline, especially as he moved into the rigors of the vigil with its intense self-reflection, completely alone in the wilderness. Aleron had left his own training before he underwent these rigors. He had left before his vigil and couldn't know what that year was like, designed to break a person down to his most elemental self and then rebuild him again.

So he didn't know, couldn't know, what Maeldoi endured. But in many ways, he did know Maeldoi the way no one else did or could. Maeldoi loved Aleron.

One of Master Bertran's last acts, before he and Maeldoi were forcibly separated, was to hand over the packet of Aleron's letters. Then, before Maeldoi could read them, the Penance Board had taken them from him.

On his release, his jailers gave back the letters, smudged but not destroyed. No doubt the Penance Board had read them all, to make sure they contained nothing incriminating.

Now Maeldoi could read them. At least he had that comfort. During his first days of freedom, he devoured Aleron's letters and couldn't help weeping, so lonely he was for his friend. Aleron's news was two years old, but Maeldoi read the letters over and over, touching them, smoothing them with his fingers. The letters consoled him. They also aroused his fears. What would Aleron say to him when he learned of Maeldoi's deep offenses?

This day he sat toying with an orange in the sunny courtyard where, he remembered, he and Aleron and Halde had last enjoyed each other's company. He lifted the orange to his nostrils and inhaled the scent of it. He wanted to postpone the joy of peeling and eating it, because then the joy would be over.

Afterward he planned to go in search of Aleron, or someone who might know where Aleron was now. At the very least, he should have new letters from Aleron. He would go to the military official in charge of the cohorts and ask there. The newest letters in the packet he fingered in the fold of his robe were over a year old.

Before he could, a herald interrupted him. An officious man with a message. *Report to me for your assignment,* Maeldoi read. He recognized the form of the message and where it must have come from. With a sigh he stood and followed the herald, who took him to the portico and the man at the desk with his quill.

As the herald turned to leave, Maeldoi handed him the orange. It would be a crime to waste such an amazing fruit.

"You have finished your years of physical discipline, then your years of mental discipline. You have finished a period of penitence I believe you were mandated to serve?"

"Yes, lord," Maeldoi told the man, bowing. He wondered how much the penitential sentence had weighed against him. Would he be given lesser work now?

With a sudden lifting of his heart, he wondered if he'd be released from the burden of the special tasks and sent to join a cohort of soldiers instead. Maybe Aleron's. Too much to hope for, but then—

The man at the desk looked down at the parchment before him. "You're to spend some turnings of the moon, as much as a year, in better learning your letters," he said.

So Maeldoi's heart sank again. Foolish, really. After what he'd been through, this was a gnat-bite only.

The man handed him the parchment.

Maeldoi glanced down at it. He needed to get himself to the great dusty library on its pinnacle at the edge of the city, hard up against the high ridge of mountains that rose around them.

"Do you understand?"

"Yes, sir," said Maeldoi with a bow.

By the time he left the official and had finished with all the parchments he had to read and sign, it was too late to go in search of Aleron's letters. Early the next morning, he was due at the library. He promised himself he'd look for the letters soon.

The next morning, he presented himself at the library. A scholar-teacher who seemed as dusty as the library itself was assigned to teach him.

"Let us begin, trainee," said this man, fitting his fingers together in a precise little pyramid and pursing up his lips. He looked like he might have heard of Maeldoi's reputation as a notable dullard and wooden-head. Mistress Pereta had cursed anyone who thought that of him. May he be tossed into a dung-heap!

Maeldoi wondered if the man had a stout stick, like his scholar-teacher back at the rectory, and whether he'd use that stick on Maeldoi, as the other man had.

But I'm not a boy any longer, thought Maeldoi. He wasn't sure how old he was. Well into manhood now. Maybe he wouldn't be beaten like a schoolboy if he didn't learn fast enough.

If this man tries it, maybe I'll beat him instead.

This thought rose up unbidden from some place stuffed deeply down into Maeldoi by the years of discipline.

There it is again, thought Maeldoi, bleakly. *It never goes away. And over something as trivial as this.*

"Maeldoi," said the scholar-teacher sharply, turning Maeldoi's attention back to himself. "You know what the disciplines are for, don't you? The physical? The mental?"

"Yes, of course, sir," said Maeldoi, mechanically.

"And?"

Maeldoi looked at the man, startled. Dusty he might be. His eyes were shrewd.

"Control," said Maeldoi, low.

"Yes. We gwrgi need to learn control, do we not?"

"Yes, sir," said Maeldoi.

"These disciplines never banish what we are. They allow us to control it. Is that not right?"

"Yes, sir," said Maeldoi.

"And you have been through the extra discipline of penance. You know how important it is for you to maintain control."

Maeldoi nodded, miserable. If he'd let them, the experiences of the penitential cells would pour in on him and destroy him. He needed control over that as much as he needed control over the rage.

"Then let us begin. Think of this—" The scholar-teacher swept out his arms to encompass the table, the books and scrolls, the whole library. "—as one more discipline for control."

Maeldoi nodded. He doubted this teacher knew what he had gone through. Almost no one did, if they hadn't been in those cells themselves.

On this first day of his new assignment, he and his teacher sat together at a table in the library's main reading room.

Maeldoi looked aside at the scrolls, the books. The slate. The piece of chalk. He looked up at his teacher, sitting there complacent, probably regretting he'd drawn the assignment of teaching Maeldoi. Probably thinking how dull it was going to be, trying to teach him. A waste of his precious time.

But I know Guillaume, and his nephew, and his giant, thought Maeldoi. *I know Man-Dog Rough-Gray.*

"Pick up your chalk, Maeldoi, and write on the slate what I shall dictate," said the scholar-teacher. He took one of the books from the table and opened it, his fingers caressing the cover and pages like a lover.

Maeldoi drew the slate closer. He took up his chalk.

Before the scholar-teacher could speak a word or Maeldoi attempt to write it down, bells began to toll.

"The Three preserve us." The teacher-scholar rose to his feet, his book dropping with a thump to the stone floor of the library.

Maeldoi had risen too.

They both knew what the bells meant. Everyone who had spent time in the city knew.

Alarm. Emergency.

"What is it?" the scholar-teacher cried out to someone rushing past them.

"We're to assemble in the main courtyard. War, it means war."

"Stay by me, Maeldoi," the scholar-teacher commanded him. As they exited the quiet of the library, the noise assaulted them almost as a physical thing. Thousands of gwrgi were pouring into the central courtyard of the capital and moiling about. "I'm not letting this crisis interrupt your training," his teacher shouted to Maeldoi over the tumult.

Maeldoi stood with his teacher as their leaders, the Grand Council of the gwrgi, pushed their way through the crowd to a raised platform to speak. They held up their arms for silence, and the roaring of the assembled men settled to a low hum and buzz.

One of the Council stepped to the front of the platform.

"Lord Jouhan, head of the Grand Council," said Maeldoi's teacher in his ear.

"Gwrgi of the capital." Lord Jouhan's words rang out over their heads. "The lower city has been attacked. It lies under a state of siege."

Maeldoi knew that a second, lesser city lay sprawling at the foot of the mountain, a city of tradesfolk and crafters, supplying the needs of the capital. He and the rector had ridden through it—*so many years ago, now,* Maeldoi thought. *A lifetime ago.* Then, with a sense of shock, he realized: only a year ago, he and Master Bertran had ridden through it. He barely remembered the boy he had been, that first time. And now, again, he'd undergone a radical change, everything he'd thought he knew about himself scoured away in the cells of the Penitential Order.

The lower city, he remembered, was much larger than the capital, but much less well-defended, only a low wall of mud bricks, not the imposing stones of the capital for protection. But it served as a buffer for the capital. Invaders would have to fight through it to get access to the road up the mountain.

If the lower city were lost, though—.

Lord Jouhan's words emphasized these conditions. "Time out of mind this has happened," Lord Jouhan cried out. "Those of the ordinary folk who hate and fear us decide they have the strength to end us. They think the gods command them to it, in spite of the favor we know from The Three, and always have had."

"Who are the invaders?" Maeldoi murmured to his teacher. The man shook his head and shrugged. Leaned forward intently.

Lord Jouhan soon settled the matter. "The Great City of the Lyre Land, whipped up by false religious fervor, has marched on us. They have faithlessly destroyed our cohorts placed with them, and now they have come to our very doorstep."

Maeldoi felt stark fear. Aleron. He and Halde were serving in one of those cohorts. Or they had been, in the last letters Aleron had written to him.

"All professed gwrgi, present yourselves to the city armory. Arm yourselves and wait to be organized into cohorts to come to the aid of the lower city, and to defend the capital if the invaders break through."

With a roar, the men in the courtyard turned for the city armory.

Maeldoi, his heart in his mouth, turned to go with them.

The scholar-teacher plucked him by the sleeve backward.

Maeldoi looked around, incredulous. "I must go! I must arm myself!"

"Maeldoi," said his teacher. "All professed gwrgi. You are not professed. You are a trainee."

"But sir, my combat skills are good. More than good. This is attested to."

"I've seen the parchment saying so, Maeldoi. Nevertheless. You are not professed."

"Sir. Can't you release me? This emergency—my friend Aleron—"

"I order you, Maeldoi. Return to the library."

Maeldoi stood, head down, mastering himself. Finally he raised his eyes to his teacher's, who stood in the emptying courtyard, watching him narrowly.

"So you and I will just go back to the library as if nothing has happened—"

"You'll go, Maeldoi. I am ordering you to go. What makes you think I'll go?" There was a glimmer of amusement in his teacher's eye. It enraged Maeldoi.

Control, Maeldoi told himself. *This is a test. Control.*

"But you're not a warrior, sir. You're only a—"

"Oh, Maeldoi. Do you think, because my task is in the great library, that I did not undergo the same training as yourself? Every man in this city is a professed man. Unless he's a trainee only hoping to become professed. As far as you know, my combat skills are as good as yours."

Maeldoi knew his mouth had gaped open. Suppose this man were, as he said, as good at combat as Maeldoi?

He thought of himself and his training. Thought of where it might lead him.

Suppose he himself were as good at letters as he was at combat. Suppose his assignment, when he came to be professed, if he ever were, was to leave combat and embrace letters as his life. Suppose, when it came time for Maeldoi to make his profession, he were assigned some task distasteful to him. And put to it for the rest of his life.

Suppose that was his teacher's situation.

All these thoughts raced through Maeldoi as he stared at his teacher.

"I see the thoughts churning inside that interesting mind of yours, Maeldoi. Trainee. Now go back to the library and await a different teacher. Your task is to hone that mind, so you will be of use to The Three." His eyes bored into Maeldoi's. They were hard but they were compassionate. "You must not risk your hard-won success. Not after all you've been through."

Maeldoi saw then. His teacher understood about the Penance Board after all.

"As for me," said his teacher. "I must get myself to the armory."

His scholar-teacher walked away from him then, and Maeldoi never saw him again.

He learned later that his teacher died in the war. He felt sorrow when he heard. *For a man I really never even knew,* he said to himself.

Now, disconsolate, Maeldoi made his way back to the library. He thought of disobeying, of getting himself to the armory using roundabout alleys and side streets. Blending in with the crowd. He imagined someone handing him a sword.

But no. It was obvious he was a trainee.

The professed men's hair was long, tied back by an embroidered band. They wore the tunic of the professed in the bright colors of their assigned tasks.

Maeldoi, a trainee, was shorn. His hair was even more close-cropped than most of the other trainees, because of his time in the cells. In the cells, they kept the penitents' hair very short there to discourage vermin.

Perhaps if he pulled the hood of his cloak well up about his face and hid his hair. . .Suppose, in the commotion, no one looked too close. . .

Maeldoi examined himself with despair. His tunic was drab. He wore trousers, not the leggings of the professed. If he presented himself at the armory, he'd be sent away.

And did he really mean to disobey? After what he'd been through? He knew his release had been a near thing. Any violation of the conditions of his release would get him re-arrested.

He was at the library now. As he gazed away from it down one of the capital's great causeways, he watched as a troop of mounted soldiers moved past some officer in review. He ached to hold a weapon in his hands. Even worse, it had been too long, far too long, since he'd melded his body with the flowing motion of a horse. Just thinking of it, just watching the manes of the war horses as they swept past up the causeway made him ache for them.

He shrugged deeper into his hooded cloak, then turned and trudged up the steps and into the library. He saw a small knot of other trainees and headed over to it.

A porter was standing there with them. Not one of the professed. A gwrgi from the lower city, who came up every day to serve the capital. "Trainees," he said, his voice respectful. "You're to stay here and wait. Soon you'll learn how your training will continue."

Maeldoi stared around him aimlessly. He looked at his fellows. He didn't know any of them. All of them were here to rectify a deficiency in letters before they could be professed. He imagined they'd all come through the two phases, the harsh physical training, the arduous mental training, culminating in the vigil, as he had.

He doubted any of them had served time in the penitential cells, though. But he didn't know. Within the walls enclosing the cells, he'd never seen any of his fellow penitents. They were all completely isolated.

Maybe one had known that experience. Maeldoi looked aside at a young man who wore a haunted expression. Maeldoi recognized that expression.

Even without any mirror, he knew it was the expression he himself must wear.

Master Bertran, his shamanic mentor, hadn't thought Maeldoi had needed such an experience. The penitential priests had other ideas.

Now, after confronting himself in their cells, Maeldoi saw that, after a fashion, according to their own obscure principles, they were right.

The old shaman had loved him. Had seen the best in him.

These priests had seen him with colder eyes.

Maeldoi started wondering how his training in letters would progress. Some older professed scholar-teacher, one of the ones retired from the world, must be coming out of retirement to teach them. Someone too old, too ill, too impaired to fight.

There was a commotion at the opening of the alcove where the trainees waited. The porter stepped aside.

A group of gwrgi stepped into the alcove toward the trainees, who, looking up and spotting them, huddled together to the rear of the alcove, backing in a panicked little knot as far away as they could get.

"We are to be your new teachers," said the one who looked to be the oldest of these gwrgi.

The trainees stared. Maeldoi stared.

Their new teachers were women.

CHAPTER THIRTEEN

Hard Lessons

Maeldoi looked warily at the two women, and they looked warily back. The older one's face was severe. Her eyes were not friendly. She was the woman who had spoken to the trainees when the women were introduced. The younger woman of the pair seemed more approachable. She was pretty. Pretty was not the word, Maeldoi thought. She looked strong and determined.

Just the same, he thought, taking in her silky clothing and the gold at her wrist, *the likes of her—not for the likes of me.* A foolish thought. No woman would have him, not a woman of the upper classes, as this one surely was, and none of the city women who glanced at him dismissively as he sat in courtyards and taverns. What did women want. He didn't know. Just that they didn't want him. He was fairly sure of it. Damaged. Battered. Little better than a beast of the caves. It must be written on his face.

As this young woman stared at Maeldoi, though, she appeared somehow intrigued.

"On your knees to us, trainee," said the older one. "We are your teachers now. Your teachers and your betters."

Maeldoi knelt to them. "My ladies," he said, hoping that was the proper address.

"Just call us Scholar," said the older one. She seemed to be the spokesperson. "Tell us about yourself. Why you are here to be taught by us."

"Scholar, I am a dullard. I have never learned my letters properly. I may not move from trainee to professed unless I can do better."

"You're no dullard," the young one exclaimed. "We have read your parchment. You are most promising."

Maeldoi ventured a look at her, then at the older woman, who was frowning at her companion.

"Someone may think me promising, Scholar, but not in this way," said Maeldoi, hoping for a conciliatory and humble tone. He was amazed. When had these women become scholars? They were just women. "I excelled in other ways, maybe. Not in the way of letters."

"Why are you so backward, trainee?" the older one asked. "Explain to us."

"Is this why you were a penitent? Because you refused to learn?" the younger one burst in.

"Really, Gisa," said the older one. "Let us stick to what we are mandated to ask this man. Nothing further."

The younger one flushed.

"So," said the older. "Speak."

"Scholar, when I was a child, I lived in a far country. My father kidnapped my mother and took her there. I had just reached manhood when the rector found me and brought me to the rectory. The Northern Rectory," he added, explaining.

"And why would the rector do a thing like that?" this older one demanded. "I know the man."

"Scholar, you must ask him that yourself. The rector and his men brought me to the rectory, but my mother and brother he sent to the caves on the coast that stretches into the northern part of the Narrows."

"Much more appropriate." The older scholar-teacher looked him up and down, judging him. Taking in his shabby clothes. He had the eerie feeling she could see through them to his scarred body and know in some uncanny way how right she was. A savage cave gwrgi.

"And you received no education as a boy, in this far country?" the young one ventured, looking to her companion. Maeldoi saw she was careful now to make sure she wasn't overstepping.

"None, lady," said Maeldoi, forgetting. "My mother and brother and I lived like animals. We were dressed in rags, we lived in a poor hut. I didn't know the language of the Baronies until the rector took me to the rectory." No point in dissembling, trying to be someone he wasn't.

"Address us as Scholar," the older reminded him.

"Scholar," Maeldoi amended.

"You spoke some other tongue?" It was the young one, and her tone was skeptical.

"Yes, Scholar."

"Speak some of it now," she demanded, as if she didn't believe him.

"I was a mere beast of the caves, before the rector found me," Maeldoi said to her, in the language of his youth.

"This is known, Gisa. They speak some barbarous tongue of their own in those caves," said the older. Her voice was impatient.

It's a different tongue than that, he told her in his mind, remembering his first days with the rector. *Similar, though.* But he didn't speak these words aloud. The less he spoke with this one, the better. And he settled himself into the classic pose of abasement, called, of course, The Penitent, because he wasn't sure how much longer they'd keep him on his knees, and he thought he should get comfortable there, comfortable enough to hold the pose for candle-measures if he had to.

It was a familiar pose by now. He'd spent two seasons and more in it, mostly, during his penance. Unless he had been, instead, in the pose of Lowest Abasement, truly groveling. He felt an involuntary shiver.

The younger one, Gisa, stood looking down at him, bemused. She prodded him with her toe. "You can get up now," she told him.

And so he unfolded himself from the pose again and rose to his feet.

He stood in the pose Underneath the Winter Rains, arms crossed about his chest, head down, so his humility would still speak for him.

"So then," the older one said, "your boyhood was spent in these conditions, and you had no chance to learn your letters. Is that what I'm hearing?"

"Yes, Scholar."

"But this was amended, at the rectory."

"Alda, if I may—" The younger one spoke hesitantly.

"Please," the older one, Alda, said now.

"What he meant when he told us he was taken to the Northern Rectory—it's not a house known much for learning. It's a house known for combat."

Alda grunted.

"Scholars, I passed my examination in letters there, but barely, and only with a great deal of help."

"And now your lax ways have caught up with you," said Alda, at the same time the other one, Gisa, was exclaiming about how great his combat skills must be, to outweigh something as shameful as that. How much his superiors must have trusted him, to pass him in spite of his deficiencies.

Maeldoi schooled himself to stay silent. He shouldn't have spoken at all, he saw that now. The two women were looking daggers at each other. Not a good beginning.

"Let us move on, then," Alda said after a sigh. "We'll do what we can with him. If he fails after that, it won't be our lookout."

They talked about him quietly as if he weren't there. They seemed to have set aside their animosity. How stupid he must be, they agreed. How difficult it was to bring someone still unlettered by manhood to any sort of understanding at all. How he would no doubt fail.

Maeldoi sank himself more fully into Underneath the Winter Rains. It was that, or his real self, his uncontrolled gwrgi male self, would flash out and confirm for them the worst they thought of him. *They might even be trying to goad me into revealing it*, he told himself.

They had been standing together at the doors of the library's great reading room. Now they entered it. Maeldoi trailed the two women to a table. When they nodded to him to sit, he took his place on a stool.

They handed him chalk and slate. They dictated. He wrote. They criticized. He erased. He wrote again. Erased. Wrote again.

I can do this all day long, he marveled to himself. Going through the Penitential Order, he now saw, had its uses. He supposed it was one more piece of evidence that the Penance Board was right about him and his shaman guide was wrong, his judgment clouded by love of Maeldoi, his pupil whom he'd come to regard, it seemed, as his child.

Maeldoi did need to undergo the Penitential Order, not the Lesser Penances his shaman had recommended for him. He was a deeply flawed person, and everyone saw it except Master Bertran.

And maybe Aleron.

And Mistress Pereta.

The scholar-teachers and their dullard of a pupil spent a long day together in the library.

Maeldoi schooled himself not to think of what was happening outside. War. The preparations for war. All those things he was best at. The things he was born to do.

"Come to us here tomorrow, as soon as you break your fast," said the older one, dismissing him at last.

As he ate in one of the courtyards later on, Maeldoi drank in all the gossip and tried not to dwell on the long candle-measures of struggle ahead of him in the library. Days. Seasons of struggle.

But he was free.

He was in this courtyard, free to move around.

Meanwhile, the very life of the city was in jeopardy. The gwrgi army had surrounded the lower city, the gossips were saying. Their army had drawn up around the lower city in a great protective crescent. Facing them, the much vaster army of the Lyre Land. The two armies had engaged in a standoff for the better part of the day. Then both sides had retired to their tents to await a diplomatic mission sent from The Three.

"Do The Three engage in diplomacy?" one man said, clearly too old to fight. His tone was skeptical.

Maeldoi, seemingly concentrated on his food, was listening hard.

"No, lackwit," said another. "They send one of the mages to do it for Them."

"Which mage?" said the first.

"Merlin," said another man, who had just joined them with his trencher and his leathern bottle of ale.

"Nah, not he," said the first man. "This is just some spat. Not important enough to bring the most important of the mages away from his seat."

Maeldoi yearned to ask them questions. How many were the enemy? Horsed or not? Siege towers?

But he knew not to. The eyes of the Penance Board were everywhere.

"We're releasing you to your training now, Maeldoi," the head of the board had told him as he stood before them on that last day. "But we will be watching you. Watching to make sure you keep to yourself. It's true we have found no evidence of our suspicions—" That vast mysterious third charge brought against him, dangerous enough to cast him from the Lesser Penances into the full-on Penitential Order—"but we will be watching for any breach telling us otherwise. And if we see one, you may be sure you'll find yourself in one of our cells again." That meant, the man emphasized, that the less Maeldoi had to do with any others in the city outside his strict needs as a trainee, the better. *Making a connection with a citizen of the city outside the prescribed activities.* Violating that condition of his release would get him re-arrested.

As he sat finishing his dinner, unable to taste a bite, he wished desperately that he had been able to talk to Master Bertran, at least once. That had been expressly forbidden him.

Maeldoi sat brooding in the courtyard over the severity of his fault.

Saying one or two words, in a moment of befuddlement, to his own brother. Surely Master Bertran was right. This was a minor breach, under the circumstances.

The other fault was grave. The way he had treated Cae in childhood. He had repented, and these experiences were long in the past.

The third charge had settled it, though. And Maeldoi was still not sure what it involved. Over and over, the members of the Penance Board had hammered their questions at him. His relationship to Gilles de Rais. The reason Gilles wanted him.

The charge was called Aiding Insurrection. It sounded bad. In fact, it was bad, a serious charge just a step away from treason. This Gilles must be dangerous to the state, although Maeldoi had only Master Bertran's few words about him to show how dangerous he was, and why. Master Bertran had assured him the Penance Board would help him understand. They hadn't.

Over and over, he had told them the truth. He did not know why Gilles would want him. Until Master Bertran had explained, he hadn't even known that Gilles de Rais was more than he seemed, a powerful overlord.

After two seasons of attempting to break him in body and mind, the Penance Board had finally agreed. They could see no evidence he was lying. But if he were telling the truth, that there was no connection, why was his own brother in league with Gilles and sent to take him?

Maeldoi had no answer.

They had released him.

They could have kept him up to a year.

They had not, releasing him just shy of that mark.

But it was also clear to Maeldoi they still believed he was lying to them.

It had become clear to Maeldoi why. Clearer, anyway. Gilles was so dangerous to them, to all gwrgi, that they didn't dare release anyone who might have been suborned by Gilles. They didn't dare entertain even the mere possibility. They wouldn't release Maeldoi. They wouldn't release anyone with that taint on him. Yet by their own rules, they had to, and that enraged them. It made them dangerous to him.

For the better part of the first season in their hands, he had felt himself more and more aggrieved. He was innocent, yet they refused to believe him. Where was justice? He had asked himself this in a fury. As the second season began, his feelings turned. From outraged, he started to feel frightened.

The Lesser Penances were nothing in comparison to his own punishment. Many underwent the Lesser Penances, and for various offenses. Some might be whipped, true, but he doubted such a punishment had been inflicted on Master Bertran, respected and old. Probably his shamanic guide had had to make some sort of public acknowledgment of fault, and maybe spend a sen'night confined to his rooms to meditate. He may have been bumped down the roster of spiritual guides and made to take on a less promising trainee for the next years of his profession.

Maeldoi gave a bitter laugh. A promising trainee. That's what everyone had told him, of himself. That's what Master Bertran had told him. Now, suddenly, for unknown reasons, he was instead a suspected enemy of the state. How far he had fallen.

Maeldoi felt himself filled not just with bitterness, but with contrition. Master Bertran had dealt gently with him, because of the promise he said he saw in Maeldoi, and this is how Maeldoi had thanked him.

Coming under the control of the Order of Penitence was a far different matter than being remanded to the Lesser Penances. Maeldoi remembered the first humiliating days. Entering the room to face the three members of the Penance Board. They read out the charges.

You have a choice now, Maeldoi, they told him. Sign this parchment, and tomorrow you will be whipped and released into the city, free to go about your business. You will never become professed. You will never be allowed to resume your training. But you can put these charges behind you very simply, and then live your life. True, the whipping is severe. Your faults are severe. But the pain will soon be over.

Or, they said, presenting him with a second parchment, Sign this one instead. Tomorrow, as with the first choice, you'll be severely whipped. Once you are able to stand before us, you'll be entered into the Penitential Order. You'll be taken to a cell. You'll stay there, undergoing penance, for no less than a full season, no more than a full year. At the end of each season, you'll be judged anew. If we judge you have atoned for your faults, you'll be released to resume your training.

If we judge you have not atoned, you'll be remanded for another season of penance. At that point, you may petition to be removed from the Penitential Order. But know that if you do, you will be cast out utterly, to make your way among ordinary folk if you can, and no gwrgi will ever acknowledge you. Otherwise, you'll agree to undergo another season of penance. And so on, for three seasons. At the end of the fourth season, though— a full year—if in our judgment you have not atoned, you will be cast out. No appeal. Out.

Which parchment will you sign? they asked him. Choose the first, one of them advised. By far the safer.

Part of him agreed. *Whip me and have done with it. I'll make my own way without the burden of profession. Perhaps a cohort will still have me.* He took up the quill to sign the first parchment.

Then something stubborn inside him said, *They want me to fail, and I will not.* So he signed the second parchment. *Whip me. Torment me. At the end of it, send me back to my training.*

At the end of the first season, though, they told him he must endure another. The stakes were higher then. The choice before him was starker. If he didn't agree to endure a second season of their torments, he'd be cast out forever from gwrgi society. So he agreed, and signed, and the torment continued.

Whipping? He thought. *I've been whipped before.* (Never like this, though, with a many-tailed whip tipped in sharp shards of bone.) *Stand me up against a wall and refuse to let me lie down and sleep? I've gone through the physical discipline training, and you will not break me.*

Nor did they.

But the other things. Burning. Cutting with knives. Worse things. At the end of the first season he thought, *Have done with me now. I've atoned.*

And they disagreed.

How can I go on? he thought.

But he went on.

At the end of the second season, he knew he had reached his limit.

Somehow, they released him.

He wasn't sure why. He knew they still didn't believe him.

Maybe because of a talk he had, one day late in the second season, with one of his inquisitors.

204 ⚹ Jane Wiseman

Every day, before the physical punishments began, he was to sit perfectly still and meditate on his faults. Every day, he took the pose of The Penitent and begged pardon of The Three for breaking his vigil and speaking to his brother. Every day, he took the pose and begged pardon for the shameful way he had treated his brother.

Every day, he took the pose and wondered and wondered. *Who is Gilles de Rais, really, and what does he want with me, and what is he doing with Cae, and why does it mean I must be punished?*

After this period of meditation, always in the pose of The Penitent, he'd stand in the pose of Underneath the Winter Rains and an inquisitor would come in and put the same questions to him and listen to his answers.

Then the physical punishments would begin.

But one day, as the day's inquisitor was asking him the required questions, the man stopped and looked at him hard. "Maeldoi," the man said. Maeldoi didn't recognize the man. Usually it was the same three or four, sometimes another one. This one—was he vaguely familiar? It seemed so, yet the man had never questioned him before.

"Yes, lord," said Maeldoi, hoping he wouldn't be beaten for speaking at all, outside his required answers.

"Sir, not lord. You say you've atoned for speaking during your vigil."

"Yes, sir."

"It looks to me as though you were startled. You didn't mean to break vigil."

"No, sir."

"You've told us this, and we have duly noted it. And second, you say you've atoned for your treatment of your brother, in childhood, and recognize the damage you must have done to him."

"Yes, sir."

"You've gone over and over it in your mind. Over and over it to us. It seems clear to us you do indeed feel remorse. You have atoned."

Maeldoi said nothing.

"But this last charge, Maeldoi. It is very serious. Aiding Insurrection. A crime that strikes at the well-being of our kind. Why do you not take this charge seriously, as you must?"

"I do take the charge seriously, sir. I just don't understand it."

"Because, as you say, until Master Bertran, your shaman guide, explained it to you, you didn't know who the Baron Gilles was, beyond the way he is perceived by the ordinary folk."

"Yes, sir."

"That's hard to believe, Maeldoi. The very name of the Baron Gilles is used to frighten our children. Hush, or the Baron Gilles will carry you off."

"We had never heard of him, where I came from," said Maeldoi. "At the rectory, I only knew that he was the overlord of the realm where the rectory was situated."

"You come from some poor, remote village."

"Yes, sir."

"Your inquisitors have gone over and over these matters with you, Maeldoi. You persist in these same fictions. Lies."

"I'm telling the truth, sir." Maeldoi began to wonder then. *Your inquisitors*, the man said. As if he were not one of him.

"Maeldoi, let me put it to you this way. You kept yourself willfully ignorant of a great danger. In this, you were culpable."

Maeldoi looked up at the man in surprise. This was new. "Willfully ignorant?" he said. He tried to make his tone respectful, as if he were only asking for clarification. He knew that instead he must be sounding dubious.

"Indeed," said the man. "Everyone else knew the baron was dangerous. Why didn't you?"

Maeldoi opened his mouth to protest that how could he know? He had never heard these things. He was just learning the language. He kept himself apart from the other boys. Many reasons.

Then he thought hard. This was some new man, and he had just given Maeldoi an out. Something Maeldoi could confess to and atone for.

"Yes, sir. I confess it. I should have known."

The man drew a great breath.

"Atonement will begin immediately."

"Yes, sir. Thank you, sir," said Maeldoi.

The next sen'night's punishments were especially savage. Maeldoi set himself to endure them. By the end of the season, though, he was sensing relief among his inquisitors.

The day he was to come before the Penance Board, he felt a burst of optimism. They'd release him.

The good feeling died as he knelt in The Penitent pose before the three men who made up the Board. He sneaked glances at them as they turned the parchment leaves of his inquisitors' report over and passed them back and forth among themselves.

Their expressions were grave.

He dropped his eyes and tried to prepare himself for the worst. For another season of penance. The third. Only one season after that, and then— But he wasn't sure he'd be able to go on. He could sign his release now. It would be over. He'd have to make his way in the world somehow. He could probably do it.

Only then did he realize how important it had become to him, to be acknowledged a valuable member of a close-knit community. A people. No matter how hard his training became, that sustained him. Now that it might be taken from him, he saw it.

In his childhood at the edge of the moors, he had known what it was to be gwrgi among those who hated his kind. To be feared. To be despised. Spat on.

It was a time out of nightmare. To go back to that—

"Maeldoi." The voice of the head of the Penance Board recalled him to himself. "Stand."

He stood, assuming the position of Underneath the Winter Rains. Now they'd ask him which paper he'd sign.

He knew that in body and mind, he could take no more torment. He thought of his inquisitors. How they'd given him an out. They'd found one for him, and he had taken it. Somehow, then, his inquisitors had seen what these men of the Board couldn't see. His inquisitors, charged with his torments, had seen he really was innocent. But the men of the Board would never see it.

He caught their stern, skeptical eyes on him. He felt their distrust as if it were a physical thing.

He'd sign the release. Then they'd drive him out.

When their words finally came at him, he nearly broke his pose and fainted.

"Maeldoi, we have judged that you have atoned for your faults. You are remanded back to training."

Surely he was dreaming. His mind had finally broken. When he came to himself, he'd find himself crouching on some midden, in rags, in some village, and the villagers would be pelting him with dung, setting their dogs on him, and shouting at him to get out before they stoned him or set him on fire.

The voice of the head of the Penance Board went smoothly on as if he were talking to an ordinary prisoner about to be set free, not the shattered object Maeldoi knew himself to be. "But know this, trainee. We will be watching you. Watching to make sure you keep to yourself. It's true we have found no evidence of our suspicions, even though you say you've atoned for what you're calling your ignorance. The report of your inquisitors confirms your sincere atonement." The man picked up the parchment by one corner in a gesture of distaste. "But we will be watching for any breach telling us otherwise. And if we see a breach, you may be sure you'll find yourself in one of our cells again."

Another of the men spoke now. "Keep to yourself, Maeldoi. Don't infect others with your unfortunate attitude. *Making a connection with a citizen of the city outside the prescribed activities*. It's a crime, Maeldoi."

The other one muttered something low.

"I know, Estienn, but here's the report, and, well. . ." said the head of the board, the Lord Penance Board himself, shrugging. He stood. "What can we do? We can't hold him after this." He turned back to Maeldoi. "Each season, you'll be required to report to us so that we may examine you in light of any new information. Do you understand?"

"Yes." That was as much as Maeldoi could gasp out. Let the man punish him for not using his proper title.

"These reviews will continue until your training is finished. When you are assigned a task, we'll review once more to see if you may be trusted to forego such close supervision."

"Assuming he passes training," the man called Estienn added, casting an ominous look at Maeldoi.

The three men rose and fiddled with their papers and their robes. They filed out of the room without a backward glance.

Maeldoi stood for a moment in silence.

He walked to the door and pushed it open. He walked out of the House of Penitence a free man, shuddering the whole time. Surely a hand was about to snake out and snatch him back in.

Now, in the quiet of the courtyard as he sat like any man with his cup of ale, a war on—a war he was not allowed to fight—and the stars coming out, hanging by their golden chains from the underside of the Spheres, Maeldoi tried, partly successfully, to banish these thoughts that kept intruding themselves into his peace.

He tried thinking instead of his new training phase. But the thought of the two women improbably set to teach him rose before him, only unsettling him further. He wondered how he could possibly succeed, with such teachers. With such distrust.

Assuming he passes training, that man Estienn had said. It was clear to Maeldoi, and had been for some time. Just looking into the man's face, Maeldoi saw it. Estienn wished him ill.

Just there at the last, before his first teacher had strode away from the library, heading for the armory to prepare for war, he'd glimpsed the face of someone who might wish the best for him.

Now that man was gone.

If I'm given a task at all, if I'm professed at all, he thought, *it will be to a lesser task.*

But at least he was free, and maybe if he worked hard enough at these letters, he'd be released to fight. After all, that's actually what he wanted.

In the morning, after he broke his fast, he headed to the library again, armed with a new resolve.

Only to discover a new surprise.

Only one of the women was there to greet him. Gisa, the younger one.

"Scholar-teacher Alda is sick," she told him. "I'm to teach you by myself, until she's well enough to join us."

Maybe a pleasant surprise, this time, Maeldoi thought.

"Don't think you can charm me," she said, sourly, as if she could read his thoughts. "You're not charming, Maeldoi."

Then again, maybe not, Maeldoi thought.

Whatever this young one, Gisa, might truly think of him, Maeldoi began to progress under her teaching.

The readings bored him. They were about matters that didn't interest him. How to dress well. Courtly manners. Things like that. But he toiled diligently away.

Day after day, he did his best. Day by day, he felt that Gisa was thawing toward him, not looking on him with quite so much suspicion and disgust, and he began feeling more hopeful, especially as Alda, the older one, never reappeared.

One day he arrived at the library to find Gisa absorbed in a book. He waited quietly in the pose of The Obedient Student.

Finally she turned to him. She seemed surprised he was there. "Maeldoi. I am to blame. I was absorbed in my book and didn't realize you were here ready to begin."

He looked quizzically at the book.

"A bit advanced for you, I'm afraid. But here. This is what I'm reading." She opened the book and showed him.

He looked. A woodcut. His eyes lit. He touched the picture with his finger. "Ah. Guillaume, and here is his nephew, and here, his giant." He looked up at her and smiled, then reached for the book.

She handed it over.

He bent over it, enthralled.

All the delights of his time with Mistress Pereta came rushing back to him. His lips moved as he read the words and took them into himself and made them his.

"What's happening in the book, Maeldoi?" said Gisa, breaking into the moment.

He looked up at her, then back down at the page. "Do you know, I read this book at the rectory, when I was a boy. The rectory was a harsh place, but in the end, it's the only place I've ever felt safe, Scholar. The only place." He pointed. "These people in the book. They are fighting, Scholar. This is my favorite part. See, just here, the foe is coming at them with sharp, curved weapons. These men of the foe are winning, but now look, the giant strides forth, and—"

Gisa's laughter rang out into the silence of the library.

Maeldoi looked up from the page, startled. A few heads turned their way.

Gisa put her hand to her mouth, stifling her laughter, but her eyes sparkled.

Laughing at me? Maeldoi felt shame.

"Maeldoi. You are wonderful," she said.

"Truly?"

"Truly."

What Maeldoi felt then was something he didn't know how to name. But it left him dizzy on his stool.

He felt as if he had split wide open. As if a brand-new person were struggling from the old shell of him.

As if Gisa were putting out her hand and drawing this new person forth.

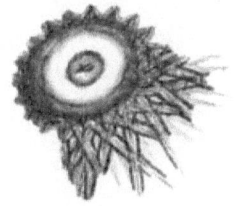

CHAPTER FOURTEEN

The Other Face of Love

Y ou failed," said Gilles de Rais to Caedon. "I don't have
Maeldoi, because you failed. Was it out of some mis-
guided feeling you needed to protect your brother from
me?"

"Never, Most High!" Caedon exclaimed, shocked.

"Now, Caedon," said Gilles, his tone changing from severe to
caressing. "You're telling me the truth. I see that. I wonder what
more you could have done, though, to bring your brother to me?"

"He has always hated me, lord," said Caedon. "He won't trust me now, even if I'm able to get to him again. Now he's back in that gwrgi city of theirs."

"What they're doing to him there may drive him into a state of despair we can use, you and I. We may have him yet."

"He hates me, lord," said Caedon, low.

"Hatred. Just the other face of love, my dear boy."

"He doesn't love me. He always tried to get the better of me, to take anything I had away from me, because if I had it, then he saw he wanted it."

"He was a savage. You both were. Now he has become civilized, in his way. I believe he is sorry for the way he treated you."

Caedon knew he'd never believe that. If Maeldoi found Caedon unprotected in a lonely place, Maeldoi would kill him if he could.

"You must trust that I know better, my boy," said Gilles, puling Caedon close to him.

"I do trust you. But we gwrgi—"

"I know who you are. I know your weak points. Your strength, too. How valuable that is to me."

For a moment Caedon felt such an intense pang of jealousy he nearly cried out. Gilles wanted Maeldoi.

"Poor boy," said Gilles. "Yes, I might enjoy feeding on your brother. I'll do that as soon as I can get my hands on him, so he'll know his true master. But I could never love him the way I love you. Especially not now, after Maeldoi has been in the hands of those severe teachers of theirs."

"Why do you need him, then?"

"You're questioning me, Caedon?"

Dangerous territory. Caedon shuddered. "No, never, lord."

"I'll answer your question, however, because you and I are about to move into a new phase of our connection. One where you'll prove of great use to me, Caedon. Would you like to hear the task I have for you next?"

"But lord," said Caedon after Gilles had finished his careful explanations and unfolded all his plans for Caedon. "I spent my childhood in the Sceptered Isle. If you send me there, the people will run me off. The people there hate and fear us gwrgi."

"The simple people. Yes, they do. As they do here in the Baronies. In that wretched little village of yours, that's what the people thought of you. But in courts and in the cities, the people there think tales about the gwrgi are just that. Tales. Fables. People may think your eyes are odd, Caedon, but they won't think beyond that. You'll hear people say things like, 'Dark Ones take it!' but they don't actually think you gwrgi will rise up and snatch them away. It's just an expression. Be easy, Caedon."

"I won't like it, being away from you, lord," said Caedon, miserably.

"I know it well, Caedon. And I will dislike being parted from you. My boy. My treasure. But it's necessary." Then the baron had turned briskly back to his plans. Caedon was to travel across the Narrows to the court of the king of the Sceptered Isle. There, he'd become companion to one of the king's sons.

"This son of the king is a pliable young man. He's stupid. Crafty, though, so be on your guard for that. He'll need a lot of stroking and reassurance about how important he is. He's puffed up. Vain. He wants to be seen as successful and grand. Your job is to make him feel he is. Flatter him over his minor successes at the court. In the meantime, you and I will be scheming to help him to the throne, and then to take it for ourselves. He's only the second son, and not even second in line for the throne. His older brother is heir to the king his father. His nephews, this brother's sons, stand ahead of him. We'll help this fellow see his advantage. How to take the throne for himself. Then you'll push him aside and take it instead."

Caedon was dazzled. To take a throne!

"You'll rule, Caedon. Everyone will see you as the king."

It hardly seemed possible or likely to Caedon.

Gilles laughed at him. "Dear boy. You don't know your own strength. I do. And besides, you'll be acting from my strength. Which, in comparison to these puny ones in control of the realm, is so immense they have no idea. They won't know what's happening to them, when you strike at them. They'll underestimate you. They won't know it's my hand doing the striking." He began lovingly stroking Caedon. "And for work like this, the gwrgi are uniquely fitted."

Later, Caedon staggered off to his own rooms. His own bed. He was having a hard time seeing how Gilles's plan could work. But he was heady with the possibilities. Everyone had looked down on Caedon. Even Maeldoi had. Especially Maeldoi. Now, Gilles promised him, he'd be powerful. One of the most powerful men underneath the Spheres. He'd take that power. He'd use it against any who opposed him. Against any who'd slighted him. He shied away from thinking, *Against Maeldoi*. Somehow, Gilles wanted Maeldoi. He must make up his mind to it, if that's what his overlord desired.

In the corner, his harp stood neglected under its cover. Just as Gilles had predicted, music was becoming ever more abhorrent to him. Even a little frightening.

But it didn't matter. He was transcending frippery things like music.

As he pinched out his candle and lapsed into sleep, Caedon forgot Maeldoi. He knew a savage kind of joy.

In the morning, his joy had faded, at least a bit. Heading off to the Sceptered Isle, for who knows how long? Daunting enough in itself.

But to be parted from his brother. The boy he'd come to think of as his true brother. Raoul. If he could only admit it, in his heart of hearts—and he knew Gilles must see it there—more than a brother.

A one-sided attraction. Gilles must see Caedon was no threat to his own possession of the boy. That must be why he never upbraided Caedon for it, or punished him. Sometimes he wondered, although he tried to stifle such a thought as soon as it rose in him, whether Gilles might enjoy watching his struggles with his unfulfilled longing for the lad.

Gilles exercised his dominion over Raoul only occasionally. He had Caedon by him now.

Gilles did continue feeding from the boy. "Very carefully," he told Caedon. "As careful with him as I am with you. Too fast, too harshly, I could end him. Or you. I want you both with me for years to come."

No telling how old Gilles himself might be. Eons. But Caedon and Raoul, being mortal creatures, would one day die.

"Even then, I'll have a use for you," Gilles purred to Caedon. Caedon flinched away from what use that might be.

He wasn't to be sent to the Sceptered Isle right away. First he needed to undergo a period of training.

"You must learn the language there, my boy," Gilles told him.

Caedon knew that when he lived in the Sceptered Isle as a boy, he lived in a part of the realm so remote that it had its own uncouth language. Now he'd learn the court language of the realm. It was a delight to him when Gilles decreed that Raoul, too, would learn alongside his brother.

"It will exercise your mind, Raoul," Gilles said to him.

Caedon could see how eager Raoul was to begin.

"Yes," Gilles said to Caedon. "That's one of the reasons I prize both of you. The bright leaping flames of your minds."

"Maeldoi thinks he's better than I am," Caedon found himself blurting out. "But I am brighter than he is."

Gilles, though, shook his head. "That jealousy, again, Caedon. You must work on that. No, Maeldoi is just as bright as you are. He's not trained to exercise his mind. They're training him. . . ." Gilles trailed off. "Soon. . . " He looked up now and smiled to himself. "And then he'll be even more valuable to me. We must try again to get him, you and I," he said to Caedon.

I'm brighter, Caedon found himself saying, inside himself, stubbornly. Then cringing because, of course, Gilles had heard.

"Lad, do you understand your parentage?"

Caedon shook his head dumbly. "No."

"Your mother was carefully nurtured. She had in her the blood of the old gwrgi wisdom keepers."

He thought of his mother and the four small objects she had given him. They were mysterious. Perhaps they were her inheritance from these wisdom keepers. He could ask Gilles what they were. He wanted to keep them to himself, though. But surely Gilles had looked inside him and had seen them.

Gilles didn't seem to be paying attention to Caedon's thoughts just then. He spoke of Caedon's father. "That man, your father, took your mother against her will. He damaged her and brought her to that little village across the sea where you were a small boy. You have his blood. But you have her blood, too, Caedon. So has Maeldoi. The gwrgi see that. So do I."

"My father is dead," said Caedon.

"I made sure of it. I made sure word of his whereabouts came to his band in the Fastnesses, so that they could hunt him down."

"Good," said Caedon.

"His criminal nature is a taint in you. I'm not as sure about Maeldoi. But the blood of your mother wins out in you, and in your brother as well."

"A taint?"

"You know the flaw of your kind. The savage thing that rises in you. It was particularly strong in your father, and you feel the strength of it yourself. As for your brother. He may be made of different stuff."

Caedon wasn't sure what Gilles meant about Maeldoi, but what he was saying made sense to Caedon when he thought of himself, and of his father's nature.

"I'm making sure to train you so you can control it."

"Thank you, my lord."

"And the gwrgi are training your brother."

"Not as well as you are training me, lord."

Gilles turned away with a smile. "They have to use harsher methods, with him. They don't have my powers, lad. You are the gainer in that, so if you enjoy the thought that you have some advantage over Maeldoi, there it is. Your advantage. But in the end, we'll have him."

His features suddenly distorted with anger, and Caedon cringed away. "Unless Merlin and Dee interfere," said Gilles.

Caedon watched as Gilles calmed himself.

"In the gwrgi community, there are forces that can destroy Maeldoi. There are forces that can help him, too. I'll make myself better acquainted with them, and see what role I can play. Have you never heard of the great gwrgi city, Caedon? I could maybe send you there, and then—"

No! Caedon cried out inside himself.

"But if I told you that you had to do it." Gilles's eyes glinted.

"Then I would obey," said Caedon quickly.

"You know," said Gilles slowly, putting his hands on Caedon and feeling around his body as Caedon made himself stand perfectly still. "I believe you'll serve me better outside their community than within it."

Caedon felt himself sagging with relief.

"That's why I need your brother, boy," said Gilles to him, sharply. "Whatever troubled role Maeldoi plays within gwrgi society, he plays one, and I can use him best there."

"So you won't want to bring him here," said Caedon.

"That's not exactly what I meant, boy," said Gilles with a slow smile.

Still, the world spun along pleasantly underneath the Spheres as Caedon prepared for his mission. Every morning, Caedon and Raoul had training in the speaking and reading of the language of the Sceptered Isle. Every afternoon, after the noontide meal, they had weapons training and combat training together. Raoul was old enough for that, now.

Gilles called them to himself from time to time, to examine them and assess their progress. He made them each converse with him in that strange language.

"You still have your Baronies accents," he said with a chuckle. "But that will endear you to those folk across the Narrows, Caedon, when I send you over. They'll see it as charming."

Caedon noticed, though, that he rested his gaze on Raoul and looked somber.

During the most recent of these examinations, one morning in early summer, he came right out with it. They were all standing together at the top of one of Gilles's towers. "Raoul. My lovely boy. You are unhappy."

Raoul tried to pass it off with his usual sunny smile.

"You can't fool me, you know, Raoul. You lack for something. It's young women you love, I perceive. And now you're just at that point in a lad's life when such matters become important to him."

Raoul blushed.

Caedon, watching, was enthralled.

"Don't think you can cease your service to me, Raoul," said Gilles. The boy's face fell. "But you must seek out young women and learn their pretty ways. I'll send you some."

Caedon found himself exchanging an amused glance with his overlord. He found they were both regarding Raoul with fond, tender eyes.

"A sweet flower," Gilles murmured.

Caedon didn't think Gilles was talking about any pretty girl.

"You lack for something else, too," said Gilles suddenly.

Raoul looked up at him, confused.

"You don't even know what it is. I think I do. Caedon, I'm sending you and Raoul off together on a little journey of your own. To the foot of the mountains." Gilles waved his arm toward the hazy blue line in the distance. He and Raoul turned to look where Gilles meant.

The two of them stepped to the tower's parapet to gaze out at these mountains. Gilles came up behind them and put his hands on their shoulders.

"There's an old goatherd there, at the foot of that big one," he said, pointing. "See the one? Not the one with the big peak. Look about three mountains over. The one standing up like a kind of loaf. I'll send you to the goatherd. He'll train you in an interesting skill. It doesn't have much practical use, but I believe it will ease your minds. Raoul's, anyway. Poor Raoul."

Raoul looked around at him.

"Raoul, those fopdoodles who believe in the gods they call The Children would take one look at you and say to themselves, 'The Sea Child's for certain.'"

"I don't understand, lord," said Raoul in his soft voice. It was just beginning to change from the voice of boyhood to young manhood.

"Look at your young brother's eyes, Caedon. How gray and wide they are. Believers in The Children would say he has Sea-Child eyes. Although the Children are only fables, their believers may have a point. The sea runs in your veins, Raoul. Yet here you are with me, land-locked. What the goatherd will teach you— maybe it will compensate you for what your body knows it is lacking."

Caedon didn't know what to make of this pronouncement of his overlord's, and he could see Raoul didn't, either.

I suppose, when we get to this goatherd, we'll find out, Caedon thought.

"You will indeed," Gilles said.

CHAPTER FIFTEEN

Climbing

Caedon saw immediately that Gilles had been right about Raoul. The old goatherd's instructions arrowed straight to the heart of the boy's restlessness.

The goatherd's task was to teach them both how to climb.

The face of the mountain towering over the goatherd's hut was steep and forbidding.

The climbing looked, to Caedon, to be impossible. But the goatherd led them to it by easy stages. He was a patient teacher.

"All in my family have done this work, herding goats," he told them. "Now my sons have gone off and have families of their own. Over there." The gnarled old fellow had waved a hand off toward a notch where the range of mountains cut south. "And one of my sons—" he faltered to a stop. One, they found out later, had died climbing the mountain.

"I've taught them all," he told them. "My sons. My grandsons. My granddaughters, too." He grinned. "In spite of their mothers screeching at me how it's not fitting." He looked from Caedon to Raoul. "I will teach you. Especially you." He fastened his eyes on Raoul. "You have the look of it about you." Then he turned back to Caedon, apologetically. "I'll teach you too, young master. I can teach anyone."

Caedon smiled at him to show he hadn't taken any offense. But when he glanced back up at the mountain, his heart quailed, and he knew the old man could see that.

The fellow took the two of them on easy hikes up the mountain skirts. Easy for the old guide, anyway. They followed narrow goat tracks up the slope, and soon they were both conditioned to the thinner air and the strenuous pace the goatherd set them.

Caedon could see how Raoul gloried in the exercise. As for himself, he learned enough to climb some of the lower parts of the cliff. Then he was content to sit by the old goatherd's fire while Raoul challenged himself to go higher and higher.

Caedon couldn't suppress a pang of fear.

"No fear, young master. The lad knows what he's doing."

In spite of these reassuring words, Caedon found that after Raoul climbed past a certain height, he couldn't even bring himself to watch.

He kept his eyes fixed on the ground and made himself recite every scrap of the verse of the Old Ones he'd ever read, over and over, until he could calm himself.

Fatal monster, who wanting to die with dignity did not fear that sword. . . .the special delight of my lovely one, you, little sparrow. . . I sing of arms and a mighty man. . . Caedon whispered the words over and over to himself, trying not to look, trying not to gasp out in fear.

If anything happened to Raoul—

But then Raoul always came back down, shining with happiness.

Once, Caedon did look up. He jumped to his feet. "Where is he?" he cried out in a panic.

"He has gotten himself to the top, good master. He just went over the lip, up there at the top," said the goatherd, turning to stoke up the fire.

At last they needed to get back. Caedon bid the goatherd a relieved goodbye, and Raoul bid him a disconsolate one.

Gilles stood at the gates to welcome them back. He held his arms wide.

Raoul rushed to embrace him. "Thank you, lord," he said. "It was wonderful."

"Welcome back, Caedon," said Gilles over the lad's shoulder. He gave Caedon a sympathetic smile.

After they had eaten, Gilles sent Raoul off to bed. Caedon and Gilles sat by the fire in Gilles's rooms. "Poor Caedon," Gilles said. "You have had an anxious time. But look how happy your endeavour has made young Raoul. Now maybe he'll be more content."

During that whole summer, Raoul made many trips to the mountain. After the first time, Caedon didn't see any need to go with him.

"I'll just worry about him the entire time. It's better that I don't watch," he said to Gilles. "I suppose I'll realize he's out there dangling by one arm from some crumbling cliff, but I won't have to watch it. I won't practically die of fright every time I think he's about to plummet to his death."

Gilles had just laughed and had shaken his head.

"You're not worried?"

"No, not I. Things like this are what Raoul was born to do. Much more risk in keeping him from them."

"I can't see it," Caedon had muttered.

"Put yourself at ease, Caedon. At harvest-tide, I'll send you over to the Sceptered Isle to begin your mission. That will take your mind off it."

"But then I'll miss you," said Caedon, feeling foolish as his eyes filled with tears.

"I see what's in you, Caedon. Yes, you'll miss me. But you'll miss that lad. That's what you'll miss."

Caedon had felt himself blushing.

"I'm glad you feel this way about our boy," said Gilles. Then his voice turned ominous. "As long as you don't touch him."

Throughout summer's end, Caedon spent many long candle-measures with Gilles going over all the strategies he was to employ in the Sceptered Isle.

"Now we set the bait," he told Caedon. "You and I will travel across the Narrows to Lunds-fort. Some of the barons will be conferring together, as we frequently do, about how best to manage our territory there across the water."

He meant the fingernail of land separated from the rest of the Baronies by the Narrows but from the realm of the Sceptered Isle, separated only by a patrolled border.

"While we're in Lunds-fort," Gilles continued, "I'll have one of my fellow barons urge King Ranulf to join us in our conferring, as a good faith gesture. So he'll see we aren't threatening his sovereignty. Of course we will be." Gilles laughed. "I will be, anyway. Just not in a way he'll be able to recognize."

"And then?" said Caedon.

"I'll introduce you to Ranulf there. My young protégé. I'll turn the discussion to the princes, his sons. I'll urge you forward as a likely companion for Prince Audemar."

"Suppose it doesn't work?"

"It will. Minions of mine are already in the realm, planting the idea. Prince Audemar is a difficult lad. He has no friends. It's a problem for his father. And you and I, Caedon, will be there to present him with a handy solution. You'll be my gracious gift to the king."

"A bondservant?" said Caedon, horrified.

"My dear boy. By no means. A noble companion."

"I'm not a noble," said Caedon.

Gilles waved a negligent hand. "Not yet. It's only a matter of time before you will be. A graceful and learned young gentleman of my household."

Gilles had new clothes tailored for Caedon. He equipped him with books. "When we get to Lunds-fort, I'll purchase a suitable horse for you, too," he told Caedon.

Caedon knew he should be happy and excited. It was his chance to climb in the social order, and to please his master. Why wouldn't he be.

But every day, as he went into the room where he and Raoul had their language lessons, and where he was beginning to teach Raoul the language of the Old Ones just as Gilles had taught it to him, Caedon would feel an anticipatory pang of grief and loss.

By then, he had taken over Raoul's combat instruction as well. Their arms master, Master Esteban, had had to leave for his own city.

"Your skills are superb, Caedon," Gilles told him. "I trust you to teach Raoul."

The whole sen'night before he and Gilles left for Londs-fort Caedon spent in mingled anticipation and dread.

Three nights before they were to sail, Gilles had kissed Raoul good night and had sent him off to his own rooms. He had drawn Caedon after him to his big bed.

Afterward, as they lay there together, he had caressed Caedon. "How disappointed I am not to be able to feed from you before we are parted, Caedon," Gilles said. "But if I were to feed, you'd be in the hands of a healer for a fortnight. Maybe just a light feeding. . . but no. It would still delay us. As soon as you are properly established with the young prince, though, I'll summon you back across the Narrows and take my fill of you."

"I yearn for that day," said Caedon.

Gilles grunted. "A lot of pain for you, my boy."

"But I will serve you, mighty lord, and that will make me happy beyond the pain."

"I don't like to see you in pain, my dearest lad. But I must have my food."

"Yes," said Caedon.

"I'm going to give you a gift, Caedon. It will be a sacrifice for me, but I want you to be happy."

Caedon waited. Some jewel or fine weapon. Maybe a precious book. Something of that kind, he supposed.

"Ah," said Gilles. "I'm enjoying this, because I'm about to surprise and delight you."

Caedon waited.

"I am going to send Raoul with you." Gilles beamed when he saw the effect this pronouncement had on Caedon. "You see how much I love and trust you, entrusting Raoul to your care."

"Thank you, mighty lord!" said Caedon, when he could speak beyond the suffocating joy he felt.

"I'm going to give you another gift, as well. Both of you lads. Come to me after we break our fast tomorrow, and bring Raoul."

When they presented themselves to him in his great room the next day, he told them to kneel.

They did.

"Now I'm about to inflict pain on both of you. But I'm sure you will endure the pain, for my sake."

Caedon looked over at Raoul, and Raoul looked back, a flicker of fear beginning to glimmer in his eyes.

"Caedon, you're the older and more obedient. You may help me with Raoul, and when your turn comes, I'll trust I will need no help with you."

Now the fear was infecting Caedon, too.

"Hold your brother quite still," said Gilles.

Caedon leaped at Raoul, who twisted from his grasp and rose to run. But Caedon was quick, and had him down, and was sitting on him while he thrashed.

"Thank you, my boy," said Gilles, stepping to them and bending over Raoul.

"Now, Raoul. You're nigh a man. Cease this unseemly racket."

Raoul just thrashed harder.

"Hold him, Caedon. That's right. Now twist his left arm behind him."

Caedon did, feeling more dread with each passing moment.

"Very well. Quieter now, Raoul. Good lad."

Raoul was making outraged yelps and still kicking out with his legs. Caedon looked down at him skeptically, his chest heaving with the effort of keeping Raoul under control. *Quieter?* he thought. All that climbing and growing was turning Raoul's muscles strong.

"Now here's the delicate part, Caedon. Move his hand right up under the shoulder blade. Yes. Left hand. Secure there? Good. Hold it still, lean across it with your right arm."

Cursing under his breath, because Raoul had landed one of his kicks smartly on Caedon's shin, Caedon made the boy's hand secure.

"Now then. Other hand, Caedon. I mean yours, not Raoul's. Pry Raoul's elbow away and back from his torso. Yes. Like that. Excellent. Raoul. Raoul. Listen to me. You can't get away from us. I'm about to do something painful to you. Do you agree I can?"

"No," Raoul screamed.

Gilles tried again. A third time. Still Raoul screamed no.

"To hell with it," he muttered to himself, although what that meant, Caedon wasn't quite sure. "Raoul," he said now, in a normal, calm, reasonable tone of voice. "Listen to me, Raoul. Who is your master?"

Silence from Raoul.

"Answer me."

A stifled, "You are, lord."

"Good enough," said Gilles. He stabbed into Raoul's left armpit with his index finger and held it there while Raoul shrieked and his face turned ashen.

After a few moments, Gilles pulled his hand away from the boy.

Raoul collapsed onto the stones of the floor, and Caedon knew he didn't have to hold him still any longer.

"Now, Caedon. You've seen. You know what kind of pain to expect. Must I get someone in here to hold you down?"

Caedon felt the blood drain from his head. He got to his feet and stood before Gilles. "No, lord." He lifted his left arm.

Gilles moved swiftly in on him.

The pain was so intense that Caedon wondered if he would survive it. He heard himself scream. When he came to, he was on the floor beside Raoul, who was writhing and whimpering.

"Caedon, you are my brave, brave lad," said Gilles, bending over him and lifting him to his feet. Soothing and fondling.

He looked down at Raoul, and his eyes were cold. "Stop that noise at once, Raoul. How you fought. Shameful. More what I'd expect from some savage gwrgi than a boy brought up in my own household."

Caedon winced.

"Get yourself off to your room and think how ashamed you are of yourself, what a big baby," Gilles told Raoul, as the lad crouched sniveling. "The boys I take into my tower have more courage than you, when I get out my implements and—Go. Go to your room, Raoul."

The boy scrambled to his feet and ran from the room.

Gilles watched him, sighing.

Later in the day, Caedon saw Raoul sitting on a bench in one of the castle's courtyards, swinging his legs and staring around. Caedon approached him gingerly.

"Raoul."

The boy looked over at him, then away.

"It hurt, Raoul."

Raoul said nothing.

"I wonder what he did to us. Would you let me—no. No. Listen, if I lift my arm, will you tell me what you see there?"

Caedon sat down a little way from Raoul on the bench and sidled carefully closer. He lifted his tunic and showed his left armpit to Raoul. He had tried to look at it in a mirror, but he hadn't been able to see, quite.

After a moment of not looking, Raoul swiveled his head around and looked. He grimaced.

"And?"

"A mark."

"A burn?"

"Just a mark. It's red. In the shape of a droplet. A raindrop, maybe."

"A drop of blood," Caedon guessed.

"I suppose," said Raoul. "Yes," he said. "A drop of blood." He got up and left the courtyard. He didn't offer to show Caedon his own.

As for Gilles, he acted like nothing at all odd or painful had happened. He ignored Raoul's sullenness. He gave Caedon extra attention, extra tenderness.

The departure day came. Caedon, Gilles, and Raoul got into Gilles's ornately carved cart to travel to the coast. Behind them came the baggage train of rich clothing, presents for Gilles's fellow barons and for King Ranulf, books, precious objects, decorated tents, rugs. Everything needful on a journey.

The trip across the Narrows was blessedly calm and rapid. Raoul was fascinated. The Sea-Child's own, he'd never seen the sea. Standing at the top strake of the cog during their passage seemed to calm him, settle him after his violent reaction to Gilles's mark.

His mark of possession. That's what Gilles called it, when he talked of it to Caedon.

Raoul could hardly be persuaded to leave the ship, when it drew into the harboring outside Lunds-fort. When Gilles spoke sharply to him, though, he came obediently off onto dry land and stood beside them.

Then the festive time that followed, in Lunds-fort. Feasting, dancing, meeting with wealthy supporters and the barons themselves. Gilles delighted in showing off the carefully polished courtly manners of his two boys. Caedon wondered if Raoul would hang back, shy and chastened. He didn't. He entered into the dancing and feasting with gusto.

Gilles arranged a little fencing exhibition between Caedon and Raoul. They held their audience enthralled, and Raoul didn't pout when Caedon won.

In fact, Caedon wondered, *did he let me win? No*, he decided. *Not possible.*

"Certainly not," said Gilles, when Caedon broached this topic with him, later. "He doesn't have the reach, and he hasn't come up to your level of skill. You're just anxious about him, lad, after his burst of disobedience."

At last, their party had its meeting with King Ranulf. A bluff and hearty man, he bestowed rich gifts on Gilles and all of the rest of them. He entertained them royally.

"May I present a fine young gentleman of my household, Master Caedon?" said Gilles to the monarch.

Caedon bowed low and then moved to kiss Ranulf's hand.

"You'll make a useful companion for my young son, Audemar," said the king.

"I look forward to that day, Your Majesty," said Caedon.

"What do you say, baron? We don't need any delay, do we? I'll take Master Caedon with me a sen'night from now, when we travel back across the border to Tam Fort," Ranulf said to Gilles.

"An excellent plan," said Gilles.

They spent the next several days making all of the arrangements.

At last they came before King Ranulf, where Gilles bid Caedon a formal farewell and presented him with Raoul. "Here's a boy of my household who will go with Master Caedon to your royal seat, Majesty," Gilles explained to the king, "to help with practical matters."

"Fine," said Ranulf. "Fine."

As they crossed the border in the king's party, Caedon realized a new phase of his life had begun.

"Don't fail me," Gilles had whispered to him, the night before. "Soon I'll summon you to me, so you can make your report. More importantly, so I can relieve my hunger. Having both of my beloved boys away from me is a hardship. But I have plenty of fresh meat in my larder," he said, with a grin that always chilled Caedon to see. "And I need you to be happy, Caedon, if you are to do your best work in my cause. Take care of Raoul. Do you promise?"

"I promise," said Caedon.

"If I find you have damaged Raoul in any way, I will be most displeased," said Gilles.

"Never, mighty lord."

"Don't touch him."

"Never, mighty one."

"But Caedon. You can see it for yourself. As he moves away from childhood, Raoul is becoming a bit disobedient and unruly. Work on that, will you? That's my dearest boy. When I say don't touch him, you know what I mean. But if you have to discipline him—" Gilles drew a deep breath. "That's another matter entirely. I always have trouble laying a hand on him, myself. He always gets right under my defenses to my soft heart."

Gilles put his hand over it and blinked. "There was a young girl on another plane. She was seen as a witch and a troublemaker. She was handed over to the authorities, to be burnt. I could have stopped them. But I knew it was necessary that she feel that pain. Do you know what I'm talking about, Caedon?" The words were coming out of Gilles in a whisper now.

Caedon nodded. Although he really didn't.

Gilles's voice strengthened. "So in the case of Raoul, Caedon." He turned grim eyes on Caedon. "Discipline him if you find it necessary. Cut yourself a stout stick, and don't spare it."

"I won't," said Caedon. *Ah*, he thought. *Now I see.*

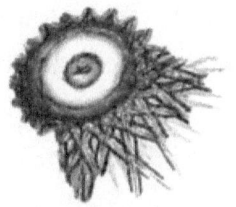

CHAPTER SIXTEEN

Bare Essentials

Caedon found Prince Audemar a highly unpleasant companion. Everyone did.

It's my job to become his friend. Caedon had to say this to himself daily. Sometimes more often. He squared his shoulders and set out to do his job. He flattered the prince. He supported him in all of the mean pranks he played on his younger brother, and suggested new ones. He sought out other young men of the court, sized up their characters, and set out to influence them, by subtle means, so that they came to realize their chances for advancement were tied to Audemar.

Such tactics didn't work for many. But there were enough opportunists at court that by winter, Caedon had assembled a nice little group of fellow louts who followed Audemar about everywhere and toadied up to him.

Actually, although he devised many means of tormenting the boy, Caedon found himself fascinated by the younger brother, Avery, who seemed to have conceived an instant dislike for Caedon.

Caedon just smiled to himself. One day the young man would be sorry for treating Caedon with disdain. Very sorry.

"But Caedon," Raoul objected. "I'm sure Prince Avery feels that way because you're Audemar's friend, and Audemar tries to make his life as unpleasant as possible, and you help Audemar think up ways to do it."

Caedon made a dismissive gesture. "How are you doing with Audemar yourself, Raoul?"

"I hate him. I hate having to sleep on a pallet at the foot of his bed in case he needs something in the night. He farts."

"This is our task, Raoul. Gilles expects us to succeed with the prince."

"Succeed how?"

"Befriend him. His father the king needs someone to befriend the prince, and we're doing the king that favor."

"Because, on his own, no one would be his friend."

"Keep that to yourself, Raoul. Actually, you don't have to become his friend. I do. All you have to do is serve him. And me, of course."

"He can't pronounce my name."

"He can't?" Caedon was amused.

"He says it has too many syllables. That's stupid. It doesn't."

"That's just how they are over here in the Sceptered Isle. They think their own language is best. They don't want to learn ours."

"I hate him," said Raoul.

Caedon turned on him. "Come here."

Sullenly the lad approached him.

"Gilles sent you here to do my bidding. He sent you here to help me with the prince. If I see you slacking, or giving the prince any reason to think he disgusts you, I'm to discipline you and make you see your duty. Gilles told me I am to do that. Just before he left to go back, he told me."

"Discipline me how?" Raoul had moved beyond sullen to truculent.

"I'll beat you, Raoul. Don't think I won't."

"You wouldn't dare."

"Oh, wouldn't I?" The rage began rising in Caedon. As quick as thought, he had Raoul pinned under him on the ground. Raoul fought and bit. The life of the cave rose up in Caedon then. He overpowered Raoul. And then he took him. In the way he was not allowed.

Raoul crept away from him to the corner of the rooms they shared, and huddled there. He wept.

Caedon wanted to weep, too. He had hurt his brother. Raoul looked up at him with eyes of fear. And hatred.

But I can't show him my remorse, thought Caedon. "Never cross me again," he said to Raoul. "Are we clear?"

Raoul nodded his head yes.

"Go on, clean yourself up. Then take yourself off to Audemar. It's nearly time for your night duties."

Raoul sidled out of the room.

When he was sure Raoul was gone, then Caedon wept, himself. He sobbed. He could not calm himself.

And I don't even really want him any more, he thought. Raoul was almost past that age when a boy becomes a young man. Caedon had realized something about himself. It was the boy he wanted, not the man, and the boy was nearly gone.

But beyond that, he felt a yearning for Raoul that had nothing to do with any of those physical feelings.

I'll find other boys, to satisfy those urges, Caedon told himself. But his deep feelings for Raoul had no outlet.

By morning, he had gotten himself in hand. *I have dominated Raoul, and he needed to understand that I have dominion over him. Now he does understand. What I did was painful, but it was necessary.* It was the way things worked in the caves, he realized. And these ways, he saw, had their uses. Others, even Gilles, had tried to convince Caedon that they were savage ways.

They're not, Caedon realized. *They are the way the world works, stripped to bare essentials. And I have an advantage, because I'm not too afraid to use them.*

It was a sorrow, though, to watch Raoul come into his rooms the next morning, his eyes down, and realize nothing would be the same between them now. *This is why Gilles is sorrowful, too,* he thought.

His feelings for Raoul were complicated by guilt. He had no time now to continue Raoul's education. He was supposed to be continuing his instruction of the lad in letters, including the language of the Old Ones. He was supposed to be continuing Raoul's combat training. But he was too busy.

When Raoul asked him about these matters, Caedon brushed him off.

As soon as the spring weather allowed fair sailing back across the Narrows, Caedon and Raoul made their trip across to pay their tribute to Gilles.

"My boys!" Gilles exclaimed. He embraced them both.

That night, after board, Gilles turned to Caedon privately. "Tomorrow, you and I will have a long discussion about our plan in the Sceptered Isle and how matters stand with Prince Audemar. I need you to be lucid for that. So tonight I will feed on young Raoul. I perceive all is not well with him."

"He has been difficult, lord."

"And you have disciplined him?"

"I have tried. I am so pressed for time that I'm afraid I never have the time to do it properly. I took a few—" Caedon gulped. "—shortcuts," he finished.

Gilles looked deep within him. "I see," he said at last. "Shortcuts you were not allowed to take."

"No, lord, I know I was not. I am to blame."

"You are indeed. We'll come to a reckoning for that. But tonight I'll enjoy Raoul. Raoul," he called, raising his voice.

Raoul stood and came to him, and bowed.

"Wait for me in my rooms."

"Yes, lord," said Raoul, heavily.

"He's at that age," said Gilles, watching him go.

"Yes, lord," said Caedon.

"Past the age you like them, Caedon," said Gilles.

"Yes, lord."

"And yet you laid hands on him in the way we agreed you would not."

"I did, lord. I confess it."

"Why."

"In the caves—"

"Ah," said Gilles. "I see it. Well, then. What you did is a slightly different matter, isn't it? You didn't act out of lust. You acted to control and discipline."

"I believed so at the time, lord," said Caedon.

"I'll think about that, Caedon. Now I am headed off to feed, and you may spend the night thinking over your faults."

"Yes, lord," said Caedon. It was his turn to feel heavy-hearted.

As it turned out, both Caedon and Raoul needed their full fortnight of recovery after Gilles had done with them.

"He was so hungry," Caedon said to Raoul, when they were able to get about. They were breaking their fasts together in one of the castle's courtyards.

Raoul didn't answer. Caedon watched as the lad's gaze wandered over the plantings and the trees and the wall of the garden and settled on some enigmatic place in the middle distance.

Caedon got up and hobbled to his own rooms in the castle. How much was Gilles's depletion of them hunger and how much dissatisfaction with both of them? Caedon debated it, but then it made his head hurt, so he stopped and just sat in a patch of sunshine and tried to recoup his strength.

Before they went back to the Sceptered Isle, Caedon had another session with Gilles where they strategized over Audemar and Gilles's grand plan for him.

"You're doing well with it, Caedon," said Gilles. "In that way, I'm most pleased with you. Less so in the matter of Raoul."

"I hope I have made amends, lord," said Caedon.

"To some degree. Caedon, do you remember when I arranged to have Raoul go off to learn climbing of the goatherd?"

"Yes, of course, lord," said Caedon.

"Remember how restless Raoul was. I sent him to learn that skill so I could channel his restlessness away from rebellion. You must do the same, Caedon." Gilles held out a forestalling hand. "I know, I know. Lack of time. That's your excuse, and I see it's no mere excuse. I'll arrange for Raoul to get tutoring in combat from Ranulf's arms master. That should help both of you. You won't have to spend the time, and Raoul's energies will be channeled in a more positive direction."

"That would help," Caedon admitted. "And lord, I have another thought. There's a powerful earl in Ranulf's court who loves learning. He has arranged for the youngest prince, Avery, and a few of his friends, to receive tutoring in letters at the temple of the Lady in Tam Fort. I wonder if he would allow Raoul to join in. The youngest prince and his friends are all around Raoul's age."

"Good," said Gilles, nodding approval. "See that done, Caedon. Just make sure you emphasize to Raoul that he isn't to undertake any of these teachings at the expense of his duties for Audemar. And his duty to you, my dearest one. Otherwise, discipline the lad." Gilles sighed. "In any way you see fit."

"Thank you, my lord!" said Caedon, leaping up to embrace Gilles.

"One more thing, Caedon."

Caedon cringed inwardly at the change of tone. It was as if the normal temperature of the day had very suddenly dropped to freezing.

"Yes, mighty one?"

"Your brother. I don't have him."

"I will try my utmost to find out where he might be. He disappeared, Mighty One. I had people tracking him, as you bid me, and suddenly it was as if he had dropped off the edge of the world."

"I have a few things I myself will try, in order to smoke him out. You and I may have to step up our efforts. Find out who his enemies are, and dangle him before them as bait." Gilles looked thoughtful. "I have an ally in the gwrgi city. No one under my absolute control, as I hope to have your brother. But a man who will prove useful. I'll start by asking him about your brother and where I might find him. How I might possess myself of him. Meanwhile, make your own inquiries."

"Yes, Mighty One. I'll look into it. I'll help in any way I can." Caedon knelt to kiss Gilles's hand.

And Gilles gave him a fond kiss in return.

Part IV: THE JAWS OF THE TRAP

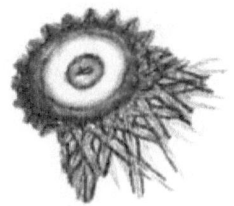

CHAPTER SEVENTEEN

Too Dangerous

Maeldoi turned away from Gisa uneasily. He wasn't sure what to say to her. Their time together was over. He knew he should be glad to be done with this part of his training. Instead, he felt himself teetering at the edge of a strange kind of despair.

Its source was Gisa herself.

He tried telling himself how frivolous his feelings were. He knew despair, didn't he? If anyone did, surely he did. He knew the despair of being thrown into a cell and mistreated and not knowing when or even whether he'd ever emerge.

What was this despair to that?

Yet it ate at him.

He played mind games with himself, trying to settle himself down. He told himself that his feelings for Gisa were perfectly ordinary and natural. Every time a teacher was kind and generous to him, he couldn't bear the parting that always seemed to come. Aleron, Mistress Pereta, Master Bertran. Now Gisa.

But with Gisa, everything felt different.

Something in him couldn't allow her to walk away without a word.

"I'm very pleased with how fast you progressed, Maeldoi," Gisa was saying. He tried to pay attention to her words instead of his feelings. "You've done everything I could have hoped," she was telling him. "I'll put that in my report. You must be pleased as well. Now that you've overcome this hurdle, I believe there is nothing now standing in the way between you and your profession."

"Yes," said Maeldoi. He decided not to tell her of his misgivings. There were many hurdles between himself and his profession.

As for his feelings. He couldn't tell her of those either. Certainly not those. *Just smile and thank her and walk away*, he told himself.

"Scholar," he said. *I'll do it now. I'll smile. I'll be calm.* He felt himself break out into a sweat.

She rose and started gathering her books from the table in the library. "Yes, Maeldoi?"

"I wanted to say—" He stopped, the words sticking in his throat.

"Yes?"

"How grateful I am to you," he made himself say. "You didn't give up on me. I know you must have thought—" *Gods protect me,* he thought. Over the course of her teaching, he'd started having intense bursts of feeling about her. Yearnings. Feelings he had always tamped down. He knew he must keep doing so, not give way at the end to some kind of shameful display. It would not be proper, especially from someone like himself. She was very obviously from a wealthy and cultured family. While he himself. . . He blushed.

She was giving him a quizzical look.

"I must not have seemed the most promising pupil, when you began teaching me. Yet you never gave up." *There,* he thought. *I've mastered myself. I sound perfectly respectable.* A grateful pupil thanking a teacher who has helped him.

"That's true. To be honest, I doubted you'd be able to learn. Many can't, when they reach your age and still don't know their letters. You did know them, after a fashion. Not well, and you hadn't practiced them lately, so I suppose you weren't a complete novice. But you surprised me, Maeldoi."

"I learned patience, in there—where I was—when I was learning discipline—" *Nine Spheres,* he thought to himself. *You are a stammering ninnyhammer.*

"In there." Gisa looked thoughtful. "You don't mean just the physical training quadrangle, or the ground on which you practiced your mental training. You mean, in the House of Penitence, don't you."

"Yes," said Maeldoi, feeling miserable. They'd never talked of it. Now here it was, out in the open. She must despise him.

"Whatever you did, Maeldoi, I confess I don't understand any of it. But we women are shut out of these matters, so why would I understand? You don't seem like a criminal to me."

"But anyway, I thank you." Maeldoi rushed past this last statement of hers. "And I think—well, I really do think that if Scholar Alda had continued with us, I wouldn't have been able to succeed, or anyway, not as well as I did. She wouldn't have been able to teach me. Might not." He stuttered to a halt.

"Really? Why is that, Maeldoi? She is a learned woman. A scholar highly respected by the library chancellors, and for a woman, you know—." She paused thoughtfully. "That's rare, for us. To get that kind of respect." She looked back up at Maeldoi. "So why, Maeldoi?"

"It's this," said Maeldoi. "Some look at me, and right away they decide I am worthless and a waste of their time. Scholar Alda gave me that look. A look I recognize." He stopped. "Maybe I misjudged her," he finished lamely.

Gisa didn't answer. Instead, she said, "I am amazed they allowed me to teach you, Maeldoi. We have only been allowed to teach you men because the war has taken all the male scholars away. Most of them. And we are only allowed to teach you in pairs. Yet when Alda became ill, I was allowed to continue teaching you. I felt honored by the library chancellors' trust."

"In pairs. I wondered," said Maeldoi.

"Maybe no trust was involved, when they allowed me to go on alone. Maybe, because of the war, they were so short-handed they had to allow it," she said. "In pairs, yes," she continued, answering his question now. "You men are dangerous to us, you know."

"We are?"

"Any child knows that, Maeldoi. Didn't you grow up in the caves, where the women rule and allow the men to buy themselves brides but make sure they are controlled?"

"No," said Maeldoi. "I didn't grow up in the caves."

She looked nonplussed. "I thought you did. That's what they told us."

He had to smile. "So you thought I must be doubly dangerous."

"You are a mysterious man, Maeldoi," she said. "And now I must get myself back to the women's quarters before someone sees us standing here talking and begins to spread nasty rumors."

She was smiling, so he realized she must be making a joke.

But he also realized that he should indeed be on his guard. He was being watched. Recently he had noticed. People following him. At first he'd thought he was imagining things. But it had happened too many times. One too many skulking strangers slinking away when he turned to look after them.

Hadn't the Penance Board warned him about any unnecessary connections with the folk of the city? It was even a crime, written into his release agreement. *Making a connection with a citizen of the city outside the prescribed activities.*

And she. She should be on her guard. He knew he'd never hurt her. Not deliberately. But suppose his very presence endangered her. The way he had endangered Master Bertran.

"Before I go, Maeldoi, I must know something. I've been burning with curiosity to know it. Where will you go now? What will you profess? The priesthood, maybe, now that you know your letters. . . ."

"No, Scholar. I don't know where I'll go. Some lowly post, I suppose. I doubt I'll be allowed to do anything very important."

"Maeldoi!" She looked shocked. "In my report, I will emphasize you must be given challenging work to do."

"Scholar, my time in the House of Penitence was spent in the Penitential Order, not the Lesser Penances."

Now he saw he had truly shocked her. "I see," she said slowly.

"Anyhow. I thank you. I have valued my time with you." He made her a formal bow, assuming the pose The Obedient Student, and then he rushed away from her before he could lose his composure, seize her by the hand, tell her he wanted to ask her mother's permission to see her after his profession.

It was a fool's dream. Never would such a shocking connection be allowed. Not by the Penance Board. Not by Gisa's family. And surely she looked on him as an apt pupil, nothing more.

He hung around his rooms in a state of misery, wondering when the herald would come to escort him to the man behind the desk to give him his next assignment. Hoping it would be soon, so he'd be distracted from his feelings. Wondering about Gisa. Thinking about her at night, yearning for her. Wondering what her body, a woman's body, would feel like if he'd ever be allowed to put his hands on it.

But he never would, so he'd never know.

He thought about getting himself to the Lower Town and finding himself a whore. Even in war time, men from the capital went down there to relieve their urges. Young men who hadn't been accepted as husbands for someone's carefully guarded daughter. And most of the men left in the capital were trainees who couldn't hope for that privilege. The elite, the highest officials, were still in the city. He supposed they must have their wives stashed away in the women's quarter. Everyone else was off fighting the enemy, if they weren't sitting around fighting their own urges.

But he couldn't find a whore. If he tried to, it would be sure to come to the attention of the Penance Board. Besides, he had no coin. The meager trainee allowance paid for room, meals, a few pieces of clothing. Barely that.

He told himself he didn't want to. Some quick sordid encounter with a stranger, a bought woman. He'd never done such a thing.

Maybe I'll be assigned at last to a cohort, thought Maeldoi. *Even though I'm professed, even though I've trained for the special tasks, what special task can they possibly find for me after what I've done. After what they think I've done. I'll get away from here, join the fighting. I'll have no time to think of anything but fighting. I won't dwell on this impossible thing, touching Gisa. Kissing Gisa. Holding her, submerging myself in her.*

A burning inside him with no possibility for relief.

As for the challenging work Gisa might recommend, he felt the irony. All the effort and pain to reach the professed state, yet he knew such challenging work would be closed to him. He could so easily have avoided the whole disaster his life had become. He could have joined a cohort immediately after leaving the rectory. Or immediately after finishing his physical training. Or sometime during those first free and easy years of the mental training, as Aleron had.

Aleron had meant well, recommending him for the special tasks. But his friend's well-meaning advice hadn't ended well for Maeldoi. It had somehow become exactly the worst path Maeldoi could have taken. He remembered his stubborn persistence through all of his setbacks.

Foolish, he told himself. *I knew I was an outsider. I should have kept my head down. Taken the easy route. Signed that parchment of theirs in the House of Penitence.*

Thinking of Aleron was painful. He'd gotten no letters from Aleron, and by now he'd been able to check. Aleron and Halde might both be dead. The war had begun when the Lyre Lands had turned on their gwrgi cohorts, Aleron's and Halde's among them.

Instead of sitting around brooding, he knew he should be doing his penitential exercises. *That will help me,* he told himself. He went into The Penitent's pose, trying to summon up every skill Master Bertran had taught him, but it was all rote. It didn't banish the thoughts tormenting him, as he had hoped in his desperation.

Finally he took himself to bed. Even pleasuring himself didn't work. He lay awake staring into the dark.

The heavy thing that kept him awake was stalking him now. A thing beyond all the other difficulties. He felt it always about him now, like a poisonous cloud.

The watchers.

Something had gone wrong, and he didn't know what it was.

As the Penance Board had promised, every season since his release he'd been called before them to account for himself. The first two seasons, the Penance Board hearings were quick, perfunctory affairs. A few bored questions, then he was back out on the street with only a nightmare tingling between his shoulder blades as he walked away from the House of Penitence and no one had seized him back. No one had whipped him or cast him in chains.

But this last time was different. Something had changed. The expressions on the faces of the members of the Penance Board were alert and hard. The questions were challenges in disguise.

As he knelt in the pose of The Penitent, the second-in-command, the sneering one named Estienn, had given him an ominous warning. "You know, Maeldoi, to be allowed to atone for a charge of Aiding Insurrection is a great privilege. The charge is a serious one. Maybe only a shade of difference between Aiding Insurrection and outright Treason. But the punishment for treason—oh, I doubt you'd want to undergo that. And for those convicted of treason, there's no atonement. It is one of the Three Unpardonable Crimes. Be warned, Maeldoi. Our eyes are on you. You will have to hope that brother of yours, and the one he serves, stay far away from you."

Maeldoi knew it would do no good to protest, once again, that he knew nothing of Gilles de Rais. That he did not know the whereabouts of his brother. His protestations hadn't been believed when he was in the cells, and they wouldn't be believed now. But somehow, the matter seemed freshly urgent.

He woke heavy-lidded. He must have slept, at least a little.

A few mornings later, after he broke his fast, there was the herald, summoning him. And soon there Maeldoi stood, before the usual desk. At least now he'd have work to do, and that would take his mind off Gisa. Off Aleron, Master Bertran, all the miseries torturing him. Maybe even the big unknown thing oppressing him.

The man behind the desk looked up at him with a bemused expression. "Maeldoi. Yes." He looked down at his parchment. "It seems you've earned a glowing report from your scholar-teacher." The man looked up again. "But I've been given no assignment for you. You may consider yourself Professed At Large."

Maeldoi could guess what that meant. It meant he was in a sort of limbo. "Is it possible I could go to the armory and join a cohort?" he asked.

"Possible," said the man, with a dubious look. "But not likely."

"There was a call at the beginning of the war for all professed men. Now I am professed."

"Yes, but you have no assignment," the man said with an evasive half-smile. "You must wait for your assignment. If you go off to war, they won't know how to find you or what assignment to give you."

"So. Wait."

"Yes. Make sure not to leave the city. The herald will find you as soon as I hear."

Maeldoi made his bow. As he turned to go back to his room, a stranger, cloaked and hooded, lounging against a pillar, had suddenly hustled away.

Maeldoi felt chilled, recalling all the other times, during the sen'night after his most recent appearance before the Penance Board, when he had felt himself watched.

Even his room did not feel like a refuge. He supposed someone would soon come around to evict him, since the rooms were reserved for trainees. He'd be without a task and without a place to live, both. Without coin, not the trainee's stipend, not the wage of any assigned work.

Then again, what possible work could they give him, a man like him?

He tried thinking over likely assignments and couldn't imagine what they'd do with him. What happened to the professed who didn't fit in?

The Hermitage. They'd send him for a hermit. He'd go into a little room somewhere and never come out. *And I'm perfectly suited to it, because that has been my strictest training*, he told himself. He began to laugh.

The thought of his time in the penitential cells stopped his laughter. He'd go mad. *But at least they won't beat me every day*, he thought. He thought of the phrase, "as mad as a hermit." *Yes*, he thought. *That's the work they'll assign me.*

What did hermits do in their solitary state? he wondered. They meditated. They took and held poses, attempting to perfect them. And they were given books to read and to copy. He felt his lips turning up in a sour smile. With his background and Gisa's recommendation, he was a shoo-in.

It would be like his vigil, only he'd be warmer, and he'd have books.

But he'd be shut into a tiny space and he'd never come out.

Maeldoi felt himself getting twitchy. Needing to move.

He found he had wandered out into the city without even thinking about it. *I need to get away from here*, he thought. Not just out of his stifling little room. Out of the city altogether. He could go to the Lower City, get a job as a laborer—but no. The Penance Board would find him there.

He remembered how horrified he had once felt at the idea he'd be cast out from the community of the gwrgi. So horrified by the thought, in fact, that he'd signed their parchment agreeing to endure the humiliation and the pain of his penance. *I myself should do it. Should cast myself out*, he thought. *I should run for it.*

For the first time in years, he thought of his father. With shock he realized. That's what had happened to his father. His father had cast himself out. Had committed a terrible crime, and had run for it. And finally they had caught him and killed him.

He didn't quite understand why his father had been killed for his crime. The gwrgi didn't practice judicial murder. Not as such. Maybe it was different for the cave bands.

But I've committed no crime, he thought grimly. *They just think I have. They still do.*

He wondered why in the Nine they'd let him out of their cells. They had. But now they were watching him.

With a kind of horror, it came to him. *They think I'll lead them to some higher-up who has incited me to this criminal act they think I've committed. Aiding Insurrection. Just this side of treason. And when they think I've led them there, they'll arrest me for treason itself, one of the Three Unpardonable Crimes, and I'll be done for.*

That's it, he told himself fiercely. *That's it.* They were just waiting to reel him in. He was still their prisoner. They just weren't letting him see it. The hook was hidden in the bait.

When they thought they really had the goods on him, they would grab him off the street and send him up for punishment.

He found his feet had taken him to the library.

He looked up at the big doors in befuddlement.

Then he went in.

His feet took him to the shelf where he'd find the information he sought.

He reached for the volume and took it down. A big volume. He hauled it to the nearest library table and flipped it open, searching for what he needed.

There.

He was reading so intently that he didn't feel the light hand on his shoulder until it gave him a hard rap.

His head whipped around. He snapped the book shut. "Gisa," he said.

"Here you are again, Maeldoi. Just when I thought I had given you your freedom."

"You're here," he said, staring at her with what he knew must be a stupid expression. *Given me my freedom? Oh*, he thought. *From the tedious study of letters. That's what she means.* "You're here too, in the library," he tried again.

"Yes, we scholars are in here a lot."

What an addlepate he was. Couldn't he think of something else to say to her?

"Gisa." Someone calling to her.

Gisa waved this person off.

"What are you reading?" she said.

Suddenly he didn't want her to see. "Nothing, really," he said.

She laughed and pushed his hand away from the cover of the book, from the title that his hand was shielding from her view.

"*Punishment and Crime*," she read. "Let me see." Her hand clamped down on his, where he was holding his place with a finger, and she shoved him aside and opened the book. She stared at the page, her whole manner altered.

The Three Unpardonable Crimes. That's what the page said, at the very top. *Murder. Rape. Treason*. Then a description of what constituted each, and then a description of the punishment for that crime.

Murder. Not accidental or in passion but with intent and plan. Punishment: The mines.

Rape. Forcing oneself on another. Punishment: Castration.

Treason: Attempted or actual and intentional damage to the state. Punishment: Sensory Annihilation and Exhibition.

"Which was yours?" she whispered.

"None of these, or I wouldn't be sitting here. Aiding Insurrection. That's what they call it. I did penance for it. Finally they allowed me to atone, although they didn't want to. Aiding Insurrection is what they call sneaking behavior that might be treason but they just can't prove it yet. That's what they think I've done. They think I'm some traitor," he said.

"And that's a foul lie," she exclaimed.

"I think so," he told her. "But truth or lie, how would you know?" He could have bitten his tongue out. He knew his words came out harsh and hostile.

She looked at him, uncertain. "You were acquitted."

"So they say." Then his heart broke, because her eyes filled with tears.

"I don't believe it. That you did anything like that. Anything even close to treason."

"Gisa. You are very kind to me."

"I have come to know you, Maeldoi. When you teach someone, you come to know that person in a way no one else does. Aiding Insurrection? Treason? You have done no such thing," she was saying.

He spoke over her, low and urgent. "You must know this, Gisa, talking to me is very dangerous. When you taught me, it was because you had to. It was your assignment. No one could hurt you or fault you for that. Meeting me now. That's different. You must step away from me. They'll come after me again, and when they do, it's because they'll think they have the evidence to charge me with treason. I won't be coming back from a crime like that. I won't be allowed to atone. Do you understand what I'm telling you?"

He stared at her, where she sat so close beside him. He was drowning in her eyes, breathing in the nearness of her.

"It's too dangerous for you to speak to me," he whispered, "and I don't want to endanger you because—"

The words kept pouring out of him. Before, he couldn't seem to get them out of his mouth. Now, he couldn't seem to stop them. "—because I care about you and wish I could put my arms around you and—"

He stood up abruptly. He rushed from the library.

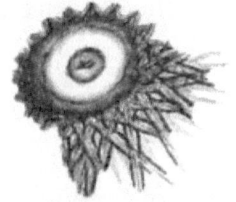

CHAPTER EIGHTEEN

Gotcha

"My Lord of the Board," said Estienn. "Good news. We have him."

"Who, the traitor?" said the head of the Penance Board. "You have evidence of treason?"

"Not exactly," Estienn admitted. "But we have enough to hold him. And I think we're right on the point of finding the evidence we need, so we bring him in, and as soon as we do get the evidence, we charge him with the crime he actually committed, not that lesser thing. We'll charge him with treason. By the time he comes to trial, we'll have the evidence. More importantly, we'll have him."

"Yes, if you're right, we'll have the legal right to hold him, and he won't be able to flee. Nice work, Estienn. What have you got?"

"He seems to have formed some kind of relationship with a young woman."

"Rape?" said the head of the Penance Board hopefully. "Two of the big crimes."

"No," said Estienn.

"Oh. What, then?"

"Well, it's not much. But it's enough to bring him in."

"Oh, right," said the head of the Penance Board. "Making a connection with a citizen of the city outside the prescribed activities. Enough to re-arrest. Who is this young woman?"

"The one assigned to teach him, when he had to remediate his letters."

"These scoundrelly cave dwellers. They know nothing, yet they're allowed around civilized men."

"And women," said Estienn, meaningly.

"And women. Indeed, Estienn. Her family will be appalled. The young woman herself, better bring her in as well."

"It may be her ruin, my lord," said Estienn gently. "How will her family find her a husband?"

"True. Bring her in under a writ of confidentiality. Bring her mother with her. That should impress upon her how serious this misstep of hers is. Unless he forced his attentions on her. Then we'd have—"

"Yes, then we'd have rape. Or something close enough to it," said Estienn, beginning to feel a rising excitement. "It will help our case. Maybe the young woman can be made to see, gently led to see, the advantage in—"

"Hush, Estienn. I may not hear anything of the sort. Nothing savoring of manufactured evidence."

"In a case of treason, though? With the safety of the state at risk? In war time?"

"Yes. I see your point," said the head of the Penance Board. "Extreme times can require extreme measures, much as we may find them distasteful. For the good of the state. Yes. Bring her in."

Once outside the door of the Penance Board's judicial chambers, Estienn heaved a sigh of relief. Sometimes it was necessary to lead his lordship of the Penance Board by easy steps to the desired conclusions.

The man's scruples did keep getting the better of him, and then criminals got off. Or got off too lightly.

A treason case didn't come along any day of the year. A case like this would be the making of him. This criminal, this Maeldoi, must not be allowed to slip out of their hands.

And besides. Estienn knew things about Maeldoi. Things that would work to his advantage. It was, he thought, using to himself the strange phrase of his mysterious contact, a *win-win*. If he could win a conviction, his reputation would be advanced considerably. But even if he could not, this contact of his would pay well to get his hands on Maeldoi. The Three knew why. Estienn shrugged. Not his concern.

But although Estienn found his superior, the Lord Penance Board, a tedious fool, Estienn did agree with his lordship about the young woman. She was no doubt an innocent victim. Surely she was, a girl of good family like that. Misled, no doubt.

And if there were even a whiff of coercion, then their case would go so much better. A gift from the gods.

Maeldoi could have violated his release agreement in any number of ways.

He could have tried to get in contact with his old spiritual guide. Or, really, anyone else. Visited a whore. Made a friend.

But this! A pure young woman.

This was a gods-send.

Best of all, of course, would have been an attempt to find that brother of his. Or anyone else connected with Gilles de Rais. Estienn suppressed a smile at the irony.

Sadly, the Penance Board's efforts to establish such a connection kept coming up empty.

All we need is time, thought Estienn. *I feel it. The lad has to make a slip-up sometime.*

Estienn went immediately to one of the inquisitors he knew. "Have a cup of ale with me, Nicodéme," he said to the man. They walked together to a pleasant leafy courtyard where a server brought them each a cup.

"Excellent ale," said Nicodéme. "Where do they get it, in these times, with the blockade? Someone must smuggle it in."

"Listen, Nico. Remember that fellow a few seasons back, tried for Aiding Insurrection, got off? the one who kept insisting on his ignorance and finally confessed to some minor thing and was allowed to atone?"

"Yes, that one. I do. Scruffy fellow. Cave fellow."

"That's the one. We think we have the evidence to bring him in again. It's just not enough. I'm worried he'll get off and evade us again. And I'm talking about treason here, not stealing some man's pig. Treason. We think we're close to getting the evidence on him."

"Let me guess. You need a little help," said Nicodéme. "That fellow, remember him well." He nodded to himself. "Kept pleading his ignorance. We kept sort of hinting to him, you know, find something you're guilty of and they'll let you go. Finally we called in his advocate to do it. The addlepate got the idea after a while. He pled. He walked. Poor silly noodle. A real rustic. You should have seen his back, after the punishers got through with him. Turned my stomach."

Estienn stared at his friend. *He's not getting it.*

"Nico, I know he seemed like a naïve harmless type to you and the others. But actually—well, let's just say that in the course of our duties, we members of the Penance Board come across information that we can't reveal and no one else knows. Information that can't be entered into evidence for reasons of state."

"Ah," said Nicodéme, laying his finger alongside his nose. "Gotcha. You're saying this prisoner played us."

"I'm afraid he did."

"That won't happen twice. Word to the wise."

"We're bringing him in, Nico. A little heads-up for you and the fellows."

"Thanks, man," said Nicodéme.

Now for Anselme, Estienn thought, after tactfully ridding himself of the inquisitor.

With an inner shrinking, he knew this next interview was going to be the hard one.

An interview with Anselme, Maeldoi's advocate.

Anselme was known to be a stickler. In fact, Anselme had a stick up his arse.

Estienn went back through the big doors of the House of Penitence and down a hallway. Outside a plain wooden door, he hesitated. He knocked.

"Enter."

Estienn opened the door and looked in.

Anselme was sitting at his desk strewn with parchments. He stood and gave Estienn a small bow.

"Your lordship. How may I help you?"

"Big caseload?" said Estienn, nodding to the sea of parchment.

"Yes, as always," said Anselme, waiting courteously for Estienn to take his seat. Then Anselme seated himself behind the desk again, casting a wary eye on his visitor.

"I wonder if you recall a case from a few seasons back. That charge of Aiding Insurrection."

"Of course. Maeldoi."

"How has he been doing? Come to your attention in any way?"

"No, not at all. The boy seems to have been, as we say, keeping his nose clean."

"I hear he passed his remediation for letters."

"Excellent news," said Anselme. "I thought he had it in him. One can never be sure, though."

Estienn nodded. "These rustic types," he said. He liked that phrase of Nico's.

"I suppose he was something of a rustic. He was very naïve. A tragedy, really. If he'd only understood, I doubt he'd have been charged at all. Wonder what kind of profession they'll allow him, after this. But I'm glad he is professed. A big step forward."

Estienn was nodding along. Yes. Yes. Yes, how admirable. Yes.

"You know, I've often thought that if poor old Bertran hadn't gone off opining about the lad's likely punishment, how light it would be, or if he had just left him out there to finish his vigil, none of these misfortunes would have happened to the lad. Or to Bertran, either. I think the whole matter has forced Bertran into retirement." Anselme was musing aloud. "The good master shaman was quite disturbed to find out what was happening to his boy. He blames himself, I believe. Aiding Insurrection. Just a hair short of treason itself."

"Master Bertran retired. My, my," said Estienn, trying to tamp down his impatience.

"Well, now. You must have come to ask me a question. You're a busy man, I know," said Anselme. "Wait," said Anselme, sitting up in alarm. "Maeldoi hasn't tried to get in touch with Bertran, has he? Or Bertan with him?"

"No, nothing like that."

"Good. I was worried." Anselme subsided back into his chair.

"I have to be honest with you, Sir Anselme. It's worrying. What your lad has done."

"Oh, no," Anselme murmured. "Tell me."

"I'm afraid we'll be dragging you back into the case, Sir Anselme. We'd hoped not. But—" Estienn spread out his hands. "There you go."

"Just tell me," said Anselme.

"As Maeldoi's advocate, you're the first I'm telling, of course. After you, I'll head over to Lord Penance Board himself. Then— well, I don't know. You can tell me how best to proceed."

"Go on," said Anselme.

"He has been found in violation of his agreement. He has been making connections outside the prescribed activities."

"What, made a friend, something of that kind? I'd hope he would. His isolation is half his problem. You're not telling me you're bringing him in for something like that, I hope. It's against the letter of his agreement to do so, even make a friend, but still."

"You're getting ahead of yourself, sir," said Estienn, striving for a stern look.

"Yes. You're right. I am. Please, my lord. Tell me the details."

"His offense involves the reputation of a young woman of good family."

Anselme passed a hand across his brow. "Go on," he said. "Please go on."

"He was assigned a scholar-teacher, of course, to remedy the problem with letters."

"Of course."

"But then, when war was declared, his assigned scholar-teacher immediately went to the defense of the city."

"Yes, I see he must have."

"In their wisdom—" Here Estienn rolled his eyes. "—the library chancellors appointed women scholars as substitute scholar-teachers for all the trainees needing remediation."

"They did what?" Anselme's mouth had dropped open, Estienn was gratified to see.

"Well, they did appoint them in teams. Two to a trainee. But early on, one of the two assigned to Maeldoi grew seriously ill. Somehow the chancellors neglected to provide the remaining woman with a new partner and chaperone. The woman assigned to Maeldoi, I mean. And she's young. And pretty. And of a good family. A very good family."

"A disaster. You aren't telling me Maeldoi paid addresses to this young woman."

"I'm afraid so. His required stint with her ended a sen'night ago, and yesterday they were seen together. Whether any coercion was involved—that I don't know. I'm trying to find out."

"Doesn't look good," Anselme muttered.

"Sir Anselme. I know how hard you worked for this young man. But we're having to bring him in."

"I understand," said Anselme.

"I'll want you to interview him as soon as you can clear your calendar."

"Yes. Of course. It may be a relatively minor thing."

"It may be. That's what we're hoping, of course. But we need to find out."

Anselme nodded. He looked a bit sick.

Estienn let himself out, congratulating himself on a sensitive job well done. The right hints dropped. The right alarms raised.

Now for his final visit. The one where he had to be most discreet.

He left the House of Penitence and went by a circuitous route to the women's quarter.

He gave his card to the majordomo and mentioned the name of the one he intended to visit.

"Whom shall I say is calling, my lord," said the servant.

"An old family friend."

"Very good, sir. One moment, my lord."

He came back shortly to escort Estienn up a shady street to a well-set-up house.

The house servant admitted him, and a woman a bit past middle years came down the stairs to greet him.

"Estienn," she said. "How good to see you. I trust our plan has borne fruit?"

"Alda," said Estienn, bowing over her hand. "My dear Scholar. I'm gratified to tell you it has."

CHAPTER NINETEEN

Back Inside

Maeldoi sat looking down at his hands. The shackles held them stiffly out in his lap. Finally he looked up at his visitor. Now he recognized the man. He hadn't, when the man had come into his cell. But now, examining him, he did. The inquisitor, the strange one, who had given him an out during his earlier time in the cells.

"Maeldoi, do you remember me?"

"Yes, my lord inquisitor."

"Maeldoi, I'm not an inquisitor. I'm your advocate."

"I'm not sure I know what that is. My lord."

"I'm not a lord. Sir will be fine. Do you not remember, when Master Bertran first brought you to our attention? I was there to take your statement."

"I don't remember those days very well. I had been—well, the penitential exercises are hard, the physical conditions of the vigil are hard, and I was forgetting to eat, and—I think I was a bit disoriented to find myself in here. Confused by it. Those early days. They're a blur. Then all the pain. Sir."

"I see. Let's begin again, then, shall we? I'm Anselme, your advocate, appointed by the Penance Board to oversee your case and make sure you do understand the charges brought against you." The man laughed a little. "I must not have done a very good job, before."

"I was very confused, Sir Anselme," said Maeldoi. "And then you helped me. I remember that part well." *This man helped me once*, he thought. *Maybe he'll help me now.*

"You look in much better shape than you did at our last meeting."

Maeldoi nodded. Not for long, he supposed. The first punishment would take place tomorrow. Fifty lashes. A lot.

"You'll need to be in fine shape. So make sure you are eating well and sleeping. You have a time ahead of you."

Maeldoi nodded again.

"Do you know why you're back in here?"

Maeldoi stared at his hands again. "I'm not sure. Maybe because I talked to my teacher, in the library. Maybe that wasn't allowed, not after our sessions had ended. I've thought about it. That's the only thing I can imagine doing wrong. I've tried to be very careful with myself, sir."

"That's the reason, Maeldoi. You're right. You violated the terms of your agreement. Now here you are again."

Suppose they talked to Gisa, Maeldoi thought with a chill. *The stupid thing he had said, about wanting to touch her. And maybe because of him she was in danger herself.*

Then a different kind of cold settled on him. A vicious sort of despair took him up. "What does it matter, sir. I think you know. The Penance Board has been biding its time, watching me, waiting for an excuse to take me up again after I somehow got out of their hands before. Now they'll hold me, and soon they'll charge me again. Not with Aiding Insurrection, some lesser thing. This time they'll charge me with treason."

"This cynical, hostile attitude won't help you, Maeldoi. Only true contrition will."

"That's a load of ox dung, and if you don't know that, you're more naïve than I am," said Maeldoi.

"Maeldoi. I'm trying to help you here."

"You could help me. You could help me understand. What's really going on? What do they really think I've done? That would help me."

"The old story, Maeldoi. You are ignorant, you are not responsible. That's not going to move them, not any longer. If it ever did," he muttered to himself.

"Let's leave that, then. They've got me back here. Now they'll convict me, and then they'll punish me. I know what they do. I was in the library to make sure. That's why I was in the library, when I exchanged words with my scholar-teacher. To read about cases like mine in books. I've heard the rumors, but I wanted to know for sure, and now that I am equipped with this skill of letters, I do."

"Treason is a fearful thing, Maeldoi. Assuming you'll be charged with committing it. We don't know that. Not yet."

"The punishment for it is indeed fearful. Sensory Annihilation and Exhibition. I didn't know what that meant, before. Not really. I do now."

Something inside him shuddered. Once, walking about the city, he'd come upon a man hung up in a cage on the city wall. Mutilated. Groaning. "Traitor," the sign above him read.

The loyal man of the city delights in the scents of the world. The man treasonous to the city has forfeited that delight; let his nose be cut from his face.

The loyal man of the city receives through his ears the many sounds of the world. The treasonous man has forfeited that delight. Let his ears be sheared from his head.

The loyal man of the city tastes and speaks. Let the treasonous man never experience the delights and uses of the tongue; cut it out.

The loyal man of the city surveys the wide world through his eyes. The traitor has forfeited those sights. May his eyes be gouged out.

The loyal man of the city touches with his fingers many delights. The traitor may not be allowed them. Cut off his fingers.

The loyal man rejoices in the joy of his loins and his seed brings offspring. May the traitor never experience those joys. May he never have offspring. Pluck up the roots of his manhood and destroy it utterly.

Carve away from the treasonous man any sensory delight.

Hoist him up in a cage so the people will see and take warning.

Maeldoi had read it.

Books are good for something after all, he thought.

"Such an extreme charge may not be brought, in the end. If it is, there may be things we can do to mitigate your punishment."

"If I'm convicted of treason, that's the punishment," said Maeldoi flatly. "And they're going to charge me. And then they're going to convict me. We both know it. I won't be able to live like that." His voice dropped low. "But they say the procedure kills most who undergo it, and if the procedure doesn't, a fever catches them and finishes them off later. So I can pray to the gods I'll be lucky. I don't want to take my chances, though. Suppose I live? They can just kill me now. I won't object."

"There's no judicial murder, among the gwrgi," said Anselme. That drew a bitter laugh from Maeldoi. "Maeldoi, sometimes there is mercy."

"What kind of mercy." That was the moment Maeldoi realized that this advocate of his believed what he himself knew in his bones to be true. The Penance Board planned to charge him with treason.

"Sometimes the mines."

"I see," said Maeldoi. "What the murderers get."

"Yes."

"We'll just have to hope for that, then, won't we?"

The book didn't say so, but he'd heard about the mines. Almost no one lasted more than a year or two, in there. He'd take it, given a choice.

He probably wouldn't be. The Penance Board wanted an example.

Hoist him up in a cage so the people will see and take warning.

But he needed to understand.

How they could bring such charges. How they could possibly think he had done such a thing. *Attempted or actual and intentional damage to the state.* "Will you please explain to me, about Gilles de Rais?"

"He is the most dangerous being underneath the Spheres, or above them."

"I thought that other mage was more powerful. Master Bertran said—"

"Yes. Merlin. But he works for the good of the gwrgi. Gilles works to enslave us. This must not happen, Maeldoi. Of course, you know more about it than I, no matter what you're telling me."

Maeldoi looked at Anselme in despair. "You don't believe me."

"The Penance Board has information I cannot have. I must trust that they understand what they're doing. I know they do not willfully chase down the innocent."

"Could have fooled me," Maeldoi muttered.

Anselme slapped his hand down on the table between them, so hard Maeldoi jumped. "Maeldoi. Stop this insolent carping. I'm your advocate. We must think together how to mitigate your crime. No, I insist. You are not taking this seriously."

"The punisher and his whip will make sure I do, tomorrow early."

"Now then," said Anselme, as if Maeldoi had not spoken. "Considering that this fresh offense has to do with a young woman, I will need to probe your past experiences with women, to see if a pattern emerges. Tell me, Maeldoi. Who was the last woman you slept with?"

"If you mean 'slept beside,' sir, that would be my mother."

Anselme sighed in exasperation. "Your mother?"

"We lived in a small hut on the edge of a waste," Maeldoi explained. "There was only one room, and a loft above. My mother, my brother, and I slept there together. I slept at her side until I was nigh a man, and the rector took me away."

"Are you being deliberately obstructive, lad?"

"No, sir, I assure you. That's just the best answer I can give your question."

"When was the first time you had to do with a woman?"

"Had to do with—" Maedoi stopped. "I see. When I was a boy at the rectory, some fellows decided to have a bit of fun with one of the nearby village's maidens. They waited for her along a lane. I went with them. They leaped out from hiding and forced her. They took turns with her. It sickened me, so I didn't join in. I watched. I was much to blame for watching and not defending the woman. Or at least objecting. I should have at least objected. I confessed my cowardice to my shaman master, and I did penance."

"Nothing else? What about later?"

"No opportunity, at the physical training quadrangle."

"I suppose not," said Anselme. "But after, before your vigil, you would have had ample opportunity."

"I thought of it. I never made any connection with a woman to try it."

"What, not even a single whore? That's hard to believe, Maeldoi."

Maeldoi shrugged. "I never had any coin for a whore. Maybe I would have tried it."

"Maeldoi. Do you mean to tell me you're a—" Anselme swallowed hard. "You're a virgin?"

"Depends on how you think about it, sir," said Maeldoi, hauling up his shackled hands with a wry smile.

"Maeldoi. Attend me."

Maeldoi could see his advocate was getting angry. He supposed it wouldn't do to make his only ally in the House of Penitence angry.

"What about men? Is it men, then, whom you prefer?" The advocate's voice was sharp.

"No, lord."

"Ever had to do with a man?"

"No, lord."

"A boy?"

"No, lord."

"Has a man or boy ever had to do with you?"

Maeldoi was smote to the heart. "Yes," he whispered at last.

"Who?"

"Does it matter? He's dead."

"It matters. Tell me the name."

"Do you know, I don't even know his name?" said Maeldoi, staring down at the table. "My father, sir."

Anselme made an inarticulate choked sound. He rose from his side of the table. "We'll talk more, later, Maeldoi," he said after a silence. "Tomorrow, you must—" He stopped. He put a hand down on Maeldoi's shackled one. "Have courage, lad."

The door made a hollow boom as he pulled it closed behind him. Maeldoi heard the grate of the bar shot to in its slot.

He supposed he should go to his pallet and sleep. Instead, he spent a long time staring into nothing.

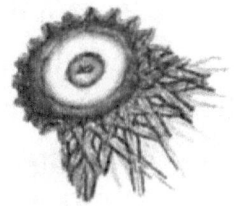

CHAPTER TWENTY

A Politic Interview

T hank you both for coming in," Estienn said to the two
women. Thank the gods the Lord Penance Board was
leaving this part to him. He knew he'd be able to extract
nuggets of pure gold from this. The Lord Penance Board would
have gone by the book, drat the man.

He could see the women were a bit frightened. The mother
came in first. Her daughter followed.

Estienn motioned them to a comfortable bench at the hearth and took his own seat opposite them. He could watch both of them, calculate his moves based on what he saw in their faces.

A servant brought in hot possets and handed the cups around.

Estienn held his up to the light filtering in from the high windows of the room. The cups were delicate green glass, some of the many treasures stored at the House of Penitence.

"My ladies, first let me assure you that your reputations are perfectly intact. Of course you've done nothing wrong, and you've been brought here under a writ of confidentiality. I trust you feel your privacy was well-protected on your way here?"

"Yes, many thanks, my lord Estienn," said the mother. "The closed cart was perfectly discreet."

"Good. Good." Estienn crinkled up his eyes in a reassuring and friendly way. "My lady, it's your daughter I'll need to question, but I wouldn't dream of doing so without you present to make her feel safe."

"I knew it, Gisa. Those books of yours. I knew they'd prove your undoing, but would you listen?" The mother turned furious eyes on her daughter.

"Now, my ladies," said Estienn soothingly. "No one is in trouble here. May I proceed?" He looked always to the mother. She was the one with whom he needed to ingratiate himself. Glancing quickly at the daughter, he saw with an intake of breath that his tactics were exactly right. She was pretty. More than pretty. *If that savage lad hasn't spoiled her. . . .* But resolutely he turned his mind to the matter at hand.

The mother gave him a curt nod. "Proceed."

He saw he'd have to be careful with her.

"Now then, my dear young lady." He turned his eyes on Gisa, the daughter. "It pains me to have to question you, but I must. The highest matters of state require me to ask you several questions."

"Of course," she murmured.

He was finding her a bit hard to read. But if all went well with the mother, it wouldn't matter.

"First let me say how much all of us at the House of Penitence, and on the Grand Council, and of course within the Library Chancellorship, appreciate the efforts you and your fellow female scholars have made in war time. If not for you amazing ladies, some of our trainees would have been left floundering."

Gisa inclined her head, accepting his words.

"Quite a sacrifice you officials have demanded of some of our finest young women," said the mother from between tight lips.

"I acknowledge your words, my lady. We have all anguished over it, believe me. Now, then." He steepled his fingers in a way he'd seen Anselme do it. He returned his gaze to Gisa. "Let me make sure I understand. When war broke out, you and twenty or so other women of learned tastes were asked to take on the remediation of letters. Is that accurate?"

"I'm not sure exactly how many we are, but yes," she replied.

"And you worked in teams, to make sure modesty and reputation were protected."

"Yes, that's right."

"I would never have agreed to this for my daughter if I hadn't been assured of such protections," the mother put in.

Nine Spheres, he said to himself. *The mother doesn't know. Here's the tricky part, then.*

He leaned toward Gisa. "You were assigned a trainee and began to work with him. But then your partner, a woman named Alda—" he hesitated, pretending to be uncertain. "Yes, that's her name. Alda, is that right?"

"Yes."

"This woman scholar, Lady Alda, fell ill."

"Yes."

"If I'm not mistaken, you were supposed to be assigned a new partner."

"That's right."

"And were you?"

He felt a little thrill of satisfaction. Gisa threw a quick, nervous glance at her mother. But she answered steadily enough. "No, I was not."

The mother made a shocked exclamation.

"Weren't you a little worried? If I may ask, why didn't you bring your situation to the attention of the authorities?"

"I didn't think it necessary."

"Gisa!" hissed the mother.

Estienn held up a genial hand. "I think I understand. The young man seemed to pose no threat, so why not just go on as you were?"

"Yes, that's what I thought," Gisa replied.

And if you had demanded a new team member, Alda and I would have seen that request snarled in endless little difficulties, as if someone had taken the red ribbon used to tie up official dispatches and had gotten it impossibly tangled around the requisition.

"This is outrageous. Why was my daughter not assigned a new partner?" burst out the mother.

"My dear lady, we all beg your pardon. We truly do. If we had only known. For—" and this, he knew, would stop her fuming and turn it to fear instead— "your seemingly harmless trainee, Lady Gisa, was far from harmless. Far from it."

"I know that's what was thought of him. But I don't believe it," said Gisa.

Perfection. Estienn arched his eyebrows. "Oh? You discussed this with him?"

He was right about the mother, he saw. The sick fear settled over her like a mantle.

"I believe, Lady Gisa, that your mandate required you to teach the fellow his letters. Nothing more. No personal contact. I believe you signed an agreement to that effect."

"Yes, you're right, I did," said Gisa. But she did not lose her composure, and she didn't volunteer more.

Now Estienn felt disappointment. Usually, once he tripped them up and forced them into an admission they didn't realize they were about to make, they began to babble.

On the other hand, Estienn felt himself admiring Gisa's self-possession.

"You seem to have violated this agreement," he said.

"You see," she said, looking from him to her mother and back. "In the process of teaching someone, especially in that intense one to one manner—"

The mother looked as if she were about to faint.

Time to ride to the rescue on his white steed. "My dear young lady. Say nothing further. You're not on trial here. We need information about that fellow you taught. We know his slippery ways, how he ingratiates himself with gullible people—"

Now her expression told him he'd made a misstep with her.

"—not that I think you're gullible, mind you. Just that the fellow is expert at getting sympathy. We believe that's how he operates. Part of his cover. I should inform both of you ladies that I believe, in sweeping him up into our cells for a relatively minor offense, we have luckily happened upon a much greater villainy. Luckily, I say, because we have gotten to him in time, prevented him from doing the damage to the state that he and his masters intended."

The mother's eyes were round with horror. The daughter's, narrowed and suspicious.

Well, well, he thought. *Maybe he has had to do with her. Then we can go for rape.* A slam dunk, as the little boys on the rectory playgrounds would say as they bounced their pig bladders around. Or was that the game where you kicked?

But he'd be sorry for it. Sorry about how that would change his own personal plans, the ones just beginning to form in his mind.

"So anyway. You see why, as painful as I find it, I must question you, Lady Gisa."

She said nothing.

"I believe you wrote a most positive report on our incarcerated fellow, once you were satisfied his deficiencies in letters had been remediated."

"Yes, I did. He did remarkably well. He is a very bright man."

"I believe you, dear lady. That's certainly not in question. You are certainly not wrong. Too bad his mental abilities have turned in a devious and destructive direction."

She said nothing.

"You did the task you were mandated to do. Admirable," he told her, with a little bow. "Here's what troubles us." He paused to let her start to sweat a bit. She didn't seem to be doing that. "After your assignment with the fellow—" He turned to the mother. "His name is Maeldoi," he told her, more to keep her focused than to inform her. He let his eyes rove back to Gisa. "After your assignment with this Maeldoi was over, the two of you met in the library. Why?"

"We didn't meet," she said sharply. "It was a chance encounter."

"Could you please describe what happened during this—" He paused and counted to three inside the privacy of his own head. "—chance encounter?"

"He was reading a book. He was in a library, and libraries have books, you know. I had taught him to read. Well, not exactly. He knew how to read. Just not important texts like that."

Now, he told himself, inwardly smiling at the turn toward the sarcastic in her voice. *Now I have her angry.* "What text?"

She blinked. Her eyes dropped.

She sees what I just did to her, he thought. *And she knows I can check.*

" 'Punishment and Crime.' "

"Ah. 'Punishment and Crime,' by the great criminologist Frobertius de Capite Ville?"

"Yes," she said, her voice dropped low.

"One of the great authorities," he said. "And what part of this text was the young man reading?"

"I don't remember," she said.

"Might it have been 'The Three Unpardonable Crimes'? No matter. Let's go on," he said. *Now you see,* he directed this thought at her. *Underestimate me at your peril, lady. At your great personal peril.*

He let the silence settle over them.

"Lady, I must ask you a very difficult question. I am grateful you have your mother by you. I wouldn't ask it for the world, if I didn't have to."

The mother sat up straighter in alarm.

"Did this Maeldoi ever put his hands on you?"

"No, never," she said, her eyes flashing.

Well, that's a relief, he thought, because it was clear she was telling the truth about it. *On the other hand, if only he had, the case would have become so much easier.*

"I am gratified to hear it. It speaks well of you, lady."

"It speaks well of him," she responded tartly.

Oho, he thought. "I disagree, lady. I believe he would indeed have laid his filthy traitor's hands on you, except that he saw what you are made of. He saw he didn't dare." But what did she just reveal about herself? *It speaks well of him?* As if, had he done it, she was the one who would have lost all restraint?

The mother sat up straighter and looked proud. Then, as the meaning sank in, she glanced at her daughter in dismay.

But now he saw another little tactic of his was about to bear fruit. The filthy traitor hands thing.

"If you know your Frobertius, my lord," said Gisa, rising to her feet, "You know you've just prejudged a man before his trial. He did not put his hands on me. The reverse, in fact. He warned me away from himself. He knows the lot of you are coming after him. He knows he's about to be charged with treason. He told me it was too dangerous for me to be seen talking with him, and he left."

Estienn nodded to a servant standing discreetly out of earshot by the door. The man came over to stand at Gisa's elbow.

"I have no more questions for you, Lady Gisa. I'm most sorry if I caused you distress." He turned to the servant. "See the Lady Gisa to her closed cart." He swiveled to the mother, who looked like she'd fall down if she tried to stand up. "A moment, dear lady?" he said to her. "Just a quick question for your ears only. Then I'll escort you myself out to the cart, and you and your lovely girl can go home."

He moved over to sit on the bench beside the mother and waited until the servant had escorted the daughter out of the room and had closed the door.

"Oh, my lord!" quavered the mother.

Estienn took her hand and pressed it sympathetically. "The young, eh? They are so passionate, so full of life. But too often much too reckless."

"Do you think that man—"

"No, my lady. Banish the thought. It's clear her qualities protect her. She is a fine young woman, that daughter of yours. Even a man as hardened as Maeldoi wouldn't have dared touch her. Not in a public place like a library."

"But could he have gotten her off alone someplace? Where were these teaching sessions conducted? Why was I not informed she was, without a partner, meeting with some felon?"

"No, no, my lady," Estienn soothed. "They would have had no possibility of being alone." He saw she was moving from abject terror to anger now.

"How would you know?" Her tongue was mordant.

"I would know. I do know. Yes, Maeldoi had gotten his freedom. Yes, he had been allowed to resume his training. No one, of course, would have dreamed this would involve your daughter. Unfortunately, it did. The war, you know. But trust me on this, lady. We have had our eye on Maeldoi. However he escaped his first incarceration in our cells, we knew he'd be back with us. We know he's a traitor. And now we have him, and can prove it. Your daughter just did us a valuable service. I'm sorry she is so distressed. I hope she'll come to realize, later, what a good service she has done for all gwrgi, and how fortunate an escape she has had from one of the world's true villains."

As he spoke, he watched the mother grow calmer and more resolute.

"And you swear to me her name won't come up, during a trial?"

"Not if I have anything to say about it, my lady."

"And you are second on the Penance Board."

"Indeed." He hesitated a fraction. Another fraction? No, that was enough. "I must in good conscience tell you something, lady."

She looked at him in alarm.

"The man himself. He might bring up her name, at trial. And his advocate, if he ever got wind of it, might do the same."

"Will he get wind of it? Oh, no," she moaned.

"Dear lady. I have a solution in mind. A bit unorthodox, but I can assure you I've given it a great deal of thought."

"Anything you can do to help will be greatly appreciated. Her marriage prospects—" The woman began moaning, just a little, just a bit under her breath.

"Suppose I made an offer of marriage for the young lady." There. Best to just say it and get it out there. The moment seemed to be right for it.

The mother's mouth gaped open.

"I have a good income, my lady. True, I'm a great deal older than the Lady Gisa, but I've conceived a great admiration for her. As I say, we've had Maeldoi under observation for quite some time, and I can't tell you how greatly I've admired your daughter's comportment. I know she got a bit overwrought and said a few rash things just now, but I can assure you she has done absolutely nothing improper. If my suit were to be accepted, it would touch my honor to know she had done anything even remotely improper. She hasn't. Even if you reject my suit for her hand, you can rest assured she hasn't done any improper thing." *Of course, no one else will know that, and when this meeting we've just had starts to leak out—as it will—everyone else will suspect. So take me now, before her value on the marriage market drops like a stone.* And what a coup for himself. He has wealth. She has the great family name he needs if he is to climb as high as he thinks he can. He has the title, but it's not an inherited title. He needs the inherited title.

Just as he expected, Gisa's mother was thinking the same thoughts he was, making the same calculations. A commoner son-in-law, but a rich one, and maybe the best her daughter can hope to catch, given her recent rash behavior. Given her willful eccentricities, the books, the thinking herself independent, the—

Estienn watched the wheels turning. He waited.

"That is a most kind, most generous offer, my lord," she said. "I'll summon my husband from the Army Board tonight. I believe he's not at the front just now. I'll talk it over with him. If I may, I'll give you my decision tomorrow."

He walked her to the closed cart, where he glimpsed Gisa sulking within—*that kind of behavior will change, my girl,* he promised her in his mind—and he and Gisa's mother parted with effusions of thanks and protestations of friendship.

What a bonus, he thought, looking after the cart as it trundled away toward the women's quarters. *On top of all her other advantages, the Lady Gisa is even prettier than I thought. When she's angry, what a fine flush, what bright eyes.*

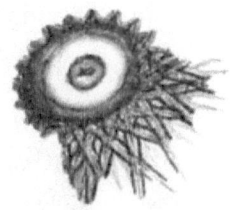

CHAPTER TWENTY-ONE

The Usual Transition

G isa, you are a lucky girl," her mother told her. Her mother had summoned her into the formal reception room of their well-proportioned stone house set back from a street in the toniest section of the women's quarter.

As Gisa entered, she was startled to see her father standing there.

"Father," she said, coming to him and dropping him a curtsey.

"Gisa," he said. He stood resplendent in his general's uniform, not his armor, he'd taken that off, but his silks and furs screamed wealth, privilege, authority.

Only outside in the city, of course. In this house, in the women's quarter, Gisa's mother ruled.

The men sniggered behind their hands and called the women's quarter "the cave." But whenever Gisa encountered one in their house, or in one of her friends' mothers' houses, these men were cowed and properly respectful. They knew they had better be, or The Three protect them.

She knew about their disrespectful jokes because she had been out in the city a bit. Other girls were hardly allowed such visits, but she was. First, because of her education. Then, because she needed to visit the library. And then—but here she shied away from thinking of it.

All night she had thought about it.

Maeldoi. Teaching Maeldoi. Maeldoi's fine hands. His fine, tragic hands. The planes of his face. The mysterious male body, built so differently from hers. The feelings that arose in her when she looked at him, drew near him. He smelled different. A man smell. She wasn't sure what was under his clothing. Something different from what was under hers. Everything about him was different, and all of it enticing.

Once, shortly after beginning to teach Maeldoi, she had gone to the library to find books about male bodies. Alda was still her partner then.

"What are you searching for, Gisa? I'll be happy to help you," Alda had told her.

"Oh, nothing in particular," Gisa remembered replying. "I like to browse around. A library is a treasure house, is it not? No telling what you might find in here."

She was embarrassed by her own unacceptable curiosity. What was she thinking? Embarrassed, but compelled. She didn't find anything about the male body, and she was too timid to ask anyone. Alda was the last person she'd ask.

How happy she was the day Alda took sick.

Gisa realized her parents were staring at her. She realized that in spite of swearing not to think about Maeldoi, there she stood like a ninnyhammer, thinking of nothing but Maeldoi.

And now, because of what she and her mother had just undergone at the House of Penitence, she felt the truth of what he was trying to tell her. How dangerous he was to her.

But yesterday, I endangered you, Maeldoi, she told herself. She understood the man from the Penance Board had set out to entrap her. She knew she must have revealed more than she realized. She had tried so earnestly not to.

She shook her head hard, to banish the whole disturbing experience from her mind. She looked from her mother to her father.

Her mother had probably discussed her shocking behavior with her father. Maybe they'd punish her somehow. Maybe that's why they had called her to them. Maybe that's why they were both standing there. A united front, and then they'd punish her.

And yet she was a woman grown.

She still lived in her mother's household. She wouldn't be able to move to one of her own unless she married. And marriage was the last thing on her mind.

"Gisa, we are here to inform you that we have signed your marriage contract. You are married," said her mother. "Soon you'll leave this house to set up your own."

"High time you entered adulthood, Daughter," said her father as she stood there gaping, wondering if she had just heard what she thought she had.

Gisa didn't know why she was so astounded. Her circle of friends had dwindled rapidly of late, as one after the other had left the house of her mother and moved into her own household. They all swore to each other they'd be friends forever, but that wasn't the way of it. The life of a young married woman was so different from that of a girl living under her mother's roof that soon the friends realized they had little in common and drifted apart. But Gisa had seen it. In married life, they often reconnected.

Some of her unmarried friends were riven with anxiety and terror. Would they be left out and stay girls forever?

When her friends did marry, sometimes they knew the man, but frequently they didn't, or only slightly. A few of her friends' parents had discussed the matter beforehand with their daughter. Most didn't.

Mostly, the marriage event followed a script exactly like the one unrolling before her now. The parents called the daughter into a room, announced they had just signed the paperwork, and handed her off to the husband.

All women needed to marry. Gisa knew this. Her friends seemed to talk of nothing else. Their parents would pick someone. They'd let the daughters know who it was. Their husbands would come to them until they conceived a child. If the child was a boy, their unpleasant duty in that department was over, unless the man was anxious for a spare part. If the child was a girl, they had to keep trying.

Gisa's younger brother had relieved her mother greatly, after Gisa turned out to be a disappointment. A girl.

Once a married couple had their boy, the man mostly disappeared except for ceremonial roles like this one. Presiding over the dickering for her marriage price. She was sure her mother had been the one to decide. But her father was necessary, to uphold appearances.

And of course fathers were necessary to secure their sons places in life similar to their own. So her brother had professed the military, just after rectory, and her father had paved the way for him to do it, with a lot of gold.

Gisa wondered when her brother would marry. It was up to the man to get the bride price together, but that shouldn't be such a hardship for her brother. In a poor family, it would. But her father would provide the necessary funds for that step into adulthood, too, even if her parents looked high for her brother and agreed to the high bride price that went along with such a gambit. They could afford it.

Often, though, young men didn't marry. They were too busy with the matters of their training and then their profession.

There was a mystery. Everyone knew men had powerful urges fixated on women's bodies, and women made use of these urges to their own advantage. What did the men do later, when their women had no further use for their male urges? Gisa wasn't sure. She knew there were women who catered to such urges.

Women had no urges. Gisa thanked the gods she was a woman and would never find herself driven by anything as brutish as an urge.

Her father had been talking at her all this time. The bride price paid for her. The honor her husband would bring to her. Then her mother chimed in. The new house she had gone to inspect, when the new husband had purchased it and presented it along with his offer. How Gisa and her mother would have to visit the street of the factors together, to choose furnishings for it.

"Are you even listening to us, Gisa?" her father said finally, exasperated.

"Yes, Father," said Gisa. But she stood astounded. She had just discovered something about herself. Realized what it meant, these last several seasons of wondering and yearning. She did have urges. Urges for Maeldoi. *No wonder my mother is ashamed of me,* she thought. Thank the gods her mother didn't know about the feelings Gisa harbored for such an inappropriate man. An animal. A savage. A beast of the caves. A criminal, even. But though her mother didn't know, she did suspect something was wrong with Gisa. Something was very wrong.

"See, this is what I've been talking about," said her mother. "Gisa walks around in a daze. She doesn't do anything the way other girls do them. I blame you, Husband. You're the one who allowed her to pursue her foolish notion about letters. So now, scandal has come to our house."

"I see it now," Gisa burst out. "Get me married off quick, before anyone hears about our little trip to the House of Penitence.

Before my price drops, and you have to settle for less, and a lesser husband. All that scandal. Oh, my."

"Yes," her father huffed. "And if you were one of my soldiers, I'd have you up on charges, and you'd be whipped."

"Husband, for shame. What coarse language. I forbid it. That's what I get for marrying a military man. What do you know about it? Nothing. Truth to tell, Husband, the scandal is what brought Gisa such a suitable husband. The fortunate gods smiled on us. I'm not sure how or why, but don't look a gift ox in the mouth, as the saying goes. Gild its horns instead and throw a wreath of flowers about its neck."

Gisa stared at her mother, puzzled.

"Now your father and I will step aside so that your husband can claim you and take you to your new household. I'll see you soon, Daughter. I'll tell you all my ideas about furnishings and the best prices. You and I have a lot of work to do so you can set up your new household properly."

Her parents withdrew from the room.

Her new husband strolled in.

Gisa's hand flew to her mouth. "No," she said.

"Yes," said this husband, Estienn.

"What have you done to my student?" she demanded.

"Who, Maeldoi? That scum? I can't believe it. I pay the bride price, every penny. I buy the best house on the block, all for you. Yet this is the first thing you ask me. Our first conversation in married life is to be about some unwashed traitor. Very well, I'll tell you, since you're so eager to know. We charged that scoundrel with treason this morning. Your answers to my questions gave me the last piece of information I needed."

Gisa stifled a cry.

"In only a fortnight, Maeldoi will be a lump of flesh in a cage, or he'll be dead." He stepped close to her and took her by the wrist. "Listen, Gisa. Wife. Your answers implicated you, too. Maybe not to the point you would have been charged with treason. But without my protection, something bad would be happening to you right now. So I'd say you should be falling at my feet in gratitude. Otherwise the punisher's whip would be flaying strips of your skin from your back at this very moment." He reached around and pulled the back of her kirtle down a little from the nape of her neck. "Such fine skin, too. Lovely. Smooth and soft. I can't wait to get my hands on it."

She was speechless, and in a state of shock.

"Enough. This is my wedding night. You may rule everywhere else in the women's quarter, but I rule in the bedroom. I've bought me a bride, and you are she. Come with me."

He took her by the arm, half-steered, half-dragged her out of her mother's house, turned the corner at the end of the street, and manhandled her into a new house. To the back of it. To the bedroom. And shut the door.

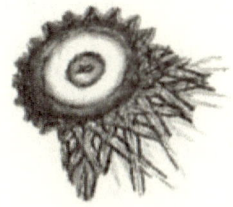

CHAPTER TWENTY-TWO

Traitor

H ow are you doing with your princess, Caedon?" said Gilles de Rais. He looked deep into Caedon's eyes. "Those fascinating gwrgi eyes of yours. Are they helping you with that one?"

Caedon stirred uneasily at Gilles's little joke about the latest episode in their scheme to possess the Sceptered Isle. Of course Gilles knew that Diera was deep in a potion-induced sleep when Caedon took her. "I am trying hard, mighty one."

"Labinia is giving you the help you need?"

"If not for Labinia, I wouldn't be able to do it at all."

"She is well-trained in all of the arts of the witch." He caught Caedon to him and caressed him. "My poor boy. This is very hard for you, is it not?"

"Yes, my lord," said Caedon, leaning into the comfort of Gilles's arms. "You see into me. You see it's so."

"Those boys around you must help you."

"They do. I can get myself into the humor, and then I—"

"As you did with the Lady Ailys."

"Yes, but this one—"

"The Princess Diera."

"Yes." Caedon, miserable. "Labinia gives her the potion, and then she just lies there. And later, she looks at me with those big trusting eyes of hers, and I think of her as she so recently was, a delectable little girl, and—"

"What about your own delectable little girl?" said Gilles, nudging him and smiling.

Caedon felt himself soften and relax into a happy state. "She is perfection. I visit her often, in her place underneath the manor. If only that silly princess weren't about the place, I could take Jillian into my own rooms."

"Patience, Caedon. Look how far you've come. Ranulf dead. Artur dead. Audemar as good as crowned. We've moved into a new phase of my plan, and it is going very well. Thanks to your skill and nerve."

Gilles's plan was bearing fruit, and Caedon had played his part well. He'd arranged the assassination of Crown Prince Artur and the death of the king, and he'd planted the evidence implicating the youngest prince, Avery. Caedon hadn't stopped there. He'd spirited away the Crown Prince's heirs, two small boys, so they'd be no impediment. Now at last Audemar was positioned to become king, with Caedon at his side.

Why, then, can't I feel much triumph? Caedon thought. *Much of anything at all.* He knew why.

And so did Gilles. "Raoul." Gilles's eyes darkened. "There you've failed me."

"Pardon, mighty lord! It hurts, to fail you. And it hurts to have Raoul so hostile to me."

"But you have him securely away from those friends, am I right? The young prince Avery and those boy-men who follow him about?"

"Yes, and Avery is branded a traitor."

"Does Raoul believe that?"

"No."

"Hmm." Gilles lifted one finger, and Caedon knew to stay quiet. "Ah. I made a quick trip into Raoul's mind. I see you're right. He doesn't believe Avery killed Diera's father the crown prince. Worse, Raoul is still thick as three abed with those lads. They call him Rafe?"

"It's Audemar's name for him, and it stuck." Caedon gave a miserable sniff. "How can Raoul be close to Avery still? I make sure to keep him where I can watch him." Caedon passed a hand over his forehead. *Rafe*, he said inside himself. It made his whole body hurt, to think Rafe loved them, those lads about Ranulf's youngest son, Prince Avery, the younger brother of the lout of a prince Caedon needed to support. Rafe loved the younger rebel prince and those others and didn't love Caedon, in spite of Caedon's mission from Gilles to prop up the middle prince, Audemar the usurper. Worse, Rafe was actually helping them.

Gilles himself had sent Rafe with Caedon to support the endeavor to usurp the throne. And this is how Rafe repaid their trust—treacherous acts against Caedon and Gilles, in spite of Caedon's tender feelings for him, and all Caedon's tender care.

"Watch Raoul harder. Rafe. Whatever you're calling him. You're calling him that too, Caedon?"

"Everyone does." Caedon felt a shiver of fear for Rafe. By whatever name he was called, the lad was treading a dangerous line. But Gilles loved the boy, too. That was some protection.

"Meanwhile," said Gilles, "keep letting Raoul—Rafe—" Gilles paused, considering. "Keep letting him believe he is guarding the princess. That should keep him occupied and out of trouble. And keep trying with the Princess Diera. All you need is one lucky shot—" He laughed and punched Caedon, "and you can stop. Hope for a boy. A royal boy, sired upon a royal mother."

"If it's a girl?"

"Then you'll bring the infant to me, and I'll enjoy what I can of it. That won't be as pleasing to me as if you sire a boy, but I do get quite a bit of enjoyment from a girl infant, as you well know."

Caedon's stomach turned. He did know.

"The princess gives birth to a girl, then you simply try again." Gilles wasn't paying attention to Caedon's thoughts just then.

Luckily. He was musing aloud. "But it may not come to that, so much effort. You're lucky, Caedon. I trust in your good luck to sire a boy of the princess. She suspects nothing?"

"She thinks she has bad dreams. She saw her father lying dead half fallen out of his bed, covered with blood, and she thinks that gives her bad dreams."

"That would indeed give a person bad dreams."

"So that's what she thinks, and she is most naïve, and Labinia's potion is very effective."

"Good. The incubus, visiting the maiden in the dead of night, taking her all unsuspecting. Ha, I like it, Caedon."

Incubus, thought Caedon, trying it on. *I've never thought of myself as an incubus.*

"Come with me, dear boy," Gilles was saying. "I'm hungry."

I'm not an incubus, thought Caedon, trailing after Gilles. *An incubus loves his work. I despise it.*

Much later on, after Gilles's feeding, a light one requiring not much recovery, as Caedon came out of his state and Gilles carefully tended him back to himself, Gilles supported him as they climbed to the top of the tower where the mountains rose in the distance, hazy and blue.

"This spot eases me, Caedon," said Gilles. "From here, I can see much of my domain, and I can imagine, looking into the blue distance, that I see it all. I can imagine I have taken it all. One day I will, and you will be my instrument." Gilles's tone changed. "Tell me, now. I need a report on your other project."

Caedon inwardly trembled. This is how their conversations about Maeldoi always began.

"Well?" said Gilles. "I'm waiting."

"I've heard back from some people I trust. I know where he is. I know why he disappeared."

"Funny, I've never been able to track him. I suppose that's because I've never actually met him, so I don't have any little essence of his to work from. I do from his boyhood, a residue I scraped up. I suppose as he has become a man, that essence is no longer effective. So tell me what you've discovered. I'm relying on you."

"The gwrgi threw him into their prison in their capital city."

"Huh. Why?"

"My attempt to find him. I did find him, remember? Somehow that made them think he's some kind of traitor."

"During that vigil of his."

"He got in a lot of trouble over it. That's what made them decide he's a traitor. So now they plan to mutilate him and display him in a cage as a warning to all traitors."

"Waste of good meat," said Gilles, with distaste. "But anyway, I want him for my own purposes. We must not let them do anything to spoil him. He's key to my plan for the gwrgi."

"That's the problem. They know that. They know your plans for them. They just think he has fallen in with those plans. Mistakenly. Because I'm his brother."

Gilles gave a bark of laughter. "I do have my sources in the gwrgi capital," he began. Then his eyes became twin gimlets. "How do the gwrgi know my plans for them. Who could have told them what those plans are? Let me see. Who knows what they are? Why, I can think of only one person."

Caedon began backing slowly away. "No, Gilles. My lord. Please, my lord. I didn't tell them, my lord!" He felt the hard stone of the parapet just at his back. One more step and he'd go over.

As suddenly as the murderous look had descended on Gilles, it was gone. He pulled Caedon to him and caressed him. "Such fear," he crooned.

Caedon stood shivering within the circle of his master's arms. Gilles's arms tightened about him like bands of steel.

"My lord," Caedon choked out.

"I see into you, Caedon. I know it was not you. Who, then?" He flung Caedon away from him in a fury, and Caedon nearly did go over. Gilles's arm shot out. He grabbed Caedon by the neck of the tunic and pulled him back from the brink of the tower.

Caedon crouched whimpering at Gilles's feet. He had pissed himself.

"It has to be Rafe," said Gilles. "He overheard us."

Caedon felt terror. Too much treachery. Rafe supporting Avery and his rebels, Rafe maybe informing the gwrgi against Gilles. How much more bad behavior from Rafe would Gilles tolerate? He'd kill the lad. But in this gwrgi matter, Rafe was surely innocent. Rafe knew nothing of the gwrgi. "No, lord," Caedon cried out. "It's not Rafe. He has no idea. He doesn't even know I have a brother. Rafe is my brother." He began to sob.

Gilles reached down, hauled him to his feet, and absently began stroking him. "Who, then?'" he said.

Caedon had no answer.

"Pah, go clean yourself up," said Gilles. "You stink."

Caedon crept down the spiral staircase of the tower to his own rooms. He supposed one day he would be king of the Sceptered Isle. Maybe king of a lot more.

Right now he felt like the king of nothing. A hollow shell someone might someday call a king, and when they did, everyone else would laugh.

I want Rafe, he cried to himself.

But he knew he'd never have him.

After he'd cleaned himself up, he wandered out to the castle's inner bailey, then down the motte to the outer bailey.

"A beautiful day, my lord," one of the guards called out to him.

"Yes, it is," said Caedon. He thought of riding through the lanes surrounding the castle. That would settle him. He was decided. He was minded to ride. He strode to the stables, picked out a horse, mounted, and soon found himself cantering with the fresh breeze blowing his long hair back and the scent of springtide in the air.

The ride soothed him. The hollow feeling in his chest eased.

After a while, he slowed and rode aimlessly. He found he had come to a little valley.

A villager walked by on the other side of the road, his maul over his shoulder.

"Good man," Caedon called out. "What's that, down there?" He pointed. Just above the trees he was able to see a squat tower made of some red stone.

"The rectory."

"The rectory? What's it for?"

"Those gwrgi. Where they send their young for schooling." The man made a quick warding gesture with his left hand. He had stepped close to Caedon to speak to him, pulling his forelock respectfully.

But now he started back as if some serpent had bitten him. He stammered something and took to his heels.

Caedon sat his horse, watching him go, mystified. Then he realized.

The eyes, he thought. *The man is gabbling on and on about the gwrgi this and the gwrgi that, and suddenly he realizes he's in the very presence of one.*

Caedon felt a prickle of curiosity. His brother had gone to a place like that. A rectory. Who knows, maybe this very one. He recalled his long-ago childhood. The men who had come to their hut. The portal that had transported them to the caves. But they'd taken Maeldoi away with them. Here, maybe.

He guided his horse down the road toward the building he had glimpsed through the trees.

As he neared the place, he heard the creak of harness, the rumble of wagon wheels. The road was narrow. He backed his horse practically into a hedge as the little convoy went by.

Two outriders. An ox pulling a strange sort of cart. It was wheeled and flat. Affixed to it by chains and leather straps was a kind of tall narrow box put together of rough wood. There was a slit at the very top.

Caedon wondered if they were somehow transporting livestock that way. As the cart went past, he got a distinct whiff of some animal odor, and there was a thumping from inside. Two mounted men followed the cart.

After it had trundled past, Caedon urged his horse out into the middle of the road and sat looking after it. He watched as it turned down the lane he was sure must lead to the rectory.

What was in the box?

A mystery.

At last he turned his horse's head. The shadows were lengthening. He wouldn't get back to Gilles's castle before dark.

He hadn't gone far before he realized how done-in he was. The events of the day rushed on him and he nearly cried out.

A near thing. Gilles about to throw him off the tower, Gilles in his fury nearly doing so accidentally, Gilles's arms about to crush his ribs into shards of bone that would have pierced his inwards.

Gilles in his fury didn't know his own strength. No wonder he was fascinated by the gwrgi, who went into their own uncontrollable rages.

Not me, thought Caedon. *Not any more*. Gilles had given him the tools for self-control. He nearly wept from gratitude. Gilles was his savior.

But Gilles was dangerous to be around, too. There was the murderous anger. The hungry feeding that might take Caedon down too far, too fast, and end him.

I walk a knife-edge, Caedon realized. The apprehension of it was destroying him from the inside out, driving him close to a kind of distraction. And. . .he made himself face it. His feelings for Rafe, completely unreciprocated. Trying to control Rafe, he had just made things worse. Caedon felt heartsick.

Right now, though. He realized that if he didn't find an inn and eat something and drink something right now, this instant, he'd fall off his horse. He hadn't eaten all day. And he needed to sleep.

There, flapping against the side of a modest house, was an inn sign. Caedon rode into the innyard, handed his horse off to an ostler, and stumbled into the dimly-lit main room.

He pulled his hood well up around his face. With the hood and the poor light, no one would realize he was gwrgi. He called for bread, stew, and ale, and devoured it all.

As he sat at his table with his back to the room, he realized something he hadn't known of himself.

He actually liked being across the Narrows in the Sceptered Isle while carefully crafting Gilles's designs on that realm, despite all the difficulties. Liked it better than here in the Baronies.

Except for remote parts of the Sceptered Isle, such as the village where he had spent his childhood, not many there knew of the gwrgi. When people glimpsed his eyes at the Sceptered Isle court and other civilized parts of their realm, they just thought he was a bit odd-looking.

Over here, any random stranger might take one look at him and run away screaming.

As he was thinking about it, voices from the table behind him intruded on his thoughts.

They're talking about that caravan, he realized, his ears pricking with interest. He began to listen hard.

"The old one died," the man directly behind him was telling someone else. "Those gwrgi hired my cousin and his friend to take their axes and mauls and chop the dead man out of his little room."

"Room? More like a barnacle on the side of that rectory of theirs."

"They wall them up in there. Their hermits. Feed them through a slot. When they die, somebody like my cousin has to chop them out. The stench like to kill him, so he told me. They're strange ones, the gwrgi."

"Oh, I see it now. That cart was bringing them a new one."

"Yes, and my cousin stayed to build a new little room. Sticks out where the old one was. They'll brick this new hermit up in there."

"Your cousin is a braver man than I."

"They pay well," said the other.

"What do you think those hermits do?"

"Dunno. Pray? Eat. Shit. Make a big stink."

"Wonder what gods they worship. Not the Lady."

"Dunno."

In the morning, Caedon went back toward the rectory. He couldn't help himself. Something drew him.

He stood a distance off, and watched. He saw some of the villagers doing the same.

Just as the man at the tavern had told his friend, they were walling someone up in some little excrescence, bricks and mud plaster, on the side of the main building's wall. They were almost finished doing it. Caedon could just see the top of the man's head. If it was a man.

Pretty soon, the fellow was completely walled in. On the front of the structure the workers had built, Caedon saw a strip of darkness. The slot the men at the tavern had described. One of the gwrgi walked over to it and spoke through it. Then he walked away.

A couple of half-grown village boys were laughing and shoving each other and daring each other to dash over to the little structure and thrust a stick into the slot.

Caedon grew more and more agitated, listening to them. At last he moved over to where they were roistering. They didn't notice him standing there. He doffed his hood.

One of them turned and caught a glimpse of him, the yellow of his eyes. The boy yelped. His friend turned. He yelped too. They went pelting back toward the village then.

Caedon stood watching them go, his yellow eyes gleaming.

No one else was about now.

Caedon edged closer. Soon he was right up against the slot. He tried peering in, but it was too dark.

A hollow voice came from within. "Get away from me, Caedon, you horse pricker. You traitor."

Caedon jumped back. He'd never heard that voice before, not in all his life.

A terror crept up his spine.

Could it be his brother? How would he even know what his brother sounded like, after all this time? They'd only exchanged a couple of words at the crevasse in the mountains where Caedon had found him, and that experience was fading into the past.

Caedon approached the slot again.

"Maeldoi?" he tried. His voice sounded hoarse in his own ears.

"No, you addlepate. But stay away from your brother or, so help me Three, I'll bust out of this place and come after you. You've done enough damage."

Caedon wanted to run for it. But he stilled himself. *What's going on here*, he wondered.

"How do you know my name?"

"Let's say a little bird told me," said the voice from the slot.

After that, no matter what question Caedon put to him, the man inside didn't answer.

In a while, Caedon wandered back up the lane, found his horse, mounted, and rode back to Gilles.

He wanted to ask about the hermit crouched inside his tiny dwelling. He wasn't sure how to frame his questions.

He did try.

"Oh, a member of the Hermitage. You gwrgi are given different specialized tasks. One is to take on the life of a hermit. You saw. They are enclosed, they never come out, they stay there til they die. I think all of the important gwrgi institutions need to have one about the place. Some decree from their gods, perhaps? The men you overheard said the former hermit died?"

"Yes."

"Well, then. There's your answer. The old one died. They needed a new one over at that rectory. They carted one in, they blocked him up, there he sits. End of mystery."

"But what do they do? What are they for?"

Gilles shrugged. "Who knows? I've never bothered to find out. So. You met one, he upset you, he seemed to have some kind of prophetic powers, he knew Maeldoi's name, he knows you are Maeldoi's brother, and he made some kind of obscure threat. I wouldn't worry about it, dear lad. The world is full of strange creatures with strange half-understood powers. Someday maybe I'll look into it."

Caedon let the matter drop.

Part V: SPRUNG

CHAPTER TWENTY-THREE

Merlin Takes a Look

M erlin. Merlin."

"What is it, John?" said Merlin, but he didn't turn around. He was absorbed in a series of complicated calculations involving the moon in its sphere, and how it would cross the path of the sun hanging from its own sphere, and how much the resulting darkness would terrify the inhabitants underneath the Spheres. He had devised an instrument that calibrated just how much.

The mage named John Dee tugged at his sleeve. "Merlin. You have to see this."

"Now what?" said Merlin, turning to his friend at last. He heaved a dramatic sigh and rolled his eyes. He punched Dee affectionately in the shoulder. "Something down there is always getting you whipped up, Dee."

"No, but look down there. No, a little to the left."

"The gwrgi city?"

"Yes. Will you look at what they're doing to that lad?"

"Oh, John. You can't go around worrying about every little thing they do down there. You have bigger observations to make. And anyway, you do have your mission on that other plane, with that young queen. Isn't that enough for you?"

"Merlin, what they're doing to that lad isn't decent."

Merlin leaned far over and looked far below. Some of the gwrgi had chained up one of their young ones, a young man, and they were tormenting him.

"You're right, John. Indecent. Good word for it."

"Can't we stop them?"

"John, we're not to interfere. You know that."

"What are we, then, if we can't put a stop to something like that?"

"Well, now, John," said Merlin in his patient voice. "Let's think it through. This young one must have violated one of their rules. That's their House of Penitence he's in, if I don't miss my guess. And I suppose the young man is being punished. Until he's properly penitent, you know."

"How could that—that thing they're doing to him— inspire anyone to penitence? I'd say it would inspire fear and hatred, myself."

Merlin looked harder. "He must have violated one of their most important rules." He thought over what he knew of the gwrgi justice system. "Must have committed one of their big three unpardonable crimes."

"You think that young man is a criminal? Have you seen his eyes?"

"John. You're too close. Back off."

Dee turned to him. "I can't. I look into that fellow's eyes, and I don't see a criminal. I see a man afraid, confused, but also angry. An injustice is being committed in that little dark room, Merlin."

"And you want to swoop in and see justice done? Dee, you know The Three discourage that. The gwrgi, the eala, the ordinary folk, all those underneath the Spheres, must be left to work out their own laws and customs for themselves. You know this."

But Dee's eyes had filled with tears.

"My friend, you are too soft-hearted to be a mage. Yet you are one of the best I know," said Merlin. "If you take on every one of the world's ills, when will you find the time to get back to your wife and son and daughter? And you know they, being of the ordinary folk, don't have the vast stretches of time you have. Don't you worry about what you're missing with them?"

"Of course I do worry," said Dee. "But now that I've seen this young man, looked into his eyes, I worry about him too."

"Listen, the gwrgi laws seem harsh to everyone else underneath the Spheres. They have to be harsh. The whole gwrgi culture is based on control and restraint. With the nature they have, that terrible rage that overtakes them, strict discipline is their safeguard. You can't fault them for exercising it."

"Something's wrong," Dee insisted. "I feel it. Something not right. It's as if they're using this young man to fight some force that is threatening them—"

"As your superior in the Magisterial Council, I order you to stop scrutinizing that lad. You must not interfere with—" But then Merlin stopped. He stared at Dee. "Some threatening force."

"See for yourself," said Dee, throwing his arms wide in exasperation. "Then tell me I'm wrong."

Merlin spent some minutes examining the details of the scene unfolding before him. The young man, beaten and tortured, dragged into a terrible room where men with knives waited to do him terrible damage. But there was an atmosphere Merlin recognized. An odor of fear and anger emanating not just from the victim but from his tormentors as well. "No," Merlin whispered. "You're not wrong, John. I sense what's behind this."

"And?" said Dee.

"Gilles de Rais."

"I thought you'd never see it. Thank The Three." Dee looked again. "Sweet Jesus, we need to stop them. They're about to gouge out that poor boy's eyes."

Merlin took another look. "They're about to do worse to him than that." He made his hand into a fist and punched it into the ether.

Below, a thunderclap shook the gwrgi city. In the terrible room, the torturers dropped their implements and abased themselves on the stones of the floor.

"There we go," said Merlin after a minute. "They're getting up off the floor and milling around. They're huddling and talking. They're dragging their victim back to his cell."

"I'm going down there to listen," said Dee.

"No, you're not," said Merlin. "I can tell you what they're talking about. They're trying to decide if my thunderclap was a natural thing or a sign from the gods. They're trying to decide what it means for their prisoner. His name, by the way, is Maeldoi."

"So in a moment or two they'll decide, hey, just a thunderstorm, and bring him back in and set back to work on him."

"Not if I understand gwrgi penitential procedure. Their punishments will have to stop until their Penance Board can issue a ruling. That will buy us some time, John."

"Time for what?" Dee said.

"Time for us to find out this Maeldoi's connection with Gilles de Rais. And then, maybe work out a solution that will allow the Penance Board to save face but preserve the hapless lad."

"I'll get right on it, Merlin."

"Meanwhile, what about your neurology practice back on your own plane? Aren't you in the middle of some fascinating case involving some softball player?"

"Fast-pitch, yes, line drive to the head, but she's a plucky young woman, and I believe she's in no danger. Mrs. Winston and her team have matters well in hand. This matter of the gwrgi is important. I'd call it time-sensitive. Send me, Merlin. I can't stand by and watch those men down there brutalize that lad."

"Oh, very well," said Merlin. "Promise to make it quick?"

"I promise, Merlin. I can fit it in between other projects. I have some ideas."

"Okay, then," said Merlin. "Just be discreet. John? John? Are you listening to me?" But John Dee was already gone.

Well, then, Merlin said to himself. Time for him to get to work. After his thunderbolt, he knew what the gwrgi were doing now. They were scurrying about, arranging for the temple's chief sortileger to read the omens. Then they'd know what to do about the lad they were tormenting.

They had dragged him gasping back to his cell, where he lay on the stones of the floor in a state of near-hysteria.

Merlin watched while he gradually calmed himself.

That's right, lad. Just as your shaman taught you. Breathe. Focus. Breathe. Put yourself under, until you see the world as if from far above it. Breathe. Breathe. Good lad.

"I'm going to have to send our envoy to Master Bertran," Merlin muttered to himself.

But now, for the most important task, he sent word for Little Bird.

Shortly she came flapping over from whatever mission she was working.

She usually assumed bird form these days, although in life she had been a sturdy and forthright woman, an admirable wife, an admirable friend. Poor thing, she had been called across that river while giving birth to her only son, so she'd never known the joy of ordinary mothering. But she had watched over young Dru his whole life.

"Little Bird, how lovely to see you," said Merlin, when she lit on a branch that jutted from the cloudland where he and Dee and a few other mages liked to take their ease.

Great to see you too, Myrddin, she said, shaping her bird language to his ears. He wasn't an ornithomancer, so he couldn't understand her unless she made an effort. Graciously, she always did.

He smiled to hear this name by which he was known in her own part of the world.

"Listen, Little Bird, I have a kind of urgent task that will detach you from your regular duties, although not for long. Will you take it on, as a favor to me?"

You know I will, Myrddin.

"How much do you know about the gwrgi?"

They are savages, like animals, are they not? Beasts of the cave. They turn into wolves when they are enraged.

"I know that's the popular idea of the gwrgi, but it's quite wrong. They are a very civilized people. Some of them, living at the fringes of their society, maybe not so much. But those who live in the great gwrgi cities are quite sophisticated.

If you say so.

"And they don't turn into wolves. They do become enraged, and when that happens, they transform into something quite frightening—not just to their enemies, but to themselves. So their entire educational system, really their entire culture, is based on inculcating control and discipline."

Interesting, I suppose. Where do I come in?

"Look down there, where I'm pointing. See that young man in some kind of trance state?"

The one who is caged in that cell? I don't like cages, Myrddin.

"That's the one. I don't like them either, Little Bird. Now, his fellow gwrgi nearly performed an entire series of atrocious acts upon this young man's person. But Dee and I stopped them."

I don't mean to question you, Myrddin. You're my superior. But is that really allowed? Interfering like that?

"I know. I know. Dee and I have discussed it. I think in this case it is justified, only because Gilles is involved in it somehow. And I don't like dividing mages faction against faction, but I think we've all seen some things—"

Gilles, you say. If a bird could hiss, Little Bird hissed. *Say no more. What do you want me to do, Myrddin?*

"I scared them all down there. Released a thunderbolt or two. Now, before they can resume going to town on that lad, they must consult their oracles to see if the thunderbolt is natural or a warning from the gods."

Going where?

"Never mind. They're going to start torturing him again unless we can stop them. I want you to rig the oracle for me."

Easily done. When?

"Tomorrow at dawn. See their temple? See the altar just outside? That's where their chief sortileger will butcher a sheep and look at its entrails. Then he'll issue a ruling."

He and Little Bird put their heads together, deciding on a strategy.

When the sun on its golden chain began moving over the gwrgi city at dawn, Dee and Merlin found themselves front row seats to watch the sortilege.

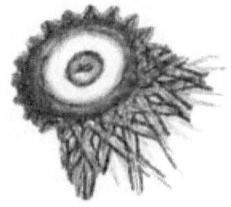

CHAPTER TWENTY-FOUR

Sortilege

This is going to work, isn't it? I've been making my own arrangements with our envoy, so it had better," said Dee.

"It's going to work," said Merlin, with maybe a touch more confidence than he actually felt. "Ok, watch now. Here goes."

Far below them, the sortileger stepped to the high altar outside the temple.

Many gwrgi filled the temple square, raising their eyes to his activities.

Beside him stood three men.

"Those are the three men of the Penance Board. That's the head of it, known as the Lord Penance Board," said Merlin, pointing.

"Strange name for a man."

"It's his title, Dee."

"I knew that," said Dee.

"That man next to him is his second, Estienn. And the other one is. . . I never can remember the other one's name. A complete nonentity. Oh, yes. Clarence. So now the three of them will watch the sortilege and listen to the oracle, and then they'll go back to our young man and act accordingly."

"Act how?"

"If Little Bird works it right, they'll have to release him or anger the gods."

"And if she can't?"

"I suppose they'll mutilate him, and he'll probably die. Mercifully. If he doesn't die—"

Dee flinched.

"Hush. Watch now."

The sortileger prayed in a loud voice to the gods.

He lifted the knife of sacrifice high, then brought it down on the softly bleating sheep, who made a startled squawk and fell limp, spewing blood from its severed jugular.

"Now he'll examine its heart. Then he'll make his ruling," Merlin told Dee.

The sortileger began gutting the sheep in a matter-of-fact way.

"He's a very accomplished butcher," Merlin observed, casting a professional eye on the man. "Did I ever tell you about my cousin in Asheville, the one who owns the butcher shop?"

But now the three men of the Penance Board were stepping to the altar and craning their necks. Another man came to the altar with them.

"Who's that one?" said Dee, pointing. "That other man."

"That's the head of the gwrgi Grand Council, Lord Jouhan. He's there to represent the secular arm. The Penance Board is a religious institution, you know."

"What the—" Dee began.

"Oh, it's Little Bird. She's getting right to work, I must say."

A kind of mist floated down over the sheep. The mist dissipated.

The sortileger looked into the carcass. His face went white with dismay.

A murmur arose from those assembled to watch.

"My lords," the sortileger stammered to the Penance Board. "The sheep has no heart."

"That's my cue," Merlin murmured to Dee. He raised his arm, dropped it.

A peal of thunder from a cloudless sky blasted the air. A sharp odor of ozone drifted over the high altar.

At that moment, an eagle soared overhead on the sortileger's left. The man pointed and moaned. The eagle stooped on a passing pipit and demolished it. A bloody bundle of feathers fell at the sortileger's feet.

Little Bird appeared breathless at Merlin's side.

"A pipit? Really? I was thinking maybe a writhing serpent."

It's all I could come up with on short notice, she said, sounding a bit put out.

"Very dramatic!" Dee enthused.

Below them, the murmur of the crowd had risen to a roar.

"My lords," they heard the sortileger said. "A sign from the gods. A very clear sign of displeasure. No heart. . . ominous signs on the left. . .thunder from a cloudless sky. . . " He was beginning to babble.

The three members of the Penance Board stood frowning and silent.

"Look how disappointed they are," Dee jeered.

The members of the Penance Board left the altar, the sortileger trailing in their wake.

Lord Jouhan began making some sort of speech to the assemblage, but by then Merlin and Dee were congratulating the bird mage, she was flitting away, and they were heading back to their usual seats to ponder next steps.

"That little performance is going to buy us at least a week of Penance Board dithering," said Merlin with satisfaction. "While they try to figure out a way around the disappointing sortilege, we will be using the time to figure out Gilles's intentions, and we can plant the idea of a better fate for Maeldoi where it will do the most good."

"Where?" said Dee.

"With Lord Jouhan. You saw it yourself. Those Penance Board members are out for young Maeldoi's blood. But Lord Jouhan is a sensible man. Here's where we call in our envoy."

In a hut halfway between the Lower City and the gwrgi capital, a modest man lived in a modest house. One of the ordinary folk, or so it seemed to the casual eye.

He wasn't a gwrgi. That was clear to his neighbors.

There were a few such ordinary folk scattered near the gwrgi capital. They lived mostly amicably with their gwrgi neighbors. In this time of war, with everyone on edge, they didn't intrude themselves. Stayed out of the Lower City's marketplace. Kept to themselves. Entertained no suspicious visitors.

So Merlin and Dee were dressed in practical traveling cloaks, like merchants on their way through gwrgi territory, stopping for the night with a fellow countryman as far the wiser move than stopping at an inn.

The modest man welcomed them inside.

Once they were all away from prying eyes, the man knelt to them both. "My lords!" he exclaimed.

"How do you, Maciotus?" said Merlin.

"Very well, Lord Merlin. Welcome. And welcome to you, too, Lord Dee."

"Did you receive my message?"

"Yes, Little Bird brought it a candle-measure ago."

"And you've heard the commotion in the capital?"

"I certainly heard your thunderbolts, Lord Merlin," the mage called Maciotus said with a grin. "One big one yesterday, another equally loud today."

"We need to get that young man out of the hands of the Penance Board."

They were interrupted by an elderly gwrgi who rushed from an inner room and flung himself at Merlin's feet, attempting to kiss them.

"Now, now, no call for that," said Merlin, doing a little quick-step.

Dee suppressed a smile. Merlin never wanted anyone messing with his feet.

In some regions, the religious leaders wanted to perform foot washing on any mages who showed up. Merlin was having none of it.

"Stand up, Master Bertran," said Maciotus. "Just bow. That will be more than enough obeisance."

The elderly man scrambled to his feet, his chin quivering. "That's my boy they've got in their cells."

"You're the lad's father?" said Merlin, with a kindly smile.

"Nay, lord, but I feel like his father."

"This is Master Bertran, Maeldoi's spiritual guide," Maciotus told Merlin and Dee.

"Oh," said Merlin, understanding. "One of the shamanic order. Your exercises are keeping your boy alive, I believe. Sane, anyway. I took a quick look inside him to see how he was coping with the strain of his situation. I saw you there. Your influence."

"Yes," Dee put in. "He's using your breathing exercises to calm himself."

"Thank The Three!" said Master Bertran. "I feared he hated and blamed me."

"By no means," Merlin reassured him. "Maeldoi reveres you, good master."

"And he fears he may have endangered you," Dee put in.

"If only I had—"

"No self-reproaches, Master Bertran. Instead, help us with our plans to get Maeldoi out of Dodge," said Dee.

"Huh?" said Master Bertran.

"Come to the fire, Master Bertran," said Maciotus. "We need to think how we'll help your boy."

Soon the four of them were sitting with their heads close together, proposing and supposing. By the end of the evening, they had a workable plan.

On the morrow, Maciotus took his safe conduct amulet from its niche and prepared to journey into the capital.

"I'll be with you every step, Maciotus, so fear nothing," said Merlin. "You, as the envoy from the mages, will beg an audience of Lord Jouhan. The amulet will let him know it's a matter of great importance and urgency. He'll hear you, and I'll be right there. Invisible to him but not to you."

"And you and I, Master Bertran, will wait here for Maeldoi when Maciotus and Merlin bring him out," said Dee, pressing the old man's trembling hand.

Dee wished Master Bertran would avail himself of his own calming exercises. The old man couldn't settle. He rattled around Maciotus's house like dice in a hazard box.

But at last they heard voices just outside. Dee stepped to the door and flung it open.

Through the door, Merlin and Maciotus bundled a skeletally thin and silent young man wrapped in a warm cloak, despite the summer heat.

Master Bertran was at his side immediately, soothing him and patting him and drawing him into the inner room of the house.

The other three stood aside.

In not even a candle measure, Master Bertran was easing the door to the inner room closed.

He came to the fire and stood looking down at the others as they sat by the hearth.

"Maeldoi is asleep, bless him!" said Master Bertran. He was beaming.

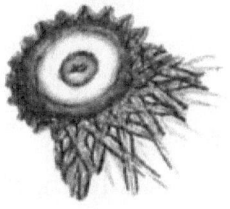

CHAPTER TWENTY-FIVE

Gone

W"e're not out of the woods yet," Dee told the other two. He, Merlin, and Maciotus were in their usual places by Maciotus's hearth. Dee turned to Maciotus. "Have you ever known any religious fanatics?"

Maciotus smiled and shook his head no. Merlin saw right away what he was thinking. "Out of the woods." "Religious fanatics." In his enthusiasm, Dee never stopped to think how his words might strike a local.

"Sure you have," said Dee. "You know, the kind of person who, rather than mix up the aumbrey with the tabernacle, would stand by and let Jesus H. Christ be nailed to the cross."

"Do what?" said Maciotus, turning pale.

"Oh, come now, Maciotus. What they were planning to do to Maeldoi was far worse than that."

"Nonsense," said Merlin. "Sneering at someone for confusing the aumbrey with the tabernacle is not religious fanaticism. It is merely behaving like a twit."

After a little more back and forth, Maciotus began to nod. "I understand. It is the kind of person who would allow a helpless young man to be tortured to death rather than admit they had got their instructions from The Three completely wrong."

"Right. Ok, then," said Dee. "So I'm afraid that even with Lord Jouhan's help, the Penance Board will still come after Maeldoi. Especially when they discover they've been snookered."

Once Lord Jouhan had understood how outraged the Magisterial High Council was over Maeldoi's treatment, he had pulled rank and insisted that Maeldoi be turned over to the secular prison authorities until the Penance Board sorted out its omens.

"Although actually," Dee had murmured to Merlin, "We're acting a bit high-handed, don't you think? We haven't summoned the Magisterial High Council."

"I didn't say that, not exactly," said Merlin, with a serene smile. "I just implied it."

"Because if we did summon the Council—"

"Yes, I know. Gilles would find out the whereabouts of Maeldoi."

Once Lord Jouhan had Maeldoi in secular custody, he let it be known, casually, during one of his own council's meetings, that he was less than pleased at the security in the secular prisons.

Then, presto-chango, Merlin and Dee and Maciotus among them had gotten Maeldoi down through a floor drain and had hustled him out of the city.

"I just hope none of the secular guards got in trouble over it," Dee had fretted.

"We can't do everything. What do you want, Dee?"

"World peace?" said Dee.

By now, of course, the Penance Board had learned that Maeldoi had absconded, and they were incensed.

Lord Jouhan was untouchable, especially in war time. He was also unrepentant. Mostly. "Those three officials of the Penance Board exercise far too much power," he said to Merlin. "They're due a come-down."

"You're not worried? They're starting to make noises about how you're letting traitors walk free."

"But he's not, is he?"

"No," said Dee. "Maeldoi is not a traitor. He is a scapegoat."

Jouhan knew what a scapegoat was, of course. He looked troubled. "Our gods tell us that in extreme times, the sins of the community can be laid upon the goat. When the goat is sacrificed at the high altar, the gods are pleased."

"The gods are displeased," said Merlin firmly. "They're calling down thunder and lightning upon you, and if you anger them further, they'll call down worse."

Lord Jouhan nodded thoughtfully. "That must not happen."

So then Dee and Merlin and Maciotus had made away with Maeldoi in the night.

Maeldoi was having a hard time of it. He seemed always cold. He huddled next to Maciotus's fire.

Master Bertran at last persuaded him to go outside for a little air. "It's a risk," he told the others. "He could be spotted. But I fear for Maeldoi's state of mind. During our exercises, and during our vigils, we try to get the trainee out into the open air. We don't hold with the ideas of the Hermitage, in my line."

"Master Bertran is right," said Dee. "It's as if the lad had been taken into a Hermitage of evil."

"Or into the regular Hermitage," Master Bertran muttered.

"With the addition of beatings and pincherings and mutilations and burnings with hot pokers," said Merlin tartly.

Master Bertran nodded unhappily.

"Have you seen his eyes?" said Dee. "They are as empty as two gold nuggets. As two orange-ade marbles. As two buttons off a sou'wester. As—"

"Point taken," said Merlin. "Get him outside, Master Bertran. Just be very cautious."

"Now then," Merlin said to the other two, after Master Bertran had gently persuaded Maeldoi to take a step beyond the threshold of the house. "I think I know where we can stash Maeldoi. It's a long-term solution, though, and you may not agree with me."

"What is it?" said Dee.

"What do you know of the Silver King? And the Wild Hunt?"

Maciotus shook his head dubiously.

"Something to do with the eala, isn't it?" said Dee.

"Yes. It's an ancient rite of the eala, drawing from the power of the very roots of the earth. The Silver King lives in the Undercroft, attended by thirty silver-clad Huntresses. On each night of the full moon, the Hunt rises out of the Undercroft and goes galloping over the land. They kill a white stag. They ritually bring it back to the Undercroft, and the Spheres are safe again til the next turning of the moon."

"The Huntresses are of the eala? I thought people were afraid of the Wild Hunt," said Dee, running a hand distractedly through his beard.

"You know, they are," said Merlin, "and the whole rigamarole might be superstitious nonsense. Might not have a thing to do with holding up the Spheres. But it's real. It does happen. There really are eala living underground, and they really are governed by a Silver King."

"These eala live underground." Dee looked baffled.

"Yes, not the usual idea of them, is it? Winged heroic creatures flying through the heavens to right wrongs and see justice done. The Silver King and his Huntresses are a much older idea about balance and how to keep it. Balance does hold up the Spheres. They got that part right."

"What does all this have to do with Maeldoi? He's not of the eala. He's the opposite. Gwrgi," Dee objected.

"Exactly. Opposites. Balance. Traditionally, the one who makes the kill, taking down the white stag, is not the Silver King. He's there to preside over the Hunt, but he doesn't hunt himself. The Huntresses assist the Hunt and assist the king. The one who kills the stag is the Dark Rider, and that post is always held by one of the gwrgi. In fact, the whole arrangement is deeply pleasing to The Three. The Three cause a gwrgi to be bound to the Hunt, and the dark and the light are held in balance."

"Wait a minute, Merlin," said Dee. "Placing Maeldoi there? You're speaking of enslaving him."

"Not as such," said Merlin.

"How much more enslaved can you get? This is a post for life, right?"

"He'll be safe down there. Safe from Gilles. Safe from the Penance Board. Safe and valued."

"And stuck underground." Dee's eyes glittered dangerously.

"That's where you're wrong, John. Every turning of the moon, the Hunt rides out. Every turning. It's exhilarating. I've seen it."

Dee didn't look convinced.

"Not only that, but one of the Dark Rider's tasks is to train the novice Huntresses. He trains them in combat and in hunting. The training in combat takes place underground, true, but the training for the hunt takes place in the fields and woodlands. Maeldoi will spend seasons and seasons of his life doing what he loves best. And then there are the horses. I hadn't really seen it, until I looked inside Maeldoi. I saw then. He has a deep connection with the horse."

"Wolves and horses?" Dee looked dubious.

Merlin rounded on him. "The gwrgi are not wolves, John."

Dee looked a bit ashamed. "I knew that."

"Look, John. Life as the Dark Rider will be perfect for Maeldoi. When we say a person is professed, we mean that person professes a skill or task or calling that speaks to his deepest self. This is Maeldoi. Trust me, John. It is."

"He'll be the only one of his kind, down there. Wouldn't you think he'd become a little lonely?"

"Well, there's that. It's not perfect. It's just almost perfect. It's not as though he has a wife or anything."

"And down there," said Dee, "he never will have one."

"Let's think about it," said Merlin. They could all agree to that, and they were content. For maybe half a candle-measure.

Master Bertran came stumbling through the door with a wild look about him.

"What's wrong!" Maciotus exclaimed.

"He's gone!" gasped Master Bertran. "I was standing there beside him, I turned aside because I thought I heard a noise, and when I turned back, he was gone. Gone." Master Bertran moaned out this last word.

"He's frightened and disoriented. He has been through hell. He is probably hiding somewhere near the place Master Bertran saw him last," said Dee, striving for calm. "Lead us there, Master Bertran. We'll fan out. We'll find him."

They did not. The next morning found them all sitting disconsolately around Maciotus's hearth.

"You know what we were saying last night?" said Merlin. "How adept Maeldoi is at hunting, things of that nature? He's good at this. Giving the slip to a pursuer. He has trained in how to do it."

"Poor Aleron trained him," said Master Bertran.

"He has had some good teachers. You. This Aleron. Tell us of him, please," said Merlin.

"He's a man who made it all the way through the early stages of the mental training. Then he fell in love and left the training before profession. But his combat, hunting, and stealth skills were all excellent. The rector—you know him?—he was Aleron's teacher. When he saw the promise in Maeldoi, he knew Aleron would be the perfect one to teach him. So Aleron went to the rectory and trained Maeldoi, just the two of them, until Maeldoi could go into the regular training program on his own. That's the pity of it all," said Master Bertran. "Maeldoi has more promise than almost anyone else I've ever trained. And this pack of hypocrites and opportunists—for that, if you'll pardon me, mages, is who the Penance Board members really are, especially that Estienn—not religious fanatics at all—" He stopped, huffing. "I've lost the thread," he said.

"I understand. They've ruined this young man. Terrible to do to any living soul. But to a young man with that much promise, tragic indeed," said Dee.

Master Bertran nodded miserably.

"And this Aleron was his teacher," Merlin said thoughtfully. "Where is he now? Could we enlist his aid?"

"That's why I was sad. Why I said poor Aleron. His unit was overrun, during the war. His lover, Haldemarus, was killed before his very eyes. He himself was terribly wounded. Worse, he was shattered by the loss of the man he loved."

"But if he values Maeldoi—"

Master Bertran was shaking his head no. "He left his military cohort. Because he was a war hero, he was allowed to resume his training where he left it off, right at the vigil. He sat his vigil. Didn't take long. Then he made his profession."

"Where, man?" said Dee, feeling impatient.

"The Hermitage."

"He got himself enclosed into one of those—" Dee sputtered to a stop.

"Yes. I tried to argue him out of it. He just wanted to shut himself up and shut the world away. And he has."

"Where?"

"The Hermitage doesn't give out that information," said Master Bertran.

Master Bertran's tale plunged them into an even deeper gloom.

"Well. We do know Aleron trained Maeldoi well. We'll have to hope the lad keeps himself safe, somehow. Do you think he could find his way back to Maciotus's house?" said Merlin.

"I doubt it. I really do. He didn't seem like he knew where he was, when he and I went outside," said Master Bertran. "His predicament, first the unjust accusations, then the severe mistreatment, then the near-escape from a grisly fate—" Master Bertran shook his head slowly. "All of it has stunned and bewildered him. He's in a state of shock."

"I'll keep an eye out for him," said Maciotus.

"And I will," said Master Bertran. "He may understand how to get to my small retirement hut. I explained it to him. It's hard to know how much he took in. You're right, Lord Dee. His eyes are just as blank as stones."

"And Dee and I will watch for him, on our travels around the Spheres. We can only hope for the best," said Merlin.

That's how they had to leave it, and they were all downhearted as they parted from each other and went their separate ways.

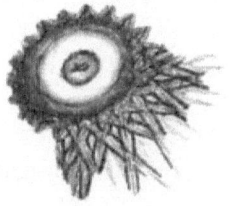

CHAPTER TWENTY-SIX

Down and Out in the Lower City

Gisa waited quietly for Estienn to wake. So far, he was staying every night at her house in the women's quarter, not going home to his own outside in the city.

"I'll get a son upon you. Only then can we back off," he declared.

She wondered for the hundredth time what life in the mines with all the other murderers might be like. Short and brutal, everyone said. But she wasn't sure how long she could hold off sticking a knife into Estienn's pompous gut.

At least during the day, he had to rush away to his duties at the Penance Board. Especially now.

She smiled, and she knew without looking in a mirror that it must be a grim smile.

He'd tried to keep the news from her for a while, but of course news like that could hardly be hidden. First, Maeldoi got a temporary reprieve when a god thundered his disapproval as the Penance Board was about to carve pieces off him and stick him in a cage.

Then Lord Jouhan demanded Maeldoi be handed over to the secular authorities until the Penance Board could figure out the meaning of the ominous sortilege the day they appealed to the gods for guidance about Maeldoi.

And now, best of all, Maeldoi seemed to have escaped.

It frightened her, though.

If he'd stayed put in the secular prison, he might have gotten off. Now, if they caught him (*when they did*, she told herself with a chill), he'd go straight to his sentence, no more reprieves. Not after an escape attempt, which attested to his guilt.

The hypocrites, she thought. He was supposed to trust to their justice, after what they'd done to him?

But at least for now he was out of the hands of the gutless and the malicious. Her husband being chief among that last.

Maeldoi is brave, she told herself.

"No kiss goodbye, Wife?" said Estienn as he left for his duties. "Perhaps if you're good to me, I'll let you have a book."

She ignored him. He wouldn't let her have a book. He was just taunting her with his ability to withhold them from her.

But ignoring him did little good. He didn't care if she ignored him or not, as long as he controlled her and made her do what pleasured him. As she was required to do.

If he gets me with child, I might figure out how to do away with it, she thought. Another way to earn a quick trip to the mines, if anyone found out she'd gone to the wise woman.

But anyway, if she shed the babe from her body, he'd just keep trying. So she was trapped.

She stood at the door of her house, looking up to the sky and the trees. Maeldoi was out there somewhere. That was the only thing that gave her a good feeling.

He was free, not in a trap or a cage. He was brave.

Slowly, an idea was dawning on her. She sat down on the step, too stunned to stand.

What a fopdoodle you are, she told herself. When had she ever done what she was supposed to do? So why in the name of the Nine was she doing it now?

Maeldoi was free. She could be free.

Maeldoi was brave. She was brave.

Her mother was coming over in a few candle-measures, to help her decide on fabrics for her big new bed.

Her big new bed. The thought turned her stomach inside out with revulsion.

Quickly, she pulled herself to her feet, went back in the house. Packed herself a small bundle. Into it she tucked a pair of Estienn's trousers, a ball of twine, and a tunic. She kicked off her velvet shoes with the turned-up toes and put on the stout leathern shoes she used for gardening.

No, she thought. She'd stand out too much, so the velvet shoes went back on. Then she minced out into the street, waving cheerfully to her near neighbor, and strolled from street to street, heading always away from the street where her mother's house stood, and closer to the most disused gate of the women's quarter.

She walked up to it. She knew the majordomo stationed there.

"My lady. I am deeply sorry. I've been told you may not leave the women's quarter," the man said, his voice shaking a bit.

"How very odd," she said. "There must be some mistake. I'll talk to my husband about this. No fear, man." The fellow was afraid he'd get in trouble for preventing her from doing as she wished. After all, his job depended on pleasing the women of the quarter. But she could see he was more afraid of Estienn. She placed a hand on his arm and smiled at him. And calmly went away.

Silly of Estienn, to think he could thwart her this way. There were many routes out of the women's quarter. She recalled her girlhood, and how she and her friends had sneaked out unchaperoned to buy sweets.

There was a broken-down part of the wall behind her house. That close. But too close to any pursuers, she decided. Instead, she headed to the other tumbledown part of the wall she knew about, the one behind the stables. In less than a candle-measure, she was out in the city. She walked purposely through it, but made sure to keep to streets where she didn't stand out.

It took her a full candle-measure to get through the city, but at last she had made it outside the city wall. She ducked down a scrubby gully and kicked off the velvet shoes with the upturned toes. She changed into the trousers, folding over the top and tying the waist off with twine so it didn't trip her. And pulled on the tunic. And the gardening shoes. She hid her regular clothes. She tied her hair back with some of the twine, as if she might be a half-grown lad. If no one looked too close, they might think she was.

So she needed to get at least as far as the Lower City before anyone raised an alarm. Her mother would do it. By now, she already had, not a doubt about it.

Gisa had never been as far away from the city as this, not on her own. As she neared the outskirts of the Lower City, she felt a flutter of unease. All the stories of criminals and low-lives began to pop into her head. What they did to young unaccompanied women.

She didn't know the Lower City. She hesitated as she came to a warren of alleys full of refuse and rotting vegetables.

She stood still, listening for footfalls or heavy breathing, any warning sign she was being followed.

None.

So she summoned up her confidence and headed down into the Lower City.

The person who was indeed following her was so skilled in the ways of stealth that she didn't even get a chance to scream before he had scooped her up, jammed a gag into her mouth, and pulled her into a noisome doorway.

He shoved her ahead of him into an abandoned, dilapidated dwelling. The light there was so dim that she didn't recognize him for a moment.

Then she did. Her eyes widened.

He shoved her into a corner, where she fell against some broken chairs.

He sat down cross-legged opposite her, and he drew a long knife that looked, in the dim light filtering in from a single grimy window, to be very sharp.

"Now then," he said. "I'm going to remove your gag. I need to talk to you. One squawk out of you, though, and I'll have no compunction about using this on you." He flourished the knife. "I'm skilled with this weapon. I spent some years as a scout in our army. Are we clear?"

She nodded vigorously, trying at the same time to remember all the gossip about the man. But truly, she had been so occupied with other difficulties that she hadn't paid much attention.

He reached over and pulled the gag out of her mouth.

She retched.

"So," he said heavily. "I've found a prize worth having. I have no idea what you thought you were doing, sneaking to the Lower City dressed like a lad. And I don't care. I'll sell you, lady. Sell you in a heartbeat, to get what I want."

"And what's that, Sir Anselme," she said, trying to make herself sound calm.

"Do you know what has happened to me?" He looked wild. His hair stood on end. He was filthy. His eyes were red-rimmed, as if he hadn't slept in days.

The other thing she knew about him she'd found out even before she got a good look at him.

He stank of unwashed body, but he stank worse of distilled spirits.

"No, I don't know what has happened to you. You're drunk, though."

"Who'd blame me. It's your husband, lady. He drove me to these straits. Now I have you, and if he wants you back, he'll need to buy you for enough gold that I'll be able to get away from here. Far away. . ." He trailed off in a string of mutterings.

"Oh, gods. Take me with you."

"No, my lady. If he won't buy you, you're no good to me, and then—" He made a couple of slashing motions with his knife.

"Really? You'll add murder to kidnapping?"

"What does it matter?" He stared at her with a look of desperation that pierced her to her core.

"It doesn't matter much to me, either," she told him. "A few more seasons with the disgusting slime-trail that calls himself my husband, and I'll be up for murder myself. Or self-murder."

"And what has brought you to this distress, lady, if I may ask?"

"You first. No, I haven't heard the gossip about you."

"It's the advocate's dis-ease. You've heard of it?"

"No. You have a dis-ease? That sounds painful. What are its symptoms?"

Keep him talking, she told herself.

"We all get it, sooner or later. All of us. Just a matter of time."

"Interesting," she said. "Tell me more."

"There will be a case that ends us. Over and over we see the injustices and the petty torments and the great torments. Sometimes they are justified. Often they are not. And then one too many, and we care a bit too much, and then we go over."

"Go over?"

"The edge, lady. The edge. Now my superiors have cast me out, and my wife has cast me off, and I have nowhere to live and nothing to live on."

"I see," she said.

She did, too, and felt pity for him.

She knew he must be talking about his job as an advocate for the accused. What he must have seen, during his career.

"But I don't care about that. It's my undoing, that I don't care. I care about that boy. That poor boy."

Now her ears pricked. "What poor boy?" she said carefully. Could this man be Maeldoi's advocate?

But his eyes grew hard. "You. It's because of you."

"Me?" she said faintly.

"I've changed my mind. I don't want to sell you after all. What I want to do to you does not bear describing."

"Sir Anselme. Are we talking about what I think we're talking about? Are we sitting here, both of us, devastated with grief, over the same mistreated prisoner? Over Maeldoi?

She might as well take the risk and say it, she thought.

If she were wrong, what matter? If she angered him into killing her, what matter?

"I was working hard for that boy. Then you lured him into a position where they could seize him up again. Then you gave the evidence against him that condemned him. Then, as your reward, his enemy married you."

"No!" she cried in horror. "I taught Maeldoi. I thought the best of him. Then that terrible man, my husband now, used the flimsy excuse of my chance encounter with Maeldoi to re-arrest him. Then he entrapped me, and mis-reported what I said to the court, and—"

She began to cry. "And he had me in a bad position, or my parents thought he did, so then he manipulated my parents into agreeing to our marriage."

Sir Anselme, too, began to cry. Great snuffling sobs. "I tried to save him. I couldn't. We try, and we almost never can, and then it breaks us. Maeldoi broke me, lady. They used you as an excuse to take him up, scandalous, some connection with a woman, how terrible, what a scoundrel, and do you know something? That boy has never had to do with a woman in his life. He is as pure as you are, lady."

"I'm not pure any longer. That man has defiled me. I want to take your knife and go home and stick it in him. Thinking about his body in any way touching mine makes me want to vomit."

Look at us, she thought. *The crazy man full of drink, and the crazy woman full of despair.*

They sat together and cried.

After a while, they had both cried themselves out.

"Well, now, Sir Anselme," she said. "Go ahead and sell me or kill me, because I have run away from that despicable man, my husband, and from the sham of my life. Maeldoi has run too, did you know that? I fear for him. He might have had some sort of chance, in the secular prison. Now, if they catch him, you know what they'll do to him. But he ran. If he can be brave and run, why can't I?"

Sir Anselme sat staring at her. "Where will you go?"

"I have no idea. And you yourself, Sir Anselme? What will you do."

"This bottle has me, lady," said Anselme, taking a leathern bottle from his cloak. "I'll just sit here quietly and drink until it kills me. That's my own plan."

"Fie, Sir Anselme. That's a coward's course." She leaned forward. "Why don't we try to find Maeldoi? Maybe we can help him."

Anselme's eyes narrowed suspiciously. "You'd like that, would you? Help me find him, Sir Anselme," he mimicked in a high, prissy voice. "You'll lead that arse licking husband of yours right to him," he growled. "You think you can fool me, but you can't."

"No." She shook her head. "I'd never do that."

She got to her feet. "I'm leaving now. So if you're minded to kill me, do it now. Before I go, I'll tell you a thing, shall I?"

"What thing?" His speech was slurring. His head was starting to nod.

He won't remember what I tell him, she realized, *but I'll tell him just the same. Because I want to hear myself say it out loud.*

"I love Maeldoi," she whispered into his ear. "Did you hear that, sir advocate? I'm in love with him."

She stepped around Anselme's slumped-over, snoring body and got herself into the alley.

Where will I go? she asked herself. *What will I do?*

She knew the approximate answer, just not the exact answer. Find Maeldoi.

But where?

She scouted out the alleys of the Lower City spread before her. Time to get going before she was taken.

She'd have to hurry.

Then she thought better of it and went back into the house where Anselme lay insensible.

She leaned down and plucked the knife from his resistless hand. She tucked it into the twine at her waist.

Where? she thought wildly. *Where will I go with my stolen knife, and no plan at all, and no hope of ever finding the one I long for.*

As her thoughts whirled about her, a half-formed notion rose up inside her. There was a thing she knew about Maeldoi. A conversation she remembered.

It's the only place I've ever felt safe, Scholar. The only place.

She set out on her journey.

CHAPTER TWENTY-SEVEN

A Voice

Where in the wide world could he go? Maeldoi crouched along a high road and waited for a party of horsemen to move by. He was dressed in rags, he had no cloak, and the weather was turning toward harvest-tide.

It reminded him of his boyhood. He wondered how easy it would be to get himself back there, to that tiny village at the edge of a moor. A remote spot, for sure. He thought of his father, on the run. It had taken years and years for his father's band to catch up with him there. Meanwhile, the man had had time to spawn two ragged brats and damage them both in various ways. *Maybe*

I can do the same, thought Maeldoi. Not spawn any brats or mistreat any. Just stay years and years ahead of his pursuers.

He kept wandering west. Someday, he supposed, he'd reach the coast. No one on his journey down remote lanes recognized him. He had even found himself in areas where no one really knew what a gwrgi was. It made him feel a bit safer.

He didn't think much about much of anything. Mostly about practical matters, how to keep himself fed and warm. A day or two of labor. Some petty thievery. Sleeping in someone's haystack or cattle shed.

In his dreams, though, he returned to the nightmare of his cell. He tried not to sleep much, to keep the dreams away.

Sometimes he dreamed of the men who came to rescue him. Those were the good dreams. They were rare, though. Had that really happened? Rescue? Escape? Of course it had, for here he was. He tried to recall faces and could not.

Master Bertran, had Master Bertran found him and gotten him out of the hands of his tormentors, or was that a dream?

He remembered the old shaman being there beside him on a beautiful hillside.

Then not there.

Then the panicky feeling of a too-wide sky and too much space, the feeling that just behind him stood a man with a chain and a whip and a knife and a poker with a glowing tip.

He remembered running and running and running. Then sleeping. Then running some more.

Sometimes, as he sat along a roadside sunk in lethargy, he felt with his fingers along the ridge of rough skin around his neck, where the collar had chafed him, and he turned his hands over to stare at the places the manacles had rubbed him raw and scarred him. And to stare at the burns. So he knew those parts of his dreams were true and not just nightmares.

He dreamed of a woman and waking, thought of her, too. Gisa. She was real. But so far removed from him by space and circumstance that she might as well be fantasy.

There came a day when he woke from a sheltered spot by a barn and as he walked, he felt some faint stirrings of memory. Through the trees he saw a squat red tower.

"The rectory." The words formed on his lips. The rector. The rector might help him. Into his mind swarmed memories. *Most of the people there hated me. The rector did not. But Aleron. My friend Aleron!*

He picked up the pace, on fire to get there.

Aleron.

Then his steps slowed. Aleron, lost in the war.

Something about the place drew him on anyway. He thought he might go as far as the gate, stand and look in.

Maybe he'd spot the boy he once had been. Savage, uncouth, just learning what it meant to have a friend and be a friend.

Now, because of his training, he needed little. Not even much food. He needed no one. He could take a pose in a woodland glade and hold it for several candle-measures, and feel himself soothed.

All he felt the need to do was move from place to place. Stay ahead of anyone who might be pursuing him. Stay ahead of his memories, because if they ever caught up with him, he paid the price in days of misery and pain.

He was coming near the rectory. He saw the gates past the trees.

A lot of villagers were milling about the gates. Many more than he remembered during his time there. The villagers had mostly avoided those at the rectory.

Now villagers trickled past him in twos and threes. A few looked around at him, noting his eyes. He saw they knew he was gwrgi, but they weren't shocked or afraid.

Here's a difference, he said to himself.

A small boy kept pace with him. "Master Gwrgi, hello," he said to Maeldoi over and over.

Maeldoi gave him a half-smile back.

"Are you coming to ask a question of the hermit, hey?" the boy said.

"What hermit."

It had been so long since Maeldoi had opened his mouth and words had come out of it that he wondered if he just imagined saying it.

But the boy answered. "He's walled up against the bricks. He tells you things through a slot. We're allowed to ask him once every turning of the moon."

"Oh, aye?" said Maeldoi. The boy amused him.

Maeldoi began to think about The Hermitage and the severity of its discipline. He supposed this walled-up man must be one of those. He had a dim recollection that the rectory had had its own poor old hermit. Most institutions did.

He remembered his long-ago worry that someone would assign him to The Hermitage when he came to be professed.

Somewhere along the way, he'd learned the truth about The Hermitage. No one professed it unless they chose it for themselves.

"It isn't like prison," he whispered to himself.

He remembered his silly notion that the hermits sat around in their cells reading books. They did not.

To enter The Hermitage was to choose to live your death in the midst of your life. You died an inch at a time alone, in the dark.

Maybe the alone part was a myth, Maeldoi thought, later on.

He saw the little bulging part of the wall where the hermit was immured. And the slot through which he must receive his food.

Maeldoi chose a sunny place at the wall and squatted with his back to it, enjoying the warmth and watching the people as they filed past the hermit's slot. One by one, they spoke something into the slot.

Maeldoi inched closer so he could hear. People asked questions. Some whispered abuse or obscenities. Some threw objects into the slot, a rock or a handful of dung.

Did the hermit ever respond? Maeldoi couldn't hear that he did.

He wondered if the hermit could predict the future. He never remembered the old hermit of his boyhood answering any questions or predicting anything. Just the same, as the line dwindled, Maeldoi found himself joining it.

Three ahead of him, some dolt of a boy stood at the slot and shouted insults into it until a man, walking past, spotted him and rushed over and grabbed him by the ear and forced him away.

The next person said something Maeldoi couldn't make out. Her voice was too soft. A woman.

He found himself staring at her. He found his mind turning to Gisa. *Stop it*, he told himself. *Just stop.*

The person ahead of him in line stepped to the slot now. He said, in a firm voice, as if it were a statement, not a question, "Will Maroie marry me this year. Will her father give us a cow."

There was no response from the slot.

After a moment, he stepped aside. He gave Maeldoi a wry smile. "I ask it every couple of turnings of the moon. I don't know why. I never get an answer."

"Does anyone?"

"Sometimes someone feels himself answered, somehow."

Maeldoi stepped to the slot for his own turn.

No one was behind him. It was nearing the evening meal. It was safe for him to ask his question.

"Will they ever catch me and chop me up and hang me in a cage?" he said, speaking the words softly and carefully, feeling like a fool.

A whisper came from the slot.

Maeldoi nearly jumped back. Instead, he stilled himself to listen.

"Maeldoi, I thought you'd never come. You must take an opportunity when it's offered. The Undercroft. Don't ask me why. I don't know why. Don't ask me what it is, what it means. I don't know."

Maeldoi ignored the words, which made little sense to him. He said in a strong voice, "Aleron. What are you doing in there. The Hermitage never does anyone any good."

"It does me good, Maeldoi. I wait here to die. Halde is dead. I am waiting to join him."

"Aleron. You could be out here doing good. Being my friend."

"Maeldoi, my good friend. I am as chopped up as you imagined you would be. The war tore me apart. I can do no one any good, out there. Go now. It's not safe for you here. You carry my love with you always."

Maeldoi looked up from the slot to see three or four robed men making their way from the gates in his direction.

"The gods bless you, Aleron," said Maeldoi quickly. "Don't think I'm leaving you here. I'll be back." He stepped away from the slot, and then he ran.

When he felt himself safe, he slowed. He slept in a ditch off the road in some underbrush.

At dawn he rose again and made his way cautiously back to the rectory. Now he had a plan.

He circled around until he was hidden by shrubbery but could look out of it to the rectory gates. He crouched, assessing the gates and walls.

There was Aleron's slot.

There were the gates, set into the rectory wall.

There, at the corner, was the mural tower where Mistress Pereta, the wonderful Mistress Pereta, tended her books.

"Guillaume. His nephew. His giant," Maeldoi whispered to himself, craning his neck to look up to the top of her tower. From where he crouched, he could reach the tower in three steps.

The tower bulged out from the wall. Maeldoi waited until the guard moved away from the gates to relieve himself. Then, quick and stealthy, Maeldoi got himself to the tower where its bulge would hide him from the guard's line of sight.

He pressed tight against the wall. With a stick he'd found, he poked around at the tower's base until he found what he was searching for. A low window, hidden by vines, that let into the tower. It was still there, still wide open.

All the boys of the rectory knew of this window. It was their way to sneak out and make mischief, and each new class of boys received the secret of it from the older boys.

Noiselessly Maeldoi lowered himself through the window into the very bottom of the spiral staircase, below the level of the entry door that let onto the rectory's courtyard. He stood listening.

No one stirring.

He got himself up the staircase as quick as some stealthy animal. At the top, he looked through the door into the room where Mistress Pereta had helped him learn to read.

A feeling of peace descended on him. Peace so deep it made him want to weep.

Mistress Pereta was not in her chair at the window.

His gaze roved to a shadowy hump of quilts in a corner. A bed. In it, a woman.

He took a hesitant step into the room.

"Who's there?" called a voice.

Mistress Pereta's voice.

In two steps he was at her bedside, kneeling down, taking her hand. The dawn light strengthened. Her eyes were open, but they were blind and white.

"Mistress Pereta," he said. "It's me, Maeldoi."

She clutched his hand hard.

Just outside, he heard a voice. "Mistress, here's hot water—"

He jumped to his feet, whirled around, stood pressed back to the wall by the bed.

A young woman came into the room, holding a steaming clay vessel.

She stopped. Her eyes widened. The clay vessel fell to the stones of the floor and broke with a crack, the hot water spewing out of it.

"Well, child," said Mistress Pereta, struggling to sit up. "Your plan worked. Here he is."

"Maeldoi," said the woman.

"Gisa," said Maeldoi.

Part VI: CLOSING IN

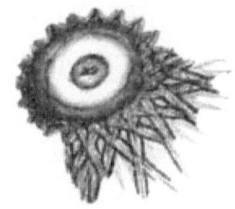

CHAPTER TWENTY-EIGHT

That Thing You Did

"Follow me," Gisa whispered. She smiled at Maeldoi and re-arranged the hood that shadowed his face. Straightened his servant's tunic. "You look fine. No one would ever guess you are a ragged unwashed escaped traitor."

Maeldoi tried to smile back. He came down the spiral stairs of the tower behind her, balancing an unwieldy pile of books in his arms.

The night before, during the scheduled bath time the few women of the rectory enjoyed, she stood guard while Maeldoi washed the filth of an entire season off him and, averting her eyes, had handed in some filched clothing to him from the servants' chest. Just this morning, she had sat him down before Mistress Pereta's window. She had chopped off most of his messy beard and had carefully shaved his face smooth. He nearly flinched away from the nearness of her. He couldn't meet her eyes. Without a word, she went about the business of transforming him, shearing his long shaggy locks into a respectable servant's cropped hair.

"There," she had said, running her hands lightly through it. "He looks perfect," she told Mistress Pereta at last.

Her touch had made him shiver.

He kept his eyes down as they went out the big gates. He heard her address the guards. "Taking these books to the binder's," she called out. "I'm borrowing Guillaume to help me."

The cheerful responses of the guards.

Maeldoi felt his tension lessen, his mouth curve into a smile. *Guillaume*. He thought he'd forgotten how to smile.

"You're not quite tall enough for the giant." She grinned. "Almost, though. To me, you're a giant. What you've done is the act of a giant. Here's the cart and mule. Load the books into the cart. I'll get in with them. You get up on the seat and drive us."

Pretty soon he was urging the mule down a weedy lane. At the end of it stood a tumbledown hovel.

He swung down off the wagon seat and Gisa climbed over the side of the cart.

"When I first got here, I wasn't sure what to do," she told him, leading the way into the hovel. "I wanted to get to the rectory, and there I was, just outside. But then what? I spent the first two nights sleeping rough in the wooded land around the rectory."

He nodded. He had done the same. He stifled his amazement that she had been able to do such a thing. That she had been able to get herself here at all.

"After a few days of watching, I knew this hovel was abandoned, and I moved into it. I knew I wanted to go to the rectory. But I wasn't sure how I'd get in. I besmirched my face and tied my hair up in a rag and found a really foul torn kirtle thrown on the town midden. Then I hung around the inn where the rectory's servants go when their work is done. They sit around with their mugs of ale, gossiping. So I hovered nearby and listened."

"Why the rectory? It seems like such an unlikely happenstance for us both to end up there."

"No, not at all." She was shaking her head emphatically. "Maeldoi, you told me, remember? The rectory was the one place you had known peace. *It's the only place I've ever felt safe, Scholar. The only place.* That's what you said to me. Do you remember?"

He nodded, and a smile stole across his lips.

"When I thought of where you might try to go, I thought of the rectory. So then," she went on, "as I listened to the rectory's servants, I learned of Mistress Pereta, the keeper of the rectory's library. How she had gone blind. How she needed help. How they'd sent for a person. But this helper hadn't shown up yet. After that, it was simple."

Maeldoi raised a skeptical eyebrow. All the while, he was bringing the books from the cart and stacking them in the hovel where she pointed. All the while he was thinking and wondering. She came here deliberately. She came here because it was where she thought he might go. She remembered the words he had spoken to her, so long ago. He wanted to exclaim to her, *You wanted to find me! You set out to find me!*

"I can't imagine getting yourself into the rectory was that simple," he said instead.

"It was," she insisted. "You don't understand. No one really looks at women, except as—" She blushed. "But anyway, no one would imagine I was anything but what I seemed to be. Women don't matter. I simply cleaned myself up, got myself in better clothes, and presented myself at the rectory gates as the helper they'd sent for."

"What will you do when the real helper shows up?"

Gisa acted out a little scene. "Oh, my!" she said, clapping her hand to her mouth. "There must be some mistake, my lords!" Then the assistant rector would march up the steps of the tower to Mistress Pereta. "Like a man with a stick up his arse," she said. "Mistress, there's been a mistake. They've sent a new helper, and this one has the proper parchment. Your woman here does not."

Maeldoi had to grin. Gisa mimicked the assistant rector's pompous accent and manner to perfection.

Now Gisa acted out Mistress Pereta's part. "No, no, don't take Gisa from me, lord! She knows her letters so well! She is so well-trained! Ahhh, how can you think of taking her from me! I'm a poor blind old woman, nooooo." She nodded briskly to Maeldoi. "It will be fine. As you told me yourself, the Northern Rectory is not known for its letters. If I'd tried to sneak in as a weapons master, now. . ."

He laughed. "Mistress Pereta knows all this?"

"Of course."

"And allows it?"

"Of course. When I told her of your fate, I thought she'd jump out of bed and run to the capital and toss my good-for-nothing husband in a dung-heap."

Maeldoi stood and turned carefully away. "Your. . .husband."

"Oh," said Gisa.

"Gisa, I—"

"No," said Gisa. "Stop. Don't say anything. Please don't. Just listen. Will you?"

Maeldoi turned to her. He assumed the pose of Underneath the Winter Rains and waited.

"Maeldoi," cried Gisa. She took him by both shoulders to make him look at her. Carefully, he did. "Let's go outside," she said. She led him by the hand out of the hovel to a grassy patch under a tree, and sat him down there. She sat down close beside him and stared at her hands.

After a moment, she raised her eyes to his. He looked uneasily away. "Maeldoi, hear me as I tell you what was happening outside your cell while inside it those men were tormenting you."

"Very well," he whispered.

"They brought me, with my mother, to the House of Penitence."

Maeldoi had to steady himself. A sick wave rolled over him. "I was afraid they'd do something to you, after we talked that day in the library. And they did."

"You were right about everything, Maeldoi. How they had pre-judged you. How they were waiting to take you. How dangerous it was for you to talk to me."

"And how dangerous for you," he said.

"Yes. In a different way. Yes." She took a deep breath. "A man questioned me. I'm sure you can guess which one."

"Lord Estienn." He dug his nails into his palms. Before his vision rose the man's pig eyes, his sneering mouth.

"Yes. He threatened me. He tried to trip me up. He made me angry, and then I made one small misstep. Nothing that would incriminate you, for there was nothing to incriminate. You'd done nothing wrong. But he knew exactly how to twist my words so it would sound like you'd made an improper connection with me, and that you had stated outright you'd be charged with treason. That you were expecting to be. And you did say those things. Just not for the reason Estienn made the court think you did. He made it sound like you had admitted your guilt to me."

"They believed him. They charged me with treason. And then they were about to—"

She put out a hand. Put it over his mouth. "They didn't, though. Don't say it. Never say it."

"Never saying it won't make it go away. That's what they'll do, when they take me."

"But they won't."

"No? I'm thinking someday they will." He thought of his father, how long it took his band to track his father down, how they did it, how they killed him.

"They won't take you," she insisted. "I won't let them."

He put out a hand to her cheek and ran his fingers down it. "Smooth," he said. "And you smell like flowers. You always do. That's maybe the first thing I noticed about you, when you sat down beside me with a book in your hand and began to teach me."

She gathered him into her arms, and he lay his head on her shoulder. She stroked his hair. Then she brought his face up to hers. "You don't know how to do this, do you?" she said.

He was shaking his head. "No," he said.

"One more thing I get to teach you. Like this," she said, and kissed him.

They sank down together into the grass. She leaned over him, toying with the thong that tied the neck of his tunic.

Abruptly, she sat up. "No," she said. "Do you know how much I've wanted you, Maeldoi? Touching you. Feeling your lips on mine, your skin against my skin. I've had feelings for you that I didn't believe it possible to have. Women gwrgi are not held to have such feelings. That's wrong. We do. I do, anyhow. But now. Now something bad has happened to me. You shouldn't touch me."

He sat up too. He took her hands in his. "Tell me."

"It's too hard. I can't," she said, not meeting his eyes.

"Gisa, I've known the worst. Almost the worst. I've seen the worst. You can tell me, and I'll understand."

"Sir Anselme told me you are as pure as I myself. Only, Maeldoi, I'm not pure."

"Sir Anselme told you that? He tried to help me."

"It destroyed him, Maeldoi."

"Everyone whose life I touch is destroyed, except the ones who mean me ill. So tell me. You're not pure. That's what you say. I don't believe you, Gisa."

"Estienn. Estienn is my husband. Now you see."

Maeldoi closed his eyes. He mastered the rage rising inside him. He folded her hands in his. He mastered himself. When he was sure he had done it, he opened his eyes again.

"I do see. I see how that man operates. I can see perfectly well what he did and said, to make that happen," he said.

"You can't know how—"

"Oh, I do. First he threatened you. I'm thinking he probably threatened your family. They probably panicked. Then they handed you over to him. You became his prisoner, Gisa. Do you think I don't know what that's like? How he tries to break a person?"

"But Sir Anselme said—"

"Let me ask you a question, Gisa. You say the word pure. What do you mean by it? I think I know what you're trying to say, but I think you have it wrong. Sir Anselme called me pure? But then, Sir Anselme knows what my father did to me, in boyhood. I think Sir Anselme meant something different by the word than you think he did."

Maeldoi studied her face. "I don't think I'm pure. And it doesn't have anything to do with some vile act of my father's upon my body. I don't know if you're pure. But if you're not, it has nothing to do with anything anyone did to your body against your will. I've done many things to be ashamed of. I mistreated my brother. The atonement I made for that was real. It's not the only thing I'm ashamed of. One thing I'm not ashamed of. How I feel about you. Allowed or not, how I've always felt about you, from almost the first moment we met." Hesitantly, he put out his hand to her. Laid it on her shoulder. Pulled her closer. "I want to try that thing you did. I want to try it again. What is it, that thing with the lips?"

"It's called kissing, Maeldoi."

"Merlin, we can rest easy," said John Dee, looking below them and pointing. "There's our boy."

Merlin looked. He catapulted from his golden seat, seized Dee by the collar, and hustled him away. "Great jumping Jehoshapat, John. What are you, some dirty-minded old coot? Get away from there. Give them their privacy. Don't look."

"Okay, okay," said Dee. He moved to the other side of their cloud platform.

"And don't grin like that," Merlin growled.

"You old hypocrite. You're trying to hide it, Merlin. Myrddin. Mervin. Whatever they're calling you this week. But you can't fool me. You're grinning too."

CHAPTER TWENTY-NINE

Mad As a Hermit

When they got back into the cart at Gisa's little hut, Maeldoi found he had a hard time taking his hands off her. He didn't want to get in the cart. He wanted to stay there at the hut. *Forever*, he decided. Yes, that was it. Forever.

But they had to get back.

She had moved down to the front of the cart so they could keep a hand on each other. But as they rode in toward the rectory gates, she gently disentangled her hand from his and moved further back, and he put both hands on the mule's reins.

"Fine morning, Mistress Gisa," one of the guards called out as they trundled past.

"Fine indeed," she replied. Then, low, to Maeldoi, "Suppose the whole world can take one look at me and see how I feel? Am I glowing all over?"

Maeldoi looked over his shoulder at her. "Yes," he said, and couldn't stop smiling.

As they toiled up the spiral staircase toward Mistress Pereta, he found himself a bit worried. "Gisa, when we were together in the grass, I didn't know what to do, I am so clumsy. . . "

"Hush it, Maeldoi. You have—" she started to dimple up. "I'd say you have great self-control."

"That's a good thing, in the matter of bodies connecting between man and woman?"

"That's a very good thing." Suddenly laughter came bubbling out of her.

His lips twitched. He had to stifle his own laughter.

By the time they got to the stop of the staircase, they could both control their expressions. Mistress Pereta could see, just a little.

They came to her bedside, where she was sitting up nursing a hot posset. "You two seemed to have had an agreeable morning," she said. Then all three of them burst out laughing, and Gisa had to lunge for the posset cup before it spilled its contents all over Mistress Pereta.

After a while, Maeldoi looked around him uneasily. "I should maybe get myself away from here."

"Certainly not," said Mistress Pereta. "Gisa is my assistant. You're my manservant. You are both perfectly safe here."

"Won't someone in the rectory notice there's a spare servant about the place?"

"When have they ever noticed anything like that? Servants come, servants go, they all look exactly the same to those scholar-teachers with their heads stuck in the clouds, and to those weapons masters with their minds intent on thwacking and stabbing and punching and slashing. The servants have been stealing this place blind for years, right under the noses of their masters, and they'll keep on doing it. When one of them makes enough coin from his thievings to open a little tavern or set up as a smith, he sends in his cousin to take his place, and none the wiser."

"Won't the other servants notice?"

"They may," said Mistress Pereta with a shrug. "But if they do, they'll think only, Mistress Pereta's young and pretty assistant has found a way to sneak her man in here."

Gisa began to giggle.

"They wouldn't be wrong, would they, my dear?"

"No," she said, reaching over for Maeldoi's hand again.

After a moment, Mistress Pereta felt for Maeldoi's other hand, and took it up and squeezed it. "But Maeldoi. Something is wrong. What is it?"

"You mean aside from all the people looking to find me and chop me into little bits."

"You can't fool me, Maeldoi. I learned your moods when you were just a lad. What is it."

"It's Aleron," he said, low.

"Ah," she said. "It always amazes me. You lads endure this place, you can't wait to leave it, but when life deals you a blow, this is the first place you think to come."

"It's because of people like you, Mistress Pereta," said Maeldoi, softly.

"Tush, lad. Well. Poor Aleron. People did chop him to bits. And they damaged him in much worse ways. They destroyed the one he loved and made him watch. That would mark a man."

Maeldoi swallowed hard. After a moment he said, "Aleron helped me, when I was almost beyond help. How can I help him now?"

"Just be with him."

"That's allowed? Beyond speaking through his slot?"

"For the servants tending to his needs, yes. One just quit, yesterday. I don't think he could take it any longer."

"How do I get to Aleron?"

"On the other side of his hermitage, there's a small door. Go in there. From the outside, he is walled in. On the inside, though, he is separated from the world only by the bars of a grille."

"Like a cell," said Maeldoi with a shudder, remembering.

"Yes, my dear one. Like that. And servants bring his food and water and tend to him, through the bars. Once a day, it's allowed."

Maeldoi got up quietly and threaded his way down the stairwell and over to the other side of the big gates. There was the small door. He pushed it open and went in.

The light was very dim. A man sat on a joint stool opposite a wall that was mostly bars, and a tiny space bulging out beyond it from the wall, lit only by any sun that could filter its way through the slot.

"I'm the new one," Maeldoi told the man as he rose from the joint stool.

"Thank the Lady," the man muttered. "I'll bring the food and water from the kitchen. Sit here."

Maeldoi slid into his place. He peered through the bars.

Aleron, in a short tunic, was half reclining on a sort of tilted board. He was strapped to it. Maeldoi put his hand to his mouth. Aleron's legs were twisted and useless, Maeldoi could see. His arms, stick-like, bent at unnatural angles, were held up to his chest by some straps. His face was perfectly serene and un-marked. Older, but Aleron's beloved face. He was staring into nothing.

Maeldoi knew that stare. Aleron was in his meditative trance.

Maeldoi took the pose Waiting Still in the Grass for the Hawk to Pass and sat perfectly quietly.

After a while, the first man opened the door. He reached in a water skin and a basket covered with a cloth. Maeldoi got up from his stool and took these things. He sat back down.

Many moments later, Aleron stirred.

Maeldoi moved close to the bars and crouched there. He un-corked the water skin.

Aleron's eyes flicked to his face. "Maeldoi," he whispered. "You're here. I thought I told you to get away."

"Yes, but I'm back. Water?"

"Yes, please, but you have to reach in and hang it about my neck with that strap."

Maeldoi angled the water skin through the bars. When Aleron lifted his head slightly, Maeldoi slid the water skin in. He eased the strap of it over Aleron's head. Aleron pinchered his arms together to get a grip on the water skin, lowered his mouth to the neck of the skin, and drank. He lay his head back down.

"Want to keep it there?"

"No, take it now."

Maeldoi maneuvered the skin back through the bars. "There's food in this basket."

Aleron's mouth quirked up in a smile. "Remember the day I taught you how to hold a spoon."

"How could I forget."

"I'm afraid you're going to have to feed me that gruel, a spoonful at a time, good friend."

"Here we go," said Maeldoi.

Aleron only ate a few spoonsful before turning his head away. "I don't eat much. The water, though. I'm always thirsty. My mouth gets so dry."

Maeldoi repeated the maneuver with the water skin.

"That's fine. Thanks, Maeldoi."

"Is it allowed, for you to speak to me?"

"Yes, it's not like our vigil. I don't talk very much. I mostly meditate."

"I thought they let you hermits have books."

"Maybe some do. I couldn't hold them, and reading would be hard. I can't hold my head up very long."

"I'll bring some in and read them to you. You wouldn't believe it. I've become a real reader."

"Maeldoi, you need to leave before they find you here."

"They won't. They think I'm a servant."

"It's always been a lax house, that way," said Aleron. "Not for the trainees, though. But Maeldoi, even though you may be able to hide here, you need to go somewhere and live your life."

"My life is here. You're here, and the one I love is here."

"The one you love." An expression of terrible pain crossed Aleron's features.

Maeldoi wished he could reach out and collect his words and stuff them back down his throat."

Aleron turned his eyes to Maeldoi's. "No, don't mistake me. I am so happy that you know love, Maeldoi. Remember? I ordered you to find it. It's just—." He stopped and swallowed hard. "Halde. You heard?"

"Yes," said Maeldoi.

"But I am here in this place to master my feelings about that. I need to. Not root them out. Everything of his inside me I keep and treasure, even that last devastating hurt. But I must master the feeling so it doesn't destroy me. What remains of me." He smiled.

"Aleron, I heard they let you resume your training where you left off. But how in the Nine could you sit your vigil, like—"

"Like this? Easy. I went into my trance state and stayed there. My shaman guide situated me by a stream, so I would have water to drink, and he came by every sen'night to leave food. He had to get a special dispensation to do that, I think."

"But if a wild beast had happened on you—"

"Yes? And then?"

Maeldoi sat silently looking at his hands.

"I prayed for one to happen by. But then I realized that was another weakness I needed to master."

Maeldoi wondered what would have become of him, if his sentence had been carried out, and he had survived it, and he had had to endure life in a cage as a broken lump of flesh. He wouldn't have been able to do it.

Aleron's body had become his cage. Aleron had set out to learn to live in his cage.

"Maeldoi, let me see something."

"What is it?"

"Your hands."

Maeldoi put them through the bars and into Aleron's.

"I can't feel anything with these fingers," he said. He levered Maeldoi's hands to eye level and stared at them. "What did they do to you."

"Those are burns. They would take my hands and put them into the fire. And then they had these pinchers, and—" Maeldoi stopped. A chill crept up his body.

"You can still use your fingers, The Three be praised. What about the rest of you."

"I am scars from neck to ankles, I think."

"Keep them hidden."

"I do." But he thought uneasily of Gisa. Suppose, in spite of everything, he repulsed her?

"What in the Nine did they think they were doing?" Aleron asked.

"They thought I was a traitor. It's because of my brother. Gilles de Rais has him. Somehow, they thought I must be some sort of spy or minion of Gilles. Nothing I could say to them would change their minds."

"So they were going to do that thing to you. The thing they do to traitors."

"They were just about to do it."

"What stopped them?"

"Here's the strange part. I'm not sure. Some men got me away from them, but I don't know how. My mind was a blank. As they took me into the place where they were going to slice me up, I went blank. Not into my trance. I just shut down. And then some men got me out. I don't remember those few days very well. I think Master Bertran was involved somehow. And three other men, very odd men. Especially two of them."

Aleron gave Maeldoi a speculative look. "Did you know that Gilles de Rais is a mage?"

"They tell me he is. I don't even know what that means, not really."

"We're fighting our war against the Lyre Lands. But another war is going on all around us, and we don't even see it. A war among the mages. This is just a guess, Maeldoi, but I think maybe some of the mages opposed to Gilles were the ones who got you out."

"That sounds pretty frightening. Blasting away at each other with wands and such?" Maeldoi thought dubiously of the two men who seemed to have had something to do with his rescue. A man with bright blue eyes and a pointy beard. Another man as dark as those who live in the Burnt Lands. Tall, dark, with a basso profundo voice. No wands, though, that he could remember.

"I don't think it's a war like that," said Aleron. "A stealth war."

"Huh," said Maeldoi.

"I've had strange dreams, in here. One of the mages came to visit me. Bird-mage. Do you know of the mages called ornithomancers? And another time, your brother came to visit me."

"Cae?" cried Maeldoi.

A creaking, grating noise interrupted them.

"Oh," said Aleron. He gave Maeldoi a wry smile. "You might want to step away, for this part. They have this pulley system rigged up, to raise and lower a bucket. You know."

"Nine Spheres, Aleron. As I lay in that cell of mine sen'night after sen'night, fortnight after fortnight, season after season, if only I'd had a bucket, I would have been a happy man."

"Why didn't you go mad?"

"I think I would have, if not for Master Bertran's training. What do poor ordinary criminals do?"

"Go mad."

"Like hermits."

"Like hermits." They grinned at each other.

Maeldoi rose to go. "I'll be back. With books, next time. I'll ask Gisa which to bring."

"Gisa."

"Mistress Pereta's assistant. Mistress Pereta has gone blind."

"I'm sorry to hear it. But Maeldoi, do you know what happens to your face and voice, when you speak this Mistress Gisa's name?"

Maeldoi blushed.

"I'm guessing this Mistress Gisa is your love."

"Yes," said Maeldoi. "I'll be back tomorrow."

He let himself out into the sunlight. Only then could he weep.

A servant emerged from a trap door with a bucket. He stood and looked with scorn at Maeldoi. "None of you lads has a spine. I suppose here's another one who can't take working with the hermit."

Maeldoi dashed the tears from his eyes. "You're wrong, man. I will work every day with the hermit. I'll be back here tomorrow, and the next day, and the next."

"Well, lad. Ye're a good lad after all. That man in there is brave."

"He's the bravest I know," said Maeldoi, turning away, making his way blindly back to the tower and up the stairs.

"Maeldoi," Mistress Pereta called, as he got to the top. "Come here to me."

He stumbled to her bedside and knelt beside it.

She smoothed his hair while he cried.

Then he stood. Gisa had come into the room and was standing quietly at the window.

"I see you are very moved, Maeldoi," she said.

"That man, the hermit, taught me combat skills, but he taught me a lot more. I was a kind of animal, and he taught me how to be a person. Between them, he and Mistress Pereta taught me to read. Then, Mistress Pereta," he said, turning back to the bed, "Mistress Gisa finished the job the two of you began."

"Mistress Gisa is a marvel," said Mistress Pereta.

Maeldoi could smile.

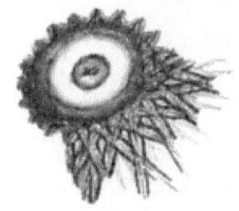

CHAPTER THIRTY

Dreams

N othing ever holds still," said Maeldoi. "Just when you think the world has quieted, and your life has quieted, suddenly there's a jolt."

Gisa nodded soberly. They had returned with the other rectory people from laying poor Mistress Pereta's wasted body to rest on a hill overlooking the red stone rectory tower. All the rectory dead lay there under a grove of trees.

"No peace for anyone," said Maeldoi.

"Except them," Gisa said, gesturing toward the hill.

"Except them."

Mistress Pereta's decline had been subtle at first. Then it progressed swiftly. She died quietly in the night, Gisa holding her hand.

She and Maeldoi walked together back to the library.

Suddenly there was the assistant rector, standing in the path before them. Maeldoi cast his eyes down, tugged at his forelock, stepped aside. On the few occasions he had encountered the assistant rector, the man had shown no signs of recognizing him. Why should he? During his time at the rectory before, the assistant rector had regarded Maeldoi as sort of an animal, a beast of the caves, not this ordinary looking servant. Maeldoi wanted to keep it that way.

"Mistress Gisa, please come with me," said the assistant rector.

"Yes, my lord," said Gisa, following after him without a backward glance at Maeldoi.

Maeldoi trundled away as if heading on his own errand. They had to be careful. If some of the servants suspected how close they were, no matter, but they must make sure none of the rectory's authorities did.

He went up to the tower and waited.

In a while he heard Gisa's light step on the stairs.

She came into the room and sank down on the bench beside him. "Mistress Pereta left the assistant rector a letter recommending me to her post. The rector wants me to accept it."

"That's perfect, Gisa!"

"Almost perfect." She gave him a sidelong glance. "The assistant rector said that now a young woman was in the post,

Mistress Pereta's manservant must be assigned to other duties. It's not fitting he should be in the tower with me."

"We'll find a way to be together anyway, Gisa," said Maeldoi.

"I told him how good you were with the hermit, and what a help the man in charge of the hermit had found you to be. He's reassigning you permanently to Aleron's care."

"See? Perfect."

But he sighed inwardly, and he saw she felt the same. While she was Mistress Pereta's assistant, she had had a tiny room off the main room of the library, and Maeldoi had discreetly moved into it with her. Now that was over, he supposed.

As for Aleron, Maeldoi was already with his friend every day.

"I'm going to move out to the hut," he said after a moment. "You'll make an excuse to go off on some errand each day and meet me there. And we'll see each other in passing, too, as I tend to Aleron. It will be fine."

She nodded. "We can't get careless." She went to a little cabinet. "But as long as you're up here now, let me rub you with the salve. No one comes up here, and if they do, we'll hear them toiling up the staircase long before they arrive."

Obediently Maeldoi took his place at the window and tugged the tunic over his head. "I don't know why you try," he said over his shoulder to her, as she set to work. "I've had some of these scars my entire life."

"Maybe I just like to look at your body and touch it. Ever think of that?"

He had to smile. A secret smile, as he thought of the early days of their love. How he was sure she would be repulsed and appalled by his body. How he had worked up the courage to tell her so. And what she had replied.

How many scars are there, do you think? Let's see how many. I'll kiss each one, and you'll keep the count. Ready?

This would work fine until she got to his hands. She'd massage them both. Then she'd start kissing his fingers. Then she'd start to cry.

"I used to stare at your hands, when I taught you. I used to have to get up and leave the room sometimes. I'd tell you I needed to look something up or find a different book. Then I'd have to collect myself, before I could come back. And now see. They did more harm to you, this last time, when they took you back into their infernal house. They hurt your hands again. They are fiends, and the worst one of all is—"

"Shh," he'd say, putting his finger to her lips. "No saying the name of that man. I don't want to think about him. Just about you."

Later that day, he went to Aleron to tell him about Mistress Pereta.

"I heard. I'm sorry for it. She was a fine old woman, and she loved you, Maeldoi. She was good to me, too."

"Now she's across that river."

"Child give her peace," said Aleron.

"Do you think the Children watch over us gwrgi?" said Maeldoi.

"I'm not sure. I know we are especially beloved of The Three, but They are a remote and frightening god."

"How is the pain today?" said Maeldoi, after a moment.

"Oh, you know. It's always there. The mental exercises help me with it. Maeldoi, do you remember the day you first got here? Not when you were a boy. This time."

"The day I spoke into your slot?"

"Yes. Do you remember what I said to you?"

"Yes, but I've never understood it."

"I've been thinking about it. I didn't understand it, either. It was something that came to me in my trance state, and I remember thinking how odd I'd have a sort of dream about you, because I hadn't seen you in so long and I doubted I'd ever see you again. And then, that very day, there you stood."

"You told me about an opportunity I'd be offered, and that I must take it. Something about a place called the Undercroft. I didn't know what that meant."

"Neither did I. I've meditated on it. I've dreamed about it again. I think I know a little more about it, now." Aleron paused. A coughing racked his body.

Maeldoi hated this part the most. He wanted to reach through the bars to steady his friend. Whenever he tried, he couldn't reach far enough in to be much help. He had to sit helpless and watch and listen. He worried that one day Aleron would choke and he'd have to watch while his friend died. Summoning help would do no good. Aleron was shut into his little hermitage, and he wouldn't be coming out, and no one would be able to get in. The day Aleron left his hermitage would be the day some big men with sledges and mauls would break through the bricks and hoist his dead body out of it.

The coughing fit subsided. As these episodes left Aleron, he would be so weak he could barely speak. Maeldoi sat absolutely still, hoping Aleron would drift off to sleep, as he often did after-ward, and not try to talk. He worried that Aleron was growing weaker.

This time, though, Aleron rallied. He summoned up the strength to speak. "No, don't try to stop me. Let me tell you my thoughts, in case the day comes when I can't."

Maeldoi hitched his joint stool closer to the bars, resolutely turning his mind away from Aleron's words. *In case the day comes when I can't.*

"The Undercroft. I realized I did know what that was. Have you ever heard of the Dark Rider?"

Maeldoi thought. He shook his head. "No, I don't think so."

"It's the oddest of all the special tasks a gwrgi may profess."

"Odder than the Hermitage?" said Maeldoi.

Aleron laughed. "If you can believe it, yes. It too involves im-muring yourself and never coming out. In a different way than this."

"Tell me about it."

"There's a special class of eala. They live underground, in a place called The Undercroft."

"I thought they all flew through the air on wings, like swans."

"I suppose most of them do. I don't know very much about the eala."

"Nor I," said Maeldoi. "I read a book once. It said they dazzled the eye, that they are too bright to look on."

"These eala of the Undercroft aren't like that, I don't think, and they aren't winged. They are women, and they are all hunt-resses. They are ruled by a man, the Silver King. Every turning of the moon, when the moon comes to full, they ride out, a vast silver sweep of them."

"The Wild Hunt!" Maeldoi breathed. "When I was a boy, my mother showed them to me once. We went out under the moon, onto the moors. We climbed the tor, and hid ourselves, and watched."

"That's a rare sight, Maeldoi. Very few can say they've seen them. When they go on their Wild Hunt, they have one task, to kill a white stag. Somehow, this symbolic act maintains the balance that holds up the Spheres."

"How would it do that?"

"I don't know. Death and beauty? Opposites in tension. That's the principle that holds up the Spheres, or so we are always taught, and that's what happens in the Wild Hunt. The Huntresses and the Silver King are all eala, but the hunt for the white stag is carried out by the Dark Rider, always. The Huntresses are women. He is a man. And he is the opposite of an eala."

"Gwrgi."

"Yes. There's only one Dark Rider. He is bound to the Hunt for his lifetime. It's a very ancient rite. An arduous task. What task did you profess, Maeldoi, when you came to make your profession."

"I was not allowed to. The man behind the desk named me Professed At Large."

"I've never heard of such a thing," said Aleron.

"I think it's because. . . well, I passed every one of their tests and conditions, and so they couldn't refuse me the status of Professed. But they had no intention of allowing me a task."

"Ah. It was a delaying tactic."

"I was being watched all the time. They were waiting for an excuse to take me. Then they found it, they charged me with treason, and the whole matter was moot."

"What task would you have chosen, do you think?"

"You know, after everything, even if they hadn't charged me with treason, I was under such a cloud that I would have been given a lesser task, or some task that would have utterly shut me away. I decided they'd force me into the Hermitage."

Aleron laughed. "The Hermitage would have stood up in force and called down the wrath of The Three upon them, if they had tried it."

"I know that now. No one enters the Hermitage unless he has chosen it for himself."

"And you undertake a lengthy process of discernment to make sure you go into enclosure with open eyes, and that no one has coerced you into it or pressured you in any way."

"Suppose you change your mind," said Maeldoi with a shiver.

"Too bad for you, if you do. You don't come out. You can never come out. I heard a story once. An enemy had overrun a part of some land with a gwrgi institution."

"Like the rectory."

"Yes. And they all have their hermit, do they not?"

"Yes."

"These enemies killed all the gwrgi. They broke open the hermitage and demanded the hermit come out. He refused. They burned down the building with the hermit still inside."

"Would you do that?"

"I don't see myself standing up and walking out of here," said Aleron with a wry smile.

Maeldoi could tell Aleron was weary. "That's all very interesting, Aleron. Especially about the Wild Hunt. It calls up an old memory from childhood. I'll leave you now, so you can sleep."

"Maeldoi. My message to you, though the slot. In my trance, I saw a vision. Do you remember the moment, in boyhood, when you realized that you and your horse were one creature? In my dream, Maeldoi, you were the Dark Rider. That was your special task."

Aleron's voice trailed away. His eyes closed. He went deeply into an exhausted sleep.

Maeldoi crept away.

He was troubled. The visions of a hermit in his trance were supposed to be sacred, so he knew he should take Aleron's words seriously.

But himself as Dark Rider?

He could imagine the deep pleasure it would give him to make a connection with a horse as noble as the one he imagined the Dark Rider rode. But to be parted from Gisa forever? That he'd never do.

Never.

The authorities would have to tear him limb from limb before he'd do it.

With a chill, he realized that's exactly what they had in mind. Not the Dark Rider part. Just the dismemberment.

Suppose Aleron's vision wasn't to be taken literally.

Suppose it meant that they'd catch him. They'd mutilate him. They'd put him in his own traitor's enclosure, and there he'd hang for the rest of his days.

◁◉▷

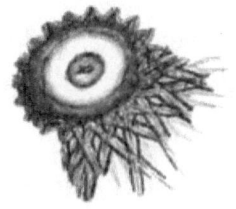

CHAPTER THIRTY-ONE

Up to Their Necks

A rider was coming up the road, and Maeldoi was walking down it, making his way to the abandoned little hut Gisa had found tucked away in the woods. Their hut now. He had finished his allotted candle-measure with Aleron. As soon as she could get away from her own duties, Gisa would join him. His heart was light.

Not as light when he thought of Aleron, though. He always hated leaving his friend, especially now, when Aleron seemed to be growing frailer.

It was a privilege to care for him. He never complained. One time, though, he whispered, "I'm so dirty."

Once a moon or so, the servants had taken to throwing a pail of water over him. The first time he saw this, Maeldoi had dashed the pail out of the servant's hands in a fury. The man had slunk away.

Aleron was laughing weakly. "Maeldoi, that's the only way I can get clean. They can't come in here to bathe me."

"But it chills you."

Even in the hot weather they were having just then, Maeldoi saw Aleron flinch back from the shock of it.

So then Maeldoi rigged up a way to get Aleron clean. The water, warmed. The only way to get it on him was to toss it through the bars, so that had to be done. But Maeldoi fastened a bunch of tow to a stick and lathered it well with soap. He could reach in through the bars, and Aleron could twist about. It worked well. A second bucket of warmed water rinsed him off.

"I shouldn't be thinking of bodily pleasures," Aleron said, afterward. "But that was fine, Maeldoi."

Maeldoi thought up other little conveniences.

Even so, he could see that Aleron was growing weaker.

"It's well with me, Maeldoi," Aleron whispered. "When it's my time, don't grieve. Promise me you won't."

"I won't promise you that," Maeldoi had growled.

Thinking of these things, Maeldoi wasn't really listening to the approaching rider. Now he realized with a start that the rider was nearing. The road was narrow, so Maeldoi stepped off it to let the man go past. But the man on the horse swerved around and leaped out of the saddle. He thrust a piece of parchment into

Maeldoi's hand and re-mounted. Rode off in a dust cloud that left Maeldoi choking behind him.

Choking, puzzled, a bit frightened. The turn-off to the hut was ahead. He hurried down it, glad to get off the road and into the forested land, where he felt more hidden and secure.

At the hut, he opened the parchment. His lips moved as he read the message.

Brother, he read. *I have found your hiding place. My master the Baron Gilles de Rais knows where you are. In the next town, there is a tavern. Come to me there tomorrow, and I will take you to Gilles. It will be much the better if you come with me willingly. If you do not, the woman you love will be killed, and you will be seized in spite of any attempt of yours to resist or flee. To avoid endangering the woman called Gisa, do not tell her of this. Tell no one. I can't vouch for the results if you do.*

Caedon.

Maeldoi felt his blood freeze. It was the last thing he was expecting. He'd opened the parchment fearing it was some sort of warning he was about to be taken up for treason. But this. This might be just as dangerous, in its way. It must be a bluff, for how would Gilles or even Cae be able to accomplish the threat. He was certainly not going off to some tavern in the next town.

But the message was still dangerous to him. If there were a copy, and the Penance Board had one, what would they make of it but more evidence against him? Worse, against Gisa. They wouldn't care if the letter implied he was coerced. They'd see the connection they were looking for.

He stepped to the lone window of the hut and looked out. All was quiet. Sunshine dappled the meadow grasses around the hut. A mist hung underneath the trees, making the perimeter around the hut sparkle.

How long before Gisa arrived, he thought, panicking. Maybe he should flee. He'd have to try it. But he'd need to let her know why he'd left so suddenly.

Otherwise, she'd run mad.

He was thinking hard. In case the threat to her was real, she'd need to hide. Maybe not here at the hut. The rider had come too close to it. Maybe Cae and this baron knew where it was. She could tell the assistant rector a sick cousin needed her. She could get away for a while, until the danger had blown over.

He would tell her as soon as she arrived at the hut.

"Ah, lad," said a voice just at his ear, in a conversational, kindly tone. "I see you're not taking your brother's message seriously. And here you are, thinking of running. I feared you'd want to run. That won't happen."

The mist had somehow infiltrated the hut. Now it infiltrated him, reeking of rot and death.

"She'll be here soon, won't she? Gisa. A lovely young woman. You don't have even a candle-measure before she's here. How much better for you, and for her, too, if you'd simply walked to the next town and handed yourself over to me. A gift freely given. The best gift. Instead, I'll take you now. So which will it be? A struggle that endangers her? Or come quietly with me."

"Who are you?" Maeldoi choked out.

"Come now, Maeldoi. Do you have to ask?"

The mist was suffocating Maeldoi. It twined about him, held him. He couldn't move. He knew the thing that had him so securely bound was Gilles de Rais.

"Decide now, Maeldoi. If I'm not mistaken, your lovely young woman has turned down the path to the hut already." The mist cleared a little. Maeldoi saw a shape coming toward the hut. Gisa. "Quickly, Maeldoi. You see my power. You see how easily I can end her. Instead, let me take you. An exchange, Maeldoi. You for her. A simple Yes will give me your consent."

"Maeldoi!" he heard Gisa call.

"Yes," he choked out. The world went dark.

"I was afraid of this," Merlin told Dee.

They sat around glumly.

Gilles had Maeldoi.

"There's only one thing for it. Gilles is going to try to use Maeldoi against the gwrgi, just as the Penance Board feared he was doing. They thought about it the wrong way round, but there it is. Gilles is indeed using Caedon against them. They were right about that. It's not enough for Gilles, that he has Caedon. You see his problem."

"Yes, I believe I do," said Dee. "Gilles needs Caedon elsewhere. He needs to use Caedon to capture power in the Sceptered Isle and then the Baronies. Maybe the Ice-realm. The Fire Isle for certain. So here's Maeldoi, and he has him now. Maeldoi is the weapon he'll send against the gwrgi. Gilles is not content to take over the ordinary folk of the realms. He's going after the other kinds. We see he has the witches. Now he is making inroads against the eala and gwrgi."

"And the mages." Merlin regarded Dee soberly. "He has his little acolytes. Even with them beside him, he's still no match for you and me, John. Our joined power."

"And the power of the virtuous mages ranged beside us. Little Bird. All the rest."

"Thank The Three for them. With Caedon, though, Gilles has a good hold on the gwrgi. With Maeldoi, even more, especially if he can place Maeldoi in the Undercroft."

"That's the key, isn't it. He'll do it through the Undercroft," said Dee.

"I'm almost certain of it. The Silver King, I'm afraid, is far gone in corruption. Gilles is already using Ailys, Queen of the Sceptered Isle, to help him with the king. If Gilles can place Maeldoi as Dark Rider, he'll have another inroad there, against the gwrgi and the eala both." Merlin stalked back and forth. "Dark Ones take that Penance Board."

"The gwrgi are the Dark Ones, Merlin. That's what the term means."

"I know that," Merlin snapped. "Let me think." After a moment, "I'm sorry, John," he said. "I'm just so worried. About Maeldoi, of course. But Gilles's grand plan worries me. He's tampering with the balance of the Spheres themselves. If he were just posturing. But no. He means business."

"I know, Merlin. I know how worried you are. I am, too."

"We need to get back to Lord Jouhan again. Get his help with the Penance Board."

"A tall order, Merlin. I'm not sure how friendly Lord Jouhan feels towards us, after we let Maeldoi escape. He lost face over that little episode."

"Yes. But if we can get Lord Jouhan to see this in the right way, I think we can thwart Gilles. So listen. Maeldoi is professed, yet he has never been assigned. That means his rite of profession is not complete. If the gwrgi can assign him to the Undercroft through the proper rite, then he'll be beholden to them, not Gilles. And once he is there, Gilles won't be able to touch him."

"But for that, the gwrgi will have to get to Maeldoi themselves," objected Dee. "And when they do, they're just as likely to seize him and carry out that treason order as help us with some cloudy matter about the Spheres."

"We need Lord Jouhan. We need to explain it all to him. He's a very intelligent man. Anyway, the worst has already happened. Gilles has gotten his filthy hands on our boy."

"No, Merlin. The worst would be that Penance Board chopping Maeldoi's fingers off, tongue out—"

"I don't need the whole catalogue, Dee. What about Gilles sucking Maeldoi dry and turning him into a shell of himself? You think that's actually better?"

"They're both pretty bad," Dee muttered. "Well, then," he said. "Let's get ourselves to Lord Jouhan."

As before, they went to the go-between mage Maciotus and slid into Lord Jouhan's headquarters invisible beside him as he showed the safe-conduct amulet to the guards.

"Here you are again, sir mage," said Lord Jouhan. His eyes were hostile.

"Indeed, my lord," said Maciotus, with a bow. "And I have brought my superiors with me."

Merlin and Dee revealed themselves.

Lord Jouhan paled, but he kept his self-possession. "Welcome, lord mages," he said.

"Lord Jouhan," said Merlin, inclining his head. Dee did the same.

"Lord Jouhan, you may recall the plight of a young gwrgi named Maeldoi a year or so back."

"Of course, my lords," murmured Jouhan with perfect courtesy, but his mouth drew down and his eyes glittered.

"We had a little trouble with the lad," said Merlin.

"Indeed," said Jouhan, with a stiff smile. "You all gave me assurances that once Maeldoi was out of the hands of the Penance Board, we would be allowed to deal with his case in a more humane and reasonable manner. That wasn't what happened, however."

"Regrettably no. I must tell you, it wasn't the lad's fault."

"Yet he ran from our justice."

"He did," said Merlin. "He was in a terrible state."

"Near catatonic," Dee put in.

Merlin threw him a warning look. "Lord Jouhan," he continued smoothly, distracting him from the confusion that Dee's psychological terms always threw the people on this plane into. "Far be it from the mages to interfere with the gwrgi justice system. The Three would be most displeased if we did. Unfortunately, the situation involves more than a simple miscarriage of justice. That's never good, of course, but justice systems aren't perfect, and we mages don't need to supervise the other kinds, eala, gwrgi, ordinary folk, what have you. You're all perfectly capable of supervising yourselves."

"Thank you, lord mage," said Jouhan. "But if we're not talking about an injustice done to our young gwrgi, and then his very unfortunate flight, what are we talking about? I'm afraid his flight had bad consequences," he went on, before Merlin could answer his question. "I'm afraid his flight just confirmed the Penance Board in their suspicions, and it undermined my authority."

Now, Merlin could see, Jouhan's anger was rising. *He's highly trained, though,* Merlin thought. *He won't let it get the better of him.* "Let me just say this, Lord Jouhan. The Penance Board's suspicions are correct. They're just not correct about the nature of Maeldoi's involvement."

"What could your meaning be, lord mages?" said Jouhan, his mouth in a tight line.

"Gilles de Rais is indeed trying to destroy the gwrgi, and he is indeed using Maeldoi to do it. But Lord Jouhan—" Merlin raised a hand to prevent Jouhan's outburst. In spite of his training, here it came.

Merlin talked over the gwrgi lord. "Maeldoi refuses to cooperate with such a thing. At first, just as he maintained, he didn't even know who Gilles de Rais was. The day his brother interrupted his vigil was the first day he began to realize. Yes, his brother is Gilles's creature. Maeldoi is not and never has been, and there's not a shred of real evidence to implicate him. Yet the Penance Board tried to torture him into admitting he was such a traitor. As you might imagine, Maeldoi has conceived a profound distrust of gwrgi justice. His flight makes perfect sense.

What do you imagine would happen to him if the Penance Board got him back into its cells? I know we all hoped the secular justice system would serve as a counterweight, and Maeldoi's name would be cleared. But he didn't trust that. I think you can see why he didn't."

"I suppose I see," said Jouhan, getting himself in hand and looking deeply unhappy.

"Now the worst has happened. Gilles has seized Maeldoi and is about to deploy him against the gwrgi. Totally against Maeldoi's will, I might add."

"That's why we're here," said Dee.

"I see," said Jouhan.

"I think we have one chance to retrieve the situation, but it will require your cooperation," said Merlin. "Gilles is about to try to insert Maeldoi into the Undercroft. Gilles has managed to corrupt the Silver King."

"Corrupt the eala. My, my. And they so virtuous and all."

"Well, as you probably know, the gwrgi have contributed the Dark Rider to the Undercroft time out of mind to prevent exactly that high-handed behavior the eala sometimes so unfortunately exhibit. But Gilles has managed to tilt the balance. And he'll tilt it further if he can get Maeldoi installed there under his own control."

"I begin to see the problem, lord mages."

"I think we can regain control if we get Maeldoi professed as Dark Rider before Gilles can implement his plan."

"Maeldoi is professed. Yes, I recall now. He had gone through every step, battling setbacks and adversity, and he had finally reached profession when he was charged with treason."

"Very wrongly charged," Dee said.

"He was professed, but given no task," said Merlin. "So the rite of profession remains incomplete. I believe we have a chance here. If the gwrgi profess him as Dark Rider, he'll be under the protection of The Three. That's a weapon—and a safeguard for Maeldoi—that Gilles will understand too well. Mess with The Three, bring his plan to Their attention, and he could destroy himself."

Lord Jouhan was nodding along.

"Let's say something goes wrong and Gilles inserts him into the Undercroft before you gwrgi can act," Merlin continued. "He's about to do it. He has suborned the Silver King. Knowing Maeldoi, if Gilles were to place him there, he'd fight Gilles with everything in him. I'm just afraid Gilles would be able to encroach himself on Maeldoi there. Few are strong enough to resist Gilles. Lord Dee here and I together must exert our utmost power against him to keep him in line." Merlin stalked back and forth, drawing his robe tight about him, deep in thought. "But if Maeldoi is professed before he goes in, and professed under the proper gwrgi rite, the attention of The Three will be drawn to him. That's what the rite does, am I correct?"

Jouhan nodded. "The priest elevates the newly professed to the attention of The Three and places him beneath The Three's protection."

"The Three will have Their eye on him. And Gilles won't want that. He'll have to back off. So will you help us, Lord Jouhan?" Merlin looked at him earnestly.

"I'm still unclear about this. I thought Maeldoi was already professed," said Jouhan. "That was part of the Penance Board's urgency. Not an ordinary traitor. One of the professed committing treason. Doubly scandalous, doubly dangerous. But you say Maeldoi's rite of profession remains incomplete."

"Professed, but not to a task. Profession At Large, it was called," said Dee.

"Poor lad. That was a ruse of the Penance Board, I'm afraid, to frighten us all into agreeing to the charge of treason," said Jouhan, and now Merlin saw he truly was angry. "Let's get him professed to the Undercroft, my lord mages. I'll begin the process."

"What about the Penance Board?" said Dee.

Lord Jouhan looked grim. "Let me deal with them. They have overstepped their authority. They have acted in bad faith, against their own vows of profession. There will be consequences for that."

"I'm glad to hear it. But this matter of Maeldoi has reached the point of utmost urgency. Let us meet at the gwrgi portal to the Undercroft. Dee has discovered Gilles will bring Maeldoi to the Silver King there in three days' time. It will be a near thing. Let us pray to The Three that we can bring this off," said Merlin. "If Gilles can insert him into the Undercroft with all of the rites of bondage before we can, even though it's irregular, it will be binding on Maeldoi, and he'll be lost to us," Merlin went on. "If we can get there in time, and insert him with the proper rite of profession, Gilles will not be able to touch him."

"Lord mages." Jouhan bowed to the two of them. Then Merlin and Dee, with Maciotus in tow, whisked away.

"I hope to the Nine this works," said Dee. He dropped his voice. "You're wrong, you know, that Gilles won't still be able to get to Maeldoi."

"Yes, but he'll do it at vastly more risk to himself. That's what I'm counting on. That he won't care to take that risk and tip his hand. Anyway, if our plan doesn't work, we're all in danger, none more so than that poor lad," said Merlin.

"We could just get ourselves into Gilles's lair and take Maeldoi away from him," said Dee.

"If only we could," said Merlin. "You and I together. Maybe out in the open, we could take Gilles on. Inside his castle, with all his wards and spells? I think we'd fail."

"A good chance we would," Dee agreed, gloom descending on him.

"A risk we don't have the luxury of taking," said Merlin. "As for the eala themselves." He sighed. "We can't march down into the Undercroft, either. It would avail nothing. Once Maeldoi is there, he stays there, however he got there, irregular means or official."

"They have some spooky thing they do to those who come there, so that they may never leave. Something with seeds."

"Yes," said Merlin. "Besides, to violate the sovereignty of the eala—it's hard enough with the gwrgi. The eala! They are so touchy. Nine Spheres. They'll rise in their legions and declare war. We'll have one chance, in the open air, as the transfer is being made."

"One chance," echoed Dee. "And meanwhile, that young girl is crying her eyes out. What's to be done about that, hey?"

Merlin shook his head. "Regrettable. Nothing we can do."

"Does she even know where Maeldoi went to?"

"I doubt it," said Merlin. "I do indeed. But Dee, perhaps you could—"

"Say no more," said Dee.

"What am I doing?" Merlin practically moaned. "We're not to interfere, yet here we are, up to our necks."

"Yes, here we are," said Dee. "When has it ever been any different?"

He went off whistling to see about Gisa.

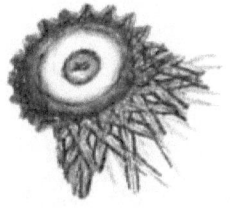

CHAPTER THIRTY-TWO

Stand-off

T here," said Gilles, pointing. "The portal. That's where we're to meet the Silver King and his Head High Huntress. They'll bind you, Maeldoi, and then they'll take you to the Undercroft with them. But all along, you'll really be mine."

Bind me, thought Maeldoi. *Not like these bonds.* He looked down at himself, his arms strapped tight to his torso with leather bands. *When Gilles says they'll bind me, he means something else.*

His brother rode close beside him in case he started to topple off his mount.

Well, he thought, *I spent a lot of my youth learning to guide my horse with my knees only. I spent the best part of my youth in kinship with horses.* He wondered whether he could pelt off across the countryside and escape his captors.

"No, you won't be able to do that," Gilles said over his shoulder to Maeldoi.

So it was true.

Gilles read his thoughts, thought Maeldoi in despair. Even those did not belong to him any longer.

"That's right, boy," said Gilles. "They belong to me. Everything you thought was yours belongs to me, including that young woman, so you'd do well to remember it and not put her in danger. There they are, Caedon. The Silver King and the Head High Huntress. Let's head over there and hand your brother over."

"Look at you," Cae said scornfully to Maeldoi, aside, as they took their mounts over at a walk toward the portal. "You look like a servant. Gilles doesn't keep me like a servant."

Maeldoi didn't respond to his brother's taunts.

"Cae," he said, low. "What did he do to me? What was that vile thing?"

"Oh, that," said Cae. He looked angry. "Gilles promised me he wasn't going to. But when it came right down to it, he couldn't resist just a taste of you."

Maeldoi wondered if he would vomit. He hadn't been able to keep anything in his stomach for a few days, ever since Gilles took him and did—what?—to him.

"He says you leave a bitter aftertaste." Cae laughed. "Me, he can't get enough of me."

"Are you boasting back there, Caedon? Bring your brother up here." Gilles sounded annoyed, and Cae hurried to comply.

Gilles circled back to them. "Better cut him from his bonds. We don't want those addlepated eala to think we've coerced him. The Silver King knows, of course, but his Head High Huntress is a stickler."

Gilles rode on ahead to greet the king and the woman riding beside him.

Cae steered himself and Maeldoi into a thicket and removed the leather bands.

As Maeldoi tensed to make a break for it, Cae hissed a warning. "Don't try it, brother. If you do, that woman of yours will be a dead woman, and don't think Gilles can't get that done. No matter where she thinks she's hidden herself."

"It took you a long time to find me," said Maeldoi, gauging his chances and putting his hands on the reins.

"But now he can track her. Through you. He has your essences. He can find her in less than an instant."

Maeldoi slackened his hands on the reins. This time, he didn't think Cae's words were a bluff.

This time, he believed his brother.

"Take it slowly, Maeldoi. We're riding over to them. When the Silver King asks if you consent, say yes. I'm warning you. Better do it. Whatever fopdoodle rite they make you undergo, do it."

I underwent penance for you, Cae. They told me I made you like this, Maeldoi cried out inside himself

And a good thing for me you did. It made my task so much easier. Gilles's words in his head were almost amiable.

"Cae," said Maeldoi. One last desperate play at hazards. "Do you really want to live like this? Debased, that man's creature?"

He felt a pain in his gut so sharp he doubled over in the saddle.

Get yourself over here, Maeldoi. Now Gilles's voice was vicious.

"When have you ever cared, brother?" said Cae, and rode up to meet the others.

Maeldoi's horse took him to them. He reeled in the saddle.

The Silver King, tall and imposing, as pale as the moon, with long lank hair as silvery as her beams, stared past Gilles. "That's the Dark Rider? He looks drunk."

"A bit indisposed," Gilles purred. "He'll be fine. Dismount and kneel to His Majesty, Maeldoi."

Cae stepped to Maeldoi and yanked him out of the saddle. He shoved Maeldoi in the back, and Maeldoi sank to his knees.

"Disappointing," said the king, "But I suppose he'll have to do. You vouch for him, Gilles?"

"Most heartily."

"Well, then," said the king. He turned to his second. "May I present Head High Huntress Théodrate?"

She inclined her head to Gilles.

She didn't bother to acknowledge Cae. She was haughty, strong-boned. She glowed as if she were made of brass, burnished to a high shine.

Maeldoi's gaze strayed from her to her mount. The horse was magnificent. He remembered the Hunt, as he and his mother watched it thunder by them.

"Head High Huntress Théodrate will conduct the rite of transfer. I assume this man has been properly professed after training in the way of the gwrgi," said the king.

"He has," said Gilles.

"This is a bit irregular, Your Majesty," Maeldoi heard the woman named Théodrate murmur to her king. "Usually it's a representative of the gwrgi who brings a new Dark Rider."

"Were you with us when our old Dark Rider came to us?"

"No, Your Majesty, as you know well."

"But I was. You can trust that I know what I'm doing, Head High Huntress Théodrate."

"Of course, Your Highness," said Théodrate.

She reached for a small chest tied to the cantle of her horse's saddle. She took it down, opened it.

Maeldoi tried to quiet himself inside.

Tried to enter the pose Waiting Still in the Grass for the Hawk to Pass.

It was no use.

Gilles had done something to him. His heart was drumming against the inside of his chest as if about to burst out of him.

She came to him as he knelt in anguish. "What is your name?"

"Maeldoi."

"Maeldoi, Dark Rider, you will be bound to the Wild Hunt for the rest of your natural life, a conduit between gwrgi and eala. Are you professed among the gwrgi?"

"Yes," he choked out.

"Do you consent to be bound to the Wild Hunt as your professed task?"

Maeldoi thought desperately of Gisa.

Beyond Théodrate, Gilles de Rais's mouth curved in a malicious smile, and he exchanged a complicit glance with the Silver King.

Maeldoi opened his mouth to say yes.

"No. He does not," thundered a voice.

Startled, Maeldoi rose to his feet.

Someone materialized just beside him and steadied his elbow. A man with piercing blue eyes and a pointed beard.

Gilles de Rais and the man who had spoken were facing off. Another who had suddenly appeared. It seemed to Maeldoi, looking from this newcomer to Gilles and back, that their bodies were lengthening, broadening, growing larger. Their eyes bored into one another's.

"Stand down, Gilles," the newcomer said, bristling and sparking with power.

Between them strode another man. A gwrgi.

I know this man, thought Maeldoi suddenly.

He remembered seeing him once, as war was declared. Lord Jouhan, chief of the Grand High Council of Gwrgi.

"Your Majesty," said Lord Jouhan, bowing faultlessly to the Silver King and introducing himself. "It seems there was an irregularity in Maeldoi's profession. I am here to rectify that, so that your rite may go forward. But I must insist it be conducted according to the laws of the gwrgi. Otherwise, I am sorry to tell you, it will be my obligation to bring the matter before the altar of The Three."

The Silver King's pale face grew paler still.

"You have brought the implements for the rite?" Lord Jouhan looked to Head High Huntress Théodrate.

"Your Lordship, I have." Head High Huntress Théodrate bowed low. "The eala salute you and honor you and your kind."

The two mages who were engaged in their stand-off—for now Maeldoi could see that's what the other must be, and he knew Gilles for a mage—had settled back into the more usual forms.

Gilles stepped aside, throwing his hands in the air. "Far be it from me to interfere with the proper conduct of the rite," he said. But his eyes had narrowed to gimlet points of fire.

For a moment, joy had risen in Maeldoi. The one who had faced off against Gilles, the one who had appeared beside him. These were the men who had rescued him before. The mages. They were here to rescue him now.

But he realized, all in a rush, that no, they weren't.

He looked aside to the one at his elbow. The man's blue eyes were full of sympathy.

"She'll be safe this way," he whispered to Maeldoi.

He knew he had to go through with it. Give his consent.

Lord Jouhan crooked a finger.

Maeldoi went to him and knelt at his feet.

"Trainee, your profession was cruelly and unfairly interrupted. Now it may continue. You have acquitted yourself with all honor. Maeldoi, the gwrgi salute you. Do you seek to be professed?"

"I do, my lord."

"Rise, Maeldoi, Professed of the Gwrgi."

Maeldoi stood.

"Maeldoi, the gwrgi ask of you a special task, to become one of the go-betweens, to mediate between our kind and others. In this special task, you will be asked to bind yourself to the

Undercroft for the term of your natural life, to serve as Dark Rider for the Wild Hunt of the eala. Do you accept this task?"

"I do, my lord."

"Freely and without reservation?"

This must have been what it was like for Aleron, when he professed himself into the Hermitage, Maeldoi thought. And this was what Aleron's vision meant.

"Freely and without reservation," he said, keeping his voice steady.

"Do you dedicate your life to the service of The Three?"

"I dedicate my life to that service."

Lord Jouhan nodded to Head High Huntress Théodrate, who came forward with her chest.

She put it down on the grass between herself and Maeldoi, and opened it. She took out a small golden plate on which Maeldoi saw a glowing red fruit. With a silver knife from the chest, she sliced it precisely in half. The two halves fell apart, revealing a glistening interior full of seeds.

She made a definitive motion with her hand. Maeldoi knew he was to kneel, and he did. She took out a silver long-handled spoon.

"Open your mouth, Dark Rider," she said to Maeldoi.

He opened it.

She fed him the seeds, and he ate them while she counted them.

"Rise, Dark Rider," she said after she had counted out twelve into his mouth. "You are bound to the Wild Hunt of the eala for the period of your natural life or until dismissed by the Silver King. Follow us into the portal."

She picked up her chest and the reins of her horse, and led the way down a passage carved into the hillside.

Until dismissed by the Silver King, he said to himself.

Maybe he could get that done, and then he'd be free.

Not likely, lad. The words echoed into his mind. *Besides, dismissal usually means the King has decided to kill you.* Not Gilles's voice. Someone else's, the mage named Merlin.

So his path was set, and there was no escape.

He squared his shoulders and moved down into the dark.

Part VII: WILD HUNT

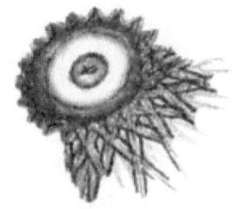

CHAPTER THIRTY-THREE

Settling In

Maeldoi knew from his experiences in the cells of the House of Penitence that a person can get used to almost anything. Maybe not live comfortably there, but know what to expect and accommodate to it.

As cells went, his pit in the Undercroft was fairly comfortable. It wasn't a cell, not exactly. He could leave it and walk around in the Undercroft. But it unnerved the eala if he did, and then they'd send some of the orderlies to politely escort him back to his pit.

He had a hearth and a bench and a bucket kept filled with fresh water by the orderlies. At morning and night, they brought him food from the Undercroft's massive kitchen. It was nourishing, filling, and often quite good. He never ate with the Huntresses or with the many people kept in the Undercroft to serve them.

When he first got there, a wardrobe sister accompanied by several orderlies arrived at the lip of his pit and looked down into it.

He got up from his bench and bowed to them.

"Dark Rider, we are here to measure you for clothing," said the sister. Later he learned her name was Sister Annet.

"Come down, then, and welcome to you, Sister." He knew by then the proper address for her.

Assisted by her orderlies, she came down into the pit using the footholds chopped into one of its walls.

He assumed the pose Welcoming the Sunrise, standing erect, arms slightly outstretched, and she scurried about him measuring him with her tape.

He could see she was shaking with fright.

He stood quietly, hoping she would see he was no threat to her, but he didn't think he had succeeded.

She whisked back up the wall with her orderlies and away down some corridor. A few days later, one of the orderlies returned and lowered clothing to him in a basket.

Maeldoi nodded his thanks and took the clothing.

There were three identical suits of black. A tunic with a high neck and tight-fitting sleeves extending to the wrists. Black leggings to the ankles. Black cloth shoes. Black gauntlets for his hands. A black band to keep his dark hair off his face.

In addition to the three suits, a stout black cloak with a hood.

The cloak was especially welcome. From his central room with the hearth and the bench radiated corridors. He wasn't sure how far back they extended. Most tapered out after a while, but a few looked like they bored into the dark and led he wasn't sure where.

He had chosen one of these tunnels for a sleeping place, but he slept on the hard rock surface, and he was cold. Now he had his cloak to wrap himself in.

The orderly still stood at the lip of the pit.

Maeldoi looked up. "Tell Sister Annet I thank her," he called to the lad.

"Sister says, put your old clothes in the basket and I will draw it up."

Maeldoi stepped into the corridor, changed into one of the sets of black clothing, and emerged to put his old servants' clothes in the basket. That was the last he saw of them.

The tunic and leggings were soft leather and fit him like a second skin, and the gloves as well. The shoes were cloth and the cloak, good wool. *The Undercroft encases me*, he thought, *and now I am encased in these clothes, too.* Layers and layers between himself and freedom. Between himself and Gisa.

His hair was just getting shaggy, growing out from its servant's crop. Soon he'd tie it back with the black band.

He began learning the ways of the Undercroft. He had no orderlies of his own—these were the servants of the place—but one was sent to him for all the necessary things. One was sent to him every few days to shave him and lead him to the bathing pool, which he then had to himself. It was a hot springs, slightly sulfur-scented, and the water was the most luxurious thing on his body he had ever felt.

Except Gisa's soft presence, he realized with an inner wrenching.

Any of his scars that still itched or bothered him or felt pulled too tight were eased by the healing waters. His hands ceased to ache.

In the Undercroft, there was no way to tell the phases of the moon, but soon he understood that the moon was growing to full. The activities of the Undercroft increased a hundred-fold.

He was measured for ceremonial black hunting leathers, richly chased with silver.

Weapons were brought to him, and he began practicing with them, as well as he could in his confined space.

A day came when an orderly arrived to take him to the Silver King.

"Your Majesty," he said, bowing to the man. He behaved toward the king as he remembered the mages and Lord Jouhan did, when he was handed over to the service of the Undercroft.

He stood in a chamber with vaulted ceilings impossibly high, and the rock walls glowed. A magnificent natural space in the depths of the cave.

Before him on a crystal glowing platform sat the Silver King on his glittering throne.

"Maeldoi, Dark Rider," said the King. The man looked him up and down. "You look much more promising than you did at the portal. I am pleased."

Not knowing what to say to this, Maeldoi bowed again.

"The moon has nearly come to full, so I have summoned you here to tell you what to expect. It's the Wine Moon, thank The Three. One of the lesser moons. The next will be the Hunter's

Moon, the most important of all to the Hunt, and that would not be a good moon for you to train on." He looked up from his scrutiny of Maeldoi, and motioned.

A woman stepped out of the shadows beside the throne. Maeldoi recognized her. The one who had administered his rite of binding and fed him the strange seeds. "Welcome, Maeldoi, Dark Rider."

"Thank you, my lady."

"Huntress is the usual title, and I am the Head High Huntress."

"Thank you, Head High Huntress," he said, unsure whether to leave any of it out but not wanting to offend her in even the least degree. He'd be with this woman for years. The rest of his life. He shivered.

"I will take you to the horse you will ride, in the Hunt, so that you and he may become familiar with each other."

Maeldoi bowed to her again.

"So then, Maeldoi," said the King, turning Maeldoi's attention back to him. "You have your proper ceremonial leathers, I believe?"

"Yes, Your Majesty."

"And Head High Huntress Théodrate is about to show you to your horse. You have your spear?"

"Yes, Your Majesty."

"When the Hunt rides out, the Huntresses and I will track the white stag. That will become your job later, but this first time, ride with the Huntresses and see how they do it."

Of course Maeldoi knew how to track game. But maybe this white stag was not like other beasts, and anyway, he'd be doing it by moonlight.

"They will beat the stag toward me, and you'll turn your horse to ride by me," the King continued. "I hope you can ride well. I hope he can ride well," he muttered aside to Théodrate.

Maeldoi wasn't sure he should respond to this. He remained silent, waiting.

"And then you will kill the stag with your spear. After that, the Huntresses and I will conduct the rite of triumph, led by Head High Huntress Théodrate, and then we will all ride back through the portal into the Undercroft. You will come in last, bearing the body of the stag across your saddle."

"I understand, Your Majesty," said Maeldoi.

"Come with me then, Maeldoi, Dark Rider," said Théodrate. "I'll bring you to your horse."

He followed the Head High Huntress down a maze of corridors to another great open space. Maeldoi marveled. A horse paddock deep underground. Looking around him, he saw a number of sturdy-looking women riding or leading their horses, all silvery white, or working with them on maneuvers.

"Here's the stable, Maeldoi."

He followed Head High Huntress Théodrate into a long shed at one end of the paddock. To the very end of the shed, where he heard the booming of furious hooves against the wood of a stall.

Maeldoi and Théodrate stepped to the stall, where the most magnificent stallion Maeldoi had ever seen was rolling his eyes and baring his teeth as the grooms sprang back. And he was a perfect midnight black.

"Glad ye're here, Head High Huntress," said one. "Phantom is in a state, so he is."

"He's missing Ditmarus," said the other.

Head High Huntress Théodrate fixed the man with a stern eye, and he quailed back. "We do not speak of Ditmarus." Under her breath, she muttered, "And I doubt that's Phantom's problem, missing that scurvy knave."

"Yes, Head High Huntress," the man stammered.

"This is Maeldoi, the Dark Rider. You will be serving him."

The grooms looked over at Maeldoi dubiously, and then they both tugged at their forelocks.

Maeldoi nodded to them both. He felt half-amused, half-dismayed. Ditmarus, he thought, must be his predecessor, and here Maeldoi was, young, with hair cropped like a servant's. He must be a sad come-down. But the Head High Huntress had called the man a scurvy knave. Still, maybe that's what she thought of all gwrgi.

He turned his attention to the stallion. Phantom. He saw instantly what a challenge it would be to ride the horse, and how he'd be judged when he couldn't do it, or couldn't do it well.

You are bound to the Wild Hunt of the eala for the period of your natural life or until dismissed by the Silver King. Those were the ending words of the rite that Head High Huntress Théodrate had administered to him. He remembered his sudden hope—*until dismissed by the Silver King*—but then the words of Merlin, in his mind, threw him into fresh despair: *dismissal means the King has decided to kill you.* He thought of the Silver King's displeasure, on catching sight of him as he reeled in the aftermath of Gilles's strange attack on him. *Is he drunk?*

The king seemed to like him better, today. But what would he think when he saw Maeldoi couldn't ride the great beast thrashing out with his hooves in the stall, and what would the king say? And what would the king do?

In the flat despair after his days in the hands of Gilles, and then the fortnight or so he'd spent in the Undercroft, Maeldoi had wondered if he'd maybe welcome that release, by the king.

But now he felt a chill.

Head High Huntress Théodrate reached over the door of Phantom's stall as casually as if he were some tame pet, and fed him a handful of oats. She stroked his noble nose.

He quieted and whinnied.

"That's right, Phantom, my dear boy. Quiet yourself. And now here's Maeldoi, the Dark Rider."

When Phantom rolled his brilliant eye in Maeldoi's direction, though, his agitation came back on him.

Maeldoi stepped up beside Head High Huntress Théodrate. Out of the corner of his eye, he caught the expression on her face.

The expression he had seen on so many faces over the course of his entire life.

I'm sick to death of that expression, he told himself. *You're going to fail, I'm going to watch you, I'm going to enjoy watching you fail.*

"Let's see if you can ride him, Maeldoi. Dark Rider." Her tone was dry.

Maeldoi felt a surge of something powerful welling up from deep inside him. Whatever Gilles had done to him—whatever that vile thing was—Maeldoi had one insight into what it aimed to accomplish. Gilles had robbed him of something inside himself.

Or tried to.

A deep sense of himself flooded into him. *But Gilles has not succeeded. Especially he has not taken from me this deep inner knowledge—that in some sense, in boyhood, the horse and I became one creature.*

He fixed the horse, Phantom, with his eye. He took the pose One Stalwart to Another. "Phantom," he said. He reached his hand out across the door of the stall. Phantom swung his great head toward Maeldoi. He bent his glossy neck and his nostrils widened. Maeldoi had taken a handful of oats from the bucket where Head High Huntress Théodrate had gotten them. Now he raised his other hand, with the oats, to Phantom and opened his palm. Phantom carefully began to lip them out of Maeldoi's hand.

Something came out of Maeldoi then. Something completely unexpected. The language of his childhood.

In that language, he said to Phantom, "Hail, O Horse. The others think you and I are beasts. We may be beasts, but we are noble beasts. We care not for the opinions of these others, only for our own. Allow me to ride you, Phantom, and I will be your good companion."

Why should I fear this wonderful animal? he asked himself. *I have at my command all of the shamanic utterances, the poses, the inner calm, the outer authority. Others have tried to strip me of them, and they have not succeeded. When I speak out of my authority as gwrgi, a natural creature, another natural creature will listen.*

He eased the door of the stall open as Head High Huntress Théodrate stood back, watching with narrowed eyes. He reached up to Phantom's halter. Phantom stood stiff-legged. "Allow me to lead you, O Horse," said Maeldoi. He waited. Phantom inclined his head and allowed Maeldoi to guide him out of the stall. "O Horse, I thank you for this courtesy," Maeldoi told him.

When he approached Phantom to mount him, the stallion began sidestepping nervously away. "Allow me to mount you, O Horse," said Maeldoi. Phantom tossed his head. Inclined it. Allowed Maeldoi to mount. Maeldoi swung up on Phantom's back. "I'll guide you with my knees only, Phantom. During the hunt, I suppose you and I will have to submit to a saddle, but as soon as we can, we'll get rid of it. We don't need it. You and I will become one beast. I'm sure of it." Under his hand, he felt Phantom shudder and then grow still.

From Phantom's back, Maeldoi gazed down on the Head High Huntress. He thought of smiling, but he didn't feel like smiling. *I'll never smile again*, he thought. *There's only one person I wish to smile on, and she is forbidden me.*

In the language of the Baronies, he said, "Where may Phantom and I practice? If we're to hunt together soon, we need to learn each other."

"I'll show you," said Head High Huntress Théodrate. She looked at Maeldoi through different eyes now. Eyes of respect.

CHAPTER THIRTY-FOUR

A Grilling

Maeldoi woke in his pit the morning after the Hunt of the Wine Moon. He was still shaken. The exhilaration he felt had still not left him. It was the thrill to his core that he'd felt as a child, watching the Hunt sweep by, but magnified a thousand-fold.

This task of his. He understood now. He wanted it now. The glory and beauty of it, the sweep of the Hunt beneath the moon, the thunder of the hooves of the horses. Most of all, his connection with his horse. He and Phantom. Just as he had promised, he and Phantom, under the glamour of the Hunt, became a single magnificent beast. He thrilled to every part of it. Every part of himself had come alive.

In the aftermath, though, as the glory of the Hunt began to fade, he began to ache. He ached for Gisa.

Not just for the physical connection with her. That he craved desperately. But their connection went much deeper. It always had, he realized, from the moment they'd met.

He realized, too, how much he missed Aleron. But in a way, this task of his was what Aleron had urged on him. In his dreams, Aleron had seen it. Maeldoi knew it was an important task, to serve as go-between, gwrgi to eala, and he knew that was important to the balance of the Spheres, dark balancing light.

Somehow, though, thinking of the times he and Aleron had talked it over, he realized Aleron's dream was more urgent still than that.

There was something Maeldoi was meant to do in the Undercroft. Something important. Aleron hadn't understood what it was, just felt it. Now Maeldoi was beginning to be stirred by the same feelings. If only he could go to Aleron and ask his help understanding these complicated feelings of his. If only he could go to Master Bertran.

Soon, he had to put his ache and confusion aside. He was too busy.

Now that the Hunt of the Wine Moon was over, everyone in the Undercroft was driven to their utmost. The next Hunt, the Hunt of the Hunter's Moon, was the most important Hunt of the year, rivaled only by the spring-tide Hunt of the Seed Moon. Even that Hunt was not as important as this.

The moon of blood and harvest. The last moon of the fruitful year, before all underneath the Spheres shut down into its winter slumber.

The Hunt would ride out on each of the winter moons, of course. Mourning Moon, Oak Moon, Wolf Moon, Storm Moon.

Then, with the Plough Moon of early spring-tide, the world underneath the Spheres would wake up again. But until the Seed Moon, no Hunt would be as joyous as this one of the Hunter's Moon.

Sister Annet and her orderlies of the wardrobe were busy refurbishing the Silver King's ceremonial robes. Cook, in the kitchen, was preparing special dishes. The Huntresses were practicing special maneuvers.

Maeldoi couldn't see that he'd need to do anything different from what he'd done before, except that this time he himself would track the stag. He watched what the Huntresses did. It was simple. The poor stag was no ordinary stag, that was clear, and he was easy to track. Then the Huntresses drove the animal toward the king. Then Maeldoi rode in and dispatched him with a single thrust of his spear.

Maeldoi tried not to think too hard about it. It hardly seemed like a fair hunt, but then it wasn't the usual hunt. It was a ceremonial hunt, and the stag was ceremonial prey.

Except for his growing love for Phantom, and Phantom for him, and his growing excitement about the next Hunt, Maeldoi was beginning to wonder whether his life in the Undercroft between Hunts would prove impossibly tedious. He saw his life stretching before him, moments of inutterable beauty and majesty punctuating long stretches of dull despair, when he would dwell on his longing for Gisa and find no way out of his cloud of gloom.

Then Head High Huntress Théodrate summoned Maeldoi to the room where she and the other elite among the Huntresses held their deliberations and made important decisions.

As he was coming into the room, Novice Mistress Mechthilde was leaving it. Maeldoi stood aside in the pose of Underneath the Winter Rain. But he saw something that amazed him. It was the look exchanged between Head High Huntress Théodrate and Mechthilde.

They are lovers, he realized. Now that he too loved someone in that same way, he recognized the look.

He released from the pose, went into the room, and bowed to Head High Huntress Théodrate.

"You disapprove," she said.

Maeldoi schooled himself to look completely neutral. "Disapprove, Head High Huntress Théodrate?"

"Never mind. I have something to explain to you," she said.

But he told himself, *yes, I do disapprove.*

No, not disapprove, he amended. What was it, the feeling that flashed through him when he identified that telling look?

As he settled into the pose of The Obedient Student, he suddenly knew.

Jealousy.

She could love, and here was her lover, right here beside her. Yet he could not, and his lover was far away; maybe, in spite of the mage John Dee's reassurances, in danger. He settled deeper into his pose, to stifle his pain.

"Maeldoi, you have more duties in the Undercroft than the duties of the Hunt," said Head High Huntress Théodrate.

He stood waiting for her instruction.

"One is to train the novice-Huntresses in the skills they will need if they are to become full members of the Hunt."

He nodded briefly to show he understood.

"They need training in hunting skills and in combat."

He nodded.

"For the combat skills, you will train the novice-Huntresses in your pit. Obviously, the training in how to hunt must be conducted in the Abovelands."

"Outside," he said carefully.

"Of course."

"Of course," he echoed.

"You will train the novices one at a time. During the training for hunting, you may not put your hands on them, except out of necessity. A safety matter, for example, or a correction of a stance in the use of the bow."

"I understand," he said, thinking *I don't want to touch any of them. They are all safe from me.*

"Hmm," she said. "Interesting. I perceive distaste in your expression."

Not as impassive as I thought I was, thought Maeldoi.

"I bring this up only because your predecessor had a problem in that area. Knowing little of the gwrgi myself, knowing only him as a representative of your kind, I wasn't sure whether I was seeing a general behavior or only his."

Now Maeldoi felt insulted.

"I beg your pardon humbly, Maeldoi, Dark Rider. I see I was much mistaken."

"It would be against all the precepts of training. Touching to correct and discipline. Only that," he said, knowing he must sound stiff and disapproving. But his disapproval was for that predecessor. Maeldoi wondered what had happened to him.

"You may not physically discipline the novices, so it's a good thing we had this little talk," she observed.

"Ahh," he said. "I understand."

"If one needs to be disciplined in that way, you must send her to Novice-Mistress Mechthilde, who will see to it. Please don't hesitate."

He inclined his head.

"Of course, combat training is a far different matter. I will be most displeased if you hold back, in that training."

"Of course not. It would be of little use, if I did. But I would also shape my contact to the novice's level of skill. No unnecessary injuries. None at all, would be my goal, but sometimes—" He recalled all the bruises Aleron had dealt him. "And the novice should try to hurt me, if she can. That's important."

"I see we are in agreement, Maeldoi. Now I'd like to discuss something else with you."

Maeldoi waited.

"Please sit," she said, indicating a bench.

Surprised, he sank down on it. Not good. It would be harder to assume a pose, if he needed to take command of himself.

She sat on a bench opposite him.

Once again, he saw how strong and sturdy she was. All of the Huntresses, nearly all, had that look about them.

"Maeldoi, during the rite of profession, I couldn't help noticing something."

He waited.

"You were perfectly obedient. Your behavior was faultless. Yet I had the uneasy feeling you were being coerced to accept this task."

Maeldoi walled the surprise away from him. He considered his answer. "Head High Huntress Théodrate, our encounter at the portal was. . ." he hesitated. "Confusing."

"How so?"

He studied her. If he answered honestly, how much danger would he be in?

"Please be honest, Maeldoi, Dark Rider. I believe your confusion can help me understand a great danger I feel we are facing here in the Undercroft."

She understands about Gilles, he suddenly realized.

"Head High Huntress Théodrate, I must say I'm not sure what was happening at the portal, not completely. I will tell you what I know and what I observed."

"Please do."

"My brother and I had an unusual upbringing, away from our kind. That was my brother Caedon, the man you saw with the Baron Gilles de Rais, when he brought me to the portal."

Her eyes burned into his.

"When I had just come of age, a man arrived at our small, mean village on the far edge of the Sceptered Isle."

"Ahh," she said, and she began to smile. "I thought I recognized that speech you used on Phantom. Go on."

"Not many do recognize that speech," he said, amazed. "Well, then, the man who came to get me, and my mother and brother, brought me to a rectory in the Baronies. That is one of the training schools of the gwrgi."

"And your mother and brother?"

"The man left them at the caves on the Baronies' northeastern coast. The more. . ." He felt his lips quirk. ". . .savage members of our kind live in caves and forests around there."

"And your father?"

"Dead."

"The rectory is the place you trained for your profession?"

"First the rectory, then the gwrgi capital city."

"And then you came here to our portal, to make your profession and take on the task of Dark Rider."

Maeldoi looked her straight in the eye. "No."

"Explain," she said softly.

"Something tells me you already know a part of what I'm about to say."

"I'd like to hear your own version of the story."

"Somehow, Gilles de Rais took possession of my brother Caedon. Do you know what I mean by possession?"

"Not completely. Enough."

"As you saw, Gilles de Rais is a powerful mage."

"One of the most powerful underneath the Spheres."

"Yes. But I didn't know that. I knew nothing of Gilles, when I was at the rectory. Just that he was the realm's overlord."

"Pardon me, Maeldoi, but it would be hard to miss what a powerful mage he is."

"So they keep telling me. All I can say, Head High Huntress Théodrate, is that I was a solitary, isolated boy from a solitary, isolated place. Throughout my training, I didn't associate much with the other trainees. They despised me for a savage."

"Yet only a fortnight ago, I saw you tame the untamable Phantom with only your voice and your will."

Maeldoi smiled a bit and shook his head. "Not my will. Never my will opposed to Phantom's. My goodwill, freely offered to Phantom and freely accepted."

Théodrate was nodding even before he finished speaking. "This is why you were chosen for your task, Maeldoi, Dark Rider. You have a true understanding of your mission. I honor that. You have something important inside you."

"My mentors kept telling me I had something inside me. I never saw it." Maeldoi shrugged. "They did."

"You say you didn't know what Gilles de Rais was. But surely, through your brother—"

"I hadn't seen my brother since the day the rector arrived to take me away to training. I thought Caedon must still be in the caves. I thought maybe he was dead. I had no idea where he was, what he had become."

"Interesting. Gilles let him live."

Maeldoi shuddered

"I see you do know what Gilles does to his victims."

"A little. Only recently, when he tried some of it on me."

"Was that what we were seeing, at the portal? You looked like—"

"The Silver King wondered if I were drunk. I was staggering. I was slurring my words. I thought I might spew. Why wouldn't he?"

"You do not imbibe spirits?"

"No, just ale, as everyone else does. I've never had strong spirits."

"But the effects we saw."

"The aftermath of what Gilles does when he— When he—" Maeldoi stopped. "I tell you truly, Head High Huntress Théodrate, I don't know what that man did to me."

"Describe it." When Maeldoi put a hand to his head, as if a vise were squeezing it hard enough to crack it like a walnut, she said hastily, "No. Don't. Please go on. You were in training, you'd never seen your brother, you didn't know about Gilles de Rais."

"Yes. No," Maeldoi whispered.

"Maeldoi, Dark Rider. My apologies. Please go on."

"Somehow, toward the end of my training, my brother found me." Maeldoi faltered on. "He tried to entice me to go with him to Gilles. He said Gilles had taken him to nurture him up. He said I could expect the same luxuries."

"And?"

"I was horrified. Speaking to Caedon at all made me break my training. I went to the city to do penance. But—"

"Weren't you glad to see your brother?"

"No, Head High Huntress Théodrate. In childhood, I had tormented him. When I was taken away from my family, I was glad. That was another thing I had to do penance for, the way I had treated him. And then all the more, when I discovered what he had become, because I felt to blame. If I had been a better brother, maybe he would not have succumbed to Gilles."

"I'm sure you weren't the only cause of your brother's bad choices."

"I suppose not. But I was to blame, and I needed to repent."

"You gwrgi are a hard people."

"That's what I'm told."

"So you repented. Speaking to your brother, mistreating him. You repented."

"It wasn't good enough. The Penance Board decides how much blame a gwrgi must bear. They decided I had committed something very like treason."

"And had you?"

"No."

"So why?"

"I pieced this together, Head High Huntress. I believe that the Penance Board regards Gilles de Rais as a terrible threat to all gwrgi."

"Not just to them. And did you come to see that they were right?"

"Yes, Head High Huntress. I saw. Especially the fortnight before Gilles himself brought me to the portal, I saw. But the gwrgi officials were very wrong about one thing. Wrong that I was complicit with Gilles. That's what they thought. All along, they believed it. Finally my advocate during the penitential proceedings advised me to confess that I was wrong not to have realized who and what Gilles was. I believe his reasoning was, confess to something, so they'll have to give you a penance and then release you. So I did, and they released me."

"But they took you back into their prison."

"Yes, and charged me with treason, and convicted me of it, and were about to punish me for it. Treason is one of the Three Unpardonable Crimes of the gwrgi, and the punishment is most severe. Most who undergo it don't survive it, and if they do, they're sorry they did."

"Yet here you stand. How did you escape your punishment?"

"Mages helped me escape."

"Gilles de Rais." Her eyes bored into his.

He shook his head emphatically no. "Those other two you saw. The Lord Merlin. The Lord John Dee."

"I have a hard time believing that, Maeldoi," she said softly.

"So did the Penance Board," he replied, feeling a sour feeling rise in his gorge.

"Help me understand, Maeldoi."

He gave her a long, level look. "Head High Huntress Théodrate. I don't think we'd be having this conversation if you believed Gilles de Rais placed me here."

"Yet he brought you to the portal."

"He did, and that was his plan. I'm not sure what I was supposed to do for him down here, but I know he planned to use me here against the eala. Against the Undercroft."

"And he deceived His Majesty the Silver King into receiving you from his hand, as if you were fully professed."

"Deceived the Silver King. Did he?"

"Did he?" she echoed softly. After a moment, she went on. "Gilles was forcing you into your task as Dark Rider. You were being coerced. Yet you said you were not."

"Gilles is holding hostage a person I love more than life itself. That coerced me."

"Think what you were about to do to us, Maeldoi, if you had come here as Gilles's bound creature."

Maeldoi went on his knees before her in the pose of The Penitent.

"But you didn't do it," she continued. "Get up, please."

He rose and assumed the pose Standing Beneath Winter Rain.

"Somehow those other two mages were there. Merlin and Dee."

"Yes," he whispered.

"And your leader, Lord Jouhan."

"Yes."

"And then he professed you with all the proper forms and rites."

"Yes."

"And you accepted your task."

"Yes."

"Why is that? I know why Gilles de Rais would violate the rule of non-interference, but why would Merlin and Dee?"

"I don't know, Head High Huntress. But I think they saw what Gilles was trying to do to me, and they stepped in to prevent it."

"You're that important."

Maeldoi shook his head miserably. "I don't know. I thought maybe—" His voice dropped low. "Maybe they'd come to rescue me, as they had before."

"And here you are, bound just as securely to the Undercroft as if Gilles had done it."

He nodded. He didn't trust himself to speak.

"Just as coerced." She stared at him. "What would you have done, do you think, Maeldoi, Dark Rider, if you had indeed found yourself bound here as Gilles's creature. Would you have betrayed us?"

"No, Head High Huntress Théodrate," cried Maeldoi and assumed the position Lowest Abasement.

"Get up, Maeldoi. No one grovels down here."

Maeldoi raised himself unhappily from the stones of the floor, but only as far as his knees.

"But you're not Gilles's creature. Merlin and Dee saw to that. They made sure your profession was regular and duly recorded. Now, if Gilles tries to reach you here, it will draw the attention of The Three, and he doesn't want that. Not yet, anyhow. I think Merlin and Dee were trying to protect you."

"By putting me here," said Maeldoi bitterly. "But Head High Huntress, even though I know in my heart I would never betray you, no matter who put me here, you can't know that. I found out how such matters work, in the House of Penitence. Underneath the Spheres, no one trusts anyone else. You'll never be able to trust me. You must tell His Majesty what you have discovered. Then he will dismiss me."

"Do you know what that means, Maeldoi."

Maeldoi nodded, his head down. "Outside, the Penance Board would capture me and mutilate me and exhibit me in a cage. Or Gilles would capture me and do that—that thing to me. What does it matter what the Silver King does to me? Any way you look at it, I'm as good as dead, and in a variety of painful ways. But worst of all—"

"You're separated from the one you love."

"You see my dilemma." Maeldoi tried to control the bitterness in him but found he could not.

"Back on the bench, Maeldoi. This is what I see," said Head High Huntress Théodrate as Maeldoi rose from his knees and sat back down on the bench. "I see that you were placed in an impossible position through foul means by Gilles de Rais. I see that Merlin, Dee, and Lord Jouhan arrived in time to make it right, because they know what Gilles is up to. They know what you know, Maeldoi. Rescuing you would simply deliver you back into the hands of Gilles, or into the hands of that Penance Board of you gwrgi. Where you are now is the only place they know you'll be safe."

Maeldoi couldn't raise his head to look her in the eye. *I am to blame*, he thought. *I must do penance.*

"Maeldoi," she said, her voice exasperated. "Put down that burden of guilt you're hauling around. We don't have time for all that gwrgi nonsense. No kneeling, no groveling. We need to act. Gilles has already made his incursions into this place, and he was trying for an even firmer grasp on us through you. It didn't work. Dark Ones take him."

Maeldoi's head snapped up at the familiar slur.

She gave him a little grin, but just as swiftly a grim expression replaced it. "And Gilles is making his incursions into you gwrgi. He has your brother. He thought he had you."

"You say he has already made incursions here."

She looked at her hands. "I fear it," she said quietly.

"The Silver King," he said.

"Why else was he going along with Gilles's irregular placement of you with us?"

"Maybe Gilles is using him and he doesn't realize it."

"Maybe. But Maeldoi, I believe you're here with us for a reason. I believe you're here to help me fight Gilles off. He wants power, Maeldoi. I believe he wants ultimate power."

With a chill, Maeldoi thought of Aleron's dream. His feeling that the dream meant something urgent and dangerous.

"I believe maybe Merlin and Dee don't just want to stash you someplace safe. I believe they see you can help us all, Maeldoi. That your gifts are meant for that."

"My friend is a hermit. He had a dream. His dream said to him what you're saying, Head High Huntress. But I. I don't think my gifts are so very important."

"I think you're wrong, Maeldoi. And let me ask you something. All the while that Penance Board was perversely ignoring the truth about you, did you ever wonder why?"

"They are frightened, Head High Huntress. They are terrified Gilles will succeed."

"All of them? Could Gilles maybe already have suborned at least one of them?"

Maeldoi's rage rose almost too fast for him to control it. With an effort, he did. *Estienn.*

"Well, we don't know. Maybe the man is simply an opportunist and a sadist."

"What must I do to help you, Head High Huntress Théodrate? Tell me, and I'll do it."

"I believe you will, Maeldoi, Dark Rider. I believe however it came to you, you take your vows of profession seriously, and hold them sacred. I am thinking of a number of measures you and I can take to ensure the safety of the Undercroft. But I'm thinking of something else, too."

Maeldoi looked at her mutely.

"I keep thinking of how you have been coerced. How that's not right. Right or wrong, the seeds have bound you here til you die. There's no getting around it. But maybe there are ways to mitigate your situation. Would you like to hear them?"

He nodded.

"Two missions. Of course, we must all get through the Hunt of the Hunter's Moon first."

"Of course," he murmured.

"But after that, I'm minded to send you out on a scouting mission to search for good places to conduct your novice training in the hunting skills. You have eaten the seeds, Maeldoi. No matter what, only death can release you from the Undercroft. However, it doesn't mean I can't send you out on special missions. I can give you special leave to depart the Undercroft for brief periods. Once every season, I want you to accomplish these two things. First, spy on your brother and report back to me. I don't want you going too near Gilles, even though he sees he can't grab you now without endangering his grand plan. Even so, I don't want you near him. But you can get close to your brother, and then we can keep our eye on what he is doing for Gilles. Agreed?"

"Agreed," said Maeldoi, with rising excitement.

"And the second one is this. You have made a promise. Maybe not even a promise in words. An implied promise. And it is to the one you love. I know this well, for I have made my own promise of that kind. Such promises are powerful, and honored of the gods. Once a season, I want you to find that one. The woman you love. I want you to spend several days with her before you return. Do this faithfully, Maeldoi, unless and until she dismisses you from her service."

Trembling all over, Maeldoi bowed. "Head High Huntress Théodrate, I will."

◉

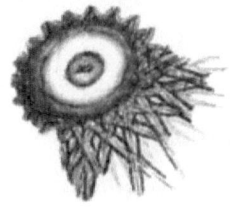

CHAPTER THIRTY-FIVE

Without Leave

Maeldoi waited patiently in the hills above the manor, watching. It was dawn. He wanted to make sure of what he was seeing before he acted.

It was his brother's manor in the Sceptered Isle. Maeldoi could travel to any place in the Twelve Realms where the gwrgi had fashioned their portals—or maybe, who knew? beyond, and the Sceptered Isle had many. Now Maeldoi could see for himself how far Gilles de Rais's schemes for the Sceptered Isle had progressed. His brother had risen to become one of the most important men of the Sceptered Isle, close advisor to its new king, Audemar.

Many muttered behind their hands that the king was a usurper, a fratricide; even a parricide. A rebel group was harrying the forces of the king, led by Audemar the Usurper's younger brother, and Maeldoi's own brother was the general who opposed those rebels.

Not bad for a dirt-poor gwrgi from a squalid village and the savage caves. He remembered his brother's enticements. *Give in to Gilles, and he will reward you handsomely, Brother, as he has rewarded me.*

Maeldoi could recall even now, with a sick lurch to his stomach, what price Cae must have paid to gain those rewards. *I've known a lot of bad things in my life,* thought Maeldoi, *but none as bad as what Gilles did to me, when he had me in his grasp.* He wouldn't exchange all the scars on his body, and the instruments of pain that made them, for that one experience of nausea, of rottenness and dread.

"Pfft, it's not that terrible," he remembered Cae telling him, afterward. "But only if you don't fight it. That's the key, Maeldoi. Don't fight it. You'll learn. Gilles will teach you."

He'll never teach me, thought Maeldoi. *I'll never let him. If he grabs me back, I'll fight and I'll keep on fighting.* But it chilled him deeply to be this close to Cae, where—he knew it—Gilles could track him. *Suppose Gilles takes me and I lose my fight,* he thought. *Suppose I'm not strong enough to withstand him.* He resolved then. He'd go to Aleron and ask his advice. As soon as he could, he'd do it, and Aleron would help him understand.

A commotion at the big gates of Cae's manor interrupted his fears. Bondservants rushing to open the gates. A man on a fine black horse came riding out.

"Not as fine as you, Phantom," Maeldoi whispered to his own horse, who knew to stand perfectly still under the dappling of light beneath the trees.

Cae and his entourage cantered off down the road leading away from the manor.

Now then, he said to himself. Cae was out of the way, and it was safer for him to reconnoiter.

Maeldoi had changed into the brown livery of one of Cae's bondservants. He had pulled the hood well up, shadowing his face. With any luck, none of the others would notice his gwrgi eyes. He was guessing only Cae had eyes like that, around here, so if anyone did spot them, it would be all too obvious to them that something unusual was going on, even if none of them understood about the gwrgi. Maeldoi had to hope for the best. Under the hood, his hair was tied well-back and clubbed.

He wrapped a cloak around himself. It was late in the year; the snows had not flown, but soon they would. A good thing, for the cloak hid the longsword at his hip. After bringing Phantom water, hobbling him so that he could safely graze, and whispering a few words to him, Maeldoi eased down the hill to the wall that enclosed Cae's lands.

He started walking along the road paralleling the wall, back away from the manor, as if he were some peasant heading off to the nearby village. Far down alongside a meadow, Cae's back fields, he spotted what he was looking for. A place where the wall was crumbling.

He climbed over it. Then he just walked in toward the manor, not concealing himself. As he neared the stables, he spotted a pail, and he picked it up by the handle and circled around to where he figured the kitchen shed must be. On the way, he drew up a bucket of water from the well.

He strolled into the kitchen shed. One of the kitchen wenches looked up. He waved a lazy hand at her, set the bucket down by the door, and stepped out again. By then he had a broom in his hands. As he came to the back doors of the manor, he began sweeping the stones. It was the middle of the day, the master was gone, everyone was sleepy and trying to capture a last bit of autumn-tide sun in the courtyard.

He went inside. If he had to, he could fight his way out. He hoped he wouldn't have to. The place was nearly deserted. He roamed the halls, listening carefully for anyone coming. Once, a bondservant went past on some errand. Maeldoi nodded to him, and the man nodded back.

Toward the back of the manor, he guessed, were the sleeping rooms. He eased a door open and looked in. A bedstead, a hearth. He closed the door again. Ahead of him stretched a corridor, and at the end of it, he spotted an ornately-carved door. If he had to guess, he'd say Cae's own rooms lay beyond that door.

He pressed himself to the wall of the corridor as one of the doors opposite him opened. A small woman came out of it, bearing a basin. Head down, Maeldoi tugged his forelock.

She threw him a bored glance and went on down the corridor.

After she had disappeared around a corner, Maeldoi pushed the door open and went in.

A young woman sat at a window embrasure. She was the very picture of grief. She looked up in surprise.

"Sorry, my lady," said Maeldoi in the speech of the Baronies. He had to hope she understood it. She seemed to. He averted his face from her and glanced quickly around. "This chair is needed in the great hall." He stepped to a chair drawn up to the hearth and hefted it.

Before he could get out of the room, the door opened again. He stood back.

A young man came into the room. He wore a strained expression. "Your Highness. Pardon this intrusion, but I have been worried of late—" He stopped. "Who are you?" he demanded of Maeldoi.

"Sorry, lord," said Maeldoi, eyes down, half-concealing himself behind the chair. "This chair is needed in the great hall." He hauled it past the young man and out the door.

"Who was that?" he heard the young man say.

A faint reply. "Just one of the servants."

Maeldoi carried the chair to the great hall of the manor and set it down, wiping the sweat from his brow. Baronies speech seemed fine here, even though these were Sceptered Isle lands.

Now he knew. *Your Highness*, the man had said. The young woman in the room must be the Princess Diera. Just as Théodrate had suspected, the daughter of the assassinated heir to the throne of the Sceptered Isle was indeed kept in his brother's manor.

He carefully reviewed the instructions he'd received from the Head High Huntress.

"Gilles and Caedon between them have successfully carried out their coup," she had told him, as he left on his latest mission of spying. "They've installed a usurper in the place of the heir to the Sceptered Isle, whom they have assassinated. They probably killed Ranulf, the king that was. They probably used poison on him, so I've no doubt they've enlisted the services of a witch. Caedon, it is said, has taken the Princess Diera, the assassinated heir's daughter, to his manor. I have reason to suspect your brother will try to corrupt the princess somehow. In this way, Gilles's plot will be furthered."

"How?"

"I'm not sure. My information is inexact."

"I'll find out if my brother has her," Maeldoi promised, "and see what I can discover about his plans for her."

Maeldoi wondered if he could somehow get the princess out of Cae's hands. He didn't know where he could take her if he did. At least he had this valuable piece of information to bring to Théodrate.

In the great hall, Maeldoi removed his longsword from under his cloak and looked around for a likely hiding place. A large tapestry hung down one wall. He nudged it aside. A cloud of dust nearly made him choke. *Perfect,* he thought. No one was going to look behind this tapestry. No one had pulled it aside for years, not even a servant bent on cleaning. He tucked his longsword there and made sure no telltale bulge betrayed it.

He might need it, later, but took a risk, carrying it in. If he had moved wrong, someone in the manor might have spotted it poking from under his cloak. That small woman in the corridor. The young man who came to the princess's rooms. The princess herself, who might have become alarmed and cried out.

Now that he'd taken a look around and felt out the sense of the place, Maeldoi got himself out of the manor and back to Phantom. He watched the road carefully. *At least I'm furthering this first mission of mine*, he thought.

He wanted to finish it. He wanted to be hurrying on to his second mission. Finding Gisa. He took the pose Split Into Two Minds. If he thought about Gisa, about Aleron, about his yearning for Gisa, his increasing fears for both of them, the bad dreams visiting him, he might fall apart. Just now, he couldn't afford to fall apart. He carefully tucked the part of his mind with the bad dreams away where the other part couldn't get at it. Right now, he needed to make sure he knew what his brother was up to.

Toward evening, he spotted Cae riding toward the manor, followed by his retainers. *You're a big man, now, brother*, thought Maeldoi.

Around the time of the evening meal, he got himself back into the manor, blending in with the other servants, helping to carry platters of meat and fruit into the main hall where the trestles were set up for the meal, but always making sure to stay well away from his brother, whom he glimpsed sitting at his ease at the head of the board. A number of the servants spoke only the language of the Sceptered Isle, the court speech and speech of the cities, not the language of Maeldoi's childhood, but Maeldoi saw right enough what to do.

"Who are you?" one of the bondservants demanded, as Maeldoi went about his tasks with the other servants. He said it in the speech of the Sceptered Isle, then repeated it in Baronies speech.

"The new man," said Maeldoi, making sure to keep his eyes down.

"One of those from across the Narrows," the man sniffed, waving a disdainful hand. "Draw water from the well and take it to the kitchen."

Not sure how to address this man, Maeldoi tugged on his forelock and hastened to obey.

In the kitchen, he crouched at the big hearth. A serving wench handed him a trencher of meat, and he ate it. He glanced to one side. There was the young man he had seen in the rooms of the princess. He looked deeply unhappy.

Outside, the wind began to rise.

The young man stepped to the hearth.

"Bad weather blowing in, young master," Maeldoi said, his face averted. He wondered what he might discover, if he could talk to this man.

"You were the man with the chair, earlier," the young man said. He spoke fluently in the language of the Baronies, as Maeldoi had heard earlier, in the Princess's chambers. Someone Cae had brought over with him, Maeldoi realized, along with some of the servants, too.

"Aye," said Maeldoi.

"Her Highness—did she seem melancholy, to you? More than usual?"

Maeldoi shrugged. But the words of this man thrilled through him.

"Listen, my good man. I need some help tonight."

"How may I help ye, young master?"

"I stand guard at the door of the princess so she will feel safe. She's had such a hard time of it."

"Aye, anyone can see it," said Maeldoi cautiously. He wondered whether he should try to get himself away. Suppose this young man became suspicious of him?

"Here's a silver piece. Watch with me tonight, if you will."

Maeldoi snapped the coin up eagerly. He knew how to play the servant, after his masquerade at the rectory.

"What do you know of Lord Caedon?"

Now all the alarm bells of the city began tolling in Maeldoi's head. But he steadied himself and went into the pose of Obedient Servant Awaiting Instruction. "None much, good master. I am new to the household."

"Lord Caedon must have brought you back with him, after his recent trip across the Narrows. I don't remember seeing you here before," said the young man.

"Aye, young master," said Maeldoi. "I saw my fortune, and I signed on and came over."

"Her Highness has a strange look about her these days," said the young man abruptly. Master Rafe was his name, as Maeldoi later learned. "I'm sure you have heard of her sorrows. I'm to watch out for her, but then I'm sent away from her door on errands. You're a man from home. If you do me good service, I'll be grateful, and you'll come out the gainer."

"Aye, of course, good master," said Maeldoi.

"If you would, stand nearby tonight and see who goes in and out of the Princess's rooms. Do that for me, goodman, and I'll be very grateful. Tell no one, and that coin I gave you might have a brother to follow."

"I want to meet the brother of this one," Maeldoi said, holding up the silver piece, rubbing it between thumb and forefinger, smiling. Always he kept his eyes down. He hoped, in the low light of the kitchen shed, that the young man, Master Rafe, would not notice his gwrgi eyes. Nor did he.

Soon Maeldoi followed this Master Rafe back down the corridor toward the princess's rooms.

"Stand here." Rafe indicated a shadowy spot around a corner, where Maeldoi could see the door to her rooms but not be seen from that doorway himself.

He leaned back against the wall to wait, and Master Rafe went to the princess's door and stood on guard there.

After about a candle-measure, Maeldoi felt himself getting so drowsy he had to pinch himself, to keep awake. Then movement roused him; someone coming out of the princess's rooms.

"Master Rafe," said the small woman who emerged. Maeldoi recognized her from earlier in the day.

"Mistress Labinia," Maeldoi heard Rafe reply. The young man's tone was perfectly courteous. Underneath, though, Maeldoi sensed hostility. The small woman headed off down the corridor on some errand.

Maeldoi was on fire to understand what was going on. He had a strong feeling that whatever it was, it would be of great interest to Head High Huntress Théodrate.

After the small woman had gone, Maeldoi watched Rafe crack open the door to the princess's quarters and look in. Apparently satisfied, he closed it again.

A bit later, Mistress Labinia came back down the corridor. "Master Rafe, Lord Caedon commands that you go to the stables. He will ride tomorrow to a most important meeting with some of the other lords, and he wants his horse perfectly groomed."

"He wants me to groom his horse?" Maeldoi heard a tinge of outrage in Rafe's voice, carefully controlled.

"By no means, Raoul." It was Cae himself, coming hard on Labinia's heels. Maeldoi heard him laugh. "I'd never ask you to do a menial task like that. But I don't trust those grooms. They have let Lebryt's caparisons get smutched and shabby. Check them for me, please."

It was not a request. It was a command. Cae had softened it a bit, but from where Maeldoi stood, he saw Rafe understood perfectly.

Cae stood beside Labinia, waiting.

Rafe bowed. He turned and walked away. As he went past Maeldoi, he gave him a nudge, and Maeldoi nodded that he understood. As Maeldoi waited, he wondered. Rafe. Raoul. Which was the young man's name?

He didn't have much time to wonder about it, because just then he heard Cae say to the small woman, "Good, he's well gone now."

Oho, thought Maeldoi. *What's this?* Rafe or Raoul or whoever he was, his instincts had not played him false. Cae was bent on some treachery.

"I'll come back in a while and see to Her Highness," said the small woman, Labinia. "Afterward," she added.

"By now the potion has done its work?"

"You should be safe with her for some time." Mistress Labinia dropped his brother a curtsey and left.

Potion, thought Maeldoi, his eyes narrowing. What was this villainy his brother planned for the princess?

Maeldoi watched Cae let himself into the room where Maeldoi thought she must be sleeping.

After several moments, when Cae didn't come back out, Maeldoi got himself to the door and listened at it. He heard the distinct click of an inner door being opened, then shut.

Maeldoi whirled and made straightway to the great hall, where he retrieved his longsword. No one was about, but he concealed it under his cloak to make sure.

He got himself back to the princess's door and eased it open. He had his hand on his sword hilt just in case. He wasn't sure what he was walking into, and that unnerved him, but he steadied himself into the pose of Ears Pricked in the Guise of a Fox.

The room was empty. As he had noticed earlier, a door seemed to lead to an inner room. Now he put his ear to that door. A faint rustling came from within.

How can I see what's going on in there? he thought desperately. *And how much time do I have?*

He took the pose Eyes Like a Hawk. He scanned the wood of the inner wall. Any crevice, any crack. *There.* A knothole in the wood of the wall.

He stepped to it and put his eye to it.

He had to stifle the sudden indrawing of his breath.

The princess lay on a bed, and his brother, naked, was stalking around it, muttering to himself. He was clearly trying to rouse himself. Just as clearly, failing.

The skamelar. Maeldoi suppressed a hiss of outrage. *That girl is deeply asleep, and there's my villain of a brother intending to force himself on her.*

Carefully, Maeldoi eased himself back from the knothole and out of the room. He resumed his post.

None too soon. Cae burst from the room, adjusting his clothing, looking a bit wild. He strode back and forth by the door, then went in again. Almost as soon, he was back out, muttering to himself again.

Then Labinia was coming down the corridor.

Maeldoi saw how his brother took command of himself.

"Everything fine, my lord?" she said to Cae.

"Fine. Fine," he responded. "I'll go in to her during this entire sen'night of her fertile time."

"Very good, my lord."

Maeldoi leaned back against the wall, stunned. It seemed his brother was trying to impregnate the girl. Failing, at least.

He thought hard about what he should do. If he told this Master Rafe what he had seen, what would the young man do about it? Would he be able to stop Cae? Maeldoi thought he would not. The young man would just reveal to Cae that he was on to him, and Cae would do something terrible to him. Kill him, lock him up, something, so that Cae's vile work with the princess could continue.

Two things I must do here, Maeldoi thought. *Find out what's going on with the princess. But also, keep this young man safe.*

He knew too well what Cae was capable of doing to any person under his authority. He'd seen it in Gilles's castle. He'd seen it when his brother helped take him to the entrance to the

Undercroft. Maeldoi wouldn't put this young man, this Master Rafe, in danger unless he had to. He saw how much the young man cared, whoever he was.

He wondered if Rafe might be in love with the princess. He remembered the look that had passed between the two of them, when he was in her rooms and had picked up the chair.

He could see his brother abhorred the young princess. But Cae was trying to force himself on her just the same. Maeldoi realized what he had learned of Cae, when he had been in the hands of Gilles. It had become clear to him, after only a few days. Cae didn't like women.

And here he was, trying to arouse himself to do villainy on one.

Maeldoi might have marveled at the irony if he hadn't been so worried and sickened. He felt sickened by what he realized Gilles had done to his brother. Turned Cae into a replica of himself.

Children. His brother craved children, as Gilles did. Maeldoi was sickened at Gilles, at Cae. He was sickened at himself, the part he had played in driving his brother into the power of such a man.

As Maeldoi kept watch, Cae returned up the corridor toward his own rooms. Labinia let herself back inside the princess's rooms.

After a while, Rafe returned from his errand, clearly make-work to get him away from the princess's door. "What did you see?" he whispered to Maeldoi.

I won't tell him everything. But I'll put him on alert, Maeldoi decided.

"Mistress Labinia came out. She returned with Lord Caedon. She left; he went into the princess's rooms. After a while, he came out again. He and Labinia had conference. Then Lord Caedon went away, and Labinia went back into the rooms of the princess."

He could see, even in the semi-darkness of the corridor, that Rafe's face was white and set with fury. He thought then that his scruples had been needless. Rafe understood what Maeldoi's observations meant. What Cae was probably doing.

"Thanks, my man," he said at last, in a suffocated voice. He pressed a coin into Maeldoi's hand. "Tell no one what you've seen."

"I swear I will not, Master Rafe," said Maeldoi.

The next day, he didn't see Rafe about the manor. But that night, he crept to his spot to observe again.

He listened as Cae and Labinia conferred outside the Princess Diera's door.

"He said he needed to go to the grain factor in the next town," Maeldoi heard Cae say, and Labinia's faint reply. "It's as well," said Cae. "Rafe will be away for a few nights, and I won't have to worry about him coming back to the door while I'm inside."

As before, Labinia left. As before, Cae entered Diera's rooms.

This time Maeldoi didn't risk going inside and watching. It was dangerous, and besides, it turned his stomach.

He was glad Rafe was not there to put himself in danger. He wondered if Rafe had gone off to inform someone or think of some strategy. He didn't think the young man would abandon the princess.

He wondered if he should have told Rafe everything he knew. Too risky. He wasn't sure who this Master Rafe or maybe Raoul was and how he figured in the treachery Maeldoi was there to observe. But with Rafe gone, at least it was safer for the young man. Safer for himself, too. Sooner or later, Rafe would have gotten a good look at his eyes. Then he might have thought Maeldoi to be an agent of his lord, playing him false.

Maeldoi shook his head. Too many loose threads. He felt he was operating in the dark, physical and otherwise. Maybe the Head High Huntress would know what to make of all he had observed.

This night, once again, Cae emerged distraught from the rooms of the Princess Deira.

The next night, Cae arrived at her door with a young boy.

What in the Nine? Maeldoi thought.

Cae took the boy inside the rooms with him. Very shortly the lad came out again, wiping his mouth and lacing up his trousers.

The sick feeling in Maeldoi intensified.

Cae emerged. He said something to the boy in the speech of the Sceptered Isle, drew the lad to him for an embrace. Gave him a coin. Gave him a kiss.

He and the boy went away toward Cae's rooms.

I can't stand watching this, thought Maeldoi. *Suppose I—*

"What are you going to do about it?" A cold voice at his elbow.

Maeldoi whirled around. Too late he wished he had brought his sword out of its hiding place.

The small woman, Labinia, was standing there beside him. "I know who you are," she said. Her dark smoldering eyes bored into him. "Help a brother out?" she said.

Quick as one of the fabled serpents of the Realm of the Asp, her hand darted toward Maeldoi's face, and Maeldoi felt himself enveloped in a sweetish, nauseating cloud of some befuddling substance.

As if he were watching someone else from high up on the ceiling, he saw Labinia lead him into the outer room. Into the inner room.

"Your brother can't do the deed," Labinia said, her voice dripping with contempt. "Not even with his boys to rouse him can he do it. You can, and none the wiser."

Wrapped within some nightmare, he saw himself approach the bed. Felt himself reach out to Diera, where she lay wrapped in a deep sleep as if death itself had wound itself, serpent-wise, about her.

Saw himself put his hands on her body.

Then he found he had done a shameful thing.

When he came back to himself, he was outside the manor. He reeled back to his hiding place in the woods above the manor, retching, the tears streaming from his eyes.

How to do penance for this? he cried out to himself.

He fell into a deep well of sleep.

When he woke, it was morning. Phantom was peacefully champing grass at his side.

"Stay away from me, Phantom. I am not worth the attention of a noble creature like you," Maeldoi whispered. He had violated the most basic of human bindings, just as that man his father had violated them. He was no better than that man. He gazed over at Phantom in anguish. Somehow he felt that the bond between himself and Phantom had been breached as well. One noble creature to another? "One of us is not noble, Phantom, if he ever was," Maeldoi whispered.

Phantom took no notice.

Now that it was too late, Maeldoi remembered the words of the Head High Huntress: that Gilles and Cae were working with a witch.

He'd known a witch was involved yet foolishly had not set any wards of protection around himself. And now he had done this deed for which he'd be atoning the rest of his days.

There was a word for the demon who preys upon a sleeping woman. Incubus.

He got water and brought it to Phantom.

He wondered how he'd ever be able to live with himself. *Incubus*, he whispered to himself.

He went into the pose Hillside of the Mountain and stayed there, only coming out to tend to Phantom's needs. He remained in the pose for three days.

He forced himself out of it.

Phantom needed him, he was due back in the Undercroft with his information, and if he didn't eat something soon, he'd be too weak to do any of those other necessary things.

Late in the day, he made his way back down to the manor. He wanted nothing so badly as to be far away from the place, but he needed to get his hidden sword.

And to find something to eat.

He got himself into the kitchen shed with a bucket of water during the evening meal. By then, the other servants took for granted that he was part of the household. The kitchen wench, with a few jolly words in that other language, handed him the meat scraps.

Afterward, he stationed himself in the shadows. From there, he could see Rafe standing guard at his usual spot outside the princess's door. Cae came past and spoke a few words to the young man.

Went on by.

Rafe seemed greatly relieved.

Maeldoi wasn't sure what that meant, but he was glad the young man seemed safe and easier in his mind. He hoped that meant the princess too was safe.

Safer.

She'd never be safe, while Cae had her. There were other villainies he could do her, even if he couldn't do that deed he was trying so mightily to force on her.

That villainy.

The villainy Maeldoi had done in his brother's stead.

A fresh wave of shame washed over him.

He must not let it master him.

He'd find his sword, and then he'd be away from there with his information.

He didn't want to be anywhere Labinia could set eyes on him and do again whatever she had done to him before.

Maeldoi shrugged his shoulders to unkink his body. He found he'd sidled down the corridor, rigid and listening. One last trip down this hallway, and he'd be gone. One last piece of luck.

Almost there.

Almost out.

He was reaching behind the tapestry for his sword, coughing a little at the dust and trying to be quiet about it, when the flare of a rush light and the hiss of steel from a scabbard froze him in place.

He whirled, longsword gripped in both hands, wrenching it across his body. *Sard it.* He'd bitten his tongue. Pulling the hilt of the sword slightly past his hip, an instinctive guarding, he rocked forward on his right foot. Found his balance.

"You." Cae, crouched with shortsword and rapier, poised to run at him and end him.

Maeldoi steadied his guard, shuddering in a breath, minutely adjusting his stance, never taking his eyes off his brother.

Alone in a circle of rushlight, the manor sleeping around them, he and Cae moved into the ritual dance of combat. They closed. Only the clashing of the blades and the hoarseness of their breathing punctuated the silence of the hall. This was between the two of them. It always had been. Stupid to think he'd avoid it.

Maeldoi's breath came hard. The sweat dripped from him. He shook it out of his eyes. His grip was slippery; he clamped his hands onto the sword's hilt so tight they felt like objects, not parts of his body. Concentrate, or die.

The world narrowed to their breathing and the heavy jostling of their bodies. Maeldoi bore down on a single moment—this one. A single act—this act.

The two of them circled each other, intent.

Control the space. Aleron's voice urgent in his head.

Cae drove at his brother. Maeldoi heaved up his sword to parry. Cae came at him. Maeldoi fought him away. Cae lunged, driving Maeldoi backward, cornering him, cutting off any escape. His every move said confidence.

Maeldoi matched Cae blow for blow. The clang of metal on metal rang out into the darkened room beyond the circle of torchlight.

Maeldoi caught a flicker of movement, armsmen hesitating at the big doors. No way out except straight past them. The smoke of the rush lights stung Maeldoi's eyes.

Cae's blade ripped a sharp line of pain down Maeldoi's side. Maeldoi swirled away, narrowly missing Cae's deeper thrust, a bigger chunk taken out of him.

Cae's eyes intent, triumphant. He came on.

Focus on Cae. Narrow everything on Cae, his eyes, his movements.

Over his shoulder Cae screamed at his men. "Out! Get out of here!" His blows redoubled. From the back of his throat, Cae's growl snarled out like a beast's. Spittle flew from his mouth, spattering Maeldoi's cheek.

Maeldoi wheezed a ragged breath in, tasting blood.

At his edges, Cae bristled, seeming to swell in size. The rancid scent of an enraged animal came off him in waves.

A heady delirium swept Maeldoi. His answering tide of rage rose to meet his brother's.

No. Maeldoi fought for concentration against it. A vein in his forehead pounded against the galloping rhythm of his heart. He gulped air.

He steadied down.

Cae's eyes gleamed with his domination.

Maeldoi flowed into the pose of Tireless Attacker, the beast-rage falling from him. Exhilaration rose, controlled and fierce and sharp, as the fatigue dropped away.

Nothing there but the sword.

He became the sword.

He came on. His breath steadied. The clashing of arms filled the silence and echoed from the rafters of the hall.

He feinted away from Cae.

"Absent from the Undercroft without leave, brother?" Cae grated. "What will the Silver King say." Cae's eyes blazed. "You're little more than a beast." His brother's voice became a guttural weapon of its own. "I'll feed you to Gilles." Cae thrust and feinted and charged Maeldoi. "They want to chop you to bits in that gwrgi city. I'll do it for them." Cae stepped back, gesturing to Maeldoi with his weapons, mocking. "Come to me, brother. Come on, then."

Maeldoi fought past the taunts.

Cae closed with him. Every blow of Cae's told. His sword, his rapier, etched patterns into the very air, they moved so fast.

But as Cae surged forward, Maeldoi stepped into the lunge, locking his sword's hilt against Cae's. In one fluid movement of leg, knee, foot, he kicked the rapier out of his brother's off-hand. It flew clattering into the corner.

Cae's eyes jerked to it, then snapped back to Maeldoi. He plowed hard into Maeldoi, his face a minim from his brother's.

The two of them strove eye to eye, blade to blade, Caedon's main-hander, Maeldoi's two-hander, the rasp of their breathing filling the space between them. Blood dripped in a thin trickle down Maeldoi's chin.

Cae's eyes glowed, a feral red light radiating out from the amber of his irises and staining them blood-tinged; his neck muscles stood out in cords.

The strain took Maeldoi, across his back and shoulders. In his biceps. In his jaw. He tasted the iron of blood; the inside of his mouth stung. He stared into his brother's eyes as they shoved and barged at each other so close together each one's fear-breath reeked in the other's face.

Cae's lips drew back, baring his teeth in a rictus of hate.

Maeldoi heaved against Cae's tension. He felt along it, a steel band connecting the two of them, rigid, quivering with the force of it.

A moment of the slightest slackening.

There.

Maeldoi jammed against his brother, hard and sudden. Cae lurched violently away from him. Maeldoi leapt to his advantage, using Cae's instant of surprise to flick the sword out of his brother's main hand with the point of his two-hander. The force of Maeldoi's attack flung Cae's sword caroming off the wall. He drove his brother back and down, pinning him with a knee in a sickening crunch of bone against bone, driving on Cae with the point of his own sword.

Cae's eyes widened in shock. His mouth opened in a soundless scream. The breath whooped out of him. He drew it in with a judder and a shriek.

Not used to losing. The thought drifted across Maeldoi as the moment splintered and stuttered to a still point. Time slowed. Stopped. Their breathing filled the void. The sharp tang of their sweat.

Cae's whole rigid body contorted and relapsed boneless to the floor.

In the rushlight, Cae's yellow eyes narrowed and glittered beneath his hooded lids. He lay splayed across the stones of the floor, his arms flung wide. Some mere beast, felled, at bay.

"End it." Cae got the words out through gritted teeth, through bloody bitten lips. "End it, brother."

Maeldoi seemed to hang over Cae an eternity, although later, as he thought about it, a minim of time.

Swiftly he reversed his sword and struck Cae on the temple with the pommel.

Maeldoi bent over, shaking, trying to suck in a breath. He pulled himself unsteadily upright to kick his brother's unconscious body away from him. The silence pooled back into the room. But then as if jolted awake from some trance, there came a rustling and a murmuring at the big doors.

Maeldoi ignored it. He wiped the blood off his chin. Absently he patted his jerkin to see how bad the gash there was. Big wet splotch, and it was spreading.

I should stomp on Cae the way I'd stomp on a noxious serpent, he thought. *But who would be left to stomp on me?*

He bent again over his brother. Cae lay dazed and crumpled like a boy. The rage was drained out of him, the beast gone, the line of his cheek softened. His hands lay flung away from him, palms upturned and helpless.

Gently, delicately, Maeldoi leaned down and kissed Cae on the forehead.

Then Maeldoi was running.

He shoved past the shocked, milling armsmen at the doors of the hall, pushing in and staring. He sprinted out of the manor, the bondservants startling behind him. He sprang up the hill, unhobbled Phantom, and flung himself on Phantom's back. Sobbing, he clutched Phantom's mane and gripped him with his knees.

They fled with the wind at their backs to the portal of the Undercroft. There Maeldoi slid off Phantom in a haze of fury and self-contempt and sorrow.

What have I done? he cried out to himself. *What have I left undone?*

Now that it was too late to choose another course, he saw what he should have seen before.

Cae was left alive in the world, knowing what he must not be allowed to know: that in spite of his binding there, Maeldoi could get out of the Undercroft.

In a frisson of terror, Maeldoi recalled the threats Gilles had made against Gisa.

I should have killed Cae, he realized. His head was swimming. Blood loss, maybe. He didn't even feel the pain.

Killed his own brother. Could he have done such a thing? He felt certain Cae would have killed him, had their positions been reversed.

But Maeldoi found something out about himself. He found he couldn't.

And now he needed to get himself to Gisa, to warn her, but there at the portal, he saw with a sick lurching of his stomach, were the Silver King's guards. Then they laid hands on him, and they were marching him to the king.

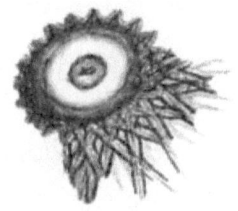

CHAPTER THIRTY-SIX

Too Late

"You left the Undercroft." The Silver King's eyes glowed red in his long, pale face. "Yet you are bound here. You wouldn't have been able to stay out. You realize that. You wouldn't have been able to escape your professed task. You have eaten twelve of the seeds. If you had stayed out long enough, you would have sickened and died. Just so you know."

Maeldoi knelt in the pose of The Penitent. His hands were bound. Phantom had been forced away to the stables by frightened grooms.

"What do you have to say for yourself? Behavior like this, in our Dark Rider, is unacceptable. It is grounds for dismissal."

Maeldoi cast a quick look at Head High Huntress Théodrate. He returned his eyes to the Silver King. He would never betray the Head High Huntress. Never say what he was actually doing on the outside, in the Abovelands.

Dismissal. The king was deciding whether to kill him. He wondered how much the king knew about his real reason for going to the Abovelands. The king had kept Maeldoi locked up for a day. In the interval, had Cae told Gilles of Maeldoi's presence at Cae's manor? Had Cae divined the reason for it, at least partly? Had Cae informed Gilles, and had Gilles gotten word to the king?

Then Maeldoi thought somberly of the last sight he'd had of his brother. How much had he injured Cae? Was he even alive? And even if he were, was he in any condition to inform Gilles?

These questions swirled through Maeldoi's head in a torrent of confused and panicky thinking. Above all, how he'd get to Gisa. He had to. How would he, what would happen to her if he didn't.

Underneath it all, he thought of the Princess Diera. How the young man Rafe had as good as enlisted Maeldoi as her protector, alongside himself. How Maeldoi had failed. How wrongly, despicably he had acted. How he deserved punishment for this ill deed, witch or no witch.

He mastered his expression. He strove for inner calm.

Now Head High Huntress Théodrate came forward. "Pardon, Most High Majesty," she said, and she too knelt. "I've just been told of the Dark Rider's fault, or I would have come to you sooner. The fault is mine. The Dark Rider is proving so useful, so trustworthy, unlike Ditmarus, that I asked him to scout out locations for the novice-huntresses' training in the hunt."

The Silver King swiveled his eyes to his Head High Huntress. He grunted. He looked back to Maeldoi, then to her again. "And this was necessary?"

"I believed so," said Head High Huntress Théodrate. Her tone was perfectly even. Maeldoi admired her self-possession.

"These matters are under your charge. Matters of training."

"Yes, Your Highness."

"Yet I received word, from a reliable source, that this gwrgi was out in the Abovelands without leave."

"There must have been some mistake, then," said the Head High Huntress. "He did have leave. My leave."

The Silver King nodded dismissively. "Keep me better informed, in future."

"Of course, Your Highness," said the Head High Huntress. "I'll be sending him out again soon."

"Very well, then. Release him." The king nodded to his guards. One of them stepped to Maeldoi to remove his bonds. "The Dark Rider's behavior during the Hunt of the Hunter's Moon was flawless. You are right about him, Head High Huntress." The king waved a gracious hand. "We are most pleased."

"Thank you, Your Highness," said Head High Huntress Théodrate. Maeldoi knew to keep his own mouth shut.

The king's words called up to him the tumult of emotions, when the Hunt had ridden out underneath that most important moon of the year. He and Phantom, one beast, one being. The silver sweep of the Hunt, in an exhilarating career over a landscape shrouded in shadow but lit by the moon high in the night sky. The rooing of the hounds. The thunder of the hooves of thirty-two horses, the thirty of the Huntresses, the tall and majestic steed of the Silver King, all ghost-white, and then himself on Phantom, black horse, black armor, Dark Rider. The thrust of the spear. The slaying of the stag. He knew himself then a kind of priest of death.

He had felt it: this is what I was born to do.

He hadn't known, not fully, until the Hunt of the Hunter's Moon. Then he saw what Merlin and Dee must have seen. What Master Bertran may have seen. What Aleron saw in his dreams.

But the sacrifice he'd had to make. It smote him to the heart. Gisa.

Aleron knew. When he gave up a great task to choose Halde instead, he was giving up something like this. Something that would have been to him: this.

Maeldoi wondered if his love for Gisa was as strong and true as Aleron's for Halde. He thought it was. But then he thought of the Hunt. He felt his heart torn in two.

Head High Huntress Théodrate walked out of the throne room and Maeldoi came after her. Outside the room, she stopped and sagged against the wall. He saw her hands were shaking.

"Dangerous work," she murmured to him.

He nodded.

"But what you saw—I think we are doing necessary work. In there, it was clear to me, the King had gotten word about your visit to your brother somehow. Maybe through Gilles or Caedon or another of their minions."

"Lucky for us he believed you and not them," said Maeldoi.

"I'm not sure he did. Just that he knew he must be cautious. We're being watched, Maeldoi, Dark Rider."

Maeldoi shivered, rubbing his wrists where the bonds had chafed the old scars. He had been watched before, and the consequences to him and the one he loved had been dire.

"We're protected by The Three. The King dares not move against us for fear his actions will draw Their attention to him."

Maeldoi saw then that Head High Huntress Théodrate wasn't just implying the king was involved in Gilles de Rais's treachery. Or might be. Or could be.

No. She was saying it outright. Out loud.

"But if he, or Gilles, or that brother of yours sees a way to silence us without drawing the attention of The Three, they're going to do it. Count on it, Dark Rider."

"Head High Huntress Théodrate, I ask your permission to go out on my second mission."

"To see that woman you love. Maybe now is not the time. Given what we both just saw. Given the danger you were just in."

"I fear the one I love is in great danger. I think I told you this. The way Gilles coerced me—in fact, the way Merlin and Dee coerced me—was through fear for her safety."

"Let me ask you this. Do you still feel coerced, Maeldoi, Dark Rider?"

They locked eyes.

"No, Head High Huntress Théodrate. This is the task the gods have meant me to do in my profession. I didn't see it at first. Now I do. I am honored to be Their chosen instrument. I am honored to ride Phantom."

He shoved aside the guilt that shadowed him, the guilt over Diera. Was he even worthy to be the instrument of the gods? Was he even worthy to ride Phantom?

But the Head High Huntress smiled at him. It may have been the first and last time he ever saw Head High Huntress Théodrate smile. "In that case," she said, "permission granted, Maeldoi, Dark Rider."

The next morning found Maeldoi stepping with Phantom from the gwrgi portal closest to the rectory. Closest to Gisa and Aleron. His heart rose.

Gwrgi portals honeycombed the lands underneath the Spheres. Maeldoi remembered the fougou of his childhood, on the moors by the tall hill everyone called Mikkle Tor.

Gwrgi portals are not like mage portals. A mage can cast a portal at will, but then, when the mage goes through the portal, nothing else goes along for the transit, and the mage steps out of it stark naked. Maeldoi was glad gwrgi portals weren't like this. You had to know how to find them—you couldn't just summon one for your convenience, as mages could—but you stepped out of it as well armed and as warmly clothed as when you went in.

The portal near the rectory was tucked into a green valley. From it he could see the red roofs and towers of the rectory.

As he stood looking out over the trees, Maeldoi froze. Something was wrong. The tower looked wrong. It looked—

Maeldoi squinted.

The tower looked caved in.

A wisp of black smoke rose from the rectory.

He urged Phantom forward, not caring who might see him. The panic rose in him. He struggled to keep it under control.

As he came to the gates, he flung himself from Phantom's back. The little bulge of the hermitage was smashed open.

Aleron's words rang in his ears. *There's a story. . . The enemies broke open the hermitage and demanded the hermit come out. He refused. They burned down the building with the hermit still inside.*

And his words to Aleron. *Would you do that?*

And Aleron's reply. *I don't see myself standing up and walking out of here.*

He stepped to the broken masonry and peered in. He could see nothing. The space inside was dark and stank of burning.

He ran through the gate to the other side of the hermitage. The bars were still intact. He gripped them hard, looking in, trying not to scream. A smoldering ruin. There were bones.

They might not be Aleron's.

He knew they were.

In the next instant, he was up the stairs to the top of Mistress Pereta's tower. Gisa's tower.

It was deserted. Books were tumbled everywhere.

He shuffled numbly around the little room. He called out once, but there was no answer.

The quiet settling around the place, the whole rectory, told him no one was there. Killed or captured, or maybe driven off. His grief threatened to overwhelm him, but he knew he couldn't let it. He needed to act, and fast.

He couldn't. He sat against the wall in the tower room as if frozen in place.

He had a vague thought he'd ask in the village.

Maybe a candle-measure went by. Maybe two. At last he got to his feet. He found he was stacking the books and tidying them. *What an addlepate*, he thought, but he kept doing it.

Gisa might be alive. Surely she was.

Where was she.

He bent down and turned over a book. *I know this book*, he thought. It was Man-Dog Rough-Gray. He picked it up, pushed it into a sack he'd found.

He went into a kind of frenzy, pawing through the books as if it were the most important mission of his life.

There it was. There it was at last. He flipped the book open to the woodcut he loved most. Guillaume. His nephew. His giant.

He put that book, too, in the sack, and went back down to the courtyard. To make certain of what he already knew, he searched the rectory. No one was there. There were signs of a struggle. A bloodstain, broken benches. The armory had been ransacked, and the kitchen shed.

No more bodies, though. No more bones.

He went back to the hermitage and leaned against the bars. For a long time he stood there. *Aleron. My friend.* He thought of trying to climb in through the smashed part on the outside, gather the bones, bury them.

There was no time. Maybe it was not too late to find out what happened, chase after the malefactors.

After a while, he got himself down the road to the village. It was a burned-out, blackened shell. One old man sat on the doorsill of a house that was just a wall with a door in it. The other walls had fallen in.

"Good man, what happened here?" he called out.

"Gwrgi," the old man said.

"The gwrgi attacked you? But whoever did this destroyed the rectory too. Gwrgi are there. Were there," he stuttered. "Why would gwrgi destroy their own kind?"

"Gwrgi," the old man repeated. Then he turned his head away and wouldn't answer any more of Maeldoi's questions.

That night, Maeldoi went back to the rectory and slept in the bed in the tower. He almost thought he could feel the warm pressure of Gisa's body into the rush-stuffed case of the mattress. He thought he wouldn't be able to sleep, but he fell asleep immediately and didn't wake til full day.

When he did, the despair descended on him. Aleron was dead. Gisa was gone.

What had happened here had happened recently.

I should have killed Cae, he said to himself. *And now it's too late.*

He realized. He still needed to act, and his need was still urgent. But he could do nothing further until he had performed a sacred task.

He went around to the outer wall of the rectory beside its ruined gates. Scraping himself on the rough and broken masonry, he climbed into the place where someone had smashed in the bricks of the hermitage and breached its enclosure.

He gathered the bones there into his arms, the tears streaming down his cheeks. Then he made his way to the rectory's hillside graveyard and dug a place for them beside Mistress Pereta's grave.

He patted the soil down and stood there for a long time. *Aleron*, he said inside himself. *Help me now, brother.* Then he felt a deep sense of despair. *But in your extremity, I could not help you*, he told Aleron, in the land of the dead. He wiped the tears from his cheeks. The time for tears was over. They'd do Aleron no good now, and he needed to move.

He headed back to the library. *There must be a clue here*, he told himself. A clue about where someone might have taken Gisa. He knew Cae and Gilles hadn't taken her. They liked little girls. They liked little boys. They didn't like women.

Who, then?

Gwrgi did this to their own.

A thought nagged at the edge of Maeldoi's mind. He was heading to the stables where he had put Phantom—water and oats were still there—when it occurred to him.

Something Head High Huntress Théodrate had said. *Maybe that man is just an opportunist and a sadist*, she had said. *But maybe Gilles suborned him.*

Maeldoi felt his eyes turning to twin pinpricks of yellow fire. *Estienn.*

He knew where he had to go. The capital.

You must be crazy, some voice in him said. *She may not be there. And if you're taken, you know what they will do to you.*

He probably was crazy, because he found he was speaking out loud to that voice. "She may be there. She is there. Estienn has her, and I'm taking her back. I'm going. Dark Ones take it, I'm going."

""Come now, Mervin. Get a grip on yourself," said Dee.

Merlin frowned at Dee, who was using the name he went by on the plane they both called home. "Insubordinate old cuss, aren't you," he sniped at Dee. He winced inwardly. *"Get a grip on yourself."* Those were the words Merlin usually directed at Dee.

"No matter what you think of Maeldoi and what he did to Diera at Caedon's manor, here's the weapon we need if we're to go after Gilles. We've been thinking of this all wrong."

"How so?" said Merlin, toying moodily with his staff. He thought again of the Princess Diera, her vulnerability, and what the brothers had done to her. A rage rose inside him. He wanted to blast someone to smithereens with it. Maeldoi, preferably. Or that misbegotten brother.

"No, you don't," said Dee. It was clear to Merlin that Dee could see his thoughts as if he were shouting them out loud. "The person you want to blast is Gilles. And now we have the means to do it. Maeldoi, our weapon."

"Maeldoi makes a poor weapon. As soon as he's in a vulnerable spot, Gilles will seize him," said Merlin in his *I know better* tone.

"Have you been watching Maeldoi, down there? He's in the capital, Mervin. Gilles knows where he is. With Gilles's powers, he could come after him. Why do you think he hasn't?"

"I suppose," said Merlin, thinking about it. "I suppose, seeing as Maeldoi has eaten the seeds and is bound to the Undercroft, Gilles wouldn't have him long, if he did seize him. Maeldoi would start getting weaker, after a few turnings of the moon, and then he would sicken, and then he would die."

"But in the meantime, Gilles could do a lot of feasting and consuming, don't you think? He could take his fill of Maeldoi, drain him dry, and then watch while he dwindles."

"Well, then. You tell me, since you know so much. Why isn't Gilles moving on him?" Merlin had a sour taste in his mouth. He wanted to spit.

"For exactly the reason we had Maeldoi professed correctly into the Undercroft. Now Trioditis protects him."

"Do you think The Three have even noticed?"

"I know They have."

"Huh," said Merlin. "The tables are turned, then, aren't they?"

"Indeed they are. Now Gilles has much to fear from Maeldoi. Now Maeldoi holds the power."

"That's going to make Gilles very unhappy. He's not used to that," said Merlin, a smile beginning to twitch at the corner of his lips in spite of all his efforts to stop it.

"In fact, as I see it, there's only one way Gilles can get at Maeldoi."

"What's that, Dee?"

"Get the gwrgi to do his dirty work for him, and then claim to the Three that he knew nothing about it. Won't be as satisfying, because he won't get to suck Maeldoi's juices, or whatever perverted thing he does to his victims." Merlin watched as Dee tried and failed to suppress a shudder. "But he can get rid of the threat that way. The gwrgi will take Maeldoi, if they can, and slice important parts off him, and put him in their cage."

"You don't think Lord Jouhan would stop it?"

"I think," said Dee slowly, "that by the time Lord Jouhan knows of it, the Traitor's Punishment will be a done deal. Because Gilles has his people in there, Mervin. On the Penance Board."

"One, anyway," said Merlin reluctantly.

"I believe two or three of them. But yes. The most powerful of all, the man who has just assumed the head of the Penance Board. The new Lord Penance Board. Estienn."

"What happened to the old one? He was hidebound, but at least he was fair," said Merlin, fretfully plucking at his robe.

"Illness, they say." Dee arched a skeptical brow. "And now, in his new capacity as head, Estienn has already done a lot of damage. He went after the Northern Rectory and destroyed it, and the surrounding villages with it, all in the name of some trumped-up charges of apostasy. A lot of trouble to go to, just to get his wife back, don't you think? Many good gwrgi destroyed, including a hermit very precious to me. And to Maeldoi."

Dee gripped the arms of his golden chair hard, Merlin saw. He saw Dee was on the point of flying into a rage. "Estienn," Dee whispered. "Gilles controls him, Mervin. All of Maeldoi's troubles with Estienn started there."

He cast a look down to the capital city. "And there's Maeldoi himself, just outside the man's back garden, waiting." Dee pointed.

Merlin looked. "Waiting for what?" he demanded. "Just a beast of the caves," he muttered.

"Love, Mervin. Remember love? Maeldoi is waiting to take Gisa away from that awful man." Dee sighed, and his eyes softened. "Even the beasts know love, Merlin. And Merlin? Maeldoi is no beast."

Merlin made a disgusted face. "Love," he said. "Bah."

He thought of his mother and the trials and sorrow she had faced. Very briefly he thought of the woman he had loved. The one who had betrayed him, humiliated him, and imprisoned him. She insisted on insinuating herself into his mind. He drove her off, but she insisted on sliding back in. Imprisoned him. Him!

He glared at Dee, as if Dee were somehow responsible. "In an oak tree," he hissed to himself.

He took himself elsewhere.

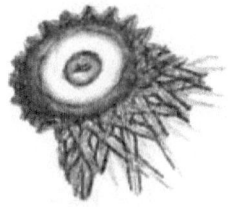

CHAPTER THIRTY-SEVEN

Seed Moon

Dressed in the drab clothing of a trainee, his hood pulled well over his face, Maeldoi sat under a tree with an apple, his slate and chalk beside him. Anyone looking at him would think him a young man who needed help with his letters.

Maeldoi turned his attention to chalk and slate whenever a passerby came down the lane. Otherwise, he studied the wall separating the city from the women's quarter. His job was to get over that wall, and now he thought he had found a tumbledown spot where he could do that job.

He had spent days hanging around the taverns where the trainees congregated, learning what he could of the women's quarter. How it was laid out. And especially the gossip about the great ones who owned houses there. Of course they didn't live there. Their wives did.

Unless he had been steered wrong, he knew he was looking, past the wall, into the back garden of Lord Estienn's wife's house. A pleached garden, a lovely spot—now that it was spring-tide again, especially lovely.

This had better work, he told himself. The Hunt of the Seed Moon was only a sen'night away. He had to be back for it, or to the Dark Ones with him. His lips curled in a sour smile.

Three other times he felt himself on the point of getting to the place where he thought Gisa might be, only to have to head back to the nearest portal in time to get to the Undercroft to bring down the stag at the Hunt for that turning of the moon.

At least by now he knew his way confidently around the city. He well knew how to stay out of the way of the Penance Board and its spies. He knew all the back lanes that led to the women's quarter, all the places where the wall was weakest.

He even had tavern acquaintances here now, people who thought they knew him and knew what and who he was. A diffident trainee who could never pass the examination in letters. A genial fellow, but kind of a wooden-head. A dullard.

His hair was cropped again.

The Silver King didn't like seeing that, whenever Maeldoi returned to his duties.

Maeldoi suspected Head High Huntress Théodrate had to do some fast talking to explain that one away.

He says the hair gets in his face as he's trying to make his kill, she tells the king.

I don't like it. It's not traditional, the king complains. *It makes him look like a peasant.*

No, only like a trainee, Maeldoi thinks. Among the gwrgi, anyhow.

Now, finding himself alone, he studied the upper windows of the big house, which he could see looming over the wall. Quite a house. But then, Estienn was quite an important man. Gossip said the Lord Penance Board was ill with some stomach ailment. Gossip said he would soon die, and Lord Estienn would take his place.

I'll just bet the Lord Penance Board has a stomach ailment. Maeldoi thought of what Cae and Gilles between them had done to whisk King Ranulf neatly out of their way, over in the Sceptered Isle. Probably with the help of some witch. *Labinia.* Maeldoi felt the sick guilt rise in him. He stifled it.

Cae himself, so it was whispered, was the one who had put Ranulf's heir to the knife. No poison for that one. A slit throat. And then Cae had taken the heir's daughter, the Princess Diera, to his own manor. And then he'd—

Maeldoi had to turn his thoughts away from his brother, so disturbing they were. And from his own sordid role.

He rose and went to the wall. There was a chink in it. When he knew himself alone, he decided he'd go over to it and look in, and think of a way to scale the wall and then the wall of the house, to one of those upper windows, maybe.

This time, he intended to act.

Before he could, he heard a voice. He couldn't make out the words. He put his eye to the chink.

A woman.

His heart stopped. Gisa.

She was talking to someone. A servant, he thought.

Then it seemed she was alone.

Now, he told himself. He vaulted over the wall.

She whirled around, startled. Stared. Made a strangled exclamation. Then she was sobbing in his arms.

Almost at once she was thrusting him away from her. "Go!" she hissed.

Footsteps.

Maeldoi looked wildly around.

She pointed furiously to some barrels at a corner of the garden, and he got himself behind them.

It was the servant again. The servant was coming toward Gisa with a bundle.

The bundle began to squall.

"Hand him here," he heard Gisa say. "I'll walk with him in the garden for a while."

"Yes, mistress." The servant, retreating.

With the infant in her arms, Gisa strolled toward the barrels.

He could see the enormous effort she was making to remain calm.

She was jiggling the infant, and the child stilled.

She leaned against the barrels, her back to Maeldoi, and began speaking quietly. "They watch me, Maeldoi. They could be watching me now. I tried to get away from them, and they caught me and brought me back." She heaved a deep breath. It sounded as though it came from her shoes. "I prayed to the gods you'd come after me. Find me. But now. You see now. You're here, but it's too late."

She bent her head over the infant and nuzzled him.

"I don't understand. I was at the rectory a few turnings of the moon ago. It was destroyed. Aleron is dead. You were gone. I thought—" Maeldoi bowed his head. "I let him down," he whispered miserably. "I wasn't there to stop them, and they broke into his hermitage, and struck him down as if he were some beast. Some nothing. One of the best men I've ever known. And then, as if that weren't an evil enough deed, they took you."

"Maeldoi." She looked at him. "What you tell me about Aleron shatters me. But as for myself. I've been here for over a year," she said. "Over a year," she repeated. "Only a sen'night after you disappeared, a man came to the rectory. He told the assistant rector I was an imposter, a runaway wife, and he was there to arrest me. The man who came. Maeldoi, it was your brother."

Maeldoi felt a sick fury. "Cae and Gilles promised me. They promised if I'd go with them and do what they wanted, you wouldn't be harmed."

"They lied to you, Maeldoi."

"I suppose when I thwarted them, they thought they were free to act against you."

She shrugged. "Do they have any scruples at all? Whatever they thought, whatever they agreed to, whatever their intentions might have been, they took me. It gave them a valuable inroad into gwrgi society."

"They are in league with Estienn."

"Yes."

He saw it. Gisa had been the prize Gilles and his brother had dangled before Estienn, to secure him to themselves more tightly. No time for the rage. Maeldoi thrust it impatiently away. "Quickly, now. I'm here to get you out."

"Maeldoi, do you see what Estienn has done to me? This is my son by him." She held the infant up, and he began to cry, so she hushed and cradled him. "You must leave me here, Maeldoi."

"Never."

"I won't leave my son. They don't even watch me that closely any longer. They know I won't run. They know I'll never leave my child."

"I won't leave him here either," said Maeldoi. "Not with that fiend who has you trapped here. Not any child. Certainly not a child of yours."

He thought of Gilles. He thought of how beholden Estienn was to Gilles, and whether he might now owe Gilles a child. After himself falling into the hands of Gilles, he'd found out what the baron did to children. He knew Gilles had children brought to him, as tribute from those beholden to him. His blood chilled.

"I am too tainted," Gisa whispered.

"And I am tainted. We've both been made to do things we abhor. But the life of that little child is not abhorrent, and you are not abhorrent, Gisa. Step closer to the barrels."

She did.

"Hand him back to me."

She did.

The child began to fuss.

Maeldoi soothed him. Not through any shamanic means. Just in the ordinary way.

"I'm going to step with him back over this broken spot in the wall. Do you know where I mean?"

"I've been over that wall several times. Never to any good effect."

"Do it, Gisa. Do it fast, before the servant comes back."

And soon he had bundled her into the spare cloak he had brought. And soon they had fled the city. And soon they were at the gwrgi portal outside the city.

But the faraway portal where they came out.

Ah, that was something different.

I never thought I'd see this spot again, Maeldoi thought, as he and Gisa stood at the entrance to the fougou, the infant in Gisa's arms.

"Where are we?" said Gisa, marveling.

"See that high hill? That's Mikkle Tor. And we are in the westernmost part of the Sceptered Isle at the edge of a vast moor."

Before he could say anything further, he felt rather than saw another person standing beside them at the entrance to the fougou. Gisa gasped and seized Maeldoi's arm. The baby started to wail.

"Quiet that infant." A large man stood beside them, as naked as he was made, his skin as dark as burnished wood, like a man from the Burnt Lands.

"Lord Merlin," said Maeldoi, bowing low, his heart quaking. Sidelong he saw Gisa put her son to her breast to suckle. She turned away from them, soothing her baby.

Maeldoi stood and whipped his own cloak from his shoulders. He handed it to Merlin.

The mage wrapped it about himself, never taking his furious eyes from Maeldoi. "What have you done?" he said in a low, penetrating, basso profundo voice.

Maeldoi knew Merlin wasn't talking about Gisa. He meant the princess Diera. "A witch, Most High—"

"And you let her. You failed to ward yourself against her."

Maeldoi assumed the position The Penitent.

"Bah," spat Merlin. "Begone, foul incubus." He raised his staff, which had blossomed into his hand.

Before he could act—to end Maeldoi completely, Maeldoi was sure of it—another figure materialized beside Merlin.

This other man, pointed beard, piercing blue eyes, put a hand on Merlin's arm. "Merlin, no."

Gisa stepped to the two of them. She looked from one to the other. She shrugged off her own cloak and handed it to this new man.

"Thank you, my dear," said the newcomer. It was the mage called Dee. He put on the cloak. Now he turned back to Merlin. "The lad was taken by surprise."

"He shouldn't have been," growled Merlin. "And then he did a despicable thing."

"I am to blame," murmured Maeldoi.

"You stay silent, if you know what's good for you," said Merlin.

"Listen, Merlin." Dee's eyes were earnest. "Here he is with this young woman and her baby. He's going to take care of them. Let him. Let him atone."

"That's what they all do, these gwrgi. They do terrible things, then they grovel, and everything is supposed to be just fine. Well, no, it isn't just fine. The damage this man has done." Merlin prodded Maeldoi with a disgusted toe. "The repercussions of his act will echo down the years, each year doing more damage than the last."

"Just as Gilles planned it," Dee said somberly. "There's your villain, Merlin. Not this one." He leaned down and guided Maeldoi to his feet.

Dee stared at Maeldoi. "The years ahead will be hard," he said to Maeldoi, his voice quiet. "Gilles will try to damage the Undercroft. He has already made his incursions on the Silver King. Already corrupted him. You and Head High Huntress Théodrate will be the only ones standing between the Undercroft and Gilles. After a while, you'll have help. But so will the Silver King. It will be a battle, Maeldoi. Are you so crippled by guilt that you won't fight?"

"I'll fight," said Maeldoi, low. "I swear I will. I want to make it right, but how can I."

"You can, and you will," said Dee. "You feared Gilles. Now he will fear you. He had the power over you. Now you have the power over him, the power to destroy him. Will you take that power and use it to protect the Spheres?"

"I promise I will," said Maeldoi.

"You amaze me, Dee," said Merlin, menace in his voice. "The only thing standing between the eala and Gilles—between the Spheres and Gilles—is this beast of the caves?" He spat. "This flawed piece of work?"

"Aren't we all, Mervin. Aren't we all."

They were still arguing when they disappeared. Not with a dramatic poof. Just gone.

Maeldoi stood staring at the place where they'd been standing. He felt a chill to his marrow.

"At least they left the cloaks behind. We're going to need those," said Gisa, collecting them from where they had puddled back to the stone floor of the fougou. "I'm cold, and so are you."

"Gisa, that mage is right. I have done terrible wrong."

"And I have. Here's your cloak."

"I should have known."

"And I should have known," said Gisa, putting hers on again. "You and I, Maeldoi. We gwrgi. We are not beasts. This little child is not a beast." She pulled aside the infant's blanket to look at him. "There may be something inside us of the beast," she said. "I wonder, though. Might not that be true for the other kinds as well?" She put a hand on his arm. "Might not that be true for all of us underneath the Spheres? But you have a job to do, looks like. Now, then. We were interrupted. You were about to explain to me where we've come."

He managed to lift his eyes to hers, the shame pressing on him. "You don't know what I've done."

"And I don't want to know. What I want to know is how I'll feed myself and this baby. How we'll shelter out of the weather. Tell me about that, Maeldoi."

Maeldoi drew a ragged breath. "I'm about to take you to a little village. If it's still there, to a small hut," he said. He gained inner command of his shattered self. "I'll have to leave you there. I was professed, Gisa. Professed at last, and my task binds me to a certain spot. I was taken to it and coerced to it. I would have never left you otherwise. Never."

"I believe you."

"But now." He dropped his eyes. "Now I feel the power and rightness of my profession. I have to tell you that, and maybe you'll think it a betrayal."

"Those two mages saw what it means," Gisa said. She made him look at her. "They saw the important role you'll play. I'm content, Maeldoi."

He swallowed hard and forced himself to go on. "Where I am bound, I'm not allowed out into the world very often. But every time I am, every time I can, I'll come to you here. I'll not be able to stay long. If I do, I'll weaken and die. So what kind of life you'll have here. . ." he trailed off. "Only if you want it, Gisa. It's a hard life. If you don't want it, just tell me, and I'll take you anywhere a gwrgi portal can. I'll even take you back to the city, back to Estienn. It may be too hard, what I'm asking of you. You may want Estienn's protection—if not for yourself, then for your son. Tell me what you want, Gisa, and I promise I'll do it. Tell me, too, if you want me to leave you here and never come to you again. Tell me, and I'll do it."

"I want to go to the village you speak of, to the hut, Maeldoi. Whenever you can get away from this task of yours, I want to be there waiting," she said. "I want to feel your arms about me and your lips on my lips. I want to make a bed and lie down in it beside you. Let's get going. This little one is asleep now, but he won't sleep long."

Maeldoi searched her eyes with his. Finally he nodded.

When they got to the edge of the village, Maeldoi smiled. A grim smile, he knew. There was the hut. It might be someone else's now. It might be uninhabitable, after all this time.

He guided Gisa to it and shoved aside the hide, stiff and brittle now, that hung over the door. It was almost as if he'd never left it. A bit more tumbledown, but still a shelter in its rude and simple way.

The villagers, he thought later, must have decided it was a cursed place, a gwrgi place, and they'd left it alone.

He made a fire in the hearth and went out to the stream behind the hut to pull up a fish from the stream for them to eat. He gutted it and roasted it on a stick over the hearth. He dipped up a bucket of water from the swift flowing waters upstream of the hut, and brought it back for them to drink.

Gisa made a soft bed of rushes for the child to sleep on. He was awake, looking around with his wide yellow eyes, waving his little arms and legs and cooing. She fed him again, and then she rocked and sang him to sleep.

Maeldoi led her up the ladder to the loft. They spread out their cloaks there. He turned to her, troubled.

She drew him down on the cloaks, pulling her kirtle over her head. She bent to unlace his leggings.

He skinned the tunic off himself and then the leggings.

"I thought I'd never see this body again, Maeldoi," she murmured, touching him. Stroking him. "Thought I'd never feel you under my hands."

She pulled him to her.

When their bodies met and joined, they cried out in joy and wonder. Maeldoi swore to himself the Spheres chimed, echoing their love. And then they slept deep in each other's arms.

In the morning, he made preparations to leave her.

"Will you be well, here by yourself with the little one?" he asked her.

"I'll be well, Maeldoi. I learned to be resourceful, when I escaped Estienn and the city to follow you so long ago. But I'll miss you terribly."

"And I'll miss you," he told her. "The Seed Moon is near to full, though, and my duties call me back to the Undercroft, the place where my task has bound me."

"What is your task?"

"You'll see. When the moon is at full, take the little one and climb Mikkel Tor. You'll see the Wild Hunt sweep by you, and feel the pounding of the hooves. The Huntresses will be silver and white, and the Silver King who leads them. They'll thunder by on their white horses. But when you see a man on a black horse, the Dark Rider, the only one in the Hunt dressed in black, in that moment think of me."

"I don't understand."

"I know. But you will. Dark horse, Dark Rider." He fixed her with the yellow of his eyes and in hers he saw the promise and pledge of her love. "I'll be back as soon as I can. Do you trust me, Gisa?"

"Do you trust me, Maeldoi?"

They smiled at each other, and they kissed.

As he got ready to go to the fougou and force himself to leave her, he turned at the door. "In your library, I found a few books. I've left them on the shelf with the porridge bowls."

"Thank you, Maeldoi! I haven't been allowed to have a book."

"I'll bring you more, Scholar," he promised her, with a smile.

"Farewell for now, Maeldoi, Protector of the Spheres." She stood at the door with the baby in her arms. He was waving his fists in the air and gurgling.

Maeldoi bent down and kissed the little boy on the forehead. It gave him a strange feeling. This wasn't his child, but he felt like he was its father.

He thought of his own mother, so long ago, waiting at this same hut for visits from an angry and violent man. It seemed to him he saw, in the shadowy corner of the hut, two frightened small boys. And he found he could love them and pity them both.

"You didn't tell me his name," said Maeldoi, gazing down on the little child in Gisa's arms.

"Guillaume," she told him, and smiled into his eyes.

◁◉▷

NOTES ON *Dark Ones Take It*

from the author

This novel is a work of fantasy, not historical fiction. Just the same, it is indebted to history. For some visual depictions of some of the scenes and ideas in this novel, visit my Pinterest board, **Medieval Life—Dark** . For a full play list of songs from the Harbingers and Stormclouds series, visit my web site, www.janemwiseman.com.

THE TIME-PERIOD is roughly early medieval, in a realm vaguely resembling several of the Celtic, Anglo-Saxon, Viking, and Norman kingdoms and military groups vying for power in the 10th and early 11th century British Isles shortly before the Norman Conquest, as well as the interlocking feudal states that would become France. There are hints of different ethnic groups and warring ethnic factions

Twelve Realms:

The Sceptered Isle stands in for the united Heptarchy (seven main kingdoms) of mainland Anglo-Saxon England, but also includes the northern part of the realm (Scotland), the Western Isle (Ireland) and the northern isles (islands off the coast of Scotland— Inner and Outer Hebrides, Orkney, and Shetland Islands). It does not include the area around Lunds-fort (London), however.

The Eastern Baronies stands in for a loose confederation of powerful feudal lords spreading across medieval France and parts of Germany. In my tale, the Eastern Baronies also own territory on the mainland of the Sceptered Isle— the land around Lunds-fort (London) and along the eastern edge of the mainland—in addition to their strongholds across the Narrows (the English Channel).

The Southern Primacy stands in for medieval territories in Italy (as well as Portugal and Spain), the homeland to which the Old Ones (ancient Romans) pulled back as their empire dwindled.

The Lyre Lands stands in for the vestiges of ancient Greece and the lands rimming the Aegean in the medieval era.

The Realm of the Asp stands in for the ancient Near and Middle East.

The Burnt Lands is a vague concept to people of the Sceptered Isle and similar northern realms. It stands in for North Africa and below, through Sub-Saharan Africa, but people in the northern realms know little of these lands.

The Ice-Realm stands in for medieval Norway and, in a loose sense, the other parts of Scandinavia.

The Fire Isle stands in for medieval Iceland.

The Mountain Fastnesses stands in for the Alpine regions of Europe.

The Trade Road Fortifications stands in for the old Silk Road of the late ancient world through the Renaissance, stretching along the Eurasian steppes.

The Silk Lands stands in for China and southeast Asia.

The Forgotten Kingdom stands in for the Indian subcontinent.

ALSO:

The New Found Lands (the Americas) across the Great Sea stretching to the west.

THE RELIGIOUS BELIEFS OF THE GWRGI: They live among worshippers of an elemental universe controlled by earth, sea, fire, and sky. In the real world, these beliefs derive from very ancient sources such as the Greek philosopher Empedocles. The head of these elemental gods, in some sources, is Trioditis, the Three, the goddess of the crossroads. For Empedocles, the three faces of this triple godhead are Strife, Love, and the overarching Harmony that binds them together. For others, they are the three faces of Hecate, or the Triple Goddess Selene, Artemis, and Hecate. (Present-day astrologers and New Age religions have their own settled ideas about these matters. I know nothing about their ideas and don't pretend to.)

THE OVERALL CONCEPT OF THE UNIVERSE is Pythagorean: nine revolving transparent crystalline spheres carry the heavenly bodies (sun, moon, stars, planets) around the earth at their center. This idea from the ancient classical Near East and then Rome (mentioned by Cicero in *De Republica*, and also by the philosopher of late antiquity, Boethius) was widespread in the medieval period and made its way into medieval Christianity and became important in the Renaissance, obviously long before anyone knew anything about the way the actual physical universe works. The Greek philosopher Empedocles envisioned this universe supported by the principle of harmony, produced when strife and serenity are held in balance.

TYPES OF BEINGS: In this fantasy work, the world contains a number of different types of sentient beings: ordinary folk, the mages, the gwrgi, the eala, the witches, and possibly more. Each has its special nature and special place underneath the Spheres.

GWRGI: See *Man-Dog Rough-Gray*, below. In the medieval lore of Western and Northern Europe, the gwrgi might have been dog-headed warriors, a kind of werewolf, or perhaps just warriors that fought as fiercely as beasts. In my fantasy world, gwrgi are werewolf-like beings, although the other types of beings harbor a lot of fears and misinformation about them.

GILLES DE RAIS is an actual historical figure. A member of the French aristocracy, he supported Joan of Arc during the Hundred Years War between France and England, fighting at her side. Despite that heroic part of his life, he dabbled in the occult, thought of himself as a sorcerer, and confessed to being one of the most prolific serial killers in history. His victims were almost all children. Most historians believe he was guilty of these crimes, although various conspiracy theorists have raised doubts. The real Gilles de Rais lived long after the time-period of this novel, but my fantasy version of Gilles de Rais had lived many lives before he came to the attention of history, and many lives after. Could he be living another of his lives still? I'm not saying!

FOUGOU: Long roofed curved passageways found in southwestern Cornwall, dating from perhaps 500 CE. No one knows what these strange passageways were for. See https://druidry.org/resources/fogous for a description and some theories.

CHOUCHENN: A type of mead from Brittany. It is made from fermented honey.

THE PLATONIC SOLIDS are a very ancient mechanism for understanding the universe, reaching back further than the Greek philosopher Plato (born around 428 BCE, or maybe a bit later; died around 348 BCE), who described them (hence the name). *The Stanford Encyclopedia of Philosophy* gives the philosophical background in its discussion of Plato's dialogue, *Timaeus* (see section 8, "Physics"):
https://plato.stanford.edu/entries/plato-timaeus/
For a readily available translation, see:
http://classics.mit.edu/Plato/timaeus.html

Euclid (maybe born around 325 BCE) described them, too, in Book XIII of his *Elements*:

https://mathcs.clarku.edu/~djoyce/java/elements/bookXIII/bookXIII.html

The math education web site MathWorld gives a mathematical explanation (far over my head):

http://mathworld.wolfram.com/PlatonicSolid.html

But the solids have been used in fortune-telling and games of chance and other gaming (think of the many-sided dice of Dungeons & Dragons, for example) since time immemorial. There are four of these geometrical solids: a cube (six faces), to the ancient world representing the element earth; a tetrahedron (four faces), to the ancient world representing fire; an octahedron (eight faces) representing air; and an icosahedron (twenty faces) representing water. There was also a fifth solid that Plato and Aristotle described very mysteriously: the twelve-sided dodecahedron, which they thought might have something to do with the composition of the heavens.

Some believe Neolithic objects discovered in Scotland may be evidence that people were thinking about the properties of the solids as far back as prehistoric times. There is quite a lot of skepticism about that from reliable sources, however:

https://studylib.net/doc/7289332/the-macplatonic-solids--mathematics-in-neolithic-scotland

GOSSUIN, also known as Gautier, wrote *L'Image du monde* (*The image of the world*) in 1245. In this book, he described the world as a ball, discussed the four elements of earth, water, air, and fire, and mentioned the dazzling appearance of the angels (in this work of fantasy, angels correspond to the eala, Celtic beings like swans that might have resembled angels).

BRETON HARP: This is the instrument Caedon learns to play. This instrument, hugely important in early Breton culture, faded away after the medieval period. It's not the same as its Celtic harp cousins in Scotland and Ireland. It's a wire-strung triangular harp that was apparently played using a plectrum, although Alan Stivell and other contemporary musicians who have revived Breton music do not adhere exactly to these medieval descriptions, which are obscure. The whole topic is quite technical and beyond me, but here are some sources, including a link to Stivell's beautiful music:

http://www.standingstones.com/bretonharp.html#telenn

http://www.cgh-poher.org/telechargement/kaier29/9-ALAN%20STIVELL.pdf

https://www.youtube.com/watch?v=s4pbYbY5iVA

THE SONG CAEDON SINGS AND PLAYS IS BASED ON a song by the French lyricist Passerat, 1580. You can hear a version of it here:
https://www.youtube.com/watch?v=qB5ZZKSbHPw

Hazard, a medieval gambling game involving dice, is the basis for the modern gambling game of craps:
https://www.lostkingdom.net/medieval-gambling-games-dice/

THE WILD HUNT, a ghostly chase of spirits through the night forest (ghosts? witches? fairies? the dead? it varies) often led by mythic or even historical figures (King Arthur, the Nordic god Odin, the Devil, Sir Francis Drake, etc.). The Wild Hunt is a folkloric motif found in many cultures worldwide. It is classified as ATU e501 in the Aarne-Thompson-Uther folk index, a codification of folk tales into categories. This tale is a prominent feature of the Middle English poem *Sir Orfeo*, a medieval recreation of the Orpheus/Eurydice myth, in which fae folk live underground and are ruled by the king of the Underworld. They ride out of their underground home, to the wonder and terror of ordinary people.

CELTIC MOON NAMES: There are many variations among the names Celtic peoples called the various moons of the lunar year. Here are some of the most common:

January, Wolf Moon
February, Storm Moon
March, Plough Moon
April, Seed Moon
May, Mother's Moon
June, Mead Moon
July, Herb Moon
August, Grain Moon
September, Wine Moon
October, Hunter's Moon
November, Mourning Moon
December, Oak Moon

Here are a few sites (some more fanciful than others) explaining these names:
http://www.ecoenchantments.co.uk/mynaming_of_moonspage.html
http://www.celticmythmoon.com/moon.html

https://www.lunarphasepro.com/full-moon-names/

MAN-DOG ROUGH-GRAY is a character in an Old Welsh poem about King Arthur, *Ymddiddan Arthur a Glewlwyd Gafaelfawr* (The dialogue of Arthur and Glewlwyd Gafaelfawr). It goes by other names as well. The poem describes Arthur's exploits against a number of foes, including the dog-headed men (maybe werewolves or creatures known as gwrgi) led by the fearsome Man-Dog Rough-Gray. The poem has been dated from the 10th century, although recent scholarly work dates it later, and it has antecedents in the much earlier Welsh Triads. One of those older texts is known as "Pa gur" ("What man") because that version begins with those words. I have used my own fanciful take on the story and the idea of the gwrgi in this novel. The material here merely uses the old texts as a jumping off point and then departs considerably from the real texts mentioning Man-Dog Rough-Gray.

GUILLAUME: The twelfth century medieval heroic tale about this hero (maybe based on a 9th century warrior) is one of the oldest known French chansons de geste, tales of noble deeds. Guillaume and his nephew are aided by a giant as they fight the foe.

ANCHORITES (and the female version, anchoress) are a particular type of hermit in medieval Europe. In my fantasy world, this is the basis for the practices of the gwrgi Hermitage. Medieval anchorites petitioned to be enclosed (locked up) for their whole lives, which they spent in contemplation and prayer, and sometimes in doling out advice to petitioners. Ruins of their cells (anchorholds) can be found attached to medieval churches. Here's a good quick description, although it focuses on the female practitioners: https://www.bl.uk/medieval-literature/articles/the-life-of-the-anchoress

APOLOGIES for my petty thefts from, modifications of, and irreverent references to a medieval song by Passerat, the ancient texts known as the Welsh Triads and the Old Welsh poem *Ymddiddan Arthur a Glewlwyd Gafaelfawr*, the medieval French writer Gautier (Gossuin), the French chanson de geste *Chanson de Guillaume*, the Middle English poem *Sir Orfeo*, and the Roman poets Horace, Catullus, and Virgil. Lawyers! When I use the word "theft," I am making a joke. The literary figure of speech I am really using is "allusion," and my novels are at least partly a kind of literary mash-up.

AND A FINAL THANK-YOU to Warren Robinett, the inventor of the easter egg.

ABOUT THE AUTHOR

I hope you have enjoyed *Dark Ones Take It*, the origin story of the villain of the **Stormclouds** and **Harbingers** fantasy novels and the companion **Betwixt & Between** novels. Please leave a review of my novel on web sites for readers and book lovers. I care about what my readers think! Please visit my author web site, www.janemwiseman.com. Follow my blog about speculative fiction, www.fantastes.com.

As always, I welcome reviews and feedback posted on amazon.com, goodreads.com, and other web sites for book lovers, and on my author web site, janemwiseman.com.

Jane Wiseman splits her time between urban Minneapolis and the Sandia Mountains of New Mexico. She loves fantasy in all its forms, enjoys her family, reads all the time, and writes in many different modes. As for fantasy, she writes books that she would like to read. She also paints (although not well).

A NOTE OF ACKNOWLEDGMENT

Thanks to my wonderful daughter, Margaret Govoni, for your editing eye. You steered me away from many mishaps and missteps, Margaret, especially in the early novels. All the remaining mistakes are mine alone.

Thanks to you, Bob, for being a faithful beta-reader!

Thanks for all the helpful suggestions I've gathered from a number of online Litreactor workshops, www.Litreactor.com (especially the ones led by John Skipp) and from other writing workshops: the Tinker Mountain Writers workshop, www.hollins.edu/academics/workshops-online-writing-courses/tinker-mountain-writers-workshop-residential/, and the (sadly now defunct) Taos Summer Writers' Conference sponsored by the University of New Mexico. The instructors' comments and suggestions were of course incredibly helpful, but I have valued beyond measure the comments and suggestions of my fellow workshop attendees. Thanks to all of you! You may not have been able to save me from all my writing sins, but you saved me from many. Thanks also to the Anam Cara Writer's and Artist's Retreat, www.anamcararetreat.com, on the Beara Peninsula of Ireland. What a peaceful and lovely place to write! Thanks, Sue!

And finally, thanks to all you Norrathians out there. You are my true battle buddies. You know who you are. You are my fantasy friends in the purest sense of all.

Thanks to the following for the public domain illustrations used in the composite art for my book cover:

Image by <a href="https://pixabay.com/users/catharina77-784204/?utm_source=link-attribution&utm_medium=referral&utm_campaign=image&utm_content=658755">Catharina77</a> from <a href="https://pixabay.com/?utm_source=link-attribution&utm_medium=referral&utm_campaign=image&utm_content=658755">Pixabay</a>

Image by <a href="https://pixabay.com/users/succo-96729/?utm_source=link-attribution&utm_medium=referral&utm_campaign=image&utm_content=2453295">succo</a> from <a href="https://pixabay.com/?utm_source=link-attribution&utm_medium=referral&utm_campaign=image&utm_content=2453295">Pixabay</a>

Image by <a href="https://pixabay.com/users/prettysleepy-2973588/?utm_source=link-attribution&utm_medium=referral&utm_campaign=image&utm_content=3251000">Prettysleepy</a> from <a href="https://pixabay.com/?utm_source=link-attribution&utm_medium=referral&utm_campaign=image&utm_content=3251000">Pixabay</a>

If you enjoyed this novel, please continue reading the Harbingers/Stormclouds fantasy novels

Stormclouds : dark fantasy about a dark world of treachery and rebellion.

Book I, *A Gyrfalcon for a King*
Book II, *The Call of the Shrike*
Book III, *Stormbird*

Harbingers : fantasy with a young adult/new adult flavor.

Book I, *Blackbird Rising*
Book II, *Halcyon*
Book III, *Firebird*
Book IV, *Ghost Bird*

Betwixt & Between : companions to the Stormclouds/Harbingers novels. There are realms and situations underneath the Spheres that don't fit into the world of men and women. They exist in some ghostly place betwixt and between.

Book I, *The Martlet is a Wanderer*
Book II, *The Nightingale Holds Up the Sky*

And this stand-alone novel set in the Stormclouds/Harbingers universe: *Dark Ones Take It* , the origin story of the villain Caedon and his brother, Maeldoi.

You might also like the urban fantasy novella *Witchmoon*. Characters from the Stormclouds/Harbingers world intrude themselves into ours!

All available in print or for Kindle and Kindle-enabled devices at www.amazon.com

Two excerpts from Stormclouds/Harbingers novels

Here are excerpts from *A Gyrfalcon for a King*, the first book in the prequel Stormclouds series, and *Blackbird Rising*, the first book in the Harbingers series. See the full list of the novels.

Excerpt from *A Gyrfalcon for a King*

An Eagle for an Emperor. A Gerfalcon for a King. A Peregrine for a Prince. A Tiercel for an Earl. A Lanar for a Squire. A Sparhawk for a Yeoman.

I t all started with a comet.

Myrddin, or Merlin, or Mervin—whatever you care to call the Arch-mage—assembled the entire Magisterial High Council, both upper and lower houses, for an emergency meeting.

He and his good friend the mage John Dee had been playing a game of chess. It was time for the meeting to begin, however, so Myrddin rose to put the board away.

"You know I had your queen in a tight spot. I was about to say garde, just as a friendly gesture," Dee groused good-naturedly.

Myrddin laughed. "Why, Dee, what an old-fashioned gentlemanly thing to do. You're something of a fuddy-duddy, you know that?" He settled his features into more serious lines. This meeting would not be pleasant. With a swirl of his robes, he strode down the corridor and into the council chambers.

Behind the two of them, another mage waited in the shadow. Gilles de Rais, almost as powerful as Myrddin. As powerful as Dee. He watched the other two through narrowed eyes, then whisked into Myrddin's private quarters.

There. The scrying stone that Myrddin kept so very close. He had just been using it. Gilles could smell it. If he moved close to it and peered in, perhaps the last vision Myrddin saw there might still be swirling in its depths.

Gilles sidled closer. He darted to the stone and peered in. He could just make it out. A young man, barely out of boyhood. A young man with a musical instrument of some sort. He was playing and singing.

That's the mage, Gilles thought with a thrill. *That's the one. Myrddin and Dee are pinning their hopes on him. He isn't born yet, but when he comes into the world, he'll be weak. Vulnerable. I'll make him mine.*

Gilles smiled. He glanced around, making sure he was not observed, then strode off to the council meeting.

The meeting was just getting under way. At the big stone pulpit, its marble facing stained with the ages, Myrddin took a steadying breath.

"I've brought you here today because of an alarming situation, a sore on creation about to fester and rot and burst underneath the Spheres," Myrddin proclaimed to the assembled mages.

Gilles de Rais made his way to his accustomed seat and sat down, looking attentive. He wasn't fooling Myrddin and Dee, he knew. He saw the apprehensive glances they cast in his direction.

Myrddin went on. "A crack in the Spheres themselves. A hairline crack, to be sure. But widening. The farwydds have foreseen this dis-ease of the Spheres, and they've called on me. They gave me warning. Now I'm passing their warning along to all of you. It's this: the Children are angry," he told them. "And if the Children are angry, there can be only one reason. The Three are angry."

Myrddin saw how shaken all the mages of the High Council were at his words. *Almost all,* he told himself with a certain despair. Perhaps he was about to lose this game, just as he was losing at chess only moments ago. But the stakes were so much higher. Worlds higher.

He kept going, past his fears and the stir his words were causing. He had to.

"Comes with the job," Dee murmured at his shoulder, seeing how unsettled his friend was.

The mages grew silent and stilled, listening.

"The farwydds have told me we need to get our people in line, or there will be trouble. Do I have to remind you what happened last time?" Myrddin's voice, a penetrating basso profundo, rang into the council chamber.

The assembled mages cringed and fearfully shook their heads. They had all read the books of lore recounting the horror of the times Myrddin spoke of. The Three had split the Spheres with Their wrath. All beneath the Spheres had died agonizing deaths. Every man, every woman, every child. After the Three had wiped the slate clean, they had angrily demanded that the Children (the other four) do better. The Three had made Them start all over. Make a new beginning. Fashion better creatures. Build a new world.

"Here we are," said Myrddin to his fellow mages, opening his arms wide. "We are that new world. And we mages, and our farwydds, are the creatures the Children have put in place to mediate between the Themselves and their creation. We're Their safety valve. Their canaries in the mine.

"For a while, the Three were placated. Now They've become displeased. When they look down upon the Twelve Realms, and the Unknown Lands, and all the other places beneath the Spheres, they see eruptions in the Balance. They see creatures who refuse Balance, who arrogantly set out to control things themselves. And they blame us, the mages, for not keeping such an explosive situation within acceptable bounds."

"Could Their anger have something to do with the star of fire we've seen streaking through the Spheres?" cried one of the mages.

"It's only a small star," said another. "It will burn itself out. Nothing to fear."

"Maybe it's a sign," said a third. "A sign of the Children's displeasure."

"The displeasure of The Three," said still another.

And another murmured, low, "Trioditis."

"Hush," another cautioned. "The likes of us do not presume to speak Their name."

Myrddin steeled himself, because the mage Gilles de Rais was rising to interrupt.

Gilles stroked his clean-shaven chin and looked around him, fixing this mage and that with his severe eye. "Why should the Children blame us? And beyond Them, the Three?" He cast a scornful eye on them all. "Trioditis. Yes, I'll name Them. I'll not cower away from Them. We mages shepherd creation as best we can. Is it our fault if some of its creatures get ideas above their station? Is it our fault if some of them want power, and seize it? That's the way of the world. Those with the power control the weak. Any of them with intelligence and will and drive? Any of them possessing those noble traits? Of course they'll try to seize control. Surely the Three must appreciate that. Must appreciate any of their creatures who have such drive. Must reward them. Such creatures are only mirroring the best qualities of their gods."

He drew a breath. His voice, its harshness concealed by a charming Baronies lilt, turned insistent. "Those who seize control aren't opposing balance. They are balance themselves, weighing their extraordinary, commendable strength against the general weakness and pusillanimity of all the others of creation. These strong ones deserve to rule over the weak." Gilles's voice vibrated with conviction. His teeth glinted as he smiled at his fellow mages. "As I'm sure we all agree."

Myrddin wondered if he should shut Gilles down. Before he could, Dee, Myrddin's friend and closest colleague, raised an eyebrow. "Sounds to me as if you're encouraging these creatures hungry for power, Gilles. And we've just been told not to. We've just been told it's dangerous. That this kind of creature creates imbalance, not balance."

"Mind your own business, and let me mind mine," hissed Gilles, the mask of his charm dropped.

Myrddin pounded his staff for order. "Dee is right. The Three want such creatures reined in. Let me speak frankly, Gilles. The Three have noticed a special disturbance originating on the plane where you've been operating. One of the planes. I know you operate on several."

"Are you accusing me, Myrddin?" said Gilles, his face darkening with anger.

"Gilles," said Myrddin. "Balance. Remember. That's the key to justice, at least the justice known underneath the Spheres."

"There's a higher justice, Myrddin," said Gilles. A number of the mages nodded and began clustering nearer him.

"There is indeed, Gilles. But you know very well, and the farwydds have warned us, that the Children reserve this higher justice to Themselves. It's not for us to meddle."

"If we don't stand together, the creatures underneath the Spheres will find themselves at terrible risk," said Dr. Dee.

"So the farwydds tell us," replied Myrddin.

"Then let's stand together for might, not cowardly abasement," said Gilles. "Besides, we must consider it's possible, just possible, that the farwydds want to keep their own power for themselves, and not share it with the others of creation. It's possible they're exaggerating."

Myrddin closed his eyes, trying to shut out Gilles's act of blasphemy. Gilles probably didn't believe his own words. But he must know that a certain coterie of the lesser mages would find him convincing. For some of them, even thrilling. Better to reason with Gilles. Too heavy a hand could lead Gilles into open rebellion, and then what?

"We have a responsibility to these creatures, especially the ordinary folk crawling helpless beneath the Spheres. We can't go running off after power, nor let the creatures do so," Dee was arguing.

"You're overruled, Gilles," said Myrddin.

Gilles subsided into his golden chair with mutterings and frowns. A few of the bolder mages of the lesser kind moved even closer to him.

"Might makes right," said one of these, looking around him for applause, seeming to think he'd invented the idea.

"Among the ordinary creatures, there are men," said another, ticking the ranks off on his fingers, "and among these men are the strongmen, the rulers. Beneath them, the followers. Next are women, mostly weak and in need of protection, ruled by emotion and irrationality. Finally, at the bottom, animals. Brutes with no understanding."

"And the other kinds of sentient creatures, all with their own ideas of hierarchy," another chimed in. "Always, the strong are on top."

Myrddin ignored them. Gilles was up to his old tricks. He sighed. He'd have to keep an eye on Gilles before his belligerent attitude got them all into worse trouble than they were in already. They'd been given their warning. They'd already come to the attention of the Three. The Children had already given their directive to the Council, and the Children would be displeased to see their express orders flouted.

Myrddin decided not to fan the flames.

"For now," he said mildly, "let's watch and wait. We'll do nothing without consultation." He seated himself in the golden chair that was his. The council broke up into small groups, milling about the chamber and talking earnestly among themselves.

Myrddin raised his voice above the hubbub. "Which of you mages operate on the plane where the Sceptered Isle is the strongest of the realms?"

The assembled mages looked over at him. A few of the lesser mages hesitantly raised their hands.

"Come here to me. I'm commissioning you to keep an eye on things." The others resumed their chatter. Myrddin looked over the ones clustered around him. They were a motley lot. He considered which one might be of best use. "Aderyn," he said, waving the others off.

"Yes, my lord?" She came to stand beside him.

"You're closest to the power struggle I fear will soon break out."

"Yes, my lord."

"But your Child is the Child of Sea, isn't that right?"

"Yes, my lord."

"Hmm," said Myrddin. "Yet most of the Sceptered Isle is under the sway of the Child of Earth." He looked around at some of the others he'd called over, already being swallowed up by this or that group of gesticulating, arguing mages. None of them seemed particularly suitable to the work he had in mind. He turned to the one by his chair. "Well, Aderyn, Little Bird, see what you can do to contain the situation. Meanwhile, I'll look around for a mage answering to the Earth Child, someone who may be able to relieve you if things get out of hand, or if you're called. . ." he paused delicately. ". . . elsewhere," he said. Myrddin didn't mention that he had already seen this mage in his scrying stone.

"Yes, my lord," said Aderyn.

"I'll expect regular reports from you, Aderyn, as the situation develops."

"Yes, my lord," she said. "There's another who can help?"

"A mage in the Sceptered Isle? Not at the moment. There will be. I've foreseen it. So try to hold on until he comes into the world."

"I'll do that. We have a thin line of defense, in our realm."

"Yes," said Myrddin with a sigh. "It's dangerous." Especially dangerous, he thought, when so many mages failed to live up to their potential, or died before they could. It was a terrible calling, full of hidden traps for the unwary.

A mage might not even know he bore unique abilities, and live out his life peaceably without ever wielding his powers. Myrddin counted such mages lucky. Or a mage might discover her powers but choose not to develop them. If she could stay quiescent and not attract the attention of the mighty through any noticeable burst of power, she too might live out a peaceful, natural life. But woe to the mage who recognized himself and set out to wield and develop and refine his powers.

At his elbow, Dee looked particularly agitated.

"What is it?" Myrddin said, more sharply than he intended.

"Someone will come, you say. Someone will be born, and he will help."

"I'm sensing this, yes," said Myrddin. "I've engaged in some discreet scrying. After the meeting, I'll see if I can find out more."

"The poor fellow," said Dee. "If his neighbors among the ordinary folk discover he's a mage, those good people are likely to cry witchcraft, especially on this plane, with all its ignorance. And then the very people he's charged with protecting may very well turn on him and kill him."

"That's true." Myrddin nodded slowly. "We know the risks, my good friend. Haven't we survived them ourselves?"

"Long ago," said Dee. He shuddered. "I remember that incident I faced, you know the one. That one time."

"Yes," said Myrddin. "Another mage on the plane where you operated."

"He got jealous. He set traps to kill me."

"You escaped him, Dee. We've all experienced the unpleasant consequences of our powers." Myrddin had his own bad memories to get past.

Only the most advanced of mages learn to use the protections of the highest spells. Only then might they live down the generations and centuries and across the planes. Few mages lasted long enough to do so. Few mages lasted long enough to cast their first spells. Myrddin knew that, and so did Dee. Few mages would last long enough and become adept enough to grow near-immortal, like Dee or Gilles or Myrddin.

And here was this young mage who glimmered at the edge of Myrddin's consciousness, a man not yet born on the plane where they needed to act. Unless he were incredibly lucky, he doubtless faced a tragic fate, if statistics were any measure. Not even great skill could save him. Not that often.

Myrddin decided he'd go to his scrying stone immediately after the council's meeting concluded, to see what else he might see of the young man.

Dee's eyes were far away. He kept on. "A jealous mage might kill this young one you envision. A rogue mage might take possession of him."

At last he fell silent. Myrddin followed Dee's gaze and saw where his friend's thoughts were leading him. A rogue mage like Gilles, one who dabbled illegally in the dark arts. One who had every reason to thwart Myrddin and Dee, and had just demonstrated it. Not for the first time.

Thank the Children for Aderyn. She was a mage of great talent, and completely dedicated. But her talents were probably limited to one time and place. Myrddin knew—and she herself knew—that she would probably live only an ordinary lifetime, subject to all of the dangers of her era. Myrddin turned back to Aderyn and placed an affectionate hand on her arm. They resumed their conversation.

Dee had stopped paying attention. He was staring with puzzled eyes over at Gilles, who was glaring back. "I don't understand Gilles," Dee murmured aside to Myrddin as Gilles looked from one of them to the other, his eyes narrowed suspiciously. "I've known you for a long time, Mervin, my friend," said Dee, "and during the course of our friendship, how many times has Gilles tried something like this? The last was the worst. Now look at him. Stirring things up again. Say he were to succeed. He'd bring the Spheres crashing down on his own head. So why?"

Forcing a smile, Myrddin dismissed Aderyn back to her family among the ordinary folk. He turned to his friend Dee. Both stood examining Gilles de Rais as he moved from group to small group of the mages who supported him. "The man's so arrogant I think he believes he'll forge a new order to replace the Spheres." Myrddin kept his voice down. That particular rumor didn't need any momentum from him, and if he took notice of it as anything more than a fool's notion, it would gain momentum.

Myrddin gazed out over the vast conclave of the Magisterial High Council. "Dismissed, all of you." His booming voice carried over the commotion the departing mages were making. "And Gilles. I'll see you in my office after the meeting."

Gilles returned a look of intense dislike.

"Unleash me, Mervin," Dee was saying at Myrddin's elbow, a familiar grim light in his eyes.

"No, good friend. I know how you feel. Not now. I need to try to reason with Gilles."

"Reason with Gilles?" Dee's voice was incredulous.

Dee was right, of course. It would be no use reasoning with the man, thought Myrddin with an inward groan. Gilles was intractable. It was as clear to Dee as it was to him. Gilles himself stood at the heart of the farwydds' warning. Gilles knew just how far to press his advantage without drawing the attention of the Three. He trod a thin line, and clearly he loved it, the danger, the rush of power he got when he manipulated himself into some advantageous position.

Myrddin pressed Dee's hand, he hoped reassuringly. He moved away to some of the others, gave an encouraging word here, a smile there.

But he never took his eyes off Gilles.

Gilles was almost as powerful in the Council as Myrddin himself. Myrddin realized he'd have to handle Gilles carefully. Diplomatically. Gilles could make trouble if he were directly confronted.

Power. Myrddin sighed.

In a way, Gilles was right. Gilles craved power, and Myrddin—with the help of the strongest of the mages, such as his friend Dee, especially Dee—needed to exercise all of his own power to keep Gilles in check.

There was a time when Gilles's power, while not overtopping his own, joined with some lesser powers to incapacitate

Myrddin. That time was over, but it didn't stop Gilles from pushing. And pushing. And pushing.

As for Dee. Myrddin looked over at his fellow-mage with affection. Not as powerful as Gilles, but vastly more well-intentioned. Still, Dee was a loose cannon.

Myrddin shrugged and set that problem aside for another day. The anger of the Three was too pressing. It threatened all underneath the Spheres. He must see how best to use his own power in the service of balance.

Power itself was not the problem. It was a tool. But a tool that could too easily be misused. He must get ahead of this most recent attempt of Gilles to overtop balance. He must do it now, while it was still a gleam in Gilles's eye.

Gilles was out to destroy them all. He had the power, and he had the will to use it.

If this new mage were born into the world, into the realm of the Sceptered Isle. . .Myrddin's mind drifted back to the glimmerings of foresight promising this. . . that might give Myrddin a bit of an advantage. But for how long? There was only so much protection Myrddin was allowed to give a new mage.

As for Gilles, he observed no such ethical boundaries. He'd have no compunctions about destroying such a person. Or luring such a person into his own orbit.

Myrddin could only hope to keep the new one away from Gilles's attention. Sneak him under the radar and hope for the best.

Dee had kept hovering at Myrddin's shoulder. "We're not to interfere. I understand, Mervin. I do. But suppose we sent a messenger, with a warning?"

"The boy hasn't even been born yet," said Myrddin.

"You know," said Dee. "These things never do start with just a boy, do they? They go back, and back, and back. Suppose we send a messenger to the father of this boy?"

"What good will that do?" said Myrddin, and strode away.

Behind him, Dee called after him. "What about our chess game? I was winning, you scoundrel."

In spite of the troubling thoughts weighing heavily on him, Myrddin couldn't suppress a grin.

But then he did head for his scrying stone, and what he saw there gave such a wrench to his inwards that he nearly doubled over with the pain of it.

Excerpt from *Blackbird Rising*

The blackbirds flap over the little rise in the meadow to set-tle and flutter and fuss.

I hear their shrieking. I stand stunned at the edge of the meadow. Past the flurry of wings and beaks I see our gutted cabin, a thin trail of smoke rising from its roof. I see the soldiers of the king poking around it, the dark form of a man on horse-back directing them. Strewn down the furlong of meadow between me and the ruins of our house, I see crumpled piles, maybe cloth, distorted and lumpy. I tell myself I don't know what they are, but in a different part of myself, I do. They are bodies.

Blackbirds perch on them. Five or six. They step delicately on and over the lumpy forms of our father and mother, cut down as they tried to run for the safety of the brushy forest verge.

And there's a smaller bundle, too. *Jillie*, I whisper, and my heart wrenches loose from me. I see, tossed out beside you, a splash of bright yellow. My mother had made you a poppet out of leftover cloth from her new yellow holiday kirtle.

You loved that doll.

From somewhere, I hear a drum pounding. I can feel the pulse beating in my ears, and I realize the sound is my own heart.

The drumbeat is so loud I think the soldiers must be able to hear it, even though they're at the other end of the meadow. Though I know in some sensible part of me that the sound is enclosed inside my body, I still find myself backing into the underbrush and crouching down.

These men patrolling the ruins of our home, they're soldiers of the king. They wear his scarlet livery. They are slashes of scarlet in and about the gray of the smoldering, stove-in cabin, almost gone back to the earth our father hacked it out of. Slashes of scarlet roaming the vivid meadow.

Down the meadow, the hovering birds bob and toss and jerk their heads. *Are they feeding?* I have a powerful urge to rush these birds, scream at them, chase them off the bodies. Something holds me back. That something keeps me alive.

The scene that is spread out before me makes no sense. The pounding drum. The ringing in my ears. Aren't we all loyal subjects of the king, all in our family? We have never done any wrong, not to the king, not to our neighbors. I want to scream at the soldiers and tell them so.

Instead, all words are driven out of me as if some massive dangerous animal has slammed me to the dirt.

From over the meadow I can see the shingles our father had split himself, still glowing on what is left of our roof. In flashes, I have a chilling notion of how the whole thing happened. I feel as if I'm rising, hovering like one of the birds, and I think I see it—the soldiers throwing burning brands on the low roof to force all of you out through the only door.

A blackness comes across me, there in the meadow, and then a flash, and in that flash I see it.

The burning shingles don't collapse at once. Our parents grab at you. You're crying in panic, Jillie. They burst to the door, help you crawl out, and try to run. They don't get far.

The soldiers ride all of you down.

Evil stalks beside these soldiers of the king. Their leader is not dressed in scarlet. He's dressed in black. The way he holds himself is wolf-like. Sinister. Like one of the Dark Ones.

I shake my head to clear it. Now my body is back crouching low to the earth, where it belongs, in its hiding place at the verge of the meadow. I'm in my leather tunic, the one our mother made for me of rabbit skins from my own trapping expeditions, and I'm wearing my brown woolen trousers. Boys' clothes, forbidden but practical for hunting. The tunic, buff and brown and mottled, blends in with the dapples and overlapping shadows at the meadow's edge. And the trousers are the same color as the forest behind me.

If I had been wearing my regular clothes, my kirtle, my white headcloth and apron, I would have stood out against the forest backdrop. I would have been dead by the third step I took into the meadow.

Though I don't understand what I'm sensing or even exactly what I'm seeing, I find myself edging backward into the brush. From there, hidden, I stare and stare at this thing I can barely fathom, something so out of the realm of possibility that I don't and can't believe it.

From where I hide, I see the soldiers moving down into the meadow toward the bodies. As they near, the blackbirds explode upward in a raucous storm of feathers and beaks and claws. I shrink down even lower, flattening myself on the ground as the blackbirds fly over, back into the woods beyond me. One stares at me, as it strafes me, one eye dark, foreboding, the other filmy white with blindness.

From wanting to rush at the blackbirds and flail at them with my hands, I become one of them. I'm rising again, soaring far overhead. I scream and scream.

The soldiers stop, look over their shoulders in my direction. They come down the meadow toward me, and as they do, one final blackbird rises shrieking from the meadow's verge, going at them with talon and beak. They duck back and hasten toward the cabin, where their leader sits his horse.

They mount up, too, and they all ride off.

I watch myself soaring on wide black wings. My eye scans the landscape for the dark leader. My beak opens wide to accuse him, and my talons spread, ready to fasten deep into his flesh.

But the bodies distract me. In a dive that bolts from the zenith of the sky, I arrow down to those bodies, desperate to reach them.

Instead, I slam back into my own body where it's standing stunned now at the ragged edge of the meadow. I'm a girl again. I turn and run. As I zigzag terror-stricken through the trees, something bangs and thwacks against me. It is my rebec, hanging from its shoulder strap.

Everything I've known and loved has just been destroyed. My rebec is the one good thing still with me in a world gone gray and horror-filled.

If only I could let you hold my rebec right now, Jillie. Somehow the feel of it might help you recall the good memories. I used to take it with me everywhere, even into the woods while I hunted. You remember this, Jillie. I know you do. When I rested under the shade of the tall trees, I played it. If I hadn't had it with me that day, that terrible day, I would have lost not only my family but the one way I know to get to the buried place inside me where my second sense dwells, the one Johnny the Traveler helped me find.

Whenever I play my instrument, I feel connected to myself. I play it to feel connected to all of you, my family, now that you're gone.

See, my rebec has four strings. Remember running your fingers across them?

Hold that memory. Please hold it.

Think about the sound the strings make. Pretty, isn't it? Think about how I used to make the strings from the guts of the rabbits I brought home. And think about how I played upon the strings for you. With this small bow.

Shall I play you a tune now? You're not here to listen to it, but in my mind, you are.

> *I'll sing you one, oh.*
> *Green grow the rushes, oh.*
> *What is your one, oh.*
> *One is one and all alone and evermore shall be so.*
>
> *Blackbirds rising, blackbird's eye,*
> *Green grow the rushes, oh,*
> *One lone blackbird in the sky,*
> *Green grow the rushes, oh.*
> *One is one and all alone and evermore shall be so.*

It's a good song, the first Johnny the Traveler ever taught me. During that winter before the soldiers came, he taught me to play other songs, but this song about the blackbirds was the first one and—I could sense, even then—the most important.

The song changed everything—everything in my life, everything in yours.

Everything in the Rising, too.

www.ingramcontent.com/pod-product-compliance
Lightning Source LLC
Chambersburg PA
CBHW030537020726
47494CB00005B/1406